PRAISE FOR

The Last Hours

"A seductive writer with an imagination that makes her dangerous to know." —*Sunday Express*

"Walters's skill and subtlety in portraying the suffering and disarray of a feudal society in which disease rampages and God has seemingly gone mad is masterly. And, as with her bestselling suspense novels, the psychological drama is gripping." —*Daily Mail*

"Vivid but flawed characters rise from the page . . . This renowned crime writer has shifted to historical fiction without faltering." —*Good Reading*

"A gripping read. Walters uses this often grisly tale to explore questions of class relations, gender relations, and the societal aftermath of the Norman conquest." —*Sydney Morning Herald*

"A riveting start to a huge story . . . [Walters] seems certain for a return to the bestseller lists." —*Herald Sun*

"A staggeringly talented writer." —*Guardian*

"Wonderful and sweeping, with a fabulous sense of place and history." —Kate Mosse, author of *Labyrinth*

"An enthralling account of a calamitous time, and above all a wonderful testimony to the strength of the human spirit. I was caught from the first page." —Julian Fellowes

"Minette Walters is a master at building engrossing tales around a single, life-shattering event." —*Washington Post*

Minette Walters is the critically acclaimed and internationally bestselling author of suspense novels, including *The Devil's Feather*, *The Sculptress* and *Acid Row*. She is the recipient of an Edgar Award and two CWA Gold Dagger awards, among other accolades. *The Turn of Midnight* is the sequel to *The Last Hours*, published in 2017. She lives in Dorset with her husband.

MINETTE WALTERS

The TURN of MIDNIGHT

HarperCollins*Publishers*Ltd

Published by HarperCollins Publishers Ltd

Originally published in the United Kingdom and Australia in 2018 by Allen & Unwin.
First published in Canada in 2019 by HarperCollins Publishers Ltd
in this original trade paperback edition.

HarperCollins books may be purchased for educational, business,
or sales promotional use through our Special Markets Department.

HarperCollins Publishers Ltd
Bay Adelaide Centre, East Tower
22 Adelaide Street West, 41st Floor
Toronto, Ontario, Canada
M5H 4E3

www.harpercollins.ca

Library and Archives Canada Cataloguing in Publication
information is available upon request.

Original trade paperback (ISBN 978-1-4434-5788-0)
Library hardcover (ISBN 978-1-4434-5791-0)

Maps by Janet Hunt
Typeset by Bookhouse, Sydney, Australia

Printed and bound in the United States
LSC/H 9 8 7 6 5 4 3 2 1

For my excellent Durham friends in Dorset
Amber, David, Geoffrey, Huw, Isobel, Jill, Josh,
Les, Mike C, Mike W, Richard

and Patrick and Lynden in Australia

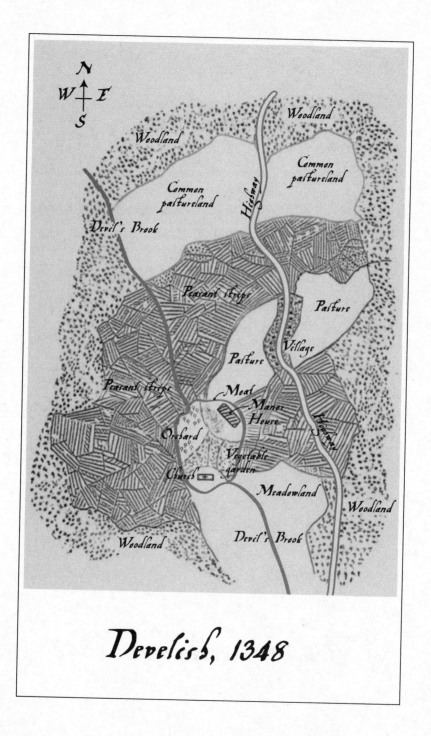

Develish, 1348

Mid-Dorsetshire, 1348

Blandeforde, 1349

So great a plague has never been heard of from the beginning of the world to the present day ... The sickness befell people everywhere ... and generated such horror that children did not dare to visit their dying parents, nor parents their children, but fled for fear of contagion.

John of Fordun, Scotichronicon

Towns once packed with people were emptied of their inhabitants, and the plague spread so thickly that the living were hardly able to bury the dead. In some religious houses not more than two survived out of twenty. It was calculated by several people that barely a tenth of mankind remained alive ... Rents dwindled and land was left untilled for want of tenants (who were nowhere to be found). And so much wretchedness followed these ills that afterwards the world could never return to its former state.

Thomas Walsingham, St Albans Abbey, Chronicle

Many villages and hamlets became deserted ... Sheep and cattle went wandering over fields and through crops and there was no one to look after them ... In the autumn [following the pestilence] no one could get a reaper for less than 8d, or a mower for less than 12d. Therefore, many crops perished in the fields for want of someone to gather them.

Henry Knighton, Chronicle

Places, people and events from
The Last Hours

Places

Melcombe, the port in Dorseteshire where the Black Death first entered England on 24 June, 1348. Within days, many of the inhabitants were dead; within weeks, the sickness had spread to the rest of the county. One chronicler described it as 'a pestilence that moved at the speed of a galloping horse'. All who contracted it died.

Bradmayne, a demesne of some four hundred and fifty people, situated a half-day's ride from Melcombe, and an early victim of the pestilence. Upwards of one hundred perished in the second week of July, 1348, amongst them Lord Peter, the betrothed of Lady Eleanor of Develish.

Develish, a demesne of some two hundred people in mid-Dorseteshire, the fiefdom of Sir Richard, a brutish tyrant, who governed until his death from the pestilence in July, 1348. To make Develish seem grander than it was, Sir Richard ordered his serfs to dig a moat around his manor house in 1338. This allowed the house and the handful of acres on which it stood to be quarantined when the pestilence came.

The nobility

Sir Richard of Develish (48), an illiterate Norman, encumbered by debt and disowned by his family. To return himself to solvency in 1334, he took a fourteen-year-old Saxon bride with a generous dowry. Twenty years older than she, and finding her unappealing, he treats Lady Anne (a noble in her own right) as badly as he treats his serfs. Within a few months of marriage, and to avoid having to make monetary reparation for rape, he forced her to adopt and raise as her own a newborn girl, sired by him to the thirteen-year-old half-sister of his brother-in-law. Named Lady Eleanor, this is his only child. While on a visit to Bradmayne to formalise Eleanor's betrothal to Lord Peter, Sir Richard contracts the pestilence.

Lady Anne of Develish (28), educated, literate and skilled in medicine, she was married out of a nunnery and follows the teachings of Christ and not the Church. From the time she came to Develish as a young wife, she has worked quietly to improve the health, lives and knowledge of her serfs through education and care. To protect them from the pestilence, and in direct contradiction of the Church's teachings, she withdraws them inside the moat and burns the bridge to prevent anyone crossing; this includes her sick husband, who is left to die in the serfs' village beyond the moat. She makes enemies of Sir Richard's steward, daughter and priest by doing this, but earns the gratitude and loyalty of her people. She assumes control of Develish on Sir Richard's death.

Lady Eleanor of Develish (14), only child of Sir Richard and adopted daughter of Lady Anne. Ignorant of her true parentage, she adores the father who spoils her and hates the mother who tries to discipline her. Wilful and cruel, her wild rages become worse after her father's death, and she denounces Lady Anne as a heretic when she learns that the woman is not her biological mother.

Lord Bourne (mid-60s), a King's treasurer from Wiltshire who plunders Dorseteshire gold with the help of eleven fighting men. On his first visit to Develish, he burns the village; on his second, his attempts to gain entry are resisted and he vows to take revenge.

Freemen

Father Anselm (mid-60s), a drunken priest. He and Lady Anne are mutually distrustful. She believes him unfit to be a priest; he believes her to be a heretic. Lady Anne cannot forgive his exoneration of Sir Richard's brutal violation in 1338 of a ten-year-old serf girl, Abigail Startout, who died from internal rupturing and loss of blood.

Hugh de Courtesmain (29), a duplicitous Norman steward hired by Sir Richard to raise extra taxes on his serfs. He comes to Develish on the recommendation of Sir Richard's sister, Lady

Beatrix of Foxcote, who speaks highly of his zealotry in whipping defaulters. Arrogant, and with little time to establish his authority before Sir Richard dies, he finds himself friendless once Lady Anne assumes control of the demesne. Stripped of his position as steward and deeply resentful of Thaddeus Thurkell for taking his place, he looks to exploit Eleanor's hatred of both Lady Anne and Thaddeus Thurkell in order to wrest power back to himself.

Serfs

Thaddeus Thurkell (21), a bastard-born slave who is hated by the man his mother marries. Dark-skinned, black-haired and a head taller than other men, he rarely speaks and gives respect only to Lady Anne, who has been tutoring him in secret for more than a decade when she makes him her steward after Sir Richard's death. As clever, literate and educated as she, he is unwavering in his loyalty and admiration for her, and together they strive to protect Develish while the pestilence rages outside. Their efforts are threatened when Thaddeus discovers the body of his half-brother Jacob, killed by a stab wound to his chest. Believing Lady Eleanor to be the culprit, and certain she intends to accuse the sons of Lady Anne's leading serfs of the crime, he persuades Lady Anne the death was an accident and, without her knowledge, removes the boys from the demesne. He leaves Lady Anne a letter excusing their absence on the need to replenish the demesne's diminishing stocks of food before winter sets in.

Eva Thurkell (37), mother to Thaddeus, she blames her son for her husband's anger at being duped into marrying a harlot from another demesne. When Lady Anne appoints Thaddeus as her steward, and Eva learns how many secrets her son has been keeping from her (most notably his admiration for Lady Anne), she develops an intense and bitter jealousy of the woman.

Will Thurkell (44), an aggressive bully whose greatest frustration stems from the recognition that an unknown man's bastard is more intelligent than he is. As resentful as his wife of the secret teaching and encouragement Lady Anne has given Thaddeus, he aids and abets Eva in trying to unseat him as steward.

Gyles Startout (48), an English serf who was raised to the position of paid fighting man in Sir Richard's retinue in 1338, when Lady Anne demanded that her husband recompense him for the violation of his daughter Abigail. The preferment allows Gyles to accompany his hated master wherever he goes, and he does so willingly to report what he sees to Lady Anne. He is the lone survivor of Sir Richard's ill-fated visit to Bradmayne and waits for fourteen days to prove he's free of the pestilence before Lady Anne permits him to cross the moat. She appoints him her captain of arms and he trains the men of Develish in the use of weapons in order to defend the demesne against attack.

John Trueblood, **James Buckler**, **Adam Catchpole** and **Alleyn Startout** (brother to Gyles), leaders amongst the serfs and members of Lady Anne's advisory council.

Martha Startout (wife to Gyles) and **Clara Trueblood** (wife to John), leaders of the female house servants.

Isabella Startout (13), daughter of Gyles and Martha Startout, and younger sister of Abigail, she is chambermaid to both Lady Anne and Lady Eleanor. Recognising her cleverness, Lady Anne teaches her to read and write and she, in turn, teaches other servants in the household. The affection Lady Anne has for her causes jealousy in Eleanor. In the final pages of *The Last Hours*, Eleanor takes Isabella prisoner and tortures the maid before Lady Anne can rescue her.

Robert Startout (11), son of Alleyn and Susan Startout, cousin to Isabella and nephew of Gyles. Because he has some sympathy for her, he speaks on Lady Eleanor's behalf when she is tried by the serfs for her wounding of Isabella. His intervention is appreciated by Isabella, who has some understanding of why her young mistress is so disturbed.

The five young men who depart the demesne with Thaddeus

Naive and bored, all are easily seduced into furtive assignations with Eleanor inside the church. Careless of her motives, they submit to her sexual games and find themselves implicated in the death of Jacob. While maintaining their innocence, they are nevertheless convinced that she plans to accuse them. At first reluctant to be taken from the demesne by Thaddeus, they commit themselves to searching out supplies for Develish.

Ian and Olyver Startout (15), identical twin sons of Gyles and Martha Startout, and older brothers to Isabella. Ian is the natural leader; Olyver the follower.

Edmund Trueblood (15), son of John and Clara Trueblood. As *The Last Hours* ends, he reveals the secret of Eleanor's birth to Thaddeus, having learnt it from his mother, who acted as wet nurse when Eleanor was first brought to Develish.

Peter Catchpole (16), son of Adam and Rosa Catchpole. Lazy by nature, he responds better to Thaddeus's leadership than his father's, though his commitment to proving himself is never as strong as his friends'.

Joshua Buckler (15), son of James and Jenny Buckler, he is the least confident of the youths. He gains in self-esteem when Thaddeus puts him in charge of seven hunting dogs found roaming a deserted demesne.

AUTUMN AND WINTER, 1348

The night of the eleventh day of September, 1348

When the hourglass tilts, midnight will have turned and a new day started. Yet I still can't bring myself to move. Once done, this cannot be undone, and the guilt will be mine. I should have been more of a mother to Eleanor, for I knew better than anyone the vileness of her father's nature. But would she have listened if I'd warned her that his love for her was unnatural? Will she listen now?

I must put an end to indecision. Despite the vicious wounds Eleanor inflicted on her, Isabella Startout came in search of help for her, and the maid's sweet generosity should be my guide. In my heart I know I must act. To do nothing will be to betray the girl I have called daughter all these years.

God forgive me. I can surely bear Eleanor's hatred more easily than she will bear the slur of incest if this misbegotten child is born.

Mea culpa.

One

THE NIGHT SEEMED DARKER WHEN Lady Anne took her leave
of Eleanor and stepped away from the serf's hut. Perhaps she'd
tarried longer than she realised in her attempts to persuade her
daughter to understand the stark choices that faced her. There
was no telling time with the moon hidden by cloud. She pulled
her cloak tighter about herself as protection against the rising
wind and felt her way blindly along the path to the manor house.
Behind her, the church was lost in blackness; ahead of her, the glow
of the six candles she lit each night in the south-facing window of
her chamber was just discernible through the panes overlooking
the forecourt. Their feeble light was all that was visible in the
enshrouding darkness.

Only John Trueblood knew of her visit, for he'd had to open
the padlock on the door of Eleanor's prison. She didn't doubt he
would speak of it to Clara but hoped both would believe that her
sorrow at being disowned by her adopted daughter had compelled
her to come. Certainly, John had seen her sadness when she left;
he'd given her arm a clumsy pat and begged her not to take Lady

Eleanor's hate-filled words of that afternoon to heart. Once the girl's strange madness passed, she would know that Milady was her true mother. Lady Anne thanked him for his kindness, but tears clouded her eyes as she made her way back to the house. She doubted Eleanor would ever come to see that an abortive of angelica, wormwood and pennyroyal was a gift of love and not hate.

She had left the girl to administer the purgative herself, saying the choice of what to do must be hers. If Eleanor decided to keep the baby, she must live with the consequences afterwards because Lady Anne could not protect her from gossip once her belly began to swell in earnest. She had warned Eleanor against repeating the lies she'd told Isabella about being raped by serf boys because all would guess the truth as soon as the infant was born. There wasn't a woman in Develish who wouldn't be able to name the real sire when she saw the baby's features and worked out from the date of delivery that Sir Richard, the girl's own father, was still in Develish at the time of conception. Dead he might be, but he still had the power to destroy any chance his daughter might have of an unsullied future.

Lady Anne trod softly as she approached the forecourt, anxious not to be seen coming from the direction of Eleanor's prison, but loose stones shifted beneath her feet and her heart skipped a beat when a beam of light shone briefly on her face as the shutter of a lantern was opened and closed. It was impossible to make out who was holding it until she heard the voice of young Robert Startout. He sounded very frightened. 'Oh, milady, milady,' he stammered. 'My Uncle Gyles has need of you. He sent my mother to your chamber, but you weren't there—and nor could she find you anywhere else.'

She placed her palm against his cheek. 'I'm here now, Robert. Where is your uncle?'

The boy caught her hand and urged her towards the moat. 'Guarding the northern step, milady. Bandits have come across the hills from the south. My father and Master Catchpole say they're circling the valley to come at us on all sides.'

It was a second or two before the import of his words registered with Lady Anne. Her mind was so full of Eleanor's woes that she couldn't conceive of worse troubles elsewhere. Her steps faltered. 'Bandits?'

'Yes, milady. My father guards the eastern step, overlooking the highway, and he saw men in numbers some half-hour since; Master Catchpole likewise from his place on the southern step.' Robert sighed in relief as a shadow moved towards them. 'My uncle can tell you better than I.'

Gyles ducked his head to Lady Anne and placed a comforting hand on Robert's shoulder. 'Don't fret before you need to,' he urged the lad. 'Are you willing to be my messenger again? Then wait by the buttress until you hear my signal. When I whistle, rouse the men in the house and send them to me here. They must bring what weapons they can and find their way without lanterns or candles. Understood?'

Lady Anne waited until the boy was out of earshot. She could barely breathe for the sudden panic that gripped her heart. 'Is this true, Gyles?'

'It is, milady. Alleyn and Adam are certain of what they saw. They've been uncommonly vigilant since a torch flared briefly to life on the road to the south. The light lasted a bare second or two, but it showed a multitude of men beneath it. It speaks of what we've always feared—an army of serfs in search of food.' He put a hand beneath her elbow to steady her. 'Our best help will be rain. They'll not be able to burn us out if God brings a downpour.'

'And if He doesn't?'

'We must fight, though I question whether our people have the will to kill Englishmen. I worry they'll hesitate if a Dorseteshire voice begs for mercy.' He felt a tremor of shock run through her. 'You need to be brave, milady. Our people will lose heart if they see you afraid.'

He asked too much of her. 'But I *am* afraid,' she whispered. 'Any courage I had is gone. I thought I could play the part of liege lord, but I was wrong. I am quite unable to shoulder the many burdens the position places on me.'

Gyles guessed Eleanor's madness was the true cause of Milady's anguish, and he cursed the girl roundly in his head. It seemed the pain she'd visited on his daughter Isabella wasn't enough for her. She must destroy the people of Develish too by destroying their mistress. Without care for the impropriety of the gesture, he placed his arm around Lady Anne's waist and drew her close.

'I remember when you first came to Develish as a young bride,' he told her gently. 'You were barely older than my Isabella is now. I was on this forecourt, summoned to watch a flogging, and I recall the look in your eye as you stepped from the wagon and saw the poor wretch who was being whipped. I knew then we'd found a friend. Inside two months such brutal flayings had stopped and you'd drawn Sir Richard's ire onto yourself. Will you show a lesser spirit tonight before a ragtag band of thieves?'

Lady Anne raised the hem of her cloak to her eyes. The last man who had held her in such a way had been her father. She took a long tremulous breath and raised her head. 'I will try my best, Gyles. Tell me what you would have me do and I will do it.'

Gyles didn't doubt her, for his faith in her was very great. 'Assist Robert in waking the house and then barricade yourself inside with the women and children, milady. Our men will fight better for knowing their families are under your protection.' He narrowed his eyes to stare across the moat, but there was no seeing the road that led to the village nor the land that lay on either side of it. 'You won't know if we've succeeded until dawn breaks, so be ruthless in keeping the door barred. In this darkness, you'll not be able to tell one Dorseteshire voice from another.'

Lady Anne didn't argue with him. He knew as well as she that their men would be no better at telling friend from foe. To fight blindly was madness, yet what else could they do? There was no future for Develish if the walls were breached and the pestilence entered. She breathed a silent prayer that Alleyn and Adam were wrong, but even that hope was extinguished when a light, as small as a pinprick, appeared in the blackness ahead of them. By its direction, it seemed to be on the edge of the village but, as they watched, it began to move, growing brighter as it came towards them.

'What is that?' she whispered.

'A burning torch, milady.'

'Who carries it?'

Gyles looked at the distorted shapes that eddied and flowed beneath the flickering flame and, with a sigh, he eased away from her and took his bow from his shoulder. He'd left it too late. 'The people we dread, milady. They've circled the valley faster than I expected. I see five or six in this group alone.'

'Why do they alert us to their presence?'

'As a signal to others in the valley that the attack is about to begin.' Gyles looked towards the west, searching for signs of movement on the peasant strips. But the night was impenetrable. 'You must leave,' he said. 'Go. Encourage our men to fight and use your cleverness against these thieves to keep our women and children safe. Even under siege inside the house, a hundred can last well into the spring on the supplies that are left.'

With the hood of her cloak about her face, Lady Anne's expression was hidden from him, but he felt the brush of her fingers against his cheek. 'You are my dearest friend,' she whispered. 'Guard yourself well this night.'

Gyles forced a smile into his voice. 'Be sure of it, milady.'

Be sure of it . . . Lady Anne knew him too well to be deceived by such lightness of tone. He was bidding her farewell and a terrible panic overwhelmed her at the thought of trying to protect the people of Develish alone. Was God not content with death from the pestilence that He must set survivors against each other until no human life remained? Where was His love in this terrible world?

A small hand slipped into hers. 'Use some of my strength, milady,' whispered Robert. 'You will fall otherwise. Do you think Thaddeus knows there are bandits in the valley?'

The question was a strange one, for Robert knew well that Thaddeus, whom he greatly admired, had left the demesne two weeks ago. The child's twin cousins and three of their friends had departed with him, but none had returned. 'Have you missed Thaddeus, Robert?'

'Yes, milady, but he's foolish to lead his horse instead of riding it. He'll be attacked more easily on foot. My uncle should call out a warning.'

She squeezed his hand by way of comfort. 'Your uncle will do what is right. He always does.'

'I don't think so, milady, or he'd have done it already. He pretends he can see in the dark, but he can't. My father's the same. Me, I'd tell Thaddeus to stop being such a numbskull. The way he's walking even I could put an arrow through his heart.'

Lady Anne told herself it was fantasy, the imaginings of a frightened child, but she drew him to a halt. 'Look again,' she urged, turning him towards the moat. 'Describe what you see. Is it one man or many?'

'One, milady. He walks with his arms spread wide like Jesus on the cross. In his right hand he holds reins and in his left a torch. I think he worries the flame will frighten the horse. He wears a high hat and a long coat.'

'Can you really make out so much? Are you sure it's Thaddeus?'

'If it's not, it's someone tall who moves like him, milady. Now he's stopped to let the horse crop some grass at the edge of the road . . . and he's staring at the ground the way Thaddeus does when he's thinking.'

Lady Anne yearned to believe him. 'It's a strange hour for him to come. He knows better than any that all in Develish will be asleep.'

'Except the men on the guard steps, milady,' said Robert matter-of-factly. 'If my cousins are dead, Thaddeus will want my uncle to hear of it first.'

The same thought had occurred to Lady Anne. But who to trust when her own sight was better at reading ledgers than seeing into the distance? 'Give me your lantern,' she said with sudden decision, 'and then take your place beside the buttress. I'm putting much faith in you, Robert. If you're wrong and your uncle is right, there will be minutes only to rouse our men to defend the walls.'

'I'm not wrong, milady,' he answered confidently, letting go her hand, 'but don't blame me if there are bandits out there as well.'

૭⁄૭

Gyles lowered his bow when the flickering torchlight showed him his nephew was right. At fifty paces there was no mistaking Thaddeus's height and long, loping stride, never mind he was dressed like a lord in a wide-skirted, fur-lined coat with a beaver hat atop a chaperon hood on his head. 'My age is catching up with me, milady. I mistook the horse for men.'

Lady Anne suppressed a smile. 'I, too, my friend. There's less to fear than we thought.'

'Except bad news,' murmured Gyles. 'He wouldn't come when all are abed if he had something good to impart.'

Lady Anne handed him the closed lantern. 'Should we open it to show him we're here?'

'Not yet, milady. Let's hear what he has to say first.' He raised his voice as Thaddeus approached to within twenty paces of the moat. 'Are you well, Thaddeus?' he called.

A familiar voice came back to them. 'Is that you, Gyles? I am blinded by this torchlight but I feared an arrow through my heart if I approached unannounced.' He stooped to quench the flames in the dirt of the road. 'Are you alone, my friend?'

The careful way he asked the question persuaded Lady Anne to step behind Gyles. She was so slight his body hid hers easily. 'Say you are,' she whispered. 'He'll tell you nothing otherwise.'

'There are guards on the steps,' Gyles replied. 'If you don't want your words overheard, you must come to the moat and keep your voice low. What troubles you?'

Lady Anne heard the stamp of hooves as Thaddeus brought the horse to a halt on the bank, and the rattle of the bridle as it lowered its head to drink. 'First give me news of Develish,' he said. 'Is it as it was when we left? I saw candles in the window of Lady Anne's chamber. Does she look forward to our return?'

'Of course,' answered Gyles in obvious surprise. 'We all do. Why would it be otherwise?'

There was a small hesitation before Thaddeus answered. 'No reason. I promised your sons I would ask is all. They worry that you and Martha are angry because they didn't seek your blessing before they left.'

'I would have refused it if they had.'

'They guessed as much.'

Gyles gave a grunt of amusement. 'You put the fear of God into me by coming at this hour. I thought you were here to tell me they were dead.'

'Far from it. All the boys live and are well. Develish can be proud of them. I could not have asked for braver companions. Their courage in the face of the pestilence has been as great as yours, and we've found plentiful supplies to restore the stocks here. Where people die, animals thrive and grain goes uneaten.'

'Is it bad out there, my friend?'

Lady Anne heard a tired sigh. 'It's a wasteland, Gyles. Death sweeps all before it. I can neither rid myself of its smell nor erase the memories of what it leaves behind. To survive is to know damnation. This night I have walked in Hell.'

The words were so bleak that Gyles opened the shutter of the lantern and held it aloft. Thaddeus had removed his hat and pushed back his hood, and the beam of light shone on his drawn, exhausted face. Seeing him flinch at the brightness, Gyles dipped the beam to the water. 'There was a glow in the sky to the south some five hours ago,' he said. 'I guessed it was Athelhelm being set ablaze. Was that your doing?'

'It was.'

'For what reason?'

'To create safe passage for the boys and two hundred sheep along the highway from Afpedle to Develish. I would have delayed the burning another few days if I could, but the rain is almost upon us and would have made the task impossible.'

It took little imagination for Gyles to read between the lines of what he said. 'Is the pestilence in Athelhelm? Are all infected?'

Thaddeus nodded. 'All those that remained.'

'And the dead lay unburied?'

'Some had been placed in a communal grave but most were abandoned to die inside their huts. The body of a monk who'd been caring for them lay in a doorway, his face eaten by scavengers. I could see no course but to cleanse the village with fire. I called a warning of what I was about to do but none answered or came out.'

'So what troubles you?'

There was a long pause. 'A man begged for mercy even as I prepared to throw a flaming torch onto his thatch. I saw him through his open door. He was lying on rushes and turned his head to look at me. I could have stayed my hand but I didn't.'

'Did he try to rise?'

'No.'

'Then perhaps death was the mercy he wanted.'

'He thought I was the Devil come to burn him. I read it in his eyes.' Thaddeus cursed quietly to himself. 'Pay no heed to me. I promised myself I wouldn't talk of it. You dealt with worse when Sir Richard and your fellow soldiers were dying.'

Gyles recalled how Thaddeus had crossed the moat at night to keep him company while he tended the sick and then buried them. The younger man had always kept his distance but his presence had been a comfort. 'And I was grateful to you for listening to me. A trouble shared is a trouble halved.' Gyles paused. 'Were my sons with you?'

'No. Their consciences were pricked enough by what I asked them to do in Afpedle.' Thaddeus painted a brief picture of the previous fourteen days, detailing the demesnes they'd visited and the supplies of food they'd found. He spoke of finding a wagon and grain at Holcombe and two hundred sheep at Afpedle, but his descriptions of the smell of corruption that lingered over all the demesnes turned the stomachs of his listeners, as did his warnings about infestations of rats in the villages where people had died. 'The stores of grain attract them, and with more food they seem to be breeding faster. I don't know if they're spreading the disease—or how—but we found a handful of survivors in Woodoak who believe they're the carriers. You'd do well to keep a close watch for any that swim the moat.'

'There were rats in Bradmayne.'

'I remember you telling me.' Thaddeus fell silent for a moment to order his thoughts. 'Ian said you're never been bitten by fleas. Is that true?'

'It is.'

'The survivors in Woodoak spoke of how sufferers scratched themselves before they fell sick, and how the skin of the living crawled after touching the dead. Full immersion brought relief, as it did for you in Devil's Brook, and I wonder if the water washed away fleas. Do you recall if Sir Richard or any of your companions complained of itching?'

'They all did. Bradmayne was a filthy place. Fleas and lice were as prevalent as rats. Sir Richard didn't know whether to envy me my thick skin or curse me for escaping my share of the bites. It's a good guess, Thaddeus, but is it true?'

Another weary sigh. 'I don't know, but it's the only explanation I can think of for why the pestilence moves so freely between demesnes. Rats stay close to food but fleas travel with their hosts. Talk it through with Lady Anne. She'll know better than I whether such a thing is possible. We discussed many times how a merchant or pedlar might carry the sickness without succumbing himself.'

Gyles half expected Lady Anne to declare herself, since there was no reason for her to remain hidden. But she didn't. 'Let me summon her so that you can talk it through with her yourself.'

Thaddeus's refusal was immediate. 'There's no time. I must leave again within the hour. I came for horse collars, harness and rope to pull the wagon from Holcombe. I believe we stored all the tackle in Sir Richard's chamber. I see you decided to leave the raft in the water, so can you send across enough for two horses? Also, put your mind to thinking which route we should take out of Holcombe. Do you have a good enough memory of the highways from when you travelled with Sir Richard to say if there's a throughway to Afpedle? It would help if we could herd the sheep and drive the wagon together.'

Gyles pictured the roads in his mind. 'I remember a drovers' lane that leads to the west some five miles down the highway south out of Holcombe, and another a mile or so to the north which comes out above Athelhelm . . . but I wouldn't advise taking either of them. You'll become bogged down in mud when the rain comes. Your best bet would be to haul the wagon to Athelhelm and meet the sheep there. How far is it from your camp?'

'Three thousand paces . . . maybe four . . . but the path along the bank is barely wide enough to take a horse. It won't take the wagon.'

'The river might. It's not deep and has a gravel bottom if memory serves me well. I recall Sir Richard riding along it once and marvelling at the trout swimming ahead of him.' Gyles shrugged. 'The work will be arduous but it'll make your journey a great deal safer than negotiating passage through demesnes you don't know. Would you like my help with the task? I'm sure Milady will grant me leave to accompany you.'

Lady Anne heard a low laugh. 'Nothing would please your sons less, old man. They want the glory for themselves.' Another hesitation. 'Is Milady well?'

'She is, and has promised a celebration to honour you and our sons when you return. She has named you as heroes and lights six candles in your memory every night. You saw them in her window as you came along the highway.'

'I did,' said Thaddeus. 'It's a kind thought, but a foolish one, perhaps, since it speaks of the presence of people here. What of Lady Eleanor? How does she fare?'

Gyles was unsure how much to say until Lady Anne whispered that he should be truthful. 'Not well. She seems to have lost her wits. In the space of a few hours this day, she attacked and wounded my Isabella; declared herself free of Lady Anne, claiming her real mother to be a child under My Lord of Foxcote's protection; and threatened to have us all burnt at the stake for refusing to acknowledge her as the true mistress of Develish. Her greatest rage was for Lady Anne's plan to give us our freedom. She'd rather watch us die of the pestilence than release ourselves from bondage.'

Thaddeus asked how bad Isabella's injuries were. 'I hate to think of her in pain, Gyles.'

'As do we all. She's pale and weak but able to walk. She took fifteen pricks from a bodkin but none was deep. Milady and Martha are caring for her and say she'll be recovered within a week.'

'I'm happy to hear that. Her brothers will be, too. Did Lady Eleanor give a reason for her behaviour?'

'Only mad rantings about Lady Anne usurping power that should have been hers. She seems unable to understand that, by keeping the secret of her birth all these years, it was Lady Anne who gave her legitimacy. Your stepfather pointed it out to her. You wouldn't have recognised him, Thaddeus. He spoke in praise of you, saying he'd rather bend his knee to you than the ungrateful mongrel Lady Anne has raised.'

There was another quiet laugh. 'I recognise very little of what you're telling me, Gyles. How long has Eleanor known that Milady is not her mother?'

'The mistress told her this afternoon in the hopes of curing her madness. Martha says she's been acting strangely since her father died but never with such lunacy as today. She promises to have Milady condemned as a heretic if she's ever given the chance.'

'Has she been confined?'

'In a serf's hut next to John Trueblood. The enclosure has rung all afternoon with her curses and complaints.'

'What form do her complaints take?'

It was Gyles's turn to be amused. 'Whatever comes to mind. Her worst slurs are against the men of the demesne—yourself included. When we're not cowards and thieves, we're base-born slaves with the appetites of dogs.'

'Is there sympathy for her?'

'Only from my daughter and young Robert. They see virtue in her that others don't, never mind Isabella was within her rights to demand a stronger punishment than Robert's suggestion of a day's imprisonment for each prick she made. No one wants her released before her madness passes. She's vicious enough to kill next time, and she'll receive no mercy from me if she harms Isabella again.'

'Then detain her until your twins return. They've grown in courage and resolve through the death and misery they've seen and won't tolerate anger against their sister from such as Lady Eleanor. Make sure she understands that.'

'You ask for the moon. She refuses to listen to anything serfs have to say.'

'Will she listen to Master de Courtesmain?'

'He's afraid of his own shadow. He can barely stand for trembling at the thought of the vengeance the High Sheriff will wreak on us for daring to put Sir Richard's daughter on trial for wounding one so far beneath her as Isabella. You did Milady no service by handing him your position, Thaddeus. John Trueblood would have made a better steward than the two-faced Frenchman.'

'I thought it wiser to keep him at Lady Anne's side. He has a jealous nature and would have caused trouble for anyone else in the position.'

Gyles nodded agreement before changing the subject. 'How long before we see you again?'

'I'll send your sons and the sons of your friends with the sheep from Afpedle in three days' time. They'll need pens on this side of the moat to take the flock, and a shelter for themselves from the rain. Can the men of Develish build so much in so short a time? And will Milady allow them to cross the moat?'

'No reason why not. She gave permission for you to cross when I returned with Sir Richard. Will you be with the boys?'

'No. I'll bring the wagon later when I've worked out how to get it here. You should make them wait two weeks on this side of the moat. I'm as certain as I can be that they don't have the pestilence, but you should still be cautious. They can use the time to slaughter the sheep and send the carcasses across on the raft.'

'Sheep won't be easy to drive through rain. A man should be in charge of such an undertaking. Let me return with you and take the lead.'

There was a brief pause before Thaddeus answered. 'I don't say I'm not tempted, but your sons have worked hard to prove themselves. Don't think of them as boys, Gyles. Greet them as men and you won't be disappointed.' He urged Gyles to make haste to bring him rope, collars and harness, also oats for the horse if there were any to spare. 'People will expect answers if they find me here, and I'm not a great talker. Any one of my companions will tell our story better than I can.'

Gyles made one last attempt to persuade Lady Anne to reveal herself. She'd seemed so keen to speak with Thaddeus when he'd first approached the moat. 'At least let me wake Lady Anne and bring her out alone. She has felt the loss of your counsel very deeply, Thaddeus.'

'And I hers . . . but I want no sweeter reminders of what I'm missing when even your gravelly old chords are tempting me to linger. Assure her of my loyalty when you tell her of this visit, but do not disturb her sleep on my behalf.'

'Is there anything else you'd like me to say?'

'Nothing you can deliver without blushing, old man. I find I'm more attached to Develish than I thought. It's not easy to break the bonds that hold us to the people and places we know.'

ᘓᘜᘓ

Lady Anne walked in Gyles's shadow to the house, slipping through the door first before instructing him to fetch the rope and tackle while she looked for oats. In the kitchen she made a package of bread, moistened with cold potage—all that was left from the night before—and added a precious hard-boiled egg, pickled in brine. Before she tied the corners of the small sacking bag, she hurried to the steward's office, lit a candle and penned a note which she folded and placed across the egg where Thaddeus would find it.

It was hard to know what Gyles made of this quiet visit by night, but Lady Anne thought she understood it. Almost every question Thaddeus asked had been designed to find out if Eleanor had made accusations of rape or murder against his companions, and Lady Anne knew he would not allow them to return if she had. She wished she could share everything with him, for he deserved an explanation of Eleanor's behaviour, but the girl's secret wasn't hers to tell. Instead, she prayed the words she had written would persuade him she had uncovered the truth about Jacob, and that Eleanor would cause him and his companions no more trouble.

Would he appreciate, or even understand, her need of his support? she wondered. She hoped most earnestly that he did, for a heaviness in her heart told her he was undecided whether to cross the moat himself once the sheep and the grain were safely delivered. He'd been so firm in his resistance to seeing her that, despite his words to Gyles, she feared his true intention was indeed to cut his ties with Develish.

ᘓᘜᘓ

My Dear Friend,

I write this letter in haste while Gyles gathers what you need for your journey. I pray you find it and will be comforted by my words when the sun comes up. I believe you removed yourself and the boys in secret to keep the harmony of Develish from being fractured, and I thank you for your kindness in doing so. I regret most deeply the manner of Jacob's passing—the details of which are known to me—but be assured he rests in peace and the problems you foresaw have not arisen. No one questions that his death was an accident or that your enterprise is noble—to seek supplies for Develish.

I envy you your freedom, Dear Friend, and will not take it from you at any price, but remember the hearts that beat for you in Develish. My guess is that you plan to leave again when you have fulfilled your promise to bring us food, but I beg you not to do so in a hurry. It will sadden me terribly if you arrive and depart a second time by night with only a wagon of grain to show you ever returned. Can you even begin to understand how much you've been missed?

You and I have achieved so much together and I believe you find my counsel wise. Please do not vanish again without allowing me to give you the benefit of my thoughts. You and I have long shared dreams of freedom for our people, but they will have little meaning if you are not amongst us when the time comes for us to break the bonds that keep us here. We depend on your strength more than you realise.

Perhaps you believe your life less necessary to the demesne than husbands and fathers like Gyles Startout and John Trueblood? If so, you are wrong. I have much need of you.

Yours in sincerity,
Anne

୧୨

It was an hour before Gyles came looking for Lady Anne in the steward's office to say Thaddeus had departed again. She was sitting by candlelight, drawing up plans to build pens outside the moat, and she smiled when he spoke of his joy on hearing that his sons were well. 'I'm glad for you, Gyles.'

'But now I have more reason to worry for their safety, milady. I informed Thaddeus of My Lord of Bourne's attack on us, and he shocked me by saying that My Lord and his fighting men were in Holcombe two days ago, a bare forty-eight hours after leaving here. He assured me that he and our sons weren't seen, but Develish will suffer badly if he's wrong. Bourne has only to bring the six of them here in chains and you'll be forced to bargain their lives against the two hundred inside the moat.'

Lady Anne's smile died. She had all but forgotten the evil old man in the tumultuous ups and downs of the day, yet she didn't doubt he would avenge himself on Develish if he could. To have his Norman army repelled by English serfs would have dented his pride, and his greed for the gold he believed to be in Develish's treasury would not have diminished. 'We watched him travel north. How could he have reached Holcombe so quickly? We killed four of his horses and injured more.'

'But not his tow-horses, milady. My guess is he did what I advised Thaddeus against and took a drovers' route. They're the shortest links between highways and, without livestock to hinder him and with enough men to keep his wheels turning, his carriage could manage them easily. Being a thief, he'd prefer them. He's less likely to be seen or challenged if he stays off the public roads.'

'But why Holcombe?'

'Thaddeus says it's all but abandoned, milady. He watched it several days ago and believes only serfs remain in the manor house. He saw horses in the fields so I'm guessing My Lord has taken them to replace the ones he lost. Weapons too, since no peasant would have the courage to gainsay him if he demanded them from their master's armoury. I fear our triumph against him was short-lived and it won't be long before we see him again—with or without Thaddeus and our sons.'

'Did you explain that to Thaddeus?'

'I did, and repeated my offer to accompany him, even suggesting we take James Buckler and Adam Catchpole. With more guards, we'll have a better chance of bringing the supplies home safely.'

'How did he answer?'

'He said you wouldn't permit it, milady. The defence of Develish is more important than sheep herding. He's right, of course, but it doesn't stop me worrying.'

'Nor I, Gyles. I hoped this day would end in the happy knowledge that all six are alive, but it seems our anxiety for them must continue a while longer.'

'Thaddeus looks to the weather to protect him, milady. He offered me a wager that Develish serfs and Afpedle sheep will take driving rain more easily than My Lord of Bourne and his men.'

Lady Anne smiled. 'Then I'll pray for a storm.'

Gyles studied her silently for several moments. 'You were quick to step behind me when Thaddeus approached, milady. What made you think he wouldn't speak freely if he knew you were there?'

There was barely a pause before she answered. 'He asked if you were alone. I understood why when he told you about burning Athelhelm. It's not something he'd want anyone else to hear.'

'Was that your impression, milady? I thought he seemed more worried about the welcome our sons would receive.'

Lady Anne placed her elbows on the desk and rested her cheek against her hands. If she confided in anyone, it would be Gyles. He had been her friend and adviser for ten years, and her affection for him and his family ran very deep. But how could she be honest without revealing why Thaddeus had removed his sons from the demesne? Gyles's pride would be much diminished if he learnt of Ian and Olyver's readiness to be whipped by Eleanor in return for a touch of her breasts.

She recalled the words Thaddeus had written in a letter Isabella had insisted on showing her when she came to tell her of Eleanor's pregnancy—*I do what I do to free your brothers and their friends, not to ensnare them in more intrigue*—and the sentiment was surely as true tonight as it had been two weeks ago.

'You must blame me for Thaddeus's caution,' she said. 'I refused him permission to leave during Jacob's funeral because I felt it spoke of a lack of respect for his brother. I imagine he came to discover if I'd made good on my threat to post him and your sons as absconders if they disobeyed me.'

Disbelief showed in Gyles's eyes. 'You're accomplished in many things, milady, but not in telling falsehoods. Perhaps it would be better to inform our people he came for horse collars and to request that sheep pens be built.'

'I'm sure that's wise.'

He made to turn away but changed his mind. 'Have I done something wrong, milady, failed you in some way, that you think I can't be trusted with the truth? If I frightened you with talk of bandits, I most humbly apologise. Young Robert was right to say my sight is not what it was.'

Lady Anne shook her head in immediate denial. 'You're my closest friend and I would trust you with my life.' She searched his face for a moment. 'Let me pose a different conundrum for you. Would you have me tell you the mysteries of your wife's heart if I knew them?'

Gyles pulled a twisted smile. 'I'd not hear anything good about myself if you did.'

'Then it wouldn't be truth—just words said in a moment of irritation—and my betrayal would be the worse for stirring up trouble where none existed.'

He was too clever to accept such an anodyne excuse. 'But what if the trouble were real, milady? Wouldn't it be a greater betrayal to stay quiet when you know that harm may come to others from your silence?'

Lady Anne spread her hands in a small gesture of apology, praying he didn't think she'd known of Eleanor's plan to attack Isabella. 'I'm less accomplished at reading minds than I am at lying, Gyles. If I knew where harm was lurking, be sure I would tell you.'

He gave a small nod then moved to the door, pausing with his hand on the latch. 'Thaddeus asked me to thank you for the package of food. He recognised the way the bundle was tied and knew you must have prepared it. He thanks you, too, for the candles you light in your window each night.'

She smiled again. 'I heard him say they were a foolish idea.'

'He was jesting. I believe he knew them for what they were the moment he saw them—as I should have done the first day you lit them.'

'And what's that, Gyles?'

He eased open the door. 'A sign that it's safe for our sons to come home, milady . . . though I'm puzzled why they or Thaddeus would need such assurance.'

∞

Two miles down the highway, Thaddeus wished he'd had the sense to bring a pack horse to carry the heavy horse collars that he wore around his shoulders and the tightly coiled ropes and harness that were balanced across his saddle and thighs. However delicately Killer picked his way around the ruts in the road, the collars drew blisters on his neck and the rope jabbed relentlessly against his groin.

The rain, which had begun as a fine drizzle when he left Develish valley, grew in strength the farther south he and Killer travelled, and both were as wet as if they'd taken a swim in the moat by the time they reached the open ground where he and the boys had left the highway a fortnight earlier. He considered looking for shelter under the trees that lined Devil's Brook but doubted he'd ever get himself or the charger moving again. Instead, he gritted his teeth and closed his mind to discomfort, thinking instead about the letter he'd found in Milady's package.

Even while Gyles had been narrating the story of how the serfs of Develish had repelled My Lord of Bourne's attack, Thaddeus had been devouring the bread and the pickled egg. Both tasted the sweeter for being absent from his diet for two weeks, and now the only parts of him that didn't hurt were his half-full belly and the patch of skin on his chest that was covered by the small square of parchment he'd tucked inside his tunic. Without light, he hadn't been able to read what Milady had written but he was sure her words were full of kindness, since she'd had no need to send him a message at all.

Gyles had been careful to hold the lantern at his side as he walked to the front door of the manor house, but Thaddeus's eyes were too well adjusted to the dark to miss the swish of a cloak behind his legs and the deference with which he shepherded a small, slender shadow inside.

He'd felt a brief hurt that Lady Anne had hidden herself from him until he remembered he'd asked Gyles if he was alone. He worried then that it was he who had hurt her by refusing Gyles's offers to fetch her, until the raft brought her package atop the rope.

'I saw you step aside to let her enter the house,' he'd confessed to Gyles as he ate the egg. 'Had I known she was behind you I would have tempered my language about what we've encountered. It wasn't my intention to frighten her.'

'She guessed as much, which is why she hid herself,' Gyles answered. 'But you're wrong to think she frightens easily, Thaddeus. My Lord of Bourne's captain gave a clear indication that the women of Develish, being free of the pestilence, would be as highly prized by his men as gold, so Milady gathered our wives and daughters in the church and armed herself with a dagger in order to kill the first soldier who entered. She knew she would suffer for it, but she intended to fight as fiercely as the men.'

And suffer she would have done, Thaddeus thought now. He could think of no quicker way to break her spirit—and the spirit of her people—than to strip her naked and force her to submit to a relay of soldiers in front of her own serfs. The same would be true if he and the boys were taken prisoner and brought to Develish for a hanging. Gyles had spoken honestly when he said that, for all her strength of mind, Milady would surrender the demesne before she allowed six of her own to be strung from a gallows on the other side of the moat.

Nonetheless, Thaddeus thought Gyles's fears more alarmist than real, for the chances of Bourne finding their camp near the River Pedle were negligible. The greater threat was to Develish, not least because it offered comfort and safety from the storm. If Thaddeus was picturing the joy of being warm, dry and fed inside the great hall, how much more would My Lord and his men be coveting the same?

With sudden impatience, he dismissed Bourne from his mind. It was all too easy to give way to imagined fears when the brain was tired. The more urgent problem was how to move the grain from their camp to Develish. He was taken by Gyles's suggestion of hauling the wagon up the river to Athelhelm, although he worried about the water rising if the downpour continued. He and the horses might keep their feet, but the boys would not. They were too slight and too short in stature.

He recalled his angry denouncing of them the previous night. His mood had darkened after Edmund related the story of Eleanor's birth—a secret known only to Clara until she'd chosen to share it with her son—but he'd lost patience when the boys began to prance about the grass in front of the camp, wearing the clothes and wielding the swords they'd stolen from Holcombe. Their carefree antics were a bitter reminder of the childhood he'd never had, and every frustration he'd ever felt about his own birth had hammered inside his head. But he'd been wrong to lose his temper, and he wished now that he hadn't. They weren't to blame for his terrible sense of betrayal because Milady had allowed him to believe he was the only bastard in Develish.

He fell asleep to the slow, gentle rhythm of Killer's walk, and the beast, unaware of his rider's inattention, continued to feel his way around the ruts and holes in the road. It was what he'd been trained for; rare had been the journey when Sir Richard of Develish was sober enough to see where he was going.

It meant neither was alert to sentries at the end of the drovers' route above Athelhelm, or prepared for the sudden beam of light from a lantern that shone on Thaddeus's face and revealed him as a Develish serf.

Two

Thaddeus's camp on the River Pedle

IAN STARTOUT SAT HUNCHED IN misery, wondering if dawn would ever break. By building a shelter amongst the trees, and positioning their stolen wagon against the side that faced the river, he and his four companions were protected against the worst of the weather, but their inability to light a fire had rendered them blind. Pressed hard against each other in the small space left to them by the twelve large barrels of pilfered grain, they stared sightlessly at nothing, preferring to withdraw into their thoughts than shout above the pounding rain.

Ian's mood was turbulent, swinging between love for Thaddeus and a deep hurt that the man he'd thought of as a friend had left without explanation. Had he not done everything Thaddeus had asked without complaint in their search for supplies? Had he not been the most dutiful and received the fewest rewards? And what should he do if Thaddeus didn't come back? Force these churls to drive sheep through the rain? He hadn't the strength to keep punching their stupid faces when they challenged his orders. The only leader they respected was Thaddeus.

Not one of the boys would have blamed Thaddeus for turning his back on Develish if Edmund's tale about Lady Anne not being mother to Eleanor was true. Any man, bastard-born, would cavil at being forced to live the life of a slave while Sir Richard's daughter, carrying the same stain of illegitimacy, was paraded as a lady. Ian understood well that Thaddeus must have been pained to hear the story from Edmund rather than Lady Anne, but were hurt feelings enough of a reason to cause him to abandon his companions without a word?

Ian's first awareness that night was coming to an end was when he saw the ghostly glimmer of faces in front of the curtain of rain that was running off the shelter's interwoven roof of osiers and fern. As the light strengthened, he saw his own emotions reflected back at him in the eyes of his friends. Wretchedness. Uncertainty. Anxiety. But with the dawn came reason. It made no sense that Thaddeus hadn't returned. He'd worked too hard to locate supplies for Develish to give up on the venture now, and he wouldn't have burdened his conscience with burning Athelhelm if he hadn't intended to herd sheep along the highway that ran through it.

With sudden decision, Ian pushed himself to his feet and began searching through the weapons, clothes and saddles that were piled on top of the grain barrels. They'd tossed everything in when the rain began to fall in earnest, and with the light still too dim to see, he used touch to select what he wanted.

His twin, Olyver, raised his voice to carry above the drumming on the roof. 'Are you planning to look for him?'

'Yes.'

'I'll come with you.'

'Me too,' called the other three boys in unison.

Ian shook his head. 'Just Olyver. If we don't return by nightfall, one of you must ride to Develish tomorrow to tell Lady Anne there's grain here and sheep at Afpedle. The other two must keep the rain off these kegs until help comes.'

'It's not possible,' protested Edmund Trueblood. 'We can keep plugging the roof, but when the ground becomes saturated the water will rise from below.'

'Then think of a way to lift the kegs,' Ian growled. '*Build* something . . . sit with the damned things on your laps, if necessary. Behave like men as Thaddeus expects, and find a solution to the problem instead of saying it can't be done. Develish won't thank us for bringing home mouldy grain.'

Joshua Buckler laid a calming hand on Edmund's arm. 'There are beds at the inn in Holcombe,' he said. 'They're low enough and sturdy enough to make a decent platform if we carry them back.'

Peter Catchpole watched Ian don a second tunic for warmth and then hand another to his brother to do the same. 'You'd better be sure you're doing the right thing,' he warned. 'What if Thaddeus comes back frozen to the bone and finds you gone?'

'Lay him down and warm him up,' retorted Olyver.

'He'll go after you.'

'It's not his job. Get off your own arses to do it.'

'There's no sense in us all dying of cold.'

'Then put your minds to keeping a fire alight and finding food,' Ian told him. 'Whatever happens, we'll need to eat—unless you want to kill Joshua's dogs and swallow them raw.' He selected a leather jerkin and buttoned it across his chest, handing a second to Olyver. 'We'll divide the arrows we made yesterday between us and tie them in bundles across our saddles,' he said, passing his brother a sword and a bow. 'They may not fly straight but they'll look threatening.'

'Where do you think Thaddeus went?' Joshua asked.

'We'll start in Athelhelm and then ride to Afpedle and on to Woodoak. If he comes back without us, follow that path. We'll be somewhere along it.' Ian dragged down a couple of saddles. 'All I know for certain is that he would come looking for us if he thought we were in trouble, so it's only right we do the same for him.'

He glanced at Joshua's hunting hounds, wondering if they'd be able to follow Thaddeus's scent, but he felt Olyver's immediate resistance. Better the twins travel alone than have Joshua's nervousness holding them back was the thought that came to him. He gave a small nod before stringing a sword and bow across his back and reaching for the bundle of arrows.

'Do your best and we'll do the same,' he told the others as he followed his twin into the rain.

They found the horses huddled within the tree line, their flanks running with water. Both boys felt momentary qualms about saddling the two they selected, knowing the animals would develop sores as the hard leather slithered to and fro across sodden fur and rain-softened skin. 'We have to do it,' Olyver shouted. 'We'll get nowhere on foot.'

Ian nodded. 'We should lead them first. There's no point mounting until we reach the highway at Athelhelm. They'll break their legs if they slip on wet grass.'

They didn't speak after that, but as Ian followed behind his brother with the river in spate on one side and dark woodland the other, he wondered if they'd ever been so in tune with each other. He felt the same fears Olyver felt. The light was too dim.

The rain too strong. The level of the river too high. They wouldn't be able to cross the ford at Athelhelm . . . It was strange. They had fought all their lives—refusing to sound alike, behave alike or look alike—yet today he knew every thought that was running through Olyver's head. *Please, God, make me brave.*

ℯ𝔁𝔬

Neither was prepared for what they found in Athelhelm. The storm had come too soon after Thaddeus had fired the village to reduce everything to ash, and charred bodies lay amongst the ruins. One had struggled to his doorway, lying half in and half out of the entrance, and the boys retched at the hideous, swollen face that lay in the dirt. It was impossible to say if it was black from smoke or the putrid blood of the pestilence, but the sight of the bulging, terrified eyes was the stuff of nightmares.

The relentless rain had caused Devil's Brook to break its banks and a stream of loosened mud and stone was washing towards the ford. Even as Ian and Olyver watched, the arm of a corpse lifted as debris passed beneath it, giving the appearance of life. Each wondered how long it would be before the stream became a flood and washed the bodies away or buried them beneath drifts of earth. Perhaps God had brought this downpour for a reason.

As they'd drawn closer to the village and seen how turbulent the water in the river was becoming where Devil's Brook was feeding into it, they'd left the path and moved through the trees in order to come out on the highway above the village. From that vantage point, they could see that the ford to Afpedle was impassable. If they'd known where safe passage was from crossing it before, it might have been different, but the river had backed up the highway, forming a lake which disguised the curve of the road.

'It would explain why Thaddeus hasn't come back,' called Olyver. 'Maybe he's decided to camp in Afpedle.'

Ian turned to look along the highway to Develish. The visibility was so poor he could barely see to the first bend but he was drawn by the idea that Thaddeus might have returned to their home demesne. Yet why? What was so urgent that he was persuaded to ride in darkness instead of waiting for daylight? And who would know he was there except the men who stood on the guard steps?

'I think he went this way,' he answered, gesturing to his right. 'Father and John Trueblood take turns to watch the approach from the village at night. I'm guessing Thaddeus wanted to speak with one of them privately while the rest of the demesne slept. He'll not take us back if Eleanor's made accusations of rape and murder against us.'

Olyver followed his gaze, questioning whether Thaddeus cared enough for any of his companions to continue protecting them. He'd been in a black mood the previous evening, cursing them roundly for their laziness and tomfoolery. 'What if it's Thaddeus she's accused?' he asked, leading his mount alongside Ian's. 'She hates him enough. Could Father have taken him in charge?'

Ian shook his head. 'He has too much fondness for Thaddeus. He'd have sent him away again. John Trueblood likewise.'

'Then where is he?' Olyver asked reasonably. 'It's not that far to Develish . . . and he'd have to have left before dawn if he didn't want his presence known to everyone.'

Ian put his foot in the stirrup and heaved himself into the saddle. 'Let's find out. He'll cuss the Devil out of us if he's round the next bend, and we'll feel mighty foolish for worrying, but we can't get any wetter than we are already.'

⊘⊘

He came to regret that statement when his teeth were chattering with cold. The sun had been up for two hours by then but its light, blocked by dark, heavy clouds was the murky grey of dusk. There was no warmth in it, and the wind sliced easily through his jerkin and double tunic. He kept narrowing his eyes against the stinging rain, searching for movement ahead, but there was nothing to see. He was close to giving up, certain he'd guessed wrongly about Thaddeus's intentions, when Olyver put a restraining hand on his bridle and brought both horses to a halt. He jerked his chin towards the woodland on their right.

'There's something in those trees. Look at the horses' ears. They can hear it.'

Ian canted his head, listening. The sound of a whinny, barely discernible over the wind, was unmistakeable. 'Do you think it's Killer?'

'Bound to be,' said Olyver with decision. 'How many other horses will be out in weather like this?' He slid from his mount. 'We should go on foot.' He adjusted his bow and sword across his shoulder and lifted the bundle of arrows Ian had given him from his saddle. 'Let's pray we don't have to use these.'

They tied their mounts to trees at the edge of the road and crept forward slowly, alert for any noise that would tell them which direction to go, but if a second whinny came, they both missed it. They felt a pounding on the ground more often than they heard anything above the wind and rain. If either had been alone, he would have turned back out of superstitious fear—such strange tremors in the earth weren't normal—but, together, they went on. They could barely see ten yards ahead, so dark was the shade inside the wood, and both gave shouts of alarm as something huge and black rose out of the ground in front of them.

They would have lost all courage if they hadn't heard the rattle of harness and laboured breathing as the creature crashed to earth again. 'Praise be to Mother Mary and all the Blessed Saints!' Ian gasped, before stepping forward and holding out a hand. 'Whoa, boy! Whoa! What's troubling you?'

'Take care he doesn't rear again,' warned Olyver. 'He's scared out of his wits.' He made a gesture to show he was going to approach the animal from the other side. 'He seems to have lost his reins so be ready to catch his head collar. It'll need both our strength to stop him from bolting.'

Perhaps Thaddeus's charger recognised their voices, because his only resistance to being caught was a half-hearted buck as their hands closed on the straps beneath his rolling eyes. Ian ran a soothing palm down his neck, feeling the heat and the trembling under the skin, but it wasn't until he looked at the back legs that he saw why the wretched creature was so frightened. For a brief moment he wondered if the rope bound tightly around the fetlocks was a badly applied hobble, but the tangle of hemp on the forest floor, caught in brambles and fallen branches, told a different story. The horse's rear hooves had become caught in the coils and his attempts to free himself had tightened the noose around his legs.

'What should we do?' Olyver called. 'He's too worked up. The rope's the only thing that's holding him. If we cut him free, he'll run.'

'Not if you go back for our two. He'll calm quicker with his own kind around him.'

'He'll smash your skull if he rears again. Thaddeus didn't call him Killer for nothing.'

'Do you have a better idea?'

'No.'

'Then go.'

All Ian could do was talk to the animal and keep running his hand down the wet neck, ever ready to jump back if Killer made another futile attempt to break free. His eyes were drawn to a breast collar, lying on the forest floor some ten paces behind Killer. The leather bore the Develish crest, much faded from being bleached by the sun, but Ian recognised it as one the serfs used to harness ponies to the plough. He knew then why Thaddeus had returned to the demesne. He'd gone for tack and rope to yoke a number of horses together in order to move the wagon and grain from their camp. He would have called Thaddeus's name if he hadn't been afraid of spooking the horse. And what would shouts achieve anyway? Thaddeus was no coward or weakling. Whatever accident had befallen him, he would have tried to follow Killer's tracks once daylight came.

It was clear to Ian that the horse had been dragging the rope for a distance because the churned-up trail in the leaf mould stretched farther than his eyes could see. Surely Thaddeus could have found it? Surely he would have heard the whinny and the intermittent pounding of the creature's front hooves as Ian and Olyver had done?

If he were able . . .

It seemed Olyver had been thinking along similar lines. 'Something bad must have happened,' he told his twin as he came to a halt with the other two horses.

Ian nodded. 'How should we do this? Killer seems calmer but he's not going to like us touching his back legs. He'll lash out as soon as we cut him free.'

'Do we have a choice?'

'No.'

Olyver's teeth flashed in a grin. 'Your turn then. At least his eyes have stopped rolling.' He tied their two mounts to a tree and stepped forward to take Ian's place at Killer's head. 'We'll need an anchor to stop him running. If you cut a length of rope from the coils on the ground, I'll make a halter to run around the trunk behind me.'

It took longer than Ian hoped. A sword was a poor substitute for a knife when cutting through fibres that were wound so tightly about flesh and bone that there was no give in them. He was mindful of time passing and even more mindful of Killer's hooves. All the while he hoped the clouds would thin, the rain would ease, and the sun would send more light into the forest. But it didn't happen. If anything, the visibility worsened, and with it their chances of finding Thaddeus. As the final strand of hemp tore apart, he rolled aside, shielding his head from lashing kicks as Killer danced away from him.

Olyver placed a foot on the trunk of the tree to brace himself as the horse fought to tear himself free of the halter. 'I'm losing him,' he shouted. 'He's too strong.'

With a groan, Ian scrambled to his feet and caught the end of the rope behind Olyver, wrapping it around his fist and digging his heels into the ground. 'If we find Thaddeus dead, I'll slit the brute's throat myself,' he muttered through gritted teeth.

'Don't tempt fate,' his twin warned as together they reeled the charger in. Once there was enough slack, he secured the rope about the tree and dropped to a squat to draw breath. 'He near scared me to death. I thought he was the Devil rising up.'

Ian walked to where he'd dropped his sword. 'Me too,' he agreed. 'Maybe this darkness is Hell . . . and we just don't know it.'

'I'm hurting too much to be dead.'

Ian followed the trail of rope that Killer had left behind him on the forest floor for twenty yards. 'There's more harness here,' he called back. 'Another breast collar and traces.'

Olyver rose to his feet, stooping to collect the bundle of arrows he'd dropped when they first saw Killer. He split the bundle in two and passed half to Ian as he drew level with him.

After two hundred yards they came across a second set of traces, and it wasn't hard to work out that Thaddeus must have been carrying them, coiled inside the rope, on the pommel of his saddle. Once he fell, the rope had unravelled and become entangled about Killer's legs, sending the creature into a frenzied charge through the trees, dragging the traces and reins behind him.

After another two hundred yards the trail began to dwindle and the twins knew that if Thaddeus wasn't at the end of it their chances of finding him were small. Killer could have travelled a mile with the coil still in place, in any direction, and neither boy was clever enough to follow a track without clear markers.

'Where next?' Ian asked as he cast around for signs of disturbed leaves. 'Do you think we mistook the trail farther back?'

Olyver shook his head. 'We should return to the highway and look for where Killer first bolted into this woodland. Thaddeus is more likely to be there than here.'

Ian couldn't fault his logic but something—instinct?—wouldn't let him give up. He drew his sword and slashed a slice of bark from the far side of the nearest trunk. 'We'll mark every fifth tree,' he said. 'Keep a count. I'll call it a day when you reach a hundred.'

Olyver hadn't reached fifty when the trees began to thin and the light, such as it was, intensified. Either they were heading back to the highway or there was a clearing ahead. He watched Ian draw to a halt and make a damping motion with his hand to urge silence. 'Did you hear that?' he asked, putting his lips to his brother's ear. 'It sounded like a laugh.'

Olyver nodded, tucking his sword into his belt and readying his bow. They didn't need to give each other instructions. They knew it wasn't Thaddeus they'd heard and neither believed that chance could have put strangers so close to where they'd found Killer.

For once the rain was their friend, hiding the sound of snapping twigs under their feet as they crept forward. As the trees grew wider apart, showing an expanse of grass beyond, Olyver spread his hands to suggest they should separate and approach the clearing from different angles. Ian gave a jerk of his chin to signal agreement. Independently, they could move more easily and find better cover behind the thinning trunks, but he swivelled his first and middle fingers between Olyver's eyes and his own to stress the need to keep in visual contact. They must act together or not all.

Ian recognised the wagon in the middle of the clearing as soon as he was close enough to see My Lord of Bourne's crest emblazoned on the side. There was no sign of My Lord or his fighting men, but it was easy to see Thaddeus. He'd been stripped of his clothes and was lying spread-eagled on the grass in front of the wagon, his wrists and ankles bound to stakes which had been driven into the earth. His nakedness, closed eyes and utter immobility told Ian he was dead. No living person could remain so still with freezing rain beating like needles on his exposed skin.

Twenty yards away Olyver was thinking the same. He looked for any flicker of life in Thaddeus and his heart burnt with anger as he made a solemn pledge to kill My Lord of Bourne. From where he was standing, he could see horses hobbled together on the far side of the clearing, but when he followed the tree line to the left and the right, looking for sight of a soldier, he realised it wasn't a clearing at all but some kind of road. The tracks of My Lord of Bourne's wagon, leading from the east, showed clearly in the grass where the wheels had cut into the turf.

He searched the trees around the horses, convinced Bourne's men must be hiding in the woodland, but if they were there he couldn't see them, and the idea entered his mind to run towards Thaddeus and cut him free. Perhaps Ian sensed the thought because he shook his head and held up his hand to signal his twin to be patient. The scene had all the appearance of trap. Yet he wondered who My Lord was expecting. Soldiers from Develish?

He was racking his brain for a plan when a second laugh came from the direction of the wagon. It was followed by the grunt of a voice and he watched the leather canopy open to allow a man to climb out. Ian recognised him as the captain of arms who had ordered his men to burn Develish village a month earlier. He was clad in the fur-trimmed coat that Thaddeus had stolen from the tannery in Holcombe, and he walked to the spread-eagled serf and kicked him in the ribs.

'My Lord grows impatient,' he said. 'Explain the letter you carry from Lady Anne. What is this freedom she speaks of? Do you carry a message of insurrection to the other peasants of Dorset? Is your treachery against God and the King to blame for the pestilence?' He jerked his head towards a couple of horse collars on the ground near the wagon. 'Why were you carrying those? Whose wagon do you plan to steal? Answer me.'

To Ian's eyes the man looked drunk as he launched another kick at Thaddeus's side, staggering slightly when he missed. There was no response at all from their friend, not even the smallest flinch to show he was aware of the other's kicks or even his presence.

'Your refusal to speak makes My Lord the more suspicious. He sees witchcraft behind it. What manner of creature are you with your height and dark skin? Did you think you wouldn't be recognised as the serf who stood with Lady Anne and lied about Develish dying of the pestilence?' He parted his coat and pulled his cock from his britches. 'You seem to find the rain easy enough to bear. Let's see how you like being used as a piss-pot again.'

The bows of the two boys came up in unison but neither had time to unleash his arrow before Thaddeus ripped his hands from the earth and lunged at his tormentor's legs, catching him behind the calves and flipping him backwards. With a tremendous heave, he pulled himself into a sitting position and reached for the stake that bound his right ankle, grasping it with both hands and wrenching it to and fro to loosen it.

On the other side of the clearing, Ian saw a shape emerge from behind an oak. Without hesitation he levelled his arrow at the man's heart and let it fly. He felt a surge of triumph as it flew straight, and he paused only to watch the man drop before feeding a second arrow onto the string and seeing with detachment that Olyver's arrow had also found a mark. He glanced briefly at the squirming body of a soldier on the grass to his right then raised his eyes to scour the woodland for further movement. There had been ten fighting men when Bourne came to Develish to burn it, and a rider on one of the horses that pulled the wagon.

But where were they?

He heard the twang of a string as his twin released a second arrow but Olyver must have missed because Ian caught a movement out of the corner of his eye and turned to see a cloaked figure running at Thaddeus with a drawn sword. He took a breath to calm himself then loosed his own, and watched with satisfaction as the man tumbled to the ground with a hazel whip buried in his thigh.

He had time to see Thaddeus free his left ankle, but it was hard to keep up with events after that. An arrow, shot from a longbow, thudded into the ground at their friend's side and the boys, seeing how defenceless he was, shouted warnings. In doing so, they gave their own positions away and, within seconds, came under attack themselves. Since their only recourse was to crouch in the lee of their trees while arrows ripped through the leaves above them, they had to interpret what happened from what they heard.

Both believed the hideous and prolonged screams that filled the air came from Thaddeus. They told themselves they should do something—move into the clearing, surrender, beg, plead—but their terror was too great. They pictured their own agony when they suffered the same fate, and looked to escape rather than intervene. But how? In the moment Ian realised the rain of arrows had ceased, he looked up to see a man approach through the woodland, bow raised and string drawn taut, frightened eyes darting to left and right.

He was of a similar age to Ian's father and was almost on top of the boy before he saw him. He stared in disbelief at the skinny youth sitting on the ground, his knees drawn up to his chin as if to make himself as small a target as possible. 'You're just a child,' he said in French, lowering his weapon. 'By what madness do you dare attack My Lord of Bourne's army?'

Ian gave a small shrug before stretching his legs to put tension on his bow and rocking backwards to lift it from the ground. The soldier watched in fascinated horror as the tightly bent arc rose horizontally from amongst the leaves, and he had time to curse himself for lowering his guard as a shaft whipped towards his chest from between the boy's feet. He felt the thud as it pierced his ribs and penetrated his lung, and with sudden weariness tried to bring up his own bow to fire back. He'd been wrong to call this youth a child, he thought, as a second shaft caught him in the heart.

Ian had no idea how long he sat looking at the fallen man. A minute? An hour? They were too close to each other. Ian could smell the sweat on his clothes and see the grizzle of grey hair about his jaw. It might have been any of Develish's elders lying there. The noise of screaming from the clearing beat upon his ears, overwhelming him with grief and guilt, and with a sigh he leant to one side and retched on the forest floor. He'd failed in everything, he thought as he rose unsteadily to his feet and forced himself to confront what was happening to Thaddeus.

He couldn't see him. Only two men writhed on the ground, screaming and clutching their bellies, but Thaddeus wasn't one of them. Ian watched their blood, diluted by rain, spread in pink pools across the grass. One wore Thaddeus's fur-lined coat, the other was the soldier with the arrow in his thigh. To their right lay the body of the man Olyver had killed. A flame of hope lit in Ian's breast. Had Thaddeus escaped? He searched to his left for his twin, and the flame became a blaze of joy when he saw Olyver running through the trees towards him.

'Why the hell didn't you show yourself when the longbows stopped?' his brother demanded angrily, jabbing two fingers at Ian's eyes. 'What was all this about if you couldn't be bothered to look at me? I thought you were dead.' He followed Ian's gaze to the crumpled body of the grizzled fighting man. 'Sweet Mary!'

'He could have killed me if he'd wanted to. He lowered his weapon because he thought me a child.'

'Don't feel bad about it,' answered Olyver sternly. 'There's not an ounce of compassion in any of them. You saw what they did to Thaddeus. I thought it was him who was screaming.'

'Me too.' Ian stared around the clearing. 'Where is he?'

'If he has any sense, he's taken to his heels.'

'Maybe we should do the same.'

But neither moved except to make their bows ready to fire again. They shared a conviction that Thaddeus wouldn't run. Ian watched the blood continue to flow from the wounded men, wondering how Thaddeus had injured them so badly until he remembered the stakes that had pinned him to the ground. They'd still been attached to his wrists when he ripped them out, and the points had been sharp. It would be a good and easy revenge to plunge them into an enemy's belly. The pain would be great and the death slow.

'The soldier you hit in the thigh was carrying a sword,' Olyver muttered, 'but it's not there now. Thaddeus must have taken it. Do you think he's gone after the rest? Five are down so there must be six still standing.'

Ian saw that his brother was right. 'Perhaps that's why the archers stopped firing at us,' he said slowly. 'Perhaps they retreated into the wood so he wouldn't be able to see them. This one looked frightened as he came through the trees but it wasn't me he was afraid of.' He paused. 'Maybe we should draw them out again—give Thaddeus a fighting chance.'

'How?'

'By attacking the wagon. Soldiers won't stay hidden if their lord's in danger.' A glint of anticipated triumph lit in Ian's eyes. 'None of his men will fire on us for fear of hitting their master. We can force the surrender of all of them.'

Olyver smiled wryly. 'You've a grand imagination, Twin. You've made him your prisoner before you've even worked out how to do it.'

Ian assessed the distance between them and the wagon. 'It can't be more than thirty paces,' he said. 'I'll lay money I can make that run and put my sword to the old devil's throat before an archer even has time to pick me out.' He laid his bow on the ground, stripping off his jerkin and second tunic to give himself more freedom of movement. He shook his head as Olyver prepared to do the same. 'We can't both go. You're quicker on the draw than I am. Someone needs to bring the fighting men down as they cross the clearing. Shout numbers as they fall.'

'Just don't run in a straight line,' Olyver cautioned. 'You'll take an arrow in the heart if there's an archer behind the flap in the canopy.' He waited while Ian picked up his sword. 'I'll not let you die,' he said with sudden emotion, gripping the other boy's shoulder. 'I'm in no mood to lose a brother today.'

Ian pulled him into a rough embrace. 'And I'm in no mood to lose you or Thaddeus,' he said. 'By God's grace, we'll all three come out of this alive.'

Three

OLYVER PUT MORE FAITH IN gut feelings than in God. He was so convinced the danger would come from inside the wagon that he trained his arrow on the side of the canopy and loosed it the minute the aperture opened. Ian, running in a curving arc, saw a man slump backwards, pulling the flap aside with his arm, and he had time to bless his brother as he leapt onto a small wooden step and hauled himself inside.

The space was confined and he hadn't thought My Lord of Bourne would have a weapon. He felt the sting of a blade against his cheek before the impetus of his leap slammed him against the old man in the far corner of the seat. His flesh recoiled before the pale eyes that looked into his own. If there was fear in them, Ian didn't see it. My Lord seemed to believe his stare alone could compel obedience.

As if to prove him right, Ian scrambled away along the seat, flicking his eyes over the chests and barrels on the floor and the fighting man who was slumped, groaning, atop a wooden box. He felt blood run from the wound on his face and saw a snarling lapdog on the floor at My Lord's feet. The first lesson his father had taught him in sword practice was never to hesitate, and the advice served him well as My Lord eased his arm away from the side of the wagon. Ian swung his sword in a backhanded arc, slicing through the ermine-trimmed cloak and cutting the flesh of the old man's shoulder.

My Lord's blade clattered to the floor as he gave a gasp of pain, but Ian's attention had already shifted to the wounded soldier. Olyver's arrow had embedded itself in his side and Ian watched as the man grasped the shaft with both hands and pulled it from his body. With more regret than he'd felt for injuring My Lord— this was another who could have been his father—he sprang to his feet and thrust his sword into the man's neck. Gyles had told him that such a cut brought instant death but he hadn't prepared his son for the hot blood that sprayed from the wound when the blade was withdrawn.

With a feeling of nausea, he heaved the man's torso across the sill of the wagon and toppled him to the ground before whipping around to place the point of his sword to My Lord of Bourne's throat. Only the dog showed fight, baring its teeth and yapping ferociously, until Ian kicked it and the yaps turned to whimpers of pain. The dead soldier's gore was everywhere. On Ian, on the canopy walls and on My Lord's face and clothes; and this time the pitiless eyes did show fear. 'A place is reserved for you in Hell,' the old man whispered in French. 'You offend against God's laws by what you do.'

Ian placed his knee on one of the barrels to steady himself. He'd never spoken to a lord in his life, not even Sir Richard of Develish, and he needed to calm himself before he did so. He felt a fizz of excitement in his veins to have taken Bourne prisoner but it was hard to forget the Church's teachings that men such as this owned him body and soul. The only sounds were the beating of the rain on the leather roof and the whimpers of the dog. Even the screams of the men in the clearing had silenced.

He ran his tongue around the inside of his mouth to produce some saliva, tasting blood as he did so. But whether it was his or the dead soldier's he didn't know. 'You should fear Hell more than I do,' he answered in English. 'Your cruelty marks you out for Satan. His evil is written in your face.'

'A murderer dares accuse me of sin?'

'I'm no murderer. You invited attack when you ordered your men to take an innocent traveller prisoner.'

'Your friend is a common thief. No serf wears such clothes or rides such a fine charger. My sentries recognised him immediately as the liar from Develish. Few men are so tall or so dark of skin.'

Above the pounding of the rain, Ian heard a cry from outside. He recognised the voice as Olyver's. 'Seven!' his twin shouted.

'Do you hear that?' he asked, leaning forward to press the blade tighter against the crepey skin of My Lord's neck, smelling the foul odour of his breath and seeing the trembling in his hands. 'You have four men left. Will you speak so arrogantly when none remains?'

'I am in God's hands.'

'As am I.'

'Not so. You condemn yourself by your actions.'

A smile flickered across the boy's face as he rested his sword point on the old man's ermine collar. 'Yet you are nothing without these trappings. Even the lowest slave would mock if you stood naked before him and claimed to be one of God's chosen.' He leant forward to part the cloak with his left hand, revealing a loose-fitting gold-embroidered gown. 'You are fashioned as other men. You bleed as readily. What is it that sets you apart except your robes?'

Bourne's pale eyes glittered angrily. 'I carry the King's warrant and am here on his business. If his armies find me dead when the danger has passed, they will search out every living person within twenty miles of this place and put them to the question with hot irons. You will have their agony on your conscience as your entrails are torn from you, and your limbs broken on the wheel.'

Was he speaking the truth? Ian wondered, trying to recall if My Lord had made mention of riding for the King when he'd come to Develish. The idea made him nervous. What if he and Olyver had been wrong about Thaddeus? What if Thaddeus knew Bourne was a King's man and had fled to save himself? He couldn't deny he was a thief. They were all thieves. Murderers, too, if the men Ian and Olyver were killing bore their orders from the King.

A smile played across My Lord's thin lips as he pushed Ian's blade aside with the edge of a gnarled finger. 'Your hand shakes with terror. You understand now how great your offence is in daring to challenge one so far above you.'

It was true. Ian could feel his courage deserting him. Whatever determination had carried him this far seemed suddenly gone, and he sought desperately for what to do next. His brain, worn out by a sleepless night and the constant battering of the weather, had no answers. His only thought was that if he left My Lord alive, he and Olyver would forfeit their lives for certain; and if he killed him, they might not.

Would he have gone through with it? He didn't know. His heart cringed at the thought of slaughtering an unarmed man, for it would make him a murderer indeed. Yet what choice did he have? A rush of weary tears rose in his eyes when Thaddeus's voice spoke from outside.

'It is I who challenges you, My Lord. The offences you have committed against the innocent people of Dorset will not go unpunished.'

A huge fist reached past Ian, grasping the collar around the old man's neck and pulling him bodily past the boy before flinging him to the ground. No words were exchanged as Thaddeus cut the bonds and stakes from his wrists and ankles and used them to bind his prisoner's hands. His concern was for Ian. 'Are you all right, my friend?'

'I think so,' said the boy, jumping from the wagon. Over Thaddeus's shoulder, he saw Olyver emerge from the trees and begin running towards them. 'What about you?' There wasn't an inch of Thaddeus's body that didn't carry lash marks, bruises or scratches. 'We saw the soldier kicking you.' He stared in fascination at the blood-stained sword in Thaddeus's hand.

'It's nothing to fret about. There are more brambles than trees in this vile forest. Does the cut on your face trouble you?'

'Not yet.'

Thaddeus stabbed his sword into the soft turf to keep it upright before bending to unfasten the jewelled clasp at the neck of My Lord's cloak and pulling the garment off him. 'This will give me some warmth at least. He's a scrawny little brute but there's width in the material.'

'Where are your own clothes?'

'Stolen by this thief and his men. I'll have them back as soon as I strip the corpses.'

Olyver arrived as he wrapped the cloak around himself, repositioning the clasp some six inches lower to allow for his broader shoulders and neck. 'I'll not forget this day or the debt of gratitude I owe you,' he promised them.

'We're not safe yet,' Olyver said urgently. 'By my count there are still four in the trees. They'll not fire on us while we have My Lord of Bourne prisoner, but I see no way to escape with our lives unless we take him with us.'

Thaddeus retrieved his sword and rested the tip against the old man's cheek, watching the rain wash gore and mud from the blade onto the grey skin. Both twins recoiled at the look of hatred in Thaddeus's eyes. 'You give him hope of rescue,' he said. 'Only these two wretches still live.' He nodded to the men who'd been screaming.

'I'm not sure every man I hit is dead,' confessed Olyver.

'Nor I,' said Ian. 'They fell but they may only be injured.'

Thaddeus looked around the clearing. 'How did you make your way here? Did you ride?' They nodded. 'Where did you leave your horses?'

'In the same place we found Killer. Half a mile inside the wood.'

A brief smile lifted Thaddeus's lips. 'Is he injured? He fought harder than I to avoid capture.'

Ian, as keen to depart as Olyver, assured Thaddeus that Killer was frightened but unharmed and begged him to make haste. 'We found the rope and traces you brought from Develish so there's nothing to keep us here,' he said. 'Let's go while we can.'

Olyver nodded. 'Our luck won't last. We'll not explain this easily if travellers come along the highway.'

Thaddeus shook his head. 'I've a score to settle with My Lord of Bourne. Fetch our horses and all the harness you can find and bring them to the edge of the woodland, then stay out of sight until you hear my call. What I choose to do here is no concern of yours.'

Ian flicked a nervous glance at the old man. 'He said he's on the King's business. It will cause trouble if he dies.'

'Only for him,' answered Thaddeus before sending them on their way with a warning to concentrate on their own tasks and ignore his. 'Guard your consciences well,' he said, 'and let me guard mine. You've done nothing this day to earn God's judgement. To kill a man in battle is not a crime.'

His words were meant for My Lord as much as for Ian and Olyver, and he took grim humour from the fear in Bourne's face. Judging by the way the old wretch cowered on the ground, he expected death within seconds.

ⲟⲥⲟ

Five miles north, in the steward's office at Develish, Lady Anne was writing in a ledger by candlelight. The rain was incessant, causing Devil's Brook and the moat around the manor house to overtop their banks. She recorded that the fathers of Thaddeus's young companions were building sheep pens and a shelter on the pastureland outside the enclosure while the rest of her people, consumed with anxiety, were gathered in the great hall. The news that Thaddeus had visited during the night to report that he and his companions had found plentiful supplies of food had been a cause for rejoicing until rumours began that he'd said this unnatural darkness was the beginning of the Black Death.

Gyles Startout, the only person to speak with Thaddeus, did his best to calm the fears, but his eleven-year-old nephew Robert proved more successful. Lady Anne paused in her writing to listen to his treble voice win laughter from the crowd by regaling them with a disrespectful tale of how his uncle's elderly eyes had mistaken a horse on a halter for a crowd of bandits. He embroidered the story wickedly, but few doubted he spoke the truth when he said Thaddeus had come only for collars and rope to pull a wagon of grain from Athelhelm to Develish.

Lady Anne had many reasons to bless the boy's level-headedness, not least his matter-of-fact observation to Gyles that Eleanor should be released from her prison when the rain began in earnest. There wasn't a serf's hut inside the enclosure which was strong enough to survive a storm, as they were built as temporary shelters when news of the pestilence first reached Develish, and the decision was made to bring everyone inside the house. With two hundred crammed into limited space, the serfs had had to sleep in serried rows on the floor of the great hall, and none had argued against Eleanor being placed in Lady Anne's charge. Better the vicious girl be confined to a chamber than allowed to wreak her madness amongst the crowd.

Robert had willingly accepted Milady's request to move amongst the rows and relay her order that no one was to enter her room while Eleanor remained inside it. She asked him how much he'd heard of what Thaddeus had said from his position beside the buttress, and when he answered 'everything', she begged him to keep the words to himself. Talk of the land being wasted and Death sweeping all before it would do nothing to alleviate fear, she explained, and there would be no peace anywhere if all began jumping at shadows because they believed rats and fleas caused the sickness.

But what if Thaddeus was right? Robert had asked. Shouldn't Develish heed his warnings if he'd ridden so far to give them? For answer, Lady Anne had urged him to have faith in the moat.

Water prevented rats from crossing to the enclosure as assuredly as it prevented strangers. Had it not kept them safe so far?

As the laughter in the hall died away, she bent again to the ledger. This was a public record which she planned to leave for others to find. In the early days she had written it only as a history of her people in the hope their names would live after them if all perished from the pestilence, but now it had become a story of survival. She dipped her quill in the ink and inscribed Thaddeus's ideas on how the pestilence was spread, adding two paragraphs of her own at the end.

If we have proved anything in Develish, it is surely that isolation is effective against the sickness. In this we have been helped by the moat. Only Gyles Startout has crossed since we burnt the bridge and cut ourselves off from the world beyond our boundaries. I instructed him to wait fourteen days on the other side to prove himself well before allowing him entry, and when the time came for his return, Thaddeus insisted he swim the water naked to prove to our people that he was free of boils and blackened blood. But I wonder if the discarding of his clothes wasn't as important as his two-week exclusion. Fleas prefer the warmth of garments to the sudden cold of bare skin.

More and more, I wonder if Thaddeus has found the answer to how a healthy man might carry the sickness upon him. Yet it's a strange irony that the person we should thank for our continued protection is the man I married. Sir Richard's desire to be admired by visitors persuaded him to order our people to forgo work on their strips in order to spend a season digging the moat and,

while many were weakened by the exercise, it may be that
they will owe their lives to his conceit.

A stir in the air told her the door had opened and she sensed who her visitor was without having to raise her head. Only one man in Develish felt entitled to intrude upon her without invitation or good reason. At times, she wondered if he thought his persistence in seeking her out would soften her heart towards him. If so, he was wrong. 'You have need of me, Master de Courtesmain?'

The Frenchman bent his neck in exaggerated deference. 'My apologies, milady. I was unaware of your presence here. I assumed you were with Lady Eleanor. She was much in need of your care when John Trueblood passed her to your charge during the night.'

'At least she was able to change into dry clothes. Not all are so fortunate. The men who guarded the walls and now build sheep pens on the other side of the moat have been wet to their skins for hours.'

Annoyed that she wouldn't look at him, Hugh de Courtesmain gave a mild admonishment. 'Peasants are better able to withstand discomfort than a nobleman's daughter, milady.'

Lady Anne laid aside her quill and raised her eyes. 'You've taught me something I didn't know, Master de Courtesmain,' she said dryly. 'I was clearly in error to think Isabella felt pain when Lady Eleanor plunged the bodkin into her breast. By what virtue do serfs feel discomfort less than Sir Richard's daughter? Enlighten me. Do they have thicker skin?'

Hugh de Courtesmain cursed himself for yet again giving this woman cause to mock him. To speak with her was to walk on eggshells. He had been trained to answer to hardened lords who knew the place of serfs, not to credulous widows who treated them as equals. 'I misspoke, milady. I should have said they are more accustomed to discomfort than Lady Eleanor.'

She nodded. 'On that we can agree. But being accustomed to hardship doesn't make it any more bearable. If you believe otherwise, cross the moat on the raft and assist our men in building sheep pens.'

'I'm not tutored in the art of building, milady.'

She smiled slightly. 'Nor I, sir, but I believe I could hold a post steady if required.' She studied him for a moment. 'For an educated man, you are slow to understand that the world is changing, Master de Courtesmain. There will be little call for stewards if the pestilence robs all England of its peasant class. The ability to build and to grow food will far outweigh an ability to read when shelter is needed and mouths want feeding.'

Hugh assumed she was signalling her intent to demote him now that she knew Thurkell was safe, and he eyed her bitterly. It wasn't his fault that her husband had chosen him for steward, nor that he had misjudged who held the power in Develish. 'I deserve better, milady. Had you granted me the same confidence you grant Thurkell, I could have served you better. I have tried these many weeks to prove my loyalty to you. Is it because I'm a Norman that you refuse to trust me?'

She shook her head. 'It's because your mind is closed, Master de Courtesmain. You interpret everything I say in terms of yourself instead of looking for the wider meaning. I sought only to advise you to learn skills while you have the chance. A man of many talents will find more opportunities to succeed when the pestilence passes than one who has few.'

'Perhaps I don't share your view of the future, milady. Should I be criticised for that? God gave me the talent of intelligence and I believe it will serve me well whatever lies ahead.'

Lady Anne held his gaze for a moment before bending to her work again. 'I hope you're right, sir. God could surely not have been so mischievous as to give the same talent to bonded men . . . or, worse, bastard slaves and women.'

Four

The drovers' route above Athelhelm

WHEN THE SERF FROM DEVELISH showed no immediate desire to kill him, My Lord of Bourne struggled to a sitting position and rested his back against a wagon wheel. His brindled lapdog crept from beneath the wagon to lick his face and, as the creature nestled on his lap and the rain drenched them both, he studied Thaddeus fearfully from beneath hooded lids.

The man wasn't human, he thought. Nothing affected him. Not pain, not cold, not lack of sleep. Only a creature of the Devil could take the beatings this serf had done and still find the strength to tear himself free of the earth to smite fighting men. Even his great height singled him out as unnatural. Not a word had passed his lips, yet by some magic he had conjured identical twins to his side. It was rare for such siblings to survive a year when no bonded woman had the milk to sustain two demanding infants. But this Develish pair had grown almost to adulthood. How so, unless through heathen practices and black arts?

Bourne felt no emotion when Thaddeus dispatched the dying by cutting their throats, but he watched in alarm as every corpse was stripped of its garments. The intention was clear: to leave the unclothed bodies above ground for scavengers to devour. If the bones were found, there would be nothing to show what manner of men had died, who they were or which lord they'd served. A shiver ran through him as he recalled the words of the boy who had entered his wagon.

You are nothing without these trappings. Even the lowest slave would mock if you stood naked before him and claimed to be one of God's chosen.

Thaddeus grew more fearsome as he re-dressed himself in the clothes that had been taken from him. All were stained with blood, even the boots, but none so badly as the fur-trimmed coat that carried the captain's gore. To Bourne's troubled imagination, the giant had the look of a warrior who wore Death with indifference. If he had a conscience at all, it would not be troubled by the murder of a frail, unarmed noble.

Thaddeus dropped Bourne's cloak into his lap before tossing all the other garments into the wagon. He followed them with the Develish horse collars he'd been wearing across his shoulders when he was captured, and the soldiers' swords, bows and arrows. As a final act of desecration, he dragged the dead deep into the woodland on either side of the drovers' lane before returning with the livery and weapons of the last four men he'd killed and those of the grizzled fighting man who had died by Ian's hand.

Persuaded his time had come, My Lord found his tongue. 'Will you treat me with the same contempt?' he asked in French.

Thaddeus paused to look at him. 'You have my contempt now,' he replied in the same language. 'What more do you fear?'

'That you'll leave me unburied.'

'What difference will a handful of earth make? You'll become food for worms whether you're above ground or below it.'

'Only the Devil would say such a thing. Is that what you are?'

A faint smile twitched at Thaddeus's mouth. 'Believe it, My Lord. Believe your crimes have found you out and Satan has come to claim you.' He watched the old man's tongue flicker nervously across his lips. 'You don't seem to share your companions' faith in the relic you wear around your neck. Why not? You persuaded your men it would protect them from everything, even the pestilence.'

'How do you know this?'

'Your captain told me of it each time he pulled out his cock. He believed a splinter of wood from the Holy Cross could ward off witchcraft and demons. He must have died wondering why you'd lied to him.'

'Your mockery proves you're of the Devil.'

'Only Develish,' answered Thaddeus. 'The spelling is not the same.' He gestured along the sunken lane. 'Is this a drovers' route? Did it bring you here from Holcombe?' When he received no response, he set off to where the soldiers' horses were tethered at the side of the road.

'Don't go,' Bourne cried in sudden terror, believing he had a better chance of life if he kept this man talking. 'You interest me. I would speak with you longer.'

'Then speak,' said Thaddeus. 'Your voice is not so reedy that I won't hear you. I caught every one of your drunken maunderings with your captain last night.' He paused to glance back. 'Begin with why I found you here when all sensible men have fled the pestilence by heading north.'

Bourne blustered about the King's warrant and God's injunction to the righteous to root out evil. Dorseteshire had brought the pestilence to England and My Lord had a duty to hold her people to account. Unheeding, Thaddeus led the soldiers' chargers two by two to the wagon, linking them with halters to a rail at the back before taking the sturdy tow-horses to the front and hobbling their legs until he was ready to harness them. He refused to answer any questions himself.

'But you insist that *I* explain myself,' Bourne snapped in frustration.

'I insist on nothing,' said Thaddeus, leaning through the leather canopy and pulling a wooden chest towards him. 'If you wish to speak, you may. If you don't, don't.' He studied the padlock and then bent to pull the neck of My Lord's gown apart. A delicate glass vial, contained in gold tracery, hung on a gold chain around the scrawny neck and, beneath it, an iron key on a leather thong. 'I've no wish for your relic,' he said, lifting the thong over the old man's head. 'Splinters come two-a-penny on any carpenter's floor.'

'You blaspheme against the Holy Cross.'

'I question your intelligence. Whoever sold you your sliver of wood must have thanked God for sending him a fool for a customer.'

Thaddeus turned the key in the lock and threw back the lid. Folded parchments, a small writing box with a quill and a stoppered bottle of ink lay on a treasure of coins. He recognised Lady Anne's handwriting on one of the squares, the seal broken, and he opened it to decipher what she'd written.

'Where is mention of treachery or insurrection in this?' he asked, showing the page to My Lord.

'Your mistress speaks of overturning God's social order. There can be no freedom for serfs.'

'The pestilence will free us. Those who survive will be in high demand when there's no one to work the land. Lords and their households will starve if they cannot attract labourers to their demesnes on the promise of payment.'

'You share her heresy.'

'I share her reasoning, as do all Develish serfs. It's incompetent fools who cling to the belief that the world will be unchanged when the pestilence ends.'

The old man's lips thinned. 'Only a sorceress could have kept her people alive so long.'

'Or a saint. You should praise God for His mercy instead of giving the honour to Satan.'

'Now you blaspheme against your Maker. Have you no fear of His anger?'

'None. There can be only one truth if the pestilence was sent by God. To die is a punishment for wickedness, to be spared is a reward for goodness. Since Develish has been spared, what further evidence do you need that Milady is loved in Heaven?'

There was a small silence. 'Do you believe that?'

'I believe what I see and know—that there are wicked amongst the living and good amongst the dead.' Thaddeus reached for another parchment. 'If you're the King's man you'll carry his mandate. Which of these bears his signature? I'll break every seal if I have to.'

Bourne's eyes narrowed angrily. 'For what reason except to damage them? They can mean nothing to you.'

Thaddeus ignored him. He snapped the wax and scanned the document briefly before reading another. 'Would these ever have reached the King?'

In the absence of an answer, he continued to break the seals and read what was written. All were addressed to His Gracious Majesty in French and all bore the names of women with their demesne titles beside them. *Lady Mary of Steynsford . . . Lady Paulann of Herringstone . . . Lady Bernadine of Chetel . . . Lady Katherine of Wolueston . . .* The writing was in the uniform script of a single hand, as if each woman had dictated her thoughts to the same person, and he didn't doubt that person was Bourne. There was desperation in every word. All spoke of the deaths of their husbands and their inability to run their demesnes alone. Some said their stewards had died, others that they'd fled when the pestilence began to wreak havoc amongst the serfs.

> *Your Majesty . . . Have mercy . . . My husband is dead*
> *and his steward gone . . . I have no one to advise me . . .*
> *You leave us destitute by this demand for gold . . . The*
> *pestilence rages across the land . . . There is nowhere to*
> *sell our produce . . . The serfs die in the fields even as they*
> *struggle to bring in the harvest . . . Your people will starve*
> *without money to buy fresh supplies . . . Have mercy . . .*
> *Have mercy . . .*

Thaddeus recalled how often Lady Anne had told him she was unusual in having an education. The only talents most women of her class possessed were skill with embroidery and the ability to manage servants. 'I wonder you bothered to record accurately what these poor ladies dictated,' he murmured. 'Were you not afraid to condemn yourself by your own hand?' He lifted a darker pigmented parchment, the seal of which was already broken. 'The King sends his respects,' he read aloud, 'and directs Bourne to collect revenues on his behalf in Wiltshire.' He ran a finger over the cracks in the vellum. 'The letter is an old one, written long before the pestilence reached our shores.'

My Lord eased his wrists inside their bonds. A nervousness bit at his belly; he'd been mistaken to think a man who could read so fluently was a serf. 'What is your name and status?' he asked. 'You seem to have some learning.'

'Rather more than you, My Lord.'

'May God strike you down for your insolence.'

'And you for yours. Does the King know you traduce his name in order to rob the people of Dorseteshire when your estates are in the neighbouring county of Wiltshire?' Thaddeus held the vellum in the water that streamed off the leather canopy and watched the ink begin to run. 'The demesnes in these parts are the fiefdom of My Lord of Blandeforde. Do you have leave to collect taxes on his behalf?'

'You speak of things you don't understand.'

Thaddeus shut the lid of the chest before relocking it and placing the leather thong around his own neck. 'You shouldn't have kept these letters, My Lord. They tell the tale of your deceit clearly enough. If it was your hand that wrote them, you're doubly condemned as a liar as well as a thief. Only the basest of men would give a woman hope of the King's mercy while leaving her destitute.' He pushed the chest aside and hoisted himself into the wagon.

'You're no less of a thief,' My Lord snapped. 'You plan to steal the gold, do you not?'

Thaddeus ignored him. 'You searched out demesnes where only widows and serfs remained, knowing an army on horseback would frighten them into bringing out their wealth. Lady Anne defeated you but few others dared try, I imagine.' He found collars and harness for the tow-horses beneath the seat and lowered them to the ground. 'How much worse are your crimes than the paltry sins of the Dorseteshire peasants who've died of the pestilence? You should have joined them long since . . . yet I'm guessing the opposite is true, and it's the wretches you've robbed who have perished.' He jumped to the ground with a bundle of traces in his hand. 'Is that why you stay amongst us? To make sure of it? If all are gone, My Lord of Blandeforde and the King will never hear of your thieving.'

Bourne turned his head.

'You were travelling away from the pestilence when you first passed through Develish. How far north did you go? What did you find? Are counties other than Dorseteshire affected?' When no response came, Thaddeus placed his heel on his prisoner's ankle. 'You have no value to me except in what you know,' he said. 'I'll kill you bone by broken bone if you choose silence now.' He began to exert pressure. 'And don't waste time with talk of God's vengeance. Worry more about mine.'

Perhaps Bourne needed to tell his story for, once started, he required little prompting to continue. He had been staying with cousins in the west of the county when a messenger arrived with news that a pestilence was sweeping the land. He was undecided about returning home until a servant died and he saw the putrid colour of her face. The journey back to his own estates in Wiltshire, some sixty miles to the north-east, would be long and perilous, but he believed it was necessary. It was clear to him that Dorseteshire was doomed, more so when travellers and mendicant friars warned with increasing alarm that nowhere was safe. From Melcombe in the south to Shafbury in the north, all were afflicted, and monasteries and grand houses were falling as easily to the sickness as the smallest of hamlets.

At times he used the words 'I have sinned', as if he hoped a sign of contrition would wring sympathy from his persecutor. He excused his actions on weakness. To see a demesne dying and to learn from a desperate woman that there was gold in her husband's coffers was a temptation. Death was written in every face and, since My Lord believed that only the wicked were being punished, it seemed a worse crime to let the money go to waste.

'We refused offers of hospitality,' he said, 'preferring to make camp in the open air. We put our faith in God to protect us.'

'Did you ever reach your own estates?'

My Lord nodded. 'They are as ravaged and desolate as any we saw here. Barely three in ten of my people survives. My foolish wife gave orders that comfort should be offered to the sick, and she brought death to my demesnes—to herself also—by doing so. She was as dull-witted as all her sex.'

'Was there no steward to guide her?'

'He was as dull-witted as she. They listened to the priest who preached salvation through good deeds and kindness, and now all are dead.'

Thaddeus wondered that the old man dared declare his hypocrisy aloud, but he was more interested in why he'd returned to Dorseteshire. He put the question to him, adding, 'Wouldn't it have been wiser to keep heading north, away from the pestilence?'

'It was too far ahead of us already. We heard word at the abbey that it had reached Oxford. The whole country trembles in fear. London has fallen to it in the east and Bristol in the west. The abbot called it a wind of destruction, blowing across the land, and

it seemed more sensible to retreat behind it than run before it.'
The pale eyes studied Thaddeus. 'Your good health suggests I was
right. Has the danger passed here?'

Thaddeus shook his head. 'You owe your life to the way you've
been living and not the capricious nature of wind.' He took
up the collars and traces and walked to the tow-horses. 'Your
saviours have been this wagon and these horses. If you'd had to
pass through afflicted villages on foot—or your conscience had
allowed you to take a woman's hospitality before you stole her
gold—you'd be dead.'

'Why?'

'We found survivors in Woodoak who say the pestilence comes
from rats, and it may be true. None has died in that demesne since
they left their houses to live in the open.' He laid the harnesses
on the ground to untangle them.

'Why do you refuse to see God's hand behind it?'

'Because good people like your wife are dead while you and
I are not,' answered Thaddeus, placing the harness across the
horses' backs.

My Lord watched him attach the traces to the collars before
easing the animals between the shafts and buckling the back straps
and girths. 'Is your plan to kill me even though I've answered
your questions?'

Thaddeus stooped to remove the hobbles. He took hold of
the lead horse's bridle, clicking his tongue to set the animal in
motion. He was afraid the wheels would bind in the wet ground,
but they moved easily enough, and he drew the convoy to a halt
after a few yards. He looked back to see My Lord fallen on the
grass, crying out in terror of the dancing hooves of the horses at
the rear of the coach.

Thaddeus dragged him clear and propped him against the wheel once more. 'Why would I want your life?' he asked, squatting on his haunches to stare into the old man's eyes. 'You're no threat to us. My young friend had it right when he said you're nothing without your trappings. Who will recognise you for a lord when you have no fighting men or servants to vouch for you?' He paused. 'I'll take your wagon and horses because they're a gift sent by God—they'll save me from having to drag my own cart along a riverbed—but I'll not take your life. It's of no value to me. I don't say I wouldn't enjoy stealing your estates in Wiltshire by claiming to be My Lord of Bourne—' a brief humour flickered in his eyes—'but even if only a handful of your people survive, they'll know me for an imposter.'

A look of disquiet appeared on My Lord's face. 'Is this the freedom your mistress spoke of in her letter?' he gasped, struggling to bring his breathing under control. 'The theft of another's birthright?'

'Why not? Do you think a rise in status less tempting than widows' gold? The pestilence makes equals of us all. A clever and resourceful serf can seize whatever opportunities are placed in his way.'

Bourne seemed genuinely shocked, and Thaddeus wondered that he was unable to conceive of a world where the rules he lived by were overturned and abandoned.

'You'll never pass for a noble,' the old man protested, while knowing he was wrong. If any serf was clever and resourceful, it was surely this one.

'I already have.' Thaddeus watched the brindled cur crawl through the grass to resume its place on its master's lap. 'You may keep your dog for company, and I'll leave you your clothes and the use of your hands and feet . . . which is more than you allowed me.'

'I'll die without food or shelter. You'll be no less guilty of murder if you leave me helpless. My death will be forever on your conscience.'

Thaddeus smiled. 'Don't flatter yourself, My Lord. I shall forget you as quickly and easily as you would have forgotten me.'

Bourne dropped his gaze. 'My intention was never to kill you,' he muttered. 'Had you answered my questions, I would have ordered your release.'

Thaddeus pushed himself to his feet, the strain of stretching bruised and stiffening muscles showing in his face. 'Before or after you took your brutish soldiers to Develish with me as your hostage?' he asked, reaching inside the canopy for his sword.

Bourne's mouth dried in fear. 'There was no such plan.'

'I heard you talk of it. You told your captain it would relieve the men's boredom to play cock-sports with witches. Lady Anne's letter appeared to express affection for me so you didn't doubt she'd offer herself and all Develish's young girls in return for my life.'

'It was said in jest. I sought to humour him with a common soldiers' fantasy.'

Thaddeus ran his finger down the edge of the blade, testing for sharpness. 'You succeeded. He liked the idea of using Lady Anne as a vessel for his Norman filth. If memory serves me right, he promised to break her for you first.'

Bourne closed his eyes. 'Your mistress was never in danger. I wouldn't have allowed it.'

'She'd have died before her people because she'd have placed herself between them and your men. She takes her oaths of fealty seriously, unlike you.' Thaddeus rested the blade against the old man's neck. 'Remind me again why my young friend committed an offence by daring to challenge you. I forget the reasons.'

There was a long hesitation. 'You know them well enough. Each person's standing is defined by his birth. You cannot alter what God has ordained.' A sigh fluttered from his lips. 'What do you want from me? Contrition for the privilege my birth gave me?'

Thaddeus smiled slightly. 'I'm not your priest, but if I were, I'd demand a more honest repentance than that.' He lowered the tip of his sword to the ground and put his hand behind the old man's neck to force his head forward. 'Your sin was to abuse your privilege, not to be born to it.' He was surprised at how violently his prisoner fought against his restraining hand.

'Have you no mercy?' Bourne cried, writhing and struggling to avoid the chop of the blade. 'At least give me time to make my peace with God before you strike.'

'I am a man of Develish,' Thaddeus answered. 'My word is my bond.' He cut the sodden ropes that tied his prisoner's hands. 'This is as merciful as I'm prepared to be,' he went on. 'In two or three days, I shall return along the highway with your wagon full of grain. If you're still alive and free of the pestilence, I'll hear your entreaties then.'

Spared one death, My Lord rushed to be spared another. 'I'll not survive that long,' he pleaded. 'The cold and wet are already deep in my bones.'

'In mine also . . . and through your fault.' Thaddeus pulled Bourne to his feet and felt the shivers in his hand and arm. With a sigh of irritation, he reached back through the flap in the canopy and pulled tunics and britches from beneath the tabards. 'You'll be warm enough in dead men's clothes,' he said, dropping them to the ground. 'The inner layers will stay dry if you wear your cloak atop them.'

Above the old man's head, he saw the twins appear amongst the trees with Killer and the other two horses. The boys paled at the sight of My Lord on his feet and the sword in Thaddeus's hand, their eyes full of anxiety that they were about to witness a murder. To set their minds at rest, Thaddeus tossed the blade into the wagon.

'Your other choice is to walk to Develish,' he said, retrieving the cloak and handing it to the old man. 'At a steady pace you should make it before nightfall. If you're willing to beg charity from a woman you've wronged, Lady Anne will float warm potage and clothing to you on the raft and allow you the use of a shelter which is being built on this side of the moat. Make no attempt to cross the water and be honest when you explain your presence there. Milady will not believe lies.'

He raised a hand to the boys, calling to them that he was ready to leave, and My Lord followed his gaze, a frightened confusion in his face, as if the reality of his situation was only just beginning to dawn on him. 'Will you do this?' he asked.

'What?'

'Leave me to die.'

'I'm not your keeper, My Lord. What you choose to do once we've gone is your business. If you lack the will to live, no one can help you.'

Trembling fingers gripped his sleeve. 'It's but a few days since my archers fired on Develish. Milady will recognise me and not offer charity.'

'Then die here,' said Thaddeus dispassionately, pulling himself free. 'You'll not be recognised when your bones are found, for no one will know they were yours. Bourne will be written out of history as surely as every poor serf who has died of the pestilence.'

He took up the reins of the tow-horses and motioned to the boys to fall in at the rear with Killer. Having never driven a wagon before, he preferred to lead the convoy on foot rather than attempt to control it from the saddle. Had he been confident of keeping the wheels moving on saturated turf, he would have turned the vehicle and taken the drovers' route to Holcombe, but common sense told him the impacted mud of the highway was the safer course. He shook his head as My Lord tried to mount the step beneath the opening in the canopy.

'Don't make me pull you out again,' he warned. 'I'll snap you across my knee the next time, and your death will be the more painful because of it. Make your way to Develish and say Thaddeus Thurkell sent you. You'll not be judged as harshly by Lady Anne and her people as you will by God.'

The thirteenth day of September, 1348

A strange event happened this afternoon. Gyles Startout summoned me to the moat with news that a cloaked figure was approaching on foot from the village. The traveller had come from the south and his progress up the valley had been slow. I recognised My Lord of Bourne as soon as he was close enough for me to see his face, but he is much diminished from the last time we saw him. He lacks presence, dressed in peasant's britches and without a carriage or fighting men to give him stature.

I had it in my heart to feel sorry for him when I saw how his teeth chattered from the cold. His garments were so drenched by the rain—which continues to fall as heavily as ever—that we could see his bony shape through the many layers of fabric. Quite a crowd gathered to watch him, and I fancy my pity was shared by others, for no one laughed to see him in such distress. He carried a small lapdog, cradled tenderly against his breast, as if he cared more for the animal's welfare than he did for his own.

Whether through fear or cold, he was unable to speak. He stood trembling on the other side of the moat with eyes cast down and his right hand stretched out in entreaty. His arm clearly troubled him, for he was unable to hold the gesture without wincing, but I couldn't tell if the seat of his pain was beneath the tear in his cloak or in the raw injuries about his wrist, which suggested his hands had been bound. He was without a head covering and scabs of dried blood were matted in his white hair, adhering so fast to the strands that the rain had not dislodged them. I looked for a wound on his scalp but could not see one.

He cut a sad and pathetic figure, and even Gyles seemed moved to sympathy. I sent Jenny Buckler for a tunic, britches and Sir Richard's heavy woollen mantle, and asked Clara Trueblood to bring a bowl of hot potage and a jar of liniment. While they were away, I explained to My Lord that we would send the items across on the raft, but that he must not attempt to board it or my archers would fire on him.

If he had thoughts of disobeying, he changed his mind when he saw the intent in the faces of my leading serfs. Even as John Trueblood and Adam Catchpole used poles and ropes to set the raft adrift and control its direction, Gyles Startout and James Buckler raised their bows and sighted their arrows on My Lord's chest. His alarm was so great that I feared he would die of fright before he could warm himself with the soup and clothes.

I gave him leave to use the hut we've built to shelter Thaddeus and his companions, but he is incompetent at performing even basic tasks. Despite our leaving dry kindling, wood and a tinderbox inside the shelter, he was quite unable to set a fire. John Trueblood urged me in a whisper to be thankful, for he didn't doubt My Lord would have set the hut ablaze had he succeeded. However, the old man's inability to warm himself obliged me to send precious fleeces across to bring colour back to his cheeks.

When he found his voice, he thanked me from inside the shelter for my charity towards him. I suggested he extend his thanks to all in Develish, since the homespun he was wearing and the food he was eating were as much my people's as mine. He did so with a show of humility, although it clearly demeaned him to bend his neck to serfs. I asked then why he had come to us without fighting men to protect him, and he answered that Thaddeus Thurkell had sent him, promising food and shelter as long as he made no attempt to cross the moat.

My Lord is unused to having his pronouncements questioned. I believe he hoped we would think that Thaddeus had found him wandering and bereft and had taken pity on him. He showed great reluctance to explain further until I asked who had bound his wrists and what manner of injury had caused blood to clot in his hair.

Few accept as true the story My Lord told us, and we will have to wait for Thaddeus's return to learn it all. My Lord would have us believe that Thaddeus and twin youths used the cover of darkness to take him and his men by surprise while they slept; but since Thaddeus was travelling alone and did not leave Develish until some 3 hours before dawn, this seems unlikely. When and where could he have met the Startout twins in order to plan and launch such an attack before daybreak?

My Lord said their purpose was to steal his wagon and horses, but when I asked him why Thaddeus would endanger himself and his companions for something he already had— namely, a wagon and horses at Holcombe—he had no answer. Nor could he give me a reason for why Thaddeus would spare his life but murder 11 defenceless men in their sleep.

Whatever the truth, it pleases Gyles to know his sons fought alongside Thaddeus—which they surely must have done for Bourne to mention twins—although John Trueblood, Adam Catchpole and James Buckler worry for Edmund, Peter and Joshua. If they live, why were they not with Ian and Olyver?

We are wary of taking My Lord's word on anything. Indeed, had he not arrived in such a parlous state, giving Thaddeus's name as the man who had sent him, we would have dismissed his tale as an old man's fantasy or, worse, a deliberate falsehood to persuade us we're no longer at threat from his soldiers.

He claims to be free of the pestilence and promises to make it known if he begins to feel unwell. It's of little matter whether he does or not. Gyles, who knows the sickness better than *anyone, will see the signs even before My Lord is aware of them. If he dies inside the hut, we will use fire arrows to set it ablaze as soon as the rain ends.*

I pray that end comes soon, for I worry that Thaddeus was overly confident to think he and his companions would survive this storm easily. Cold and damp kill as mercilessly as the pestilence.

Five

Develish, Dorseteshire

ELEANOR WATCHED MY LORD OF Bourne's arrival from the window of Lady Anne's chamber. She knew his face from the first time he came to Develish but little else about him was recognisable. He seemed frail and shrunken and cupped his hands in entreaty more often than he asserted dominance. Indeed, were it not for Lady Anne's courtesy in giving him his title and urging him to accept the only hospitality she could give him, strangers would have said he was a person of no account.

She was still at the window a half-hour later when Lady Anne sought her out. 'He should be raging at you for denying him entry,' she said harshly, her stance rigid and unforgiving. 'He disgraces himself by showing so little spirit.'

Lady Anne stood beside her and watched Bourne, huddled in fleeces in the gloom of the shelter, stroke the little dog in his lap. 'Do you have no pity for him, Eleanor?'

'Why should I?'

'He's alone and afraid. His men are gone and his only comfort is his pet.'

'Does it please you that Thaddeus Thurkell killed them?'

'If he did, it would have been for a reason.'

Eleanor rounded on her, eyes glittering with tears. 'For the same reason you would have me kill Sir Richard's baby? To be rid of a nuisance?'

With a sigh, Lady Anne reached for her hand. 'The choice isn't mine to make, Eleanor. I have given you the means, but the decision on whether to take it must be yours.'

The girl drew back, as if fearing Lady Anne's touch would cause her pain. 'You'll judge me whatever I do,' she said bitterly. 'You forgive Thaddeus Thurkell everything, but never me or my father.'

This time, Lady Anne wouldn't allow her to escape. She reached for Eleanor's hand again and caressed it gently between hers. 'You've committed no fault, daughter, so I've no reason to judge you. It's I who should beg forgiveness of you.'

Eleanor's tears spilled on to her cheeks. 'Why?'

'For failing as a mother. I should have worked harder to earn your love instead of leaving you to seek comfort from your father. You would not be in this unhappy situation if you'd felt able to trust me. Do you think you might be able to trust me now? I beg you to believe, I have always thought of you as my daughter and truly do have only your best interests at heart.'

Perhaps pain was indeed what Eleanor felt, for she snatched her hand away, as if from a burning flame. But the racking sobs that consumed her thereafter suggested her anguish was based in regret; though whether for what might have been or for what she faced now, Lady Anne didn't know.

ॐ

Pain had featured largely in the decisions Edmund, Joshua and Peter had made that day. Left to find a solution to keeping grain barrels dry inside a shelter with a leaking roof and water rising from the ground, they had opted to take them back to where Thaddeus had found them: the inn at Holcombe. But since Thaddeus was the only one strong enough to lift a hundredweight barrel on his own, the work was laboured and arduous.

Peter, the most workshy of the three, took every opportunity to scold Joshua for not supporting him the previous day when he'd urged Thaddeus to leave the barrels where they were. It had been hard enough moving the damned things in sunlight; to do it again in a storm was well nigh impossible. Nevertheless, he put his back into the task when Joshua reminded him that the inn had a hearth and enough furniture to keep a fire going for days. The place was a palace compared with their sodden camp, which was close to being submerged by the rising waters of the River Pedle.

The wagon had proved worse than useless, becoming stuck in the sodden sward before they'd loaded a single barrel, and they were forced to do the job by hand. To spread the weight, Edmund fashioned a triangular litter out of hazel whips to allow each to take a corner, but they could only manage one barrel between them and the inn was some two thousand paces from their camp. Peter estimated they'd have to walk more than twenty-four miles to complete the task, twelve with the weight of a barrel and twelve without, but Joshua said it had to be done so there was no point complaining. On each trip they added some of what they'd stolen from the tannery, spreading the wet garments and cloth over the stools and tables in the inn's hall to dry.

When they lowered the last keg to the floor, Peter announced his intention of lighting a fire and stewing the remains of the sheep that Thaddeus had slaughtered two days ago. But Joshua shook his head. 'We must go back to the camp. The others won't know where to find us.'

Edmund agreed. 'There'll be no light at all in a couple of hours. If they're not there already, we'll have to go looking for them.' He took a sword from one of the tables and tucked it into his belt. 'You made the same promises we did,' he reminded Peter, seeing the reluctance on the other boy's face. 'Do I have to fight you to make you honour them?'

Grudgingly, Peter pulled on a second tunic. 'It'll be a waste of energy,' he grumbled, heading for the door. 'We'll not be able to search in semi-darkness.'

He regretted his words when they reached the camp and discovered Ian's pony standing listlessly amongst the trees and the boy unconscious inside the shelter. He lay in a ball on the ground, blue-lipped and pale-skinned, a crusted gash scarring his cheek, and no amount of Joshua's shaking or calling woke him. Yet he seemed to be breathing and a pulse throbbed in his wrist.

'What's wrong with him?' asked Edmund. 'Has the cut robbed him of blood?'

'He's cold,' said Peter, dropping to the ground and manhandling Ian onto his lap so that he could pull him tight against his chest. 'We need to warm him. One of you must kneel on his other side and press up close.'

Joshua obeyed readily but Edmund shook his head. 'We'd do better to carry him back to the inn.'

'There's no time,' countered Peter. 'If Ian's in this state, Olyver will be worse. Sleep like this isn't good. My grandfather never woke from it that winter we had three feet of snow in Develish.'

Watching Peter's efforts to bring colour to Ian's cheeks, Edmund wondered what made him so contrary. There was no telling which tasks he would choose to shirk and which to embrace. Seemingly oblivious to the saturated ground and the rain dripping through the thatch, he put all his energy into ministering to their friend, instructing Joshua to breathe warm air onto the nape of Ian's neck while he did the same to each hand, and urging Edmund to rub the boy's arms and legs in order to heat the sluggish blood. When, finally, a flutter began in Ian's lids, Peter dug his finger and thumb into an earlobe and spoke in a good imitation of Gyles Startout's gravelly voice.

'It's past time to wake, boy . . . We need to find your twin . . . Your mother's tears will never end if Olyver dies . . . Tell me where he is so that we can look for him . . .'

A whisper of sound came from Ian's mouth. 'On the highway.'

'Which part of the highway?'

'Above Athelhelm . . . too much mud.'

Peter urged him to say more, but his speech was slurred and impossible to understand.

Edmund rose to his feet. 'He's given us enough,' he said. 'Joshua and I will head through the woods and hope the dogs can pick up the scent once we reach the road. What about Ian? Can you manage him alone?'

Peter nodded. 'If I can't wake him enough to walk to the inn, I'll lay him across the pony.' He jerked his chin towards the sward where the remaining horses were hobbled. 'You should take one of the others in case you have to do the same with Olyver.'

The advice was good but, without a halter, there was no way to implement it. Nor was it possible to lead a horse along the footpath towards Athelhelm. The river had risen so high the water was lapping inside the tree line. Edmund searched for sizeable pieces of chalk on the sward, handed some to Joshua, took what bearing he could from where he judged the sun should be and then entered the woodland in a direction he hoped would bring them to the road.

'Make crosses on the far side of every tree we pass,' he told his friend. 'That way we can look back and see if we're heading in a straight line. We'll move in circles otherwise.'

After that, they spoke little. Edmund checked behind him constantly to make sure their path was true but, since he had little confidence in his estimate of the sun's position, his greatest fear was that they were travelling due north instead of north-west. His worries grew as the light faded and the chalk marks on the trees became harder to see.

Joshua sensed his anxiety. 'Don't lose heart,' he called. 'I've been counting paces. We've done three thousand so far, which is well short of the two miles we know we have to walk . . . probably more, since we'll be coming out above Athelhelm. The time to fret is when we pass six thousand.'

From then on he spoke the numbers aloud. Edmund found the sound reassuring, though he doubted Joshua had told the truth about counting the first three thousand. He had yet to reach five when a road, awash with water, opened out in front of them.

⁂

Ian opened his eyes to see Peter kneeling before a blazing fire inside a great hearth and stirring a cauldron. He had a vague recollection of reaching the camp and finding it empty, but none at all of being brought to a building. His exhausted mind would have lapsed into sleep again had Peter not turned and seen that he was awake.

'Oh, no, you don't!' the boy said firmly, shuffling across on his knees and linking his arm through Ian's to pull him into a sitting position. 'You'll stay awake long enough to eat, then you can sleep as long as you like.' He pulled forward some rushes and wedged them behind Ian's back before returning to the cauldron and ladling some mutton stew into a bowl.

'Where are the others?'

Peter squatted beside him and fed a spoonful of shredded meat into his mouth. 'Looking for Olyver. You woke long enough to tell us where you'd left him. What happened? How did your cheek get sliced?'

But Ian's only interest was the story of My Lord of Bourne's wagon, and Thaddeus's single-minded determination to keep it moving. 'The highway became impassable a half-mile above Athelhelm. Devil's Brook had overrun its banks and the wheels became stuck in ruts filled with silt and debris. I told Thaddeus we should give up and head for the camp but he wouldn't listen.'

'Why not?'

'He said we hadn't come all that way to abandon the wagon on the highway. He persuaded the horses to pull it another few paces by lifting the front and walking backwards, but I swear to God I've never been so scared. He thinks he can do everything . . . and he can't. His face turned grey with the effort. I thought he was going to die.'

Peter offered him another spoonful of meat. 'He needs to succeed. I'm guessing it comes from being called a bastard slave all his life. I'd not accept that title either if I were Thaddeus.'

'He has nothing to prove to us.'

'We're not the ones he wants to impress.'

'Who then?'

Peter thought the question foolish. 'Lady Anne,' he said. 'He'll break his back getting food to Develish if that's what he's told her he'll do. Was it your idea to ride for help or his?'

'Mine. I thought we'd have better luck with six of us moving the wheels. He'll not be happy to see just Edmund and Joshua.'

'He'll be mighty glad to see anyone if he's anything like you when we found you,' Peter retorted bluntly. 'Where did you leave him?'

'By the roadside. Olyver said he'd get him into the wagon but I don't know if he did. They'll be all right, won't they?'

Peter gave a reassuring nod but, in his heart, he doubted it. There was a big difference between the half-hour it had taken him to hoist Ian's limp body across his pony and lead him back to the inn and the much longer time it would take Edmund and Joshua to do the same for Thaddeus and Olyver.

Assuming they found them.

☙❧

Edmund looked from left to right, but the road was empty in both directions. 'We must separate. I'll head towards Athelhelm and you for Develish. If I don't find Olyver before I reach the village, I'll turn and follow you.'

'And if you do find him?'

'I'll shout. The pack will hear me even if you don't.'

Joshua gestured to the dogs who stood together, hindquarters quivering, muzzles pointing to the left. 'They sense something already. We should both go towards Athelhelm.'

Edmund nodded. 'And we must hurry,' he said, setting off at a run. 'The light's all but gone.'

It was a quarter-mile to the first bend and the pack rounded it well ahead of the boys. With no barks or howls to alert them, and with heads lowered against the driving rain, Edmund and Joshua followed blindly and were amongst the horses at the rear of Bourne's wagon before they knew it. Each thought the same as he jumped away from the stamping hooves and buffeting rumps of the nervously recoiling animals: where there was a wagon, there would be soldiers.

Dry-mouthed, Edmund pulled his sword from his belt and made ready to fight, but Joshua laid a hand on his arm. 'The dogs aren't anxious,' he whispered. 'Look at the mastiff. He recognises someone in the wagon.'

Edmund watched the creature scent the air at the side of the vehicle then rear up on its hind legs, tail wagging, to place its paws on the sill. 'Olyver?'

'More likely Thaddeus. That dog has a real liking for him. I think Olyver's over there.' Joshua pointed some twenty paces along the road to where the rest of the pack was milling around something in the shelter of the trees. 'I see an arm.'

Edmund swore under his breath. Every instinct told him he was entering a trap, but he raised his sword anyway and took an unsteady step forward. He could barely produce a croak as he approached the back of the wagon, demanding that those inside show themselves. He pounded the hilt of his sword against the canopy to inspire fear, but the only response came from the mastiff, who gave an excited whine before dropping to the ground again.

Edmund positioned himself to the side of the opening and used the point of his sword to lift the flap. When nothing happened, he took a deep breath and glanced through the aperture. To his left were clothes, boots, tabards and weapons, piled on top of barrels and chests. To his right lay Thaddeus, curled in a crumpled heap on the floor, his knees drawn tight against his chest and his feet twisted awkwardly beneath the seat. There was no one else.

The pallor of Thaddeus's skin and the blood and gore on his sodden clothes suggested death and, with a sense of dread, Edmund reached beneath the cuff of the fur-lined coat to feel for a pulse. His fingers touched raw flesh where Thaddeus had pulled and strained against his bonds, and he wasn't prepared for the groan that issued from the big man's mouth or the speed and strength with which a vice-like grip fastened on his throat.

'Who are you?' Thaddeus whispered in a grating rasp.

Edmund cast a pleading glance at Joshua as he tried to pull away. 'Edmund Trueblood, son to John and Clara,' he gasped. 'Joshua Buckler is with me. We're here to assist you, Thaddeus. You'll die of cold if you can't rouse yourself. Do as we say and we can lead you to safety.'

When Thaddeus made no answer, Joshua climbed onto the step beside Edmund and reached inside to force Thaddeus's fingers apart. He spoke in the same firm tone that Peter had used with Ian. 'Wake up!' he ordered. 'You must be strong. Olyver lies by the roadside and his need of warmth is more pressing than yours. We can't save you both unless you help yourself. You're too heavy for Edmund and me to lift from this wagon. When we bring you a horse, you must pull yourself onto it. Do you understand?'

Thaddeus half opened his eyes and Joshua was relieved to see recognition in them. 'What of Ian?'

'He's safe,' answered Edmund. 'He told us where to find you. We expected soldiers when we saw the wagon. Should we still?'

'Not unless the dead can walk.'

Perhaps it was fortunate his legs became racked with cramps once Joshua and Edmund succeeded in hauling him to a sitting position. The air turned blue with his blasphemies but the pain restored intelligence. He took a key from around his neck and unlocked a chest at his side, muttering that he cared nothing for the gold but he'd have the letters. One he placed inside his tunic, the others he gave to Joshua, telling him to put them in Killer's saddle pack. He then sent Edmund to help Olyver and instructed Joshua to release Bourne's horses into the woodland. They'd not wander so far they couldn't be found again.

Edmund persuaded himself that Olyver looked no different from Ian, closing his mind to the coldness of his friend's wrist and the absence of a pulse. He knelt at his side, watching the relentless rain fall on the upturned, unresponsive face, and then, with a grunt of effort, hoisted Olyver over his shoulder and rose to his feet. 'Is Thaddeus mounted?' he called to Joshua. 'Do you have Olyver's pony?'

Receiving a yes to both questions, he carried the body across the mud of the road and laid it face down over the pony's saddle before clambering through the canopy to fetch tabards and rope. 'They'll keep him warm,' he said as he draped the tabards over the boy's back and wrapped the rope over him and under the pony's belly to secure them. 'He'll be fine once we get him back to the inn.'

Joshua heard the tremor in his voice and knew he was lying. 'We should head towards Athelhelm,' he answered gently. 'From there, the route through the woodland will be shorter. As long as we keep the river on our right, we can't fail to find our way to Holcombe.'

ೲ

They left the highway after rounding the bend above Athelhelm, too scared to draw any closer to the turbulent scene that confronted them. A river of mud and stones pounded against what remained of the buildings, and neither had the stomach to dwell too long on the dimly seen shapes that bobbed and rolled in its flow.

Inside the trees, they walked in single file with Joshua at the front, leading Killer. Every so often Edmund moved alongside the charger to put up a hand to keep Thaddeus in the saddle. He took heart from the fact that Thaddeus responded to his prodding, for it suggested he was fighting sleep rather than surrendering to it.

There was so little light in the forest that Joshua allowed the dogs to pick a path. They seemed to understand the need for a track wide enough to take the horses, for only rarely was he brushed by a low-hanging branch. Each time, he held it aside to allow Thaddeus and Killer to pass before alerting Edmund to do the same for the pony carrying Olyver. They spoke little, because the sound of the river would drown their words, but both shed unashamed tears of relief when the pack took them unerringly to the stretch of grassland that led to Holcombe.

As they moved along it, Joshua wondered if it was the snickering of their hobbled horses that had drawn the dogs. The whinnies and snorts grew louder the closer they came to the camp. One of the mastiffs darted forward with a yap of excited acknowledgement, receiving an answering yap in return, and suddenly the woodland was alive with sounds. The swelling crow of a rooster. The contented grunt of pig. Most sweetly, the song of a robin.

Edmund's face cracked into a tired smile when Peter appeared out of the darkness in front of them, his hands cupped in front of his mouth.

'I swear I've never been so bloody pleased to see anyone in my life,' he declared as Peter, the master mimicker of sounds, put a thumb and finger between his lips and the robin's chirrup gave way to the trill of a skylark, ascending into the blue of a summer's day.

ᘓᕽᘒ

The hall of the inn was sweltering after the weather outside. Peter had stacked the fire high with broken stools and added more as Edmund and Joshua carried Olyver inside and laid him on the floor in front of it. Ian slept peacefully a few paces away, the colour in his face a stark contrast to the deathly white of his twin's.

'I couldn't leave him out there alone,' said Edmund with a break in his voice. 'We all need to say our goodbyes, but Ian most of all. He'd not have forgiven me if I hadn't brought him back.'

Peter pressed his fingers to Olyver's wrist, and like Edmund felt nothing. Milady had taught every serf in Develish how to tell the difference between a strong beat and a weak one, but with Peter's grandfather, she had also searched for a pulse in his neck. He tried the same with Olyver and wondered if he was imagining the intermittent flicker. With sudden decision, he ordered Edmund and Joshua to return outside for Thaddeus while he stripped Olyver of his clothes and dressed him in dry ones. Lady Anne had worked so hard to bring life back to his grandfather, and it had broken Peter's heart when she failed—the old man was his truest friend—but her failure was no excuse not to try as hard for Olyver.

He moved the boy closer to the fire and pulled him into a tight embrace as he'd done with Ian. He watched Edmund and Joshua walk Thaddeus inside with his arms draped across their shoulders, and told them to bring him close to the fire and give him dry clothes. But Thaddeus would only allow them to remove his coat. Even half-asleep, he guarded the square of parchment that was pressed against his chest, unwilling for anyone else to read Lady Anne's words. His awareness improved as the heat of the fire warmed his blood, but not enough to move or speak. He saw Ian lying on the floor and Olyver, white and unmoving in Peter's arms, but he lacked the will to do anything about it.

All the industry came from Peter. While Edmund and Joshua were saying prayers for their dead friend, he was rubbing and pinching Olyver's exposed skin. Every so often a blush of pink appeared beneath his fingers, and he told his friends it was what Milady had looked for in his grandfather. 'I think it means the blood's still flowing in his veins.'

He instructed them to take his place so that he could feed Thaddeus. 'Work as hard as I did,' he told them, filling another bowl from the cauldron of mutton stew. 'Grandfather looked a lot worse, but Milady still thought she could warm him enough to save him.' He carried the bowl to Thaddeus and began feeding him spoonsful of shredded meat and gravy. 'When a body loses heat, it must be warmed from within as well as from without. Milady was very clear about that. When Olyver opens his eyes, we must force him to eat whether he wants to or not.'

The method had worked with Ian, and it seemed to be working with Thaddeus. Joshua and Edmund were alarmed by the violent shivers that suddenly rocked the big man's body. Peter said Ian had reacted the same. A person only shivered when he knew he was cold.

There was no shivering in Olyver; no movement of any kind. If he was breathing at all, his breaths were too shallow to lift his chest. When Edmund said as much, Peter moved to kneel beside Joshua at Olyver's side. 'I once saw Lady Anne bring a newborn to life,' he told them. 'It was a little girl. She lay still and unmoving until Milady blew warming air into her mouth.'

'Which little girl?' asked Edmund.

'My sister. I asked Milady how she'd known to do it and she said it's written in scripture that God formed man from the dust of the earth and breathed life into him. When I told Father Anselm what she'd done, he said only a devil would do such a thing. Do you think he was right?'

Edmund shook his head. 'Your sister wouldn't have lived if God hadn't wanted her to.' He eased his arm beneath Olyver's shoulders to raise him up and the small elevation caused the boy's throat to arch and his lips to part. 'It's a sign,' he said. 'If Lady Anne showed you the way, I believe you should try. It can't be a sin to want to save a friend.'

☙

In a corner of Lady Anne's chamber in Develish a darker scene was unfolding as an infusion of angelica, wormwood and pennyroyal leaf dislodged the foetus from Eleanor's womb. The pains that cramped her belly and the blood that flowed from between her legs would have brought forth screams had Lady Anne not held a hand over her mouth for fear of waking the household. There was so much distrust of the girl that cries of any kind would lead Milady's people to think violence was being done. The door would be forced and all hope of keeping the incestuous pregnancy secret would be gone.

Eleanor lay on a pile of linen napkins to absorb the blood, tears of distress coursing down her cheeks. There was nothing Lady Anne could say to ease her mind. All she could do was change the napkins and lessen Eleanor's pain with birch-leaf oil and white willow bark liniment. Had she thought it would help to say the purgative was working as it should, she would have done so, but the girl needed no reminders that her decision to take the infusion meant a life was being washed away.

Lady Anne had neither looked for, nor wanted, gratitude for her part in this tragic story. It had surprised and moved her, therefore, when she returned to her chamber and Eleanor had thanked her in a tearful whisper for not abandoning her to deal with the miscarriage alone. Lady Anne had expected anger, even accusations that the murder of the foetus was her crime and not Eleanor's; and, in truth, she'd have thought that a rightful penance, for she had held herself to blame from the moment she'd learnt of Eleanor's condition the previous evening. She had protected her servants from her husband's lust but hadn't thought to protect his daughter. Even in her worst imaginings she had never believed Sir Richard so vile that he'd lie with his only child.

When the flow of blood ceased, Lady Anne fetched a bowl of water from a table and washed Eleanor clean before dressing her in a shift and assisting her to the bed. She gave her chamomile and valerian to help her sleep and then returned to the corner to remove all evidence of the aborted birth. She placed one of her shawls on the floor, laid the bloodied napkins on top and tied the corners to form a tight bundle. As she opened the window which overlooked the moat and dropped the shawl into the fast-flowing water, she could only pray it would stay afloat long enough to be carried away from the demesne by Devil's Brook. Too many of the female serfs would recognise the fabric and ask questions if it became snagged on weeds in sight of the house.

She remained where she was, allowing the rain to wet her face. Eleanor would continue to bleed for several days, but the servants would think it was her natural cycle. In time, Lady Anne hoped Eleanor would believe the same, because her life would be happier if she persuaded herself the pregnancy had never happened. When the weather improved, she would be returned to her prison to serve the allotted time of her sentence for harming Isabella—fifteen days in a hut beside John Trueblood's on the path to the church—and her forced absence would allow the serf boys she had hoped to blame for her condition to come home to plaudits for driving two hundred sheep from Afpedle.

Was it wrong to hope for such outcomes? Lady Anne knew the Church would condemn her harshly if she ever confessed to her actions this night, but did God? Was He so set on every misbegotten life being born that innocent youths must be accused of rape to excuse their lord's wickedness? Was Sir Richard's depravity so easily forgiven that his daughter must play both mother and sister to his child?

With a sigh, she closed the window and drew a stool to the side of the bed. She was loath to trouble God with entreaties, believing the duty of solving problems was hers alone, but she had prayed so many prayers these last twenty-four hours. For Eleanor. For Develish. For Thaddeus. For rain. Would it be wrong to add another? She placed her hand over Eleanor's and bent her head.

In nomine Patris et Filii et Spiritus Sancti, may something good come out of this sad and terrible night.

The first week of October, 1348

*T*haddeus and his companions have been with us 7 days now. The boys came first with 200 sheep from Afpedle. *They were delayed by the River Pedle flooding, and had to wait for the water to subside before they could cross the ford at Athelhelm. They stayed long enough to pen the sheep, exchange greetings with their families and speak briefly to My Lord of Bourne before departing again. They returned 2 days later with Thaddeus, bringing My Lord's wagon filled with grain and flour, a column of horses, a pack of hunting dogs, fine clothes, weaponry, jewellery and 2 black cats in wicker cages.*

Thaddeus has allowed My Lord the use of the hut and has built a second shelter twenty paces from it for him and his companions. They have used their time to harvest what was left of the beans and vetch after the torrential downpours, and to truss sheep for safe carriage on the raft. 20 of the animals have been slaughtered and preserved, 30 are in the pens behind the church, 50 in the orchard, and some 100 graze the pastureland outside the moat.

Each night, the boys build a fire close to My Lord's hut and regale us with stories of their adventures. The young girls swoon to hear of their heroism, apparently unaware that the tales are growing in the telling! Edmund Trueblood would have us believe there are rats as big as foxes roaming the land, Peter Catchpole that he is able to demolish buildings single-handedly and Joshua Buckler that his hounds are so ferocious they would put an army to rout.

The only story Develish hasn't heard is how Thaddeus and the Startout twins defeated My Lord of Bourne's army. The details are known to me and our leading serfs after Gyles crossed the moat by night to speak with Thaddeus in secret, but Thaddeus has asked us to keep it to ourselves. He believes there is more to be gained by allowing My Lord of Bourne to keep his dignity than making the full extent of his crimes and cruelty known to our people.

A strange friendship has developed between the two, despite the circumstances under which they met. It may have something to do with a treasure chest which Thaddeus removed from the wagon and returned to Lord Bourne, along with a key that hung on a thong around his neck. Neither has any concern that the other may carry the pestilence and, while the youngsters entertain us with their stories, Thaddeus sits with My Lord and shares a meal with him. What they speak of is anyone's guess, but Bourne seems less fearful of us since Thaddeus's arrival.

Six

WHEN A LOW WHISTLE CAME from the peasant strips, Clara Trueblood flicked the shutter on her lantern twice to confirm that it was she who was waiting. She stood at the outside door to the kitchen and heard a gentle ripple as a body slid into the moat and began swimming. Until now, the door had served only to allow the drawing of water for the washing of pots and pans or, on occasion, the dousing of fires when careless maids scattered glowing embers from the hearth, but at Lady Anne's request it was becoming a thoroughfare.

Clara's authority was such that she could do as she pleased in her own domain, and if it pleased her to bar the door to the great hall at night in order to sleep in private once in a while, then so be it. None questioned her on it. Behind her, a candle burnt on the table that ran the length of the kitchen, lending a soft glow to the room, and her broad shoulders shook with suppressed laughter as Thaddeus, naked and dripping, heaved himself across the threshold a few minutes later.

'You'll make Milady swoon,' she said, taking a woollen blanket from the table and wrapping it around his waist, tying the corners tightly to prevent it slipping. 'Could you not have retained your tunic and britches at least?'

Thaddeus's dark face split in a pleasing grin. 'Not without giving Bourne reason to question why I'm dressed in wet clothes when the sun comes up. Did Gyles not ask you to provide something dry for me to wear?'

'He did,' said Clara, sorting through a coffer in the corner. 'The pair of you will turn me into a common laundress before this is over.' She handed him a loose smock and the largest britches she could find. 'You'll be lucky if they fit. I swear you've grown another inch since I last saw you.'

He took the garments gratefully and shrugged the smock over his head before pulling the britches on beneath the blanket. 'You're a good friend, Clara.'

She chuckled. 'If I can tolerate Gyles's wrinkled old frame dripping all over my floor, I can certainly tolerate yours. There'd be no end of questions if naked men began running about the forecourt.' She reached up to button the smock about his neck and then did the same at his wrists. 'We must hide your scars and bruises. If Milady sees them, she'll waste the little time you have searching out liniment to make them better.'

'Is she happy to meet me, Clara? The request was mine, for there's much I should tell her before she gives permission for Bourne to cross, but I've had no word of agreement. I hoped she might send a note with the food on the raft.'

Clara tut-tutted. 'There'd be no quicker way to set tongues wagging. Every woman in the kitchen would have been curious about why she did it. Bourne, too, when it reached the other side,

I don't doubt. Did Gyles not tell you that my lantern would signal her willingness?'

'He did.'

'Then stop fretting, my dear. She's had nought but Master de Courtesmain's counsel these last few weeks and has grown weary of it.' She untied the blanket at his waist and then took up a napkin to dry his hair and beard.

She'd known Thaddeus all his life but he'd always been a mystery to her. Like many of her neighbours, she'd stepped in to curb Will's brutality towards him when he was a child, but he'd never shown gratitude to be spared a beating. Sometimes, Clara had thought he'd welcomed the pain because he needed constant reminders to hate the man who wielded the cudgel; other times, she had wondered if it was simple ignorance of how to express thanks that had kept him dumb.

Silence came more easily to him than speech. Clara still remembered the day he'd wrested the cudgel from Will's hand on the last occasion the man had raised it against him. All who witnessed the scene had expected Thaddeus to take a violent revenge but, instead, and without a word, he had turned his back on Will and carried the cudgel into the wooded hills above Develish. It was never seen again, though gossip said Will had searched long and hard for it.

Clara had little difficulty understanding this incident once Lady Anne made Thaddeus her steward. If anyone could teach a brutalised child that nurtured hate was destructive, it was surely Milady. Some had resented Thaddeus's advancement, claiming Milady had favoured him unfairly through her quiet care and teaching, but Clara, who knew the secret of Eleanor's birth, understood why he'd been singled out. It was not in Lady Anne's nature to ignore the plight of one ill-conceived child while protecting another, though she was fortunate the boy she'd felt obliged to help was Thaddeus.

Even at six years old, when Will first set him to work in the fields, his intelligence had been obvious. It made no matter what task he was given, he had picked it up quickly and performed it well. He was also the only serf in Develish who would never betray Milady's secret support by flaunting his learning, because he would have invited a beating if he had. Nevertheless, as Clara squeezed the water from his hair, and felt him tense against the intimacy, she wondered if he or Lady Anne would ever be able to express their feelings openly. They were two of a kind, each with natures so reserved that neither would presume fondness in the other.

With sudden tenderness, she raised her palm to his cheek and gave it a brief caress before turning away to wring out the napkin. 'Do you think Milady any less excited to hear your stories than the rest of us? We listen to our sons tell theirs each night but have yet to hear yours.'

'I don't have their gift of embroidery, Clara.'

'Perhaps not, but I, for one, would wish to know what magic you've used to turn them into men. I barely recognise them as the surly churls who left Develish with you a month ago.'

Thaddeus moved towards the glowing embers in the kitchen hearth. If he answered honestly, he would have to say he'd removed them from Eleanor's malign influence, but there was another truth which was just as valid. 'I asked them to show courage and they did.'

She smiled. 'You also, Thaddeus? If what the boys say is true, you played a lord in Woodoak in order to save women and young maids from terrible abuse. Did you know it's treasonable to pretend a rank you don't have? Were you not afraid you'd be found out?'

He shook his head. 'It helped that I was riding Sir Richard's charger and had a sword in my hand.'

'Well, you won't need either to persuade Milady. She tells me our sons have convinced her you make a compelling lord. It pleases her greatly to know her teaching hasn't gone to waste.'

☙❧

Clara trod softly past sleeping bodies towards the steward's office. She eased the latch and slipped inside. 'Are you ready, milady?' she whispered. 'We must walk in darkness. If you take my hand, I can lead you.' She saw the same shy hesitation in Lady Anne's face that she'd seen in Thaddeus's and, with a smile of encouragement, she raised her beloved mistress to her feet and drew her soft brown curls about her face. 'Trust your heart, my dear. It hasn't led you false yet.'

☙❧

Hugh de Courtesmain witnessed Lady Anne's entry to the kitchen from the other side of the hall. He had been drawn to descend the stairs when he noticed the glimmer of candlelight beneath the steward's door. Seeing it, he had reasoned it was Milady's steps along the corridor that had woken him, and that she was writing in her private journal. He had always suspected her of keeping one but had never caught her working on it. To wait quietly in the shadows to see if she emerged with it in her hands would at least confirm his belief that she kept it concealed in her chamber.

He wanted to know what secrets it contained, most particularly why Thaddeus Thurkell had removed the serf boys from the demesne. Hugh had never believed the explanation Lady Anne had given, which had painted them as heroes. Their departure had followed too quickly on the death of Thurkell's brother, and Hugh felt certain the two were connected. He didn't doubt either that Lady Eleanor had some involvement, for her rages had become ungovernable in the weeks afterwards. Nonetheless, it was Lady Anne's recently altered attitude towards the girl that intrigued him. From being willing to be disowned by Lady Eleanor, she now held her closer than ever before. But why?

As Clara Trueblood opened the door to the kitchen to usher Lady Anne inside, Hugh saw a tall figure step forward to greet her. It hardly needed the candlelight to tell him it was Thurkell. No other man could have drawn Milady into a secret assignation at the dead of night, and Hugh's heart burnt with jealousy as his hated rival dropped to one knee and pressed a kiss into each of her palms. He turned away as the door began to close again, unable to watch as Lady Anne moved her hands to cradle his face. Such a bitterness grew in Hugh's heart that his only thought was to expose her for the harlot she was.

His eyes now well adjusted to the darkness in the hall, he watched Clara Trueblood place a stool in front of the entrance and seat herself upon it. He was willing to wait as long as was necessary to make his way to the steward's office but estimated a bare quarter-hour passed before the woman's head began to nod. Work and slumber were all serfs knew, and Clara Trueblood was a poor guard of her mistress's honour.

Search as he might, however, Hugh found nothing resembling a private journal in the office. It seemed Milady's industry had been dedicated to working out the sleeping arrangements when Bourne entered the demesne. My Lord was to be given

Sir Richard's chamber, and Hugh and the men who slept in it now were to be relegated to the great hall with the women, children and greybeards. There was no mention of where Thurkell would lay his head.

⚬⚬

Clara was startled awake by the brush of fingers on her hair. She opened her eyes to see Eleanor standing before her, barefoot and dressed only in a shift. Certain she had come to cause trouble for Lady Anne, Clara rose to her feet and caught the girl's hands in hers. 'There's nothing for you here, Lady Eleanor,' she murmured. 'Return to your mother's chamber. She'll not be happy if you disturb the household.'

Eleanor stared straight ahead, making no attempt to release herself or give a response. Indeed, she seemed oddly content to be held by Clara. A small smile played across her face as if she were remembering a time from infancy when the woman had been her nursemaid. It was clear to Clara that the girl was asleep, and she loosened her grip so as not to rouse her. But how disturbed Eleanor's mind must be, she thought. In daylight, she sought to capture Milady's attention through intemperate rages; at night, she felt impelled to wander through rooms in search of her. It was strange. Stranger still that, in slumber, she had known Milady was not in her bed.

But what to do about it? Keep her here, or take her back upstairs? She chose upstairs. There was no predicting how Eleanor would react if she woke. With a light hand on the girl's back, she guided her around the walls towards the stone steps in the far corner, then circled her arm about Eleanor's waist to assist her in mounting them. It wasn't uncommon for serfs to walk in their sleep. The need to work was so ingrained that some rose from their beds in the dark and headed for the fields with their eyes closed. Most came home of their own accord, others needed guidance, but Clara couldn't remember any being as compliant as Eleanor.

She took care to walk softly down the corridor and ease the latch on Milady's door without a sound, and it was arguable who was the more surprised when she pushed it open and found Hugh de Courtesmain searching through one of the coffers. He looked at her with an expression of horror, and Clara blessed Milady's foresight in continuing to light candles in her window each night until Thaddeus and his companions proved themselves free of the pestilence and crossed the moat. Without their glow, she wouldn't have known of his presence.

She pulled Eleanor close. 'What outrage is this, sir?'

He lowered the lid of the coffer. 'What I do here is no concern of yours, Mistress Trueblood. You overstep the mark by questioning Milady's steward.'

He tried to push past her but she stood her ground and, seeing an easier route, he put his hands on Eleanor to move her aside. Her awakening was violent. Eyes previously glazed and unblinking snapped back to intelligence, and, hissing words of fury to find him in her mother's room, she attacked de Courtesmain with uncontrolled ferocity, slapping and kicking him until he retreated to the far side of the chamber.

He pointed a trembling finger at Clara. 'She's madder than I've ever seen her. Hold her in check before she kills me.'

Clara folded her arms defiantly. 'I see no madness, sir. She acted as any daughter would do to find a man in her mother's chamber. Is it your custom to inspect Milady's garments when she's absent from her room?'

'I was looking for documents.'

'On whose command?'

'I need no command. I am steward of Develish.'

'Not for much longer,' said Clara, drawing Eleanor to her side again and leaving de Courtesmain's exit clear. 'Be gone, sir. You will never serve Develish as well and honestly as Milady and Thaddeus Thurkell do.'

Eleanor clung to Clara, wrapping her arms about the woman's waist and talking in riddles about blood and guilt. Whatever troubles beset her, they clearly filled her with remorse, for Clara didn't doubt the guilt of which she spoke was hers. She whispered *mea culpa* too often to believe otherwise. Unsure of what to do for the best, Clara led her to Lady Anne's bed and lay on it beside her, cradling the girl tight against her side. Within minutes, Eleanor had fallen asleep again, but it was a shallow, disturbed sleep, and any attempt Clara made to move brought forth whimpers and tears.

It seemed safer to stay with her. Dawn could not be far off and Lady Anne knew she must leave the kitchen before the first rays of the sun woke the serfs in the great hall. Better Milady find Clara gone from her stool than Eleanor set off in search of her again. She was as likely to attack Thaddeus as de Courtesmain if she thought the handsome giant was stealing her mother's affections. Thief was the least of what she'd called de Courtesmain, and Clara spent time wondering what documents he'd hoped to find. Whatever they were, he'd have used them to control Milady. His single ambition was to have her listen to him and not her serfs.

She made a gesture of apology when Lady Anne entered the chamber some quarter-hour later. 'I had no choice but to remain, milady. I found Eleanor wandering in her sleep and feared she might do it again if I left.'

She tried to ease the girl away from her, but Lady Anne pulled forward a stool and begged her to remain where she was. 'She'll not wake while you hold her. I allow her to sleep in the bed with me and she only becomes agitated if I move to the table to write in my journal.'

'Would that be what Master de Courtesmain was looking for, milady? I caught him going through your coffer.' Clara described what she'd seen when she opened the door. 'I'm guessing he knew you were absent and took a chance on entering when he saw Lady Eleanor leave. Guilt was written into every bone of him.'

'He fears Thaddeus's return. He doubts he'll keep his place as steward.'

'Nor should he, milady.'

Lady Anne shook her head. 'He'll cause less trouble if he remains in the post. His nature's too frail to want Bourne thinking him a serf.' She watched Eleanor for a moment. 'Did he wake her?'

Clara nodded. 'And reaped a bad reward by doing so.' She told the story with a smile. 'You couldn't have asked for a more dutiful daughter, milady. She cast slurs at him while speaking only good about you, and the praise surprised him, I think.' She paused. 'I, too, if I'm honest. I can't remember the last time she had anything kind to say about you.'

If she hoped Lady Anne might offer an explanation, she was disappointed. Both Milady's expression and answer were carefully controlled. 'I'm the only constant in her life,' she said. 'Her father is lost to her and she doesn't know whom else to trust. Her greatest fear is to lose me as well, I think.'

'She seemed more troubled by guilt than loss, milady. Before she fell asleep, her talk was of blood. I made no sense of it but her remorse was clear. If she said *mea culpa* once, she said it a hundred times.'

Lady Anne placed her elbows on the edge of the bed and rested her chin in her hands. How comforting it would be to confide in Clara and share the burden of Eleanor with another woman. If anyone could understand the tumult of emotions the girl was experiencing, it was surely Clara who had helped other women through the terrible anguish of miscarriage and stillbirth. But to do so would be to reveal everything, and Eleanor's slow steps towards believing that Lady Anne had her best interests at heart would end.

'I let her down at the time of her father's death, Clara. So much changed for her so quickly and I gave no thought to how it might affect her. Her guilt is for wounding Isabella and renouncing me, and she is deeply remorseful for both. By keeping her close, I hope she will learn that my love isn't easily broken.'

Clara wondered if that was the truth. 'Maybe so, milady,' she said bluntly, 'but she'll make you her captive if you allow her to become too dependent on you. You need a man in your bed, not a troubled child whose passions can swing between love and hate in a single moment.'

A glint of mischief danced in Lady Anne's eyes. 'You shock me, Clara. Would you have your liege lady take a serf to bed and destroy any chance Develish has of forging her future?'

Clara smiled. 'I would have a man who loves you, milady.'

'So would I, my dear friend, but a lover would be more appealing and useful if he were a wealthy noble, approved by Blandeforde, who sees merit in freeing his serfs.'

'Does such a man exist, milady?'

'Not yet, but with My Lord of Bourne's help, he might.' She smiled at the puzzlement in Clara's face. 'If he holds to the agreement Thaddeus has made with him, we have a chance of gaining our freedom lawfully.'

'What sort of agreement?' asked Clara suspiciously. 'I'd sooner remain a serf than have you marry that vile old man. No one's more deserving of freedom than you.'

Lady Anne squeezed her fingers affectionately. 'Have faith in Thaddeus,' she said. 'He hasn't supped with the Devil every night to hand him the keys of Develish. I have a request that you may not like, however.'

'You have but to ask, milady.'

'We must forget our grievances against Bourne and show him only respect when he crosses the moat. Will you spread that word amongst our people? Thaddeus has persuaded him he has nothing to fear from educated serfs, and he will know it for certain if he's treated with courtesy.'

⊘⊘

Clara gave the instruction the following day, saying it came from Milady, but in private she questioned what sort of agreement Thaddeus had made that allowed Bourne to think his sins forgiven. Many cavilled at showing respect to the Norman who had burnt their homes and attacked their demesne, but Gyles lent his authority to the request, saying nothing would be gained by giving Bourne reason to fear them. When the time came for My Lord to leave, better he went as a friend than an enemy. It would not bode well for Milady or her people if he took unfavourable tales of Develish to Blandeforde.

This argument was accepted, and the old man received a warmer welcome than he might have expected. He chose to wait for Thaddeus and his companions to serve their fourteen days' exclusion before entering with them, and there was so much joy from mothers at the prospect of being able to clasp their sons to their hearts again that he seemed to feel himself included in the happiness. It helped that Thaddeus had instructed his companions to introduce him to their families before accepting their mothers' embraces, and Lady Anne's leading serfs and their wives were more than willing to set the example for others to follow.

When it came to Clara's turn, she bobbed a deep curtsey and said she trusted My Lord was looking forward to the feast Milady had ordered in celebration of his arrival. He declared that he was, urging her graciously to rise, and she wondered if he was really so arrogant that he believed it was *his* arrival Milady wished to salute. Perhaps so, for he accepted Lady Anne's offer of her husband's chamber as his due, together with fine garments from Sir Richard's coffers to replace his homespun tunic and britches.

Dressed in a gown befitting her station—sewn from russet-coloured silk with softly falling skirts and a gold circlet about her waist—Lady Anne allowed him to precede her into the house in recognition of his superior status. Inside, she asked Master de Courtesmain to accompany My Lord to his room and assist him with any requests he might have. Gyles whispered to Thaddeus that he thought it a bad idea to give the Frenchman such free access to Bourne. Who knew what poison he'd whisper in the old man's ear?

Thaddeus placed a comforting hand on Gyles's arm. 'Milady knows what she's doing, my friend. De Courtesmain will find a way to speak with Bourne whatever she does—most likely in the church with Father Anselm's blessing—and Bourne will listen more closely if de Courtesmain claims he's being kept from him.'

'He'll say nothing good about us, Thaddeus.'

'For certain, but Bourne is neither blind nor foolish. He'll learn soon enough that what I've told him about Develish is the truth. De Courtesmain will do himself no favours by trying to persuade him otherwise.'

And as the days passed, this proved to be true. For all the Frenchman's attempts to snare the old man, Bourne showed more willingness to consort with Lady Anne and her people. As often as not, he sat in the great hall, watching Isabella Startout teach the children, taking pleasure in hearing them read aloud from the English translations Lady Anne had made of the parables. Each day, he expressed new wonderment that urchins as young as ten were as fluent in letters as he was himself.

Thaddeus's companions were made uncomfortable by the welcome they received. The young girls swooned over them, begging to hear more of their stories, but they seemed to prefer each other's company and took no advantage of the maids' shameless flirting. As Clara said, Thaddeus's influence over the boys was so strong they broke every heart with their courteous indifference. To Lady Anne's private relief, they showed no interest in Eleanor, seeming more preoccupied by their ambitions to forge a future outside Develish.

For her part, Eleanor was content to avoid them. She spent her days in Lady Anne's chamber and only appeared for an hour or two in the evenings to sit with her mother and My Lord of Bourne. Her demeanour was always appropriate, and her affection for Lady Anne obvious, perhaps because Milady never failed to refer to her as her daughter. Some thought she'd forgiven the girl too readily for her bitter words of hatred; others pointed to Eleanor's unlikely friendship with Robert Startout, which seemed to have had a soothing effect on her temper. Few understood why the eleven-year-old had spoken on Eleanor's behalf at her trial for imprisoning and wounding Isabella, but there was no doubting she paid him more mind than anyone else.

Most days, he visited her in Lady Anne's chamber and, together, they played with the cats that Thaddeus had brought from Holcombe. At Milady's request, Thaddeus had gifted them to Eleanor, and under Robert's guidance, she learnt to love and not fear them. Father Anselm called them the Devil's creatures, but Eleanor saw only good in them and found solace in feeding and nurturing them. And with this first small rebellion against the priest, her self-centred vision of the world, where her place was God-ordained by virtue of her birth, seemed to soften towards an acceptance that earthly life was not as intelligible as her father and the Church had led her to believe.

Thaddeus and his companions built a shelter for themselves in the orchard, preferring to sleep outside as had become their custom. Thaddeus showed no interest in reclaiming his post as steward, speaking courteously to de Courtesmain whenever they met but he drew the man's ire by spending an hour each morning alone with Lady Anne in the office. De Courtesmain's frustration at being barred on these occasions, displayed by an impatient tapping of his foot until the door opened, amused every serf who saw it. He should have been grateful that Milady hadn't stripped him of his duties and title; instead, he sulked and pouted because the counsel of a bastard slave was preferred to his.

His irritation was further inflamed by Lady Anne's willingness to allow Joshua's dogs to roam freely about the compound. When she withdrew her people inside the moat, she had commanded the mongrels from the village to be destroyed in order to preserve food for human consumption. Now she humbly accepted Joshua's argument that that decision had been wrong, agreeing that the curs would have guarded the walls as faithfully as his hounds were doing now. It mattered not that Hugh's irritation had more to do with his fear of dogs than that Milady demeaned herself by admitting error to a serf.

Not that Thurkell's companions behaved like serfs. They conducted themselves well, listening when others spoke and showing consideration to all. Clara was not alone in finding it hard to recognise her son in the respectful young man who offered to perform chores that he'd have thought beneath him a month ago. James Buckler, more used to criticising Joshua for failing at tasks, found himself in awe of his son's ability to control his pack and speak with confidence of acting as Thaddeus's master of hounds. Meanwhile, Peter Catchpole, known for his laziness, astounded his parents and everyone else by his dedication to learning the skills of medicine from Lady Anne. A story circulated that he had brought Olyver Startout back from the dead by breathing warm air into his mouth, and most believed it must be true when Father Anselm went out of his way to warn that such practices were heretical.

De Courtesmain demanded the truth of the story from Isabella Startout. 'I don't doubt you're aiding and abetting your brothers and their friends in the lies they're telling,' he said angrily. 'But to what end? Does Thurkell seek to make himself master here by winning the hearts of the credulous with myths and falsehoods?'

Isabella lowered her head 'All are loyal to Lady Anne, Master de Courtesmain. There's not a person in Develish who would wish to have anyone other than her as their liege lord.'

'Except Thurkell. He makes his ambitions clear.'

Isabella stepped away and her answer was so quiet he wasn't sure he'd heard it correctly. 'But not as clear as you make yours, sir.'

St Andrew's Day, last week of November, 1348

It has been agreed. On the first day of January, 1349, Thaddeus Thurkell, Ian and Olyver Startout, Edmund Trueblood, Peter Catchpole and Joshua Buckler will escort My Lord of Bourne to his estates in Wiltshire. They will remain with him one month in order to secure his property, bring his surviving bondsmen to live on his principal demesne and introduce some method to his affairs.

As payment for this service—and in recognition that he is compromised by the letters he wrote on behalf of the ladies of Dorseteshire, which will stay with me in Develish—My Lord has agreed to prepare a scroll, bearing his signature and seal, introducing the man who carries it as My Lord of Athelstan. He will recommend Athelstan's honesty and good character to all he encounters. My Lord is willing to write this falsehood but has warned Thaddeus it will be no protection if imposture is suspected. Thaddeus must play the noble at all times if he is to avoid detection.

I have chosen Athelstan because the title was in my family until my maternal grandfather died without male issue. His ring came to me and I have kept it these many years, along with his crest and lineage. They show descent from Godwin of Wessex, father to King Harold, who was defeated in battle by William of Normandy. It may be that Thaddeus will be more in danger of exposure through claiming royal English blood, but My Lord of Bourne believes the opposite to be true. Few Normans have knowledge of Saxon ancestry, though most are acquainted with their own.

I have taught Thaddeus all I know of my family's history and have inscribed a new lineage, showing him to be descended from an invented younger brother of my grandfather, who departed these shores over half a century ago. I have urged him to say that his grandmother's family is of Spanish-Moorish descent, for this will explain his dark complexion.

My leading serfs, whose sons will accompany him, worry that the pretence will be uncovered, but Thaddeus has persuaded them it's a gamble worth taking. To risk all is to win all. Nevertheless, so much faith is being placed in my belief that land will be cheap once the pestilence passes that I feel a weight of responsibility upon my shoulders. Only God knows if Eleanor's dowry remains where Gyles left it on his journey home with Sir Richard. And only God knows if a base-born slave can pass for a lord and purchase the demesne of his choosing.

❧

Christmas Day, 1348

Ishall look back on this day as the happiest of my life. For
the first time, the people of Develish were able to celebrate
Christ's Nativity together as equals. Father Anselm called us
to prayer early so that the long-awaited games could take place
at noon. We all laughed as fathers and sons vied for the laurel
wreaths, since there was more cheating than competing in each
event. Afterwards, we feasted on roasted mutton and warm
bread while the children sang to us. How sweet their voices are
and how ably Isabella has taught them. My Lord of Bourne has
great admiration for her and remarked that she would make a
better wife to a lord than most women who are born to the role.

Thaddeus and his companions paraded themselves in the
garments I and my seamstresses have stitched for them from the
clothes they brought from Holcombe. Thaddeus looked every
inch a lord and the boys—who seem to grow in stature with each
day that passes—every inch his soldiers. For fun, they invited
us all to join them in a merry jig. Neither Thaddeus nor I knew
which steps to make, for we are sadly lacking in dancing skills,
but Adam Catchpole's rhythmic drumming of a goatskin was so
enticing that I could not resist taking Thaddeus's hand. It's my
greatest joy that my dear friend's time out of Develish seems to
have conquered his shyness.

*It can't be wrong to feel such enjoyment, however
ferociously Master de Courtesmain frowned to see us smile!*

ೞ

The first day of January, 1349

S o many of our hopes have gone with the convoy that set
off at dawn.

My Lord of Bourne thanked me for the hospitality he has
received in Develish, and gifted me the horses and tackle of his
dead fighting men by way of compensation for my generosity.
It amuses me that he is still unable to look me in the eye when
he speaks to me. Thaddeus says he's shamed by my refusal to
accept a portion of the stolen gold, but I think it more likely that
he continues to suspect me of practising black arts. Women have
been inferior to men so long that it frightens him to see one such
as I managing a demesne.

Perhaps, more simply, he doesn't trust me not to use his
letters against him, though why he thinks I should be the first to
break our bargain is anyone's guess. Unless because I'm a witch!

I have allowed Master de Courtesmain to accompany him
to act as his steward in Wiltshire. Bourne has more need of a
scribe than I, and Develish will benefit from de Courtesmain's
absence since his only ambition seems to be the sowing of

discord. Father Anselm will miss him, since de Courtesmain is his single confidant, but I can't imagine anyone else will regret his departure.

Winter is well set in and I hope it stays with us for several months. If Thaddeus is right about rats and fleas spreading the pestilence, the journey will be safer with the ground frozen. Vermin and parasites dislike the frost and snow as much as we do.

I bid farewell to the fear and misery of 1348 with a gladsome heart and pray most earnestly that my people, Dorseteshire and England will enjoy better fortune in 1349.

1349

Seven

Bourne, Wiltshire

HUGH DE COURTESMAIN HID HIS irritation behind a thin-lipped smile as he watched Thaddeus Thurkell take his leave of the peasants who crowded around him. It was the fifth day of February and past time the slave and his men allowed Bourne's estates to be managed by their rightful steward. But how it galled Hugh to watch the hated giant's departure. Thurkell might be a god for all the adulation being showered upon him. Even after a month of behaving no differently from the serfs who sought to kiss his hand, none of Bourne's people questioned that he was My Lord of Athelstan.

His height, his bearing, his dress and mannered speech, whether in French or English, suggested a person of privilege, and Hugh's heart burnt with envy because he knew he lacked the ability to play such a part himself. Even now, he had a yearning to reveal the imposture, though he doubted these fools would view the harlot-hatched bastard differently if he did. The idea that one lower than they could rise above his station in life was more likely to excite than annoy them. It was only Hugh who felt demeaned by having to bend his neck to an imposter. He would have betrayed Thurkell gladly these last four weeks had he not feared Bourne's anger at the secret of his protégé's birth becoming known. Hugh had worked too hard to ingratiate himself with Bourne to lose his position out of momentary pique.

He comforted himself that his time of being eclipsed by Thurkell was over. In minutes, the slave and his five companions would be gone, and the only commands these serfs would hear then would be Hugh de Courtesmain's. Out of the corner of his eye, he spotted the figure of My Lord of Bourne at the top of the stone stairs, leading to the upper chamber, and he took satisfaction from the look of disquiet on the old man's face as he watched the scene below. Could it be Bourne had finally come to understand the danger of allowing an English serf to gain such ascendancy over his people?

No one who entered the great hall of Bourne would question that the owner's loyalties lay with France. My Lord had spent his wealth on dressing the walls and floor with the finest hangings and most elegant of French furniture, and the sight had warmed Hugh's heart when he first arrived. Even as a young student in Normandy, he had never visited a house so fine. There were tapestries from Arras, armoires and tables from Limousin, stools from the Breton province and a carved oaken throne from Rheims. By comparison, Develish was spare and humble, and Hugh was certain Thurkell couldn't understand the value of what he was looking at until he heard him murmur under his breath to Ian Startout that he saw now why My Lord had felt it necessary to steal from Dorseteshire widows. To My Lord's face, he was less offensive, saying only that serfs could feed as well from a French table as from an English one.

Whether through shame at having his thieving discovered or a genuine belief that treating his people with kindness would bring results, My Lord had given Thurkell leave to introduce Develish practices to his own estate. Hugh had questioned the sense when he saw the group of filthy, undernourished field serfs who assembled in the great hall within an hour of their master's return. Of what use could education be to these cowering shadows? Their community had once numbered over six hundred but a bare hundred and twenty remained, and none looked capable of productive labour. The pestilence had destroyed their families and broken what little spirit they had left.

Hugh had wanted to run at the sight of them, sure they carried the pestilence, but Thurkell, who had first addressed them outside, had accepted their word that a month had passed since anyone had died of it. He had already made enquiries of the servants in the house and all had given the same testimony. The last death had been at the end of November. Since Lady Anne had insisted on only two weeks exclusion to prove a person free of the sickness, he had persuaded Bourne that four weeks was long enough to believe his people, too, were free of it. And he didn't doubt the cold winter was to thank for this blessing.

My Lord's long absence in Dorseteshire, coupled with the death of most of his household, meant his serfs had been without direction for months. Where Hugh would have set them to work immediately to cure them of idleness, Thurkell began by instructing the handful of remaining house servants to prepare food to feed them. He and his companions assisted in the task by butchering five sheep and milling grain on the castle's quern-stones to make flour for bread, and the serfs seemed entranced to see a lord and his squires buckle to tasks usually reserved to bonded men. A ripple of curiosity ran through the assembled mass.

It was a first stirring of life, as if something out of the ordinary was all that was needed to wake them; but what they made of the orders Thurkell gave when their bellies were full was anyone's guess. Most stood with downcast eyes as he listed the tasks he wanted them to perform. Their village must be burnt to kill the vermin in the thatch, and new homes erected in another location. Their habit of defecating and urinating outside dwellings and in woodland would end. Instead, latrines would be dug at a distance from the new village to bury human waste beneath ground to deter scavengers. Great importance would be placed on the cleanliness of bodies and clothes. The women would run a communal laundry and manufacture thin-toothed combs to pick lice and fleas from the heads of all, including their own.

Athelstan understood these ideas might seem strange, but he urged compliance. Spring planting was a good two months away and there was time to complete the building work and grow accustomed to the new rules before the call came to return to the fields. For his part, My Lord of Bourne pledged food and shelter for all and an abandonment of the whip for any but the most serious of crimes.

This last brought looks of disbelief to several faces but only one man dared voice his doubts aloud. Some forty years of age, he stood at the centre of the crowd, his arms laid protectively across the shoulders of children, and he advised his neighbours in an undertone to question everything they were being told. Hugh would have challenged such insolence, but Thurkell saw courage and stepped forward to seize the serf's hand and make him an ally.

Did it gall Hugh now that his assessment had been wrong and Thurkell's right? Not so much as it had galled him to watch Robin Pikeman grow in stature over the weeks that followed. The peasant might never learn the skills of reading and writing, but Thurkell's patronage and Pikeman's own knowledge of his master's demesne won him the ear of My Lord. His fear of Bourne was obvious but, assisted by Thurkell, he found his voice and demonstrated a keen grasp of the difficulties My Lord faced through the loss of so many of his field serfs—not least the inability of one hundred and twenty to farm land that had required six hundred to make profitable before the coming of the pestilence.

He raised other issues which were rightly the preserve of the steward. The necessary redistribution of peasant strips which had become redundant through the deaths of entire families. The support of orphaned sons, too young to work, who were nevertheless heirs to their fathers' land entitlements. The protection of orphaned daughters. A recognition of the rights of the elderly to a share in the fruits of their families' strips whomever was appointed to farm them. The impossibility of selling surplus livestock with markets closed and drovers and merchants too frightened to travel the highways.

Pikeman numbered My Lord's sheep and cattle at well over two thousand beasts and argued that slaughter was essential before predicted births in the spring put an even greater burden on already scarce pastureland. Where the pestilence killed humans, it allowed stock to flourish, and My Lord would lose his flocks and herds to starvation if he continued to allow his ram lambs and bull calves to live.

Bourne studied the serf's gaunt face and frame and asked why he hadn't slaughtered and eaten the animals himself, and

Pikeman reminded him of the edicts he had issued which listed the punishments for thievery. To hide a handful of grain when taxes were being counted earned twenty lashes. To tickle a trout from the river, forty. To steal a sheep from the pastures or a deer from the forests, death.

Perhaps the old man felt shame for his own misdeeds, because he ordered the surplus male animals to be slaughtered and preserved as food for his people before turning to the problem of how to farm the demesne's land without sufficient labour. My Lord of Athelstan had suggested bringing the surviving serfs from his vassal estates to make their homes in Bourne. Did Pikeman foresee difficulties in such an exercise? Would the serfs of Bourne accept strangers in the place of those who had died?

The serf answered that My Lord's people would do as they were ordered whether they liked the new arrangement or not but, encouraged by Thurkell to say how best to create one community from four, he advised that leading men from each of the vassal demesnes should be brought to Bourne first. 'They will know the number and names of those who still live, the size of their present holdings and the rights to which each family is entitled, sire. If they're persuaded that the distribution of plots and strips in Bourne will be fair, they will take that message to their villages.'

'And My Lord's own people?' Thaddeus asked. 'How will they feel about newcomers?'

Pikeman hesitated, clearly questioning how bold he could be. 'To increase each family's portion by a third will ease any tensions, sire. When a man has the ability to grow more food, his fear of hunger decreases and taxes become less onerous. If the vassal demesnes have suffered as badly as we have, there's more than enough land to be generous.' He ducked his head to

Bourne. 'Be assured your people have done their best to till and plant your virgates, sire. We honoured our oaths of fealty even without instruction, for none of us wished you to return and find your own fields uncultivated.'

Hugh thought the churl overreached himself to pretend such work had been done out of loyalty rather than fear of a flogging, but My Lord readily accepted the lie as reason to offer rewards. He instructed Hugh to make preparations for the reallocation and enlargement of the peasant strips, appointed Pikeman overseer of the digging of latrines and the building of the new village and tasked Thurkell with bringing worthy men from the vassal demesnes. All three estates lay on the highway to Sarum, the farthest some thirty miles distant, and Thurkell requested the use of My Lord's carriage to bring the selected serfs from their villages.

At least on this My Lord showed caution. 'Is that necessary? Surely such privilege will convince them they're superior to my own people?'

Thurkell gestured to Pikeman. 'They'll be no stronger or better fed than this man, sire. Even to ride a horse saps energy when the body is unaccustomed to the saddle. To request those from the farthest demesne to walk thirty miles will be to kill them before they arrive.'

Pikeman found the courage to speak without being prompted. 'They'll be more afeared than honoured to travel in your wagon, sire. It makes no matter what reasons they're given for the journey, they'll expect your anger when they arrive.'

'Why?'

'For bringing the pestilence to your demesnes, sire. The priest told us it was God's punishment for sin.'

'The Church teaches us so.'

'Yet my wife was a better person than I am, sire, and my children quite innocent. I should have been taken before them . . . and certainly before the priest.'

Thurkell answered when Bourne stayed silent. 'It wasn't by God's will that your family died, Robin. It was through misfortune. In Develish, where your master took refuge during the autumn, none has fallen to the pestilence. They've kept it at bay by using the same methods I'm asking you and your people to follow. If you rid yourselves of vermin and parasites, you have a goodly chance of survival.'

Pikeman searched his face. 'We've never died of such things before, sire. Why should it be different now?'

'I can't tell you that, my friend. My understanding of the sickness is very limited. I know only what I've seen and heard. You and your fellows must decide for yourselves if the advice I give is good.'

He couched his explanation in words the serf would understand, only falsifying the details that related to his status, claiming cousinship with Lady Anne of Develish as his reason for being on her demesne when news of the pestilence first reached them. He explained the measures Lady Anne had taken to protect her people and then told of how he and his soldiers had ventured out in search of grain and livestock to replenish Develish's dwindling stores as autumn drew in.

ରୁୋ

Hugh had first heard the story some three months previously, when he and Develish's leading serfs had been summoned to the church shortly after Lady Anne had given leave for My Lord of Bourne, Thurkell and his companions to cross the moat. My Lord and Lady Anne were seated in the prayer stalls and the tall figure of Thaddeus Thurkell stood by the chancel window, staring towards the land beyond the moat. He seemed more imposing for his near month-long absence and, as always, Hugh resented having to look up to him. God had dealt him a poor hand when He'd made him a head shorter than a bastard-born English slave.

At Lady Anne's invitation, Thurkell had spoken of his journey, neither tempering his language nor sparing his listeners a true picture of what he'd observed. He had described a land almost barren of people. There was evidence that lords and freemen, able to travel at will, had fled north to escape the pestilence while bolder serfs, willing to live by their wits, had seized the opportunity of their lord's absence to abscond; but the size of the plague pits in abandoned villages were testimony to how many had died. He dismissed any suggestion that the sickness was carried on the wind or in the water, since he and the youths who rode with him remained well, and he respectfully challenged Lady Anne's belief that sufferers must pass the infection to others on their breath or through their touch.

Had the disease been confined to Melcombe, where it first appeared, Thurkell would have agreed with her, but the speed with which it had spread made him question whether afflicted travellers could be the carriers. Survivors spoke of the pain sufferers endured from the moment the fever took hold. Boils erupted within hours, and death followed in three to four days. Not even the strongest and most determined of men could have journeyed far enough from Melcombe to cause the whole of Dorseteshire to be wasted in under ten weeks.

In the demesne of Woodoak, where he and his companions had found people still alive, Thurkell had asked how they'd escaped the pestilence. Not one had claimed goodness as a reason, telling Thurkell their beloved priest had been amongst the first to die. Instead they blamed rats, quoting the words of a wise woman— as versed in medicine as Lady Anne—who had devoted herself to nursing the sick on the priest's death. Her reward had been to die of the pestilence herself, but her fellow serfs had followed the instructions she'd given them and none had succumbed since. Burn your houses to rid yourselves of rats, she had urged. Immerse yourselves fully in water to cleanse the feeling of dirt on your skin. Sleep outside in the open air, and build a fire each night to keep vermin away.

Thurkell would have given these warnings little credence had rats been less evident in the demesnes he and his companions visited. The creatures bred faster where peasants had died or fled, leaving easy sources of grain on unharvested strips or in sacks inside abandoned huts. As to how they might pass the pestilence to people, he repeated the descriptions the Woodoak serfs had given of the sick. Some had complained of terrible itching before boils erupted on their necks, and all, including survivors, had spoken of their skin crawling in the presence of the dead and the dying.

Some five days later, while his companions delivered sheep to Develish, Thurkell had returned alone to Woodoak. This time he had asked only about the itching. What had caused it? All cited fleas, having seen the bites on the skin of their dear ones. One spoke of how her small daughter had scratched and clawed at the virulent eruptions on her arms until painful pustules broke out around her neck. The woman was no stranger to fleas and couldn't account for why these eruptions had been so inflamed, but her husband and son, similarly afflicted, had both died within a week of her daughter.

Challenged by My Lord of Bourne to explain if it was rats or fleas that passed the pestilence to humans, Thurkell had argued for both. He knew of no illness that moved from animals to humans, but to stand near a mangy cur was to invite a legful of bites. It was the same when humans shared their living space with rats. As a child, he'd found a dead one in his bedding and the straw around it glistened with escaping fleas as he'd lifted it by the tail. To prevent the infestation spreading, his mother had seized a burning brand from the fire and set his bedding alight. Every serf in Develish had suffered similarly until Lady had instructed them on how to rid their homes of vermin and parasites.

He returned to the question of how the pestilence had spread so quickly through Dorseteshire. If sin wasn't the determiner of death, and sufferers were too weak to travel, then it must be the healthy who carried the sickness. Yet how? It was inconceivable that a man could be ignorant of a rat in his knapsack, but he could carry a flea without knowing it. Thurkell had pulled back his sleeve to show the darkness of his skin. Whether because of its colour or toughness, he was never troubled in the way that the fair-complexioned were. He could journey many miles with a flea in his clothing before losing it to a more palatable, softer-skinned host.

My Lord of Bourne had been party to Thurkell's thoughts during the time they'd spent together outside the moat, yet he still remained wedded to the idea that divine punishment was the reason for the pestilence. Nothing else made sense to him, and he appealed to Lady Anne to explain how a single flea could infect a whole village. She had answered seriously that it wouldn't be just one. Fleas must breed like any other creature, for God had no cause to make them different. If rats grew in numbers when there were ample supplies of grain, then the fleas that lived on the rats would multiply also. She had no explanation for why they had suddenly become deadly to man, but nor could she say why one pox was mild and another fatal, though experience told her it was so.

Lady Anne went on to speak of the ease with which the pestilence had entered Melcombe. There had been rumours of a killing sickness in France even before her husband had died, and it made good logic that it had crossed the sea in a ship. If the source of the infection had been dying sailors, they would have had limited contact with people ashore, but rats, bearing fleas, would have disappeared into the sewers and houses of Melcombe where colonies of their fellows already lived. The same was true of every town and village where waste lay above ground and food was unsecured.

'Are you so convinced of God's hatred for man that you cannot conceive of a different agency being responsible for this sickness?' Lady Anne asked Bourne. 'You're surely not blind to the fact that the moat has kept Develish free both of rats *and* the sickness?'

'Do you always trust what your eyes tell you, milady?'

'I do, sire. Is there a reason why I should not?'

'God's truths are as much invisible as they are visible.'

'The Church would have it so,' she agreed, 'but it's written in Proverbs: *The hearing ear and the seeing eye, the Lord made them both.* And to what purpose would He bestow such wonderful gifts upon us if He didn't intend us to have faith in what they reveal?'

'It's a great arrogance to presume to know the mind of God, milady.'

'Indeed,' she said lightly. 'The bishops took much responsibility upon themselves when they declared sin to be the cause of the pestilence. I grieve deeply for the caring priest of Woodoak who must have breathed his last in terrible distress, wondering how he had erred.'

ෙ෬ෙ

Hugh had felt tainted by heresy every time Lady Anne questioned the authority of the Church. He experienced the same sense of dread listening to Thurkell assure Robin Pikeman that his family had not been found wanting. It made no matter that he used reason to support his arguments. Hugh had been taught that the Bible could only be read and interpreted by the clergy and to hear a disbeliever dismiss the Church's teachings on sin was to conspire in his blasphemy.

He had struggled long and hard to accept that a Saxon dissenter might have right on her side but, much as he longed to, he could not avoid the truth: that Lady Anne's methods of protecting her people had worked. While all in Develish—sinners to their cores—still lived, the records in Bourne showed that eight-tenths of Bourne's servants and serfs had died.

Robin Pikeman needed little persuasion that something other than wickedness had caused his family's deaths. He even endorsed Thurkell's belief that fleas were the culprit, describing how his eldest son, the first to die, had complained of vexatious itching in the days before he fell to the fever. Nevertheless, he had little confidence that others would agree.

'Most here are persuaded that God intends all men to die, sire, with the worst being kept to last. The youngest still have hope, and may accept that washing will keep them free of the pestilence, but the adults have none. They await death in the belief that their punishment was to endure the loss of those they loved before being taken themselves.'

This bleak prediction touched a chord in Hugh, for he had always feared God's wrath, but Thurkell would have none of it. And neither, it seemed, would Bourne. With My Lord's approval and encouragement, Thurkell tasked himself with restoring the survivors' faith in the future. The following day, he and his companions assisted Pikeman in building the first house on the plot reserved for the new village. They had it finished by nightfall and attracted a crowd of curious watchers when Thurkell asked Pikeman whose home it should be. The serf consulted with his fellows and all nominated a woman who had made herself responsible for orphaned girls under twelve years old.

The day after, they began a second house and, whether drawn to help by the sight of a lord in rolled-up shirtsleeves or fuelled with new energy from the communal meals they were consuming, twenty men joined them in the enterprise, setting to work on multiple buildings. Watching from a distance, Hugh wondered what sedition Thurkell was preaching, for he knew the man well enough to know he wouldn't be arguing in favour of God's social order. Lady Anne had indoctrinated him too well in the profane belief that an accident of birth was the only difference between a noble and a slave.

He suspected more sedition a week later when Thurkell returned from a two-day journey with six greybeards comfortably seated in My Lord of Bourne's carriage. The elders showed none of the fear of punishment that Pikeman had predicted, and Hugh was certain Thurkell and his companions had tutored them in how to behave and speak along the way. They greeted their liege lord gravely and listed the names and ages of those who still lived in his vassal demesnes. Hugh recorded the names in his ledger and, when all were counted, the number of serfs remaining from a population in excess of three thousand a year previously was five hundred and three, some fifty of whom were too young to work.

The elders were unable to say whether their own lords—vassal knights to Bourne—were alive or dead. Each had departed with his household when news came that the sickness had crossed the border between Dorseteshire and Wiltshire. Two were thought to have headed west and the third north, but no word had come from them since. One of the stewards had died, two had fled, and all three priests had perished. There were no bailiffs. Responsibility for My Lord's demesnes had fallen to his bonded men and they had done their best to safeguard his land, livestock and property.

After being shown the demesne by Pikeman, and consulting with him at length, the elders had expressed their willingness to bring their fellows to live and work in Bourne on the same terms that My Lord had agreed with his own serfs. Hugh watched in disbelief as Bourne signed a writ, prepared by Thurkell, which not only granted them extra land but rights of access to education, medicine and a meal of meat every seven days. It was a world in disarray when base-born men, sworn to obedience through their oaths of fealty, could expect rewards in return for their labour.

The next two weeks saw columns of tired humanity and livestock shepherded into Bourne by Thurkell and his companions. Those too old or young to walk rode with caged poultry on open-sided bullock carts while the able-bodied drove their demesnes' sheep, pigs and cattle ahead of them. Secured inside My Lord's covered wagon were the gold reserves, weaponry and fine garments which had been abandoned by his vassal knights in their haste to flee. My Lord, watching the arrival of the first convoy, remarked to Hugh that Thurkell had the air of Moses, leading the Israelites to the Promised Land, and Hugh's heart soured when he saw the description was accurate. The words 'blessed saviour' ran in whispers through each weary throng as Thurkell urged them to rest and eat the food that was brought to them.

Brought back to the present by the weeping of maids at Athelstan's departure, Hugh raised his eyes again to the shadowy figure of the old man, standing half hidden behind a pillar to watch the scenes in the great hall. Did Bourne understand now that the slave was less Moses than Judas? He should. It was a powerful betrayal to persuade a noble he could keep his people's allegiance by rewarding them with kindness, only to take their gratitude to himself.

One young maid clung desperately to Thurkell's hand and begged him to stay. He had found her amongst the remaining house servants, a shy and frightened orphan of some twelve years whom others said had a knowledge of letters. She had learnt the skill from the priest but was fearful of admitting to it until Thurkell praised her for her cleverness and urged My Lord of Bourne to appoint her tutor to the children. He had sat at her side for seven days, helping in the teaching of the young ones, and she had grown in confidence under his guidance. But now she wept and shook with grief, for she had no belief My Lord of Bourne's approval would continue once her protector was gone.

The same apprehension was in every face.

ഇൻ

Edmund Trueblood turned in his saddle for a last look at the demesne before a bend in the highway hid it from view. The burnt--out remains of the old village lay like an ugly scar on the land but the new houses, some five hundred paces to the west, stood clean and fine as if to prove that life would go on. 'Do you think My Lord cares enough about his people to continue what you've started?' he asked Thaddeus.

'It depends what you mean by caring. He understands the value of their labour well enough.'

'They'll abscond if he doesn't keep his word,' said Peter Catchpole. 'I answered more questions about journeying the roads than I ever did about burying turds or getting rid of fleas. There isn't a lad in Bourne who hasn't thought about slipping away at night to make his fortune as a freeman.'

Olyver Startout nudged his horse to the left to avoid a rut. 'And Thaddeus will be blamed when they do. Master de Courtesmain will make sure of it.'

Peter gave a snort of derision. 'He's a weaselly little fellow. It galls him that even Joshua tops him by a couple of inches now. He puts it down to eating meat. I heard him tell My Lord of Bourne it was a bad idea to add mutton to a serf's diet.'

Joshua grinned. 'How did My Lord reply?'

'Coldly. He advised the steward to count the number of surplus rams and explain what he planned to do with them if they weren't eaten. He's no more enamoured of de Courtesmain than Lady Anne was.'

Edmund glanced at Thaddeus. 'Is that true?'

'For the moment . . . but de Courtesmain's no fool. He'll work his way into the old man's favour in time. My guess is the elders will be blamed for failing to meet My Lord's hopes of the harvest before I'm blamed for absconders.'

'Have you warned them?'

Humour glinted in Thaddeus's dark eyes. 'No need. They've laboured under stewards like de Courtesmain all their lives. I've left him a letter, urging him to make them his allies, but he'll not heed the words. It pleases him to think peasants too ignorant to merit his respect. He'll cite their laziness and stupidity for producing lower yields than he predicts.'

'What if My Lord believes him?'

'He won't. He has a keen understanding of what his land can produce.'

'You shouldn't put so much faith in him,' Peter scolded. 'He has no more liking for his serfs than de Courtesmain has. I saw it in his eyes. He can't stand to be near them.'

'Maybe so, but he's willing to tolerate them as long as his greed's satisfied. He made a bargain with the elders that if his people, working together, can increase the yield on his land by in excess of one-fifth on previous years, he'll award them the profit on the surplus. There's no better spur to persuade men to work. Rightly or wrongly, they all believe they can surpass a fifth quite easily.'

'De Courtesmain will hate you even more if you're right,' said Olyver. 'Did you tell him we were going in search of Eleanor's dowry?'

Thaddeus shook his head. 'It's not his business. I let him believe we're returning to Develish, looting what we can from every deserted demesne we pass. The idea pleased him.'

'Why?'

'He'd rather remember me as a common thief than a serf who passed for a lord. It galled him more than he could bear to have to bend his neck to me.'

'Then you'd better not have signed your letter Athelstan,' Olyver warned, 'or he'll be feeding it to the pigs by now.'

Thaddeus laughed. 'I did not. My intention was to help him, not provoke him. He needs to open his eyes to the future and stop yearning for a past that is gone.' He nodded to the road ahead. 'I suggest you do the same. I don't care how many young maids won your hearts in Bourne, everything we do from hereon in, we do for Develish.'

(THADDEUS THURKELL'S LETTER TO HUGH DE COURTESMAIN)

Honoured Sir,

I write in the hope that you will see advantage to yourself in upholding the pledges My Lord of Bourne has made to his people. He is more receptive than you realise to the ideas he encountered in Develish, and to argue against them may cause him to doubt you. He understands well that the future of his estates depends on the goodwill of his serfs to work his fields and seeks ways to encourage their loyalty rather than weaken it.

He is persuaded that our world will look different when the pestilence ends, and I advise you to give some thought to this yourself. I have tried several times to engage you on the subject, but your clear resistance to men being rewarded for their work suggests you believe that obedience can only be won through the whip. If so, you are wrong. No whip has been wielded in Develish for over a decade. Instead, Lady Anne has allowed her people to share in the profits of their labour, and the yields per head have been significantly higher, year on year, than anything Bourne has managed to achieve.

Before the pestilence, a nobleman's wealth was assessed by how many serfs he owned. The greater the number the more profitable his land. Yet, even by merging four demesnes into one, My Lord still lacks the workers to return Bourne to profit. The same will be true of every landowner in Wiltshire because none will have taken the measures Lady Anne did to protect her people. I beg you to ask yourself how this shortage will be managed except by lords luring their neighbours' serfs away on a promise of payment for work and an end to their oaths of fealty. Should this happen, My Lord of Bourne will look to you to keep his people true to him, and your success in the venture will earn his gratitude.

That task is already begun. Robin Pikeman tells me he and his neighbours dare to believe in a future since My Lord gave his undertakings, and their confidence in him will only increase as their health and strength improves. You may not agree that the dark ages of serfdom are almost over, Master de Courtesmain, but you must surely accept that every landowner, including My Lord of Bourne, will welcome skilled workers who declare themselves free and willing to work for a small imbursement. No questions will be asked about the truth of the claims when fields need planting and crops harvesting.

I urge you most strongly to put aside your doubts and suspicions of the English peasant class and seek allies amongst the elders. Not one is your enemy unless you choose to make him so. Robin Pikeman has the ear of all and will be an honest adviser on how to draw the best from My Lord's people. Robin's family is buried in Bourne and he has made himself responsible for the many young boys who've been orphaned by the pestilence. He and they will have no cause to leave unless the pledges they've been given are abandoned.

Our paths are unlikely to cross again, Master de Courtesmain, since our loyalties lie in separate directions, but please accept my sincere hope that you enjoy good fortune in the weeks, months and years ahead.

Your obedient servant,
Thaddeus Thurkell

FEBRUARY, 1349

Eight

Pedle Hinton

THEY RODE TWO DAYS TOWARDS the south-west, sleeping in
woodland by night and taking to the road again when the sun
came up. The weather had been cold for weeks but a change in
the wind on the second night presaged snow. By mid-morning
of the third day, they shivered under an icy blast from the east
which snatched at breath and bit at exposed skin. The youths
drew their chaperon hoods about their faces and looked warily to
their left, where leaden clouds were building in the sky. Thaddeus
took a firmer hold on the pack pony he was leading and urged
his companions to pick up the pace while the going was good.
There would be no steering their horses clear of ruts and holes
when the roads were blanketed with snow.

He kept to himself that he was beginning to question whether
they were on the right highway. It was one thing to memorise a
list of landmarks, described to him more than a month ago by
Gyles Startout in Develish, quite another to recognise them now.
He was confident they'd ridden the Shafbury to Sherborne road
because milestones along the way had told him so, but he was

deeply concerned he'd chosen the wrong crossroads to turn south towards Pedle Hinton. *You'll know it by an oak tree which stands at the north-east corner,* Gyles had said. *It's as wide as it's tall and casts such deep shade that nothing grows within twenty paces of it.*

But had Thaddeus been right to assume the burnt and blasted trunk of a once-great tree was the landmark Gyles had meant? It was three years since Gyles had ridden this road from the north as part of Sir Richard's retinue, and a bolt of lightning could well have cleaved the mightiest oak in the meantime, but there was little else to recognise along the way. If milestones had ever existed, they'd been long hidden by encroaching foliage.

Ian drew alongside as Thaddeus slowed before a shallow ford. 'We'll have to make camp soon,' he said, gesturing to the sky. 'The snow's almost upon us.'

Thaddeus nodded.

Ian looked to some woodland on their right. 'Wouldn't here be a good place? There's water close by and no one to see us.'

Thaddeus ignored him to stare up the incline ahead. 'Your father spoke of a ford in the valley before Pedle Hinton. He said the highway would veer to the south-west on the other side of the river.'

Ian followed his gaze. 'We've crossed several fords already and the road has continued south or south-west each time.'

'Mm.' Thaddeus turned to study the advancing line of cloud. 'We've another hour yet. We'll strike camp when we've breasted the hill.'

'It'll be harder to build a shelter if we leave it too late,' Ian warned.

'Then make haste,' said Thaddeus, clicking his tongue to set Killer going again. 'We'll need dry kindling if we want a fire tonight.'

The snow began to fall when they were halfway up the incline, soft flakes that melted as they came to rest on the chaperon hoods and woollen coats. Before long, the boys felt the icy water penetrate through the fabric to their skin and watched in growing dismay as a wispy veil of white began to shroud the road and the hedgerows. Joshua, bringing up the rear with his pack of dogs padding miserably at his horse's heels, muttered that the poor beasts would die of cold if they didn't find shelter soon.

Thaddeus, fifty paces ahead, halted on the breast of the hill to lean forward in his saddle and stare through the falling snow at the valley below. Gyles had said he would know Pedle Hinton by the way the manor house was situated and built. Standing on a bend of the River Pedle, the structure had the appearance of a cross with an elongated entrance porch on one side of the great hall, a kitchen and buttery on the other and part of a church showing behind it. The village would be clustered to the right of the highway with a hunting forest to the east and vast acres of cleared land to the west.

He scratched his beard thoughtfully as he waited for his companions to draw level. The swirling flakes were nigh impenetrable, but he thought he could make out the walls of a large building some thousand paces distant. He gestured into the valley when Ian and Edmund drew level. 'What do you see?' he asked.

Ian narrowed his eyes. 'Not much,' he admitted. 'Ask Edmund. He has the best sight for distance.'

Edmund linked his hands across his face like a visor and studied the valley through a slit between his fingers. 'There's a river behind the tree line on the southernmost boundary. I see a gap where the highway crosses it to the left of what must once have been a manor house. The walls still stand but half the roof has gone. There's a church behind it.'

'What shape is the house?'

'Long and thin with protrusions on both sides.'

'Like a cross?'

'Yes. There's cleared land to the right but I can't tell which are peasant strips and which pastures. There's the remains of a village beside the road and a mound about a hundred paces beyond.' He dropped his hands. 'It's huge. If anyone's still alive here, it'll be the poor wretch who buried the bodies.'

They'd come to recognise that a feature common to all demesnes was the bank of earth that spoke of a mass burial site. 'The pestilence was in Pedle Hinton even before Sir Richard reached it,' said Thaddeus. 'Gyles told us some forty had died in the week before they arrived.' He aped Edmund's trick with his fingers. 'I wonder what caused the roof to collapse.'

'Flames,' said Ian. 'Maybe the gravedigger went mad and set fire to everything. The village too. Burning seems to be the only way to cleanse a place.'

By then, the other three boys were lined up beside them. 'Are we there?' Peter asked hopefully. 'Does it look right this time?'

Thaddeus nodded. 'As close as anything we've seen.' He gathered up his reins. 'We'll know for certain when we've crossed the river. There should be a track into the forest some quarter-mile beyond which was wide enough to take Sir Richard's wagon.'

Joshua glanced at his shivering dogs. 'What if we find the track but not the wagon?'

'Worry more that we will,' said Thaddeus unsympathetically. 'When Sir Richard abandoned it, there were five dead bodies inside. I doubt they've been removed.'

The snow fell relentlessly as they pushed on to the river, but if Thaddeus felt the biting wind through his sodden clothes he didn't show it. The boys consulted in whispers about encouraging him to look for shelter before the river, but none voiced the idea aloud. They all knew what his answer would be. *Do as you like. I'm not your keeper.* And the last they would see of him was when he was swallowed by the blizzard.

He had warned them often enough that they must accept his decisions or be left behind, but even Ian, his most loyal supporter, questioned the sense of continuing. The purpose of their journey was to recover a chest of gold—Lady Eleanor's unpaid dowry—which the twins' father had left in woodland outside Pedle Hinton some seven months previously. He had given Thaddeus directions on how to find it, but neither believed it would still be there. Half a year was a long time to abandon a coffer of coins, unprotected, on a forest floor.

Most of what Ian knew of his father's journey home with Sir Richard had come from his mother. She gave him answers in return for a promise that he wouldn't pester Gyles for explanations. Better he be allowed to forget, she said, than relive his anguish in nightmares. Yet it was a strangely misdirected anguish. For reasons Ian didn't understand, his father felt he should have died along with his companions and started out of sleep with shouts against God's injustice. Sometimes, he muttered prayers for the men Sir Richard had chosen to forsake, feverish but still alive, inside his wagon on a woodland track.

There was no honour in Sir Richard. He had discarded his men with as little care as he took the pestilence into Pedle Hinton. His intent was to secure a bed for the night, but he feared the doors being closed to him if there was any suspicion he'd been in contact with the pestilence. By then, just three of his retinue of eleven remained—his captain of arms, his bailiff and Gyles—and he ordered them to say they'd come from Develish, where all were well. To his host, he feigned good health, blaming the flush of fever in his cheeks on a surfeit of ale, and upon learning that forty of My Lord's field serfs were already dead, had shamelessly requested My Lord to bar the rest from his house for fear they would pass the sickness to his guest.

Martha said it was right and just that God had condemned so venal a man to die. Not content with infecting Pedle Hinton, he had ordered Gyles to drive the wagon, the dying soldiers and surplus horses to Develish, threatening him with a flogging if he failed. She had kinder words for the captain of arms and bailiff, who were as feverish as their master the next morning. Too weak to do anything but support Sir Richard in his saddle, they had begged Gyles's pardon for leaving him to manage such an impossible task alone. There was no way of turning a heavily laden wagon in the narrow confines of a woodland track without assistance.

Gyles wouldn't have done it even if he'd been able; he'd rather be flogged for disobedience than take a killing disease to Develish. He told Martha of his relief to find the five soldiers dead, for it was easier to turn his back on corpses than it would have been to watch men suffer in the stinking Hell the vehicle had become. The stench of suppurating boils and putrid blood, made worse by the heat of the sun, had attracted blowflies, and the horses hobbled around it were near driven mad by their bites and stings. He had cut the horses free to find water and pasture. There was no better way to excuse his failure to drive a pestilence-ridden vehicle to Develish than to lack the means to pull it.

His mind and flesh recoiled against climbing amongst the stiffening bodies to remove Lady Eleanor's dowry, but he baulked at allowing thieves to enrich themselves at Develish's expense. He gave the dead what dignity he could by closing their eyes and folding their hands, and took some comfort from the peacefulness of their faces. Had the chest been lighter and more manageable, he might have been tempted to carry it home across his saddle, but he was as wary of displaying it too openly along the highway as leaving it in the wagon. Instead, certain he couldn't escape the pestilence himself, he chose to hide it in the woodland, pledging himself to live long enough to pass the secret of where he'd left it to Lady Anne, the one person he trusted to use Develish's wealth to benefit her people before herself.

Martha believed it was this unselfishness that had persuaded God to spare Gyles. For the same reason, she had faith that God would have kept the gold hidden from thieves. Neither conviction was shared by Thaddeus, who rarely saw God's hand in anything, and yet he continued on, seemingly oblivious to the cold and the wet. His obstinacy made sense when they reached the river. On either side the banks were pushing into the stream as plants and rushes bent under a weight of snow, causing the waters to narrow and run fast across the slabs of stone that had been laid on the bed to provide secure footing to wheeled vehicles. The crossing looked dangerous now and would surely be impassable by the morning.

Thaddeus chose to dismount and wade through the freezing flow ahead of his horses, advising his companions to do the same. 'You'll not get far if your animal slips on the stones,' he said, removing his boots. 'Better a few moments of discomfort than a mount with a broken leg.'

'A few *moments*?' Ian echoed sarcastically, sliding from his saddle and tugging at his own boots. 'We've been in discomfort for *hours*.'

'Not for much longer. The track we're looking for is ahead on the left.'

'Assuming this is Pedle Hinton.'

'Assuming that,' Thaddeus agreed dispassionately as he felt for safe passage with bare feet.

ℭℭ

They located Sir Richard's covered wagon some two hundred paces inside the forest, half drawn into the trees at the edge of the track. Thaddeus halted twenty yards short of it, and motioned to the others to do the same. He was as surprised as the boys to see it there, wondering why the Pedle Hinton serfs hadn't made use of it long since. There was enough oak in the structure to make a multitude of stools.

'Could the dead soldiers have frightened them off?' said Edmund.

Thaddeus shook his head. 'They'd buried forty of their own already, and all in the same state. Why cavil at another five? It speaks more to the wagon never being found than it does to fear of corpses.'

Olyver glanced back down the track. 'It's not that far from the demesne. Women and children out looking for firewood couldn't have missed it.'

'If they were well enough,' answered Thaddeus thoughtfully. 'Perhaps the village was worse afflicted than Gyles realised. The sick wouldn't have had the strength to walk a mile.'

He examined the woodland to the left. The trees were largely ash and oak, and, though leafless, their tight canopies offered good protection from the falling snow. He gestured towards a high-domed, wide-branched oak which had a sizeable stretch of dry ground beneath it. 'We'll camp there tonight,' he said, easing himself from Killer's back and lifting off the leather saddlebags which had been crafted for him in Develish. He tossed them into the shelter of a low-growing hazel then unbuckled the girth and divested the animal of its saddle and harness. 'You have spare clothes in your own bags,' he told the boys as he looped a rope halter about the horse's neck and muzzle before stripping the pack pony of its burdens. 'Take off anything wet and dress in dry tunics and britches before you go looking for firewood. You'll warm up soon enough if you put some effort into your search.'

Olyver lowered his own saddle beside Thaddeus's and replaced the reins with a halter. 'What will you be doing?'

Thaddeus waited while the others did the same and then took charge of the halters. 'Feeding and watering these poor brutes. There was meadowland to the south of the river. I'll hobble them there.'

They watched him walk the horses down the track.

'Doesn't he feel the cold?' asked Edmund.

'He shuts his mind to it,' said Ian. 'He says a person can withstand anything if he forgets how much he's hurting and applies himself to what he has to do.'

They put the doctrine to the test in the collection of firewood, but the promised warmth never came. The frosts of winter had permeated the forest floor and nothing was dry enough to take a flame, not even leaves. The twins began paring away the damp outer layers of fallen branches to reach the unsaturated wood inside, but Edmund said they'd have more success if they looked in the wagon. Sir Richard had never travelled anywhere without chests of clothes, barrels of brandy and hessian sacks full of sweetmeats. All and any would be dry as long as they were still there.

Ian couldn't fault his logic. The wheels had kept the base from sucking water from the ground and the leather canopy had prevented rain and snow coming in from above. Nevertheless . . . 'Have you forgotten what's in there and how they died?' he asked.

'They'll be bones by now.'

'With fleas in their clothes.'

'Not to mention rats,' murmured Olyver. 'There could be a whole colony of them feasting on Sir Richard's sweetmeats.'

Edmund selected a six-foot long branch from the stack of firewood and trimmed it to form a sharp-pointed stave. 'There's no harm looking if we keep our distance. Most of the studs holding the roof to the sill seem to have rotted.'

He approached the side of the wagon and used the pointed end of the stave to jab at the head of a carved wooden peg to the left of the opening flap. Protruding some two inches clear of the side, the peg served the double purpose of anchoring the main canopy to the sill and providing a knob for the loop of rope that fastened the flap closed. He remembered his father saying that Sir Richard would come to regret not choosing English oak for his embossed dowels but, even so, he was surprised at how few strikes were needed to knock the head from its shaft.

Ian joined him a few moments later with a stave of his own, and between them they fractured enough of the studs to prise the canopy away from the side of the wagon. When the vehicle had been in constant use the wax coating which had kept the leather stiff was regularly renewed but, after being at the mercy of the elements for more than half a year, the fabric had become soft and pliable. Together, Edmund and Ian hooked their staves beneath the edges and flipped the cover up and over the wooden hoops that formed the supports.

'Mary Mother of God!' said Peter in disgust, staring at the tangle of half-chewed bones and ripped and stained livery on the floor. 'What happened to them?'

'Scavengers,' said Edmund, pointing to a wide, splintered gap at the base of the far wall. 'Probably badgers . . . they're the only ones strong enough to claw through wood.' He turned to the stack of boxes and barrels at the front, raising his stave to point at a smaller cask atop the pile. 'That looks like a brandy keg. Will it start our fire?'

'Should do,' said Joshua. 'You can set fire to brandy. My mother saw it done in the kitchen once.'

'We'll have to hook it out,' said Olyver, kicking the stack of firewood apart and choosing a branch with a strong lateral spur at one end. He positioned the spur behind the keg and flicked it to the ground, but the ease with which he did it and the way it bounced told them it was empty. Joshua said it was probably for the best, since his mother had described the brandy flames as blue and unnatural. He took the branch from Olyver and skimmed a rag-topped torch some twenty paces clear of the wagon.

'What do you think?' he asked the others, walking across to examine it. 'Is it safe to touch? Do you see any fleas? Will it light?'

'Should do,' said Ian. 'There's still resin in the rags.' With sudden decision, he stooped to pick up the torch and told Olyver to roll the keg towards the oak tree. 'Who cares? We'll die of cold before we ever catch the pestilence if we can't make a fire.'

Thaddeus returned with a dead sheep across his shoulders; he'd culled it from a flock in the meadow where he'd left the horses. He made a strange sight with his wide-skirted coat turned white by snow and his dark eyebrows and beard glittering with frozen flakes. As he passed the wagon, he paused to look inside and then heaved the sheep to the ground and changed out of his sodden clothes, remarking idly that more steam than heat seemed to be coming from the boys' niggardly blaze.

'Blame the logs,' Ian told him, patiently paring wet bark from a branch.

'We'd do better to burn the wagon except none of us fancies eating food cooked on dead men's bones,' said Edmund.

'It's the chests and barrels we want,' said Olyver, 'but there's no way of getting them over the sill without climbing in, and none of us wants to do that in case the pestilence is still inside.'

'Mm.' Thaddeus knelt to open one of the sacks from the pack pony. He removed an axe and a coil of rope. 'It'll be easier with the side removed.'

Rather than chop against the grain of the planks, he chose to strike through the mitred joints that held the sideboard to the front and tailgates, but cold and weariness caused him to miss his aim as often as find it. Edmund took the axe from him. 'You're not made of iron,' he said gruffly. 'Take what heat you can from the fire and watch us do it.'

Given permission to destroy, the boys set to with a will. When enough of the sideboard had come away at both ends, they inserted the rope behind it and used their combined strength to tear it free of the joints which held it to the bottom. Thereafter they threw loops behind the chests and barrels that were stacked at the front beneath the driver's perch and pulled them to the ground. The three barrels, all with broaching taps, had once held wine or ale. As he used Olyver's branch to bowl them towards the fire, Peter said he hoped the soldiers had drunk them dry. Death would be easier to face if the brain was numbed.

Still wary of touching anything, Edmund used the axe blade to prise open the metal clasps that held the lids of the chests closed. Some, which had contained dried food or sweetmeats judging by the dusting of detritus on their bottoms, were empty; others were packed with articles of clothing that had once belonged to Sir Richard. Certain they were flea-ridden, Ian and Olyver scooped out shirts, gowns and hose on the points of the staves and tossed them into the rear of the wagon before pushing the chests ahead of them.

Joshua kicked the damp wood off the embers of the brandy keg and relit the torch. He motioned to Peter to push one of the barrels onto the glowing cinders and then held the torch to the staves to encourage flames. 'Be ready with the next when it takes,' he told Peter. 'Once we have a goodly blaze, we can start feeding the damp firewood into the mix. We need the fire to last the night not burn itself out in an hour.'

'More like seven nights,' Thaddeus corrected as he ran the blade of his knife down the belly and breast of the sheep which he'd strung by its back legs from a branch of the oak tree. 'The last time we saw snow like this it fell for three days and lay on the ground a week. I doubt we'll see Develish tomorrow.'

'We'll not keep anything alight that long,' said Peter.

Thaddeus nodded. 'We'll look for shelter in the church or manor house tomorrow.' He grasped the top left edge of the fleece in one hand and used the side of the other to chop at the membrane between the skin and the meat, pulling the coat away in one piece. 'Our first task come daybreak will be to look for the gold.'

Ian was performing the same actions as Thaddeus on the right-hand side of the carcass. 'How?' he asked.

'Your father built a cairn on the other side of the track. We begin with four hundred paces due south.'

'I didn't see a cairn.'

Thaddeus gave a grunt of amusement. 'It's a bare foot high and he didn't bargain for snow. I could just about make it out when we arrived but not when I came back. We wouldn't have found it if the wagon hadn't been here.'

Ian eased the rest of the skin from the carcass then crouched to slice through the spine and sinews at the neck. 'Or you hadn't forced us to keep going.'

'That too.'

Peter levered another barrel onto the flames. 'It'll all be for nothing if the gold's been stolen.'

'Let's hope it hasn't.' Thaddeus took the skin from Ian and laid it fleece down on the ground beneath the carcass before using his blade to split the sheep's belly and breast to allow the still-warm entrails to drop. 'I'll have the skin back when your hounds have done feeding,' he told Joshua. 'I want something dry to sit on while the mutton's roasting.'

Joshua knelt to cut away the liver, heart and lungs. 'What about the rest of us?'

'Get your own,' Thaddeus said unfeelingly. 'There are plenty more sheep in the meadow.'

They settled for the wagon's sideboard, laying it on the ground across the fire from Thaddeus. There was some debate about whether fleas might be hiding in the joints between the planks until Thaddeus said they could never have survived half a year. Fleas lived on animals and humans, he said, not on wood. If it were otherwise, My Lord of Bourne's furniture would have given them the pestilence.

The air grew colder as the night lengthened, yet despite filling their bellies with half-raw sheep, none of them slept. The sound of the wind in the trees dropped but the snow continued to fall in eerie silence, and the fire became increasingly difficult to keep alight. By dawn the tangled livery inside the wagon was hidden by a clean white shroud, and a two-foot drift covered the track beyond it. Peter glanced nervously at the translucent sheet that covered their oak and said it wouldn't be long before the branches sagged under its weight.

Thaddeus nodded. He was on his feet, moving the packs, harness and saddles against the trunk of the tree. 'We'll need the horses to carry these,' he said. 'We'll come back when the weather improves.' The damp clothes of yesterday were frozen stiff, but he told the boys to shake and pummel them to loosen the ice crystals and then pull them over what they were wearing. 'With luck the inner layer will stay warm long enough to reach the manor house. Bring your weapons and tools but nothing else.'

If they thought this meant he was planning to make shelter a priority, they were quickly disappointed. He stamped out the embers of the fire and used the tip of his sword to draw lines in the ash. 'Gyles used the sun as a guide,' he explained. 'Due south, four hundred paces . . . due east, five hundred paces . . . and due south again, one thousand paces. At each change of direction, he placed a ring of stones beneath a tree.' He drew circles around the points where his lines moved at right-angles to each other. 'Here and here . . . and another halfway down the long stretch.' He touched the tip to the centre of the last line. 'We need to find the rings to have any hope of locating the chest.'

'Why should that be difficult?' asked Edmund.

'We can't predict due south with the sun obscured,' said Thaddeus, marking another line which veered away from the first he'd drawn. 'If we stray west . . . like this . . . we could spend all day looking for the first ring of stones.'

'Wouldn't it be more sensible to make the search when we return for our packs?' suggested Olyver. 'Won't the sun come out when a thaw sets in?'

'More likely the snow will turn to rain and cover the ground with ice,' said Peter. 'That's what happened after grandfather died.'

'Do you have a plan?' Ian asked Thaddeus.

Thaddeus nodded. 'We know south lies beyond your father's cairn.' He placed the tip of his sword at the point that indicated the cairn and drew six lines radiating away from it. 'Edmund is the same height as Gyles. If he takes one of the centre lines and counts off four hundred paces, and the rest of us angle away from him, the chances are good that the first ring of stones will lie somewhere between the six of us when he calls to us to stop. I'll take the outermost line towards the west and work my way east. The rest of you stay put until I reach you.'

The task was easier imagined than performed. Thaddeus insisted on looking beneath every tree for twenty paces on either side of the median in the lengthy gaps between the boys and, all too predictably, he found the stones in the last stretch to be searched. They were more obvious than he'd expected, a foot-wide ring of lightly coloured flints, placed on dark earth in the cleft between the twisting, muscular roots of an ash tree, and he blessed Gyles for his common sense. It was surely no accident that he'd chosen a spot which was protected from drifting leaves.

'You should have let me work in from this side,' said Ian, who had taken the outermost line to the east and had cursed freely about boredom and cold by the time he was allowed to move. 'We'd have found it sooner if you had.'

'Now that we know what we're looking for, you can,' said Thaddeus. He stood sideways to the tree, raised his left arm to point towards where he believed the wagon to be and squared his right to indicate due east. 'Edmund, follow this line for five hundred paces, and the rest do as we did before. Don't skimp on searching,' he warned Ian. 'We'll none of us thank you if we have to return to your father's cairn and start again.'

Whether by chance or through Edmund's accuracy in judging direction, the second and third rings were within thirty paces of where he halted. Thaddeus asked how he was managing to keep his line so true, and he said he didn't know. He was simply choosing the most direct route through the trees to be sure of walking the measured distance.

Olyver said his father would have done the same. 'He told our mother the chest weighed a tonne . . . and he'd have cursed to Hell and back if he'd kept bumping into trees with a load like that on his shoulder.'

A smile creased Thaddeus's dark face. 'He'll have cursed anyway, trees or not. The chest is carpentered from three-inch-thick oak and contains four hundred gold nobles. It required two men to lift it into the wagon.'

'*Four hundred*?' Peter echoed in amazement. 'No wonder you're so keen to retrieve it.'

'And Gyles to hide it, since it was earned by the sweat of Develish serfs. We'll spread out as before for the last five hundred paces. We've not come this far to go awry at the end.' He turned to

Ian. 'We're looking for a fallen tree. Your father pushed the coffer into a space beneath the trunk where it forms an arch with the torn-up roots. Seven months ago the tree was rotten to its core and it may have broken apart since, so be sure to search under every piece of sizeable deadwood you encounter.'

As Ian dutifully turned every log, he listened for shouts of excitement from the other end of the line. When none came, he wondered what Thaddeus would do if they failed to find the gold. The woodland canopy was protecting them from the worst of the snow, but in parts, where tall, slender birches had taken the place of oak and ash, the flakes fell freely through the thinner branches and the ground beneath them was deeply carpeted. He began to fear that the mile-long walk to the manor house was already impassable. Joshua expressed similar worries when Ian released him to join the search, muttering that his dogs would die of exhaustion if Thaddeus expected them to breast drifts three feet high.

By the time they reached Peter, he was jumping up and down and swinging his arms in a vain attempt to keep warm. 'You've been bloody ages,' he growled, motioning behind him. 'There's a fallen tree with its roots still attached about thirty paces back. It's pretty much buried by snow but it's worth a look. I'm thinking your father's paces probably shortened as he grew tired.'

Ian removed his bow, scabbard and arrows and propped their tips together to form a pyramid, denoting Peter's spot so they could find it again. 'I'll wring your neck if you're right,' he snapped crossly. 'We'd be halfway to the manor house by now if you'd left a marker and made the search yourself.'

Nevertheless, he planted a hearty kiss on Peter's cheek when a small amount of scrabbling through windblown leaves and a scattering of snow exposed a carved wooden chest with its padlock intact.

⊘⊘

Four miles to the east, Eleanor was watching the falling snow through the window of the steward's office. In her arms, she cradled one of her cats as tenderly as a baby, planting kisses on its head and rubbing her cheek against its soft fur. As ever, the soft, rumbling purr that answered her honest love brought a sweet smile to her face.

She had only the dimmest memories of the last time snow had fallen on Develish and she was entranced by its prettiness. The land was white as far as the eye could see and the unsightly remains of the burnt-out village were softened and cleansed. She drew Lady Anne's attention to a group of men on the other side of the moat who were moving three abreast across the pastureland.

'What are they doing?' she asked.

Lady Anne left her desk to stand beside her. 'Tramping a path to the sheep.' She pointed to where the flock was huddled against some wattle fencing. 'Do you see how the snow is beginning to bank over them? We must move them now or they'll be smothered.'

'Why don't they move themselves?'

'They believe they're safe. It's their nature to stay together.'

'Where will the men take them?'

Lady Anne turned her towards where Gyles Startout, John Trueblood and James Buckler were enlarging the shelter My Lord of Bourne had used. 'They've taken the timber from the serfs' huts in the orchard to build a low-roofed barn.'

'Where will the serfs sleep?'

'In the house. No one can live outside while this cold spell endures.'

With unexpected tenderness, Eleanor slipped her arm around Lady Anne's waist. 'You must be worried for Thaddeus,' she said gently. 'You told me he will have left Bourne a week ago but his journey home seems overly long.'

'I expect his work in Bourne has delayed him.'

'I hope that's true, Mama. Robert is greatly worried for him. He says he and his companions could freeze to death if they've become trapped in the snow without a fire to warm them.'

For once, Lady Anne believed Eleanor's concern was sincere. Certainly, her soft embrace seemed kindly-meant. 'Robert frets unnecessarily,' she answered with a light laugh to disguise her own fears. 'Thaddeus is more of a wolf . . . and they thrive in weather like this.'

Nine

EVIDENCE THAT THE GREAT HALL of Pedle Hinton had been destroyed by fire was seen in the soot-blackened walls and the charred rafters that had once supported a timber roof. The heavy oak doors of the entrance porch stood wide open, revealing a pristine covering of snow lying like a downy coverlet on the floor. Here and there, undulating folds suggested something buried, but Thaddeus ignored his companions' superstitious mutterings about corpses as he walked through the porchway to look towards the southern end of the house which retained its roof.

A set of stone steps in the farthest corner led to upper chambers which opened off a railed gallery, and two doors in the supporting wall below to lower ones. He looked for footprints in the snow but couldn't see any. If people still lived here, they hadn't left their quarters last night or this morning. He called out a greeting. 'My Lord of Athelstan and five of his fighting men ask hospitality of My Lord of Pedle Hinton. We are free of the pestilence but need shelter from the blizzard. Does anyone hear me?'

Perhaps it was only an echo of his own voice, but he had a strong sense that he'd been answered. He stood listening, his hand reaching for the sword that hung at his side. Ian and Olyver did the same, motioning to Joshua to send his dogs forward. At the rear, Edmund and Peter, who were carrying the chest of gold between them, lowered it to the ground and lifted their strung bows over their heads.

'Try again,' urged Joshua. 'The pack will tell us soon enough if you get a response.'

The dogs reacted even before the words had left Thaddeus's mouth, racing for the stairs and bounding up them two at a time, giving vent to mournful howls as they paced the gallery and sniffed at doors. Joshua prepared to follow, but Thaddeus caught his arm. 'Summon them back,' he said. 'Whoever's up there must think the hounds of Hell have arrived.'

Joshua gave a piercing whistle. 'What will you do?'

'Try to coax our hosts into revealing themselves. If they're from Pedle Hinton, they're more entitled to be here than we are, and if they're not—' Thaddeus unsheathed his sword—'we'll have to agree temporary rights of tenure.' He beckoned the other boys forward and motioned to the doors at the end of the hall beneath the gallery. 'See if those rooms are occupied, but let the dogs enter first.'

He trod quietly up the steps and looked along the landing. Four chambers opened off it but there was nothing to tell him whether one or all were occupied, since there were only paw prints in the dusting of snow on the floor. He moved softly to the first door and placed his ear to the planking, waiting through the sound of Joshua's warnings outside a room below and the wrench of rusted hinges as Ian forced entry. In the hush that followed, he heard a child's whimper and the whispered tones of women, urging silence.

He walked on light feet to the other doors, listening outside each for several minutes. From downstairs, the intermittent conversation of the boys was clearly audible, yet there was no reaction to it inside these chambers. He positioned himself to the right of the first door and used his sword hilt to tap lightly against the wood. 'I am My Lord of Athelstan, cousin to your near neighbour Lady Anne of Develish and related through marriage to Sir Richard, her deceased husband. Be assured that I and my men mean you no harm. If one amongst you remembers Sir Richard from his visits or knows anything of Develish, then ask me questions so that I may prove my truthfulness.'

There was some whispering before the tremulous voice of an elderly man spoke. 'Sir Richard was sick the last time he was here. Did he die of the pestilence?'

'Yes. Three days after leaving Pedle Hinton. Lady Anne worried that he brought the pestilence to you, but Gyles Startout, who rode with him, told us you'd buried forty of your own in the week before they arrived.'

'I know Gyles. Is he well?'

'He is, as are all in Develish. Only Sir Richard and his Norman fighting men are gone. Gyles's twin sons, Ian and Olyver, form part of my retinue. Two of the voices you hear downstairs are theirs.' He paused to allow time for a reply, but none came. 'How many are you? We will assist you if we can.'

'We do well enough on our own, My Lord. Pay heed to your affairs and leave us to ours.'

There was a whispered altercation before a woman spoke. 'We are eighteen, sire. One elder, seven women and ten children.

We have lived in this chamber since bandits fired the village and a malign wind carried burning thatch to the roof of the great hall. We thought the whole house would be razed, but God saw fit to leave us this part as shelter.'

'When was that?'

'I can't tell you, sire, for we have lost count of the sun's rising and setting. Three weeks and more, I think. We stay together for warmth but grow weaker as each day passes.'

'When did the last of your neighbours die of the pestilence?'

'Before Christmas, sire. We are all that is left, though we don't know why God has spared us. We are much in need of assistance.'

Briefly, Thaddeus closed his eyes. He knew full well what he would find when he opened the door, for he had seen starvation in the hollow faces of the peasants of Woodoak and Bourne. He reached for the latch. 'Do I have your permission to enter, mistress? Lady Anne judges a person free of the pestilence after two weeks. Were she here, she would tell you it's time to embrace life.'

ோ

There was no understanding people like this, Ian thought, as he took an adult woman from Thaddeus's arms and carried her down the steps to where Edmund had lit a fire in the largest of the ground-floor rooms. She had so little flesh on her bones that she weighed as lightly as a child and only the grime on her face gave her skin some colour. He placed her carefully on the floor, afraid of breaking her, and her eyes filled with tears as she thanked him. He smiled and spoke comforting words but, in truth, his mind rebelled against her stupidity. By what reasoning did anyone choose death from hunger when there were sheep aplenty in the fields beyond the house?

He, Olyver and Thaddeus had caught and slaughtered two ram lambs within a hundred paces of the front door, and Joshua had found the means to cook them simply by putting his shoulder to the door of the kitchen. Little of the roof remained, but shelves around the walls were piled with iron cauldrons, pewter plates and earthenware tankards. A heavy oak table, miraculously unscathed, stood in the centre. Once swept of snow, Joshua used it to butcher the carcasses while Edmund and Peter, having looted every room of furniture to make fire, dug out a mighty stack of wood beside the kitchen's outer door and brought the logs inside to dry.

The first to be brought downstairs in Thaddeus's strong arms had been a shrivelled greybeard who took deference as his due. He seated himself on a pile of rushes and gestured towards the floor each time Thaddeus, Ian or Olyver appeared with another wraithlike figure clasped against their chests, apparently believing that women and children must always sit beneath him. He was more alarmed than grateful to see his master's furniture being broken up for firewood.

'We'll suffer for this,' he warned the women as Ian fed the legs of a stool into the blaze to keep Joshua's cauldron of diced mutton at a rolling simmer. 'They compound theft with wilful destruction by what they do.'

Olyver entered the room and placed a barely alive toddler in the lap of the woman Ian had carried. He was as impatient with these people's foolishness as his twin. 'Whose judgement do you fear?' he asked the old man. 'If God's, you can escape sin by allowing me to return you to the upper chamber without food.'

'The offences have been committed. You have made us party to your crimes whether we like it or not. Removing ourselves will make no difference.'

Olyver gave an involuntary laugh. 'You have a strange way of reasoning, sir. Do you think God doesn't know who the true culprits are? Why should He punish the innocent when My Lord of Athelstan and his men are willing and able to take the blame upon themselves?'

Thaddeus paused at the bottom of the stairs. Cradled in his arms was the last to be rescued, a woman of some thirty years with sunken eyes and transparent skin. It was she who had spoken to him through the door, and she who had insisted on the old man going first, using the opportunity of his absence to urge the women and children to pay heed only to My Lord of Athelstan. Together they listened to the exchange between the twins and the elder.

'I am acquainted with your father,' the old man told the youths severely. 'He would not approve of your behaviour.'

'You're mistaken,' answered Ian, kneeling to touch the cold, pale cheek of the toddler. 'Gyles Startout would endure an eternity in Hell before he let a babe such as this die from lack of warmth and nourishment . . . as will his sons, if that is to be our punishment.'

'Then accept God's judgement when you appear before Him.'

'We will do so gladly if this little one survives.'

'He will not. His only salvation was freedom from sin. Ours also. Now God will punish us all for your misdeeds. Boils will break out on our necks and our bodies turn black—and you will bear our suffering on your conscience along with your other crimes.'

A young maid began to weep.

'You must take me in, sire,' begged the woman in Thaddeus's arms, plucking urgently at his sleeve. 'They will crawl from the fire and eat nothing if he continues. He has a powerful hold over them.'

'Yet you seem ready to defy him. Could you not have done so sooner?'

'Not on my own, sire. He is my father.'

Thaddeus needed no further explanation. In a social order created and governed by men, women learnt obedience early. 'What is your name, mistress?'

'Alice Bartram, sire.'

'And your father's?'

'Harold Talbot, sire. He is persuaded God means us all to die. If you know differently and have the words to change his mind, I beg you to use them.'

With a nod, Thaddeus carried her into the room and sat her amongst the women and children. He dropped to one knee in front of the old man. 'Why do you deny yourself food and warmth, Master Talbot? Is the sin of self-killing not greater than the sin of theft?'

'If God wants me to live, I will.'

'He has saved you from the pestilence and placed these seventeen women and children in your charge. What more proof do you need that He wishes you to keep serving Him on earth?'

'We serve Him best by following his commandments. To prolong our lives through theft and wanton destruction will invite punishment. We are judged by the manner of our living not by the span of our years.'

Thaddeus was reminded of his stepfather, whose mind, once set, was impossible to change. 'Then you have a fine advantage over the rest of us,' he said lightly. 'We could all wish a half-century of enjoyment before being asked to account for ourselves.'

Harold's eyes glittered angrily. 'The older we are the harder we are tested,' he snapped. 'Innocents such as these—' he gestured dismissively to the toddler—'have places reserved for them in Heaven. Old men such as I have to earn our redemption through privation and suffering.'

A cynical smile flickered briefly at the corner of Thaddeus's mouth. It was a shameless tyranny that exploited weakness for its own benefit. 'I doubt redemption comes through the wilful neglect of children, sir.' He turned to the women. 'Without a priest to guide you, you must decide for yourselves what God expects of you. If you truly believe you'll be judged more harshly for stealing a sheep than leaving a little one to die, then do nothing; if you do *not* believe it, you must act.'

Ian, seeing the way the women dropped their eyes, worried that Thaddeus had pushed them too far too fast. Even men needed courage to gainsay an elder, and there was no spark of resistance in any of the faces before him.

A breath of time passed before Alice raised her head. She addressed Thaddeus. 'We grieve for our families and long to see them again, My Lord. All were lost to the pestilence, but my father assures us that the youngest and least sullied will be waiting for us in Heaven. He urges us to keep pure hearts so that we may join them. It makes death more welcome to believe we can once again clasp our newborns to our breasts.'

Thaddeus wondered if even Lady Anne could have said so much in so few words. He knew now how the old man had gained a hold over her companions' minds—grief for lost children never went away—but he had little idea how to loosen it. To urge them to live the life they had rather than yearn for an uncertain Heaven would be to take all hope away. He looked to Ian and Olyver for inspiration.

'Our father, Gyles Startout, would tell you all your family will be waiting for you, mistress,' said Ian. 'He heard the confessions of dying soldiers because there was no priest to do it, and he found only good in them. He has no belief that God caused their suffering in order to send them to Hell.'

The old man stirred. 'They were punished for the sins of all mankind, as were my grandchildren. It was the same when the Flood covered the earth and caused every living thing to perish. God saw that His creations were evil and corrupt, and He repented of making them. Only Noah, a man without blame, was saved.'

Tears wet Alice's lashes. Again, she addressed Thaddeus. 'Our priest told us this before he breathed his last, sire. He thought it would comfort us to know our families paid the price for others' sins and not their own.'

'When did he die, mistress?'

'Some six weeks after the pestilence arrived, sire.'

'Did he tend the sick?'

'Every hour of every day. We mourned his passing deeply.'

Thaddeus nodded. 'We hear the same story everywhere we go. God's servants die early.' He took her hand in his. 'Why do you think that is?'

He felt a trembling in her fingers, as if his touch made her uneasy. 'To keep their suffering short, sire. The greatest anguish is to watch others endure terrible pain, knowing you can do nothing to help them.'

'To believe that is to believe that Christ's agony on the cross was less than His mother's pain to watch it. Is that not a heresy, mistress?'

Alice glanced nervously towards her father. 'We try only to make sense of why a good man died early, My Lord.'

Thaddeus reached for her other hand to encourage her to look only at him. 'In Develish, where Lady Anne protects her serfs by refusing entry to strangers until they prove themselves free of the pestilence, every man, woman and child still lives. Here, where no such measures were taken, eighteen remain. Your priest died because he honoured his vows. He gave himself unstintingly to those who needed him and he caught the sickness through his closeness with them.'

She took so long to answer that her father spoke into the silence. 'He utters the Devil's words. You'll not escape Hell if you heed him, daughter.'

Alice ran her tongue across her dry lips. 'I nursed my husband and all my children, sire, but they died and I lived. How can that be if the sickness is caught through closeness?'

Ian held his breath, praying that Thaddeus wouldn't talk about rats or fleas. Precious few in Bourne had believed him, only following his rules on cleanliness because they were rewarded with food for their obedience. To expect this woman, so steeped in submission to her father and the Church, to understand a strange, new reasoning would be to lose her.

'In the same way that you didn't catch the sneezes every time your husband had them, or the pox from your children. Not all fall to every sickness.' Thaddeus nodded to Ian and Olyver. 'These twins' father nursed Sir Richard and two of his fellow soldiers as they lay dying, and remains healthy to this day, yet he rejects any idea that God singled him out for favour. He knows his flaws too well to believe himself more deserving of life than those who have perished.'

'But does God not ordain everything, My Lord? How else was I spared the sneezes except by His mercy?'

A smile lit Thaddeus's eyes. 'If I knew that, mistress, we could be free of them forever.' He paused. 'I have few answers except to remind you that Jesus gave us only two commandments: *Love the Lord your God with all your heart and your neighbour as yourself.*' He released her hands to cup his palm under the chin of the toddler. 'This is your neighbour. If you abandon him, you abandon God.'

⁀∾⁀

It was another two days before the snow stopped falling. By then, the church had become a stable for horses and the great hall a pen for as many sheep as Thaddeus and his companions had been able to shepherd through the blizzard. All were in need of fodder. On the first morning of clear skies, Edmund, Joshua, Peter and the twins located a barn stacked with hay on the edge of the pastureland, and used wooden spades from a shed beside the manor house to dig through the drift in front of the double doors.

They stood for several minutes, contemplating the sheaves that were piled inside and the two pitchforks impaled in the ground on either side of the doorway. The pack's lack of interest suggested there was nothing to find, but Joshua said dogs responded to movement as much as scent. If rats had burrowed into the hay to sleep through the winter, they'd emerge as soon as the sheaves were disturbed. Fleas too.

Edmund, always the most reluctant to encounter rats, gave a groan of anguish before seizing a pitchfork and using it to stab a sheaf. 'Bloody well set your animals on to anything that twitches or I'll wring their necks myself,' he warned Joshua, as he slung the bundle onto the snow behind them. 'I'm damned if I'll catch the pestilence to keep Pedle Hinton serfs alive.'

He made a fine show of proving differently, Ian thought with amusement, as he watched his friend make deeper inroads into the stack. But whether Edmund wanted to keep sheep alive for the sake of the women or the toddler was anyone's guess. He'd become the women's favourite after patiently coaxing the infant to open his eyes and take nourishment, and there was no question he enjoyed their praise. They said his voice and face must resemble the child's father's, for the little boy responded more to him than to anyone else—so much so that he would only eat if Edmund cradled him in his lap and fed him from his plate.

Thaddeus asked the child's name and how old he was, but none of the women knew. He'd been found wandering the village one morning in November, but no one could say if he was from Pedle Hinton or had become detached from a family fleeing north to escape the pestilence. From his size, he was believed to be some two years old, but he couldn't tell them his name. Before the pestilence, Pedle Hinton field serfs had numbered above five hundred, and toddlers had been hard to distinguish when some families ran to eight or ten children, with half being lost in the first three years of life. Alice thought he might be a Blount, the last of whom was believed to have perished in the week before he was discovered, but the other women were doubtful. He hadn't the look of John Blount and they couldn't recall Jeanne binding a suckling babe to her breast in order to work the fields in any of the previous eight seasons.

Out of curiosity, the following morning Thaddeus searched the church for the parish register after he and his companions had hobbled their horses in the nave. He found it in the priest's quarters, beneath the dead man's blood-and-pus-stained stole, which he flicked to the floor with the point of his sword, along with the wooden cross that lay on top. He bent his head in apology to the altar before he left, as much for turning God's house into a stable as for his affront to the crucifix. He harboured no heresies against Christ, only against the Church which claimed to speak for Him.

That afternoon, by the light of the fire, he traced the Blount family's history in the register. The last child to be born to John and Jeanne had been a son in the winter of 1346, but his early death was recorded six months later. In the eleven years before, Jeanne had given birth to nine babies, only three of whom had survived long enough to see the pestilence. The priest had recorded their deaths before he, too, had succumbed.

Since sons were valued more highly than daughters, Thaddeus found it hard to believe the toddler had been abandoned by fleeing serfs, and he combed the register for every boy born between the summer of 1346 and the spring of 1347. Eight had died within a year of their births, leaving sixteen unaccounted for. He read their names and the names of their parents aloud. In most cases, particularly where peasant strips adjoined or huts were close, one or other of the women was able to say with certainty that the whole family had perished, including babes in arms. But the fate of four was unknown.

'I heard it told that Tom Halfpenny chose to abscond and take his wife and son with him,' said Alice. 'They were young and had more courage than the rest of us.'

'Jacob Cooper did the same after his daughter perished,' another woman said. 'He and Molly swore an oath that they'd not let any more of their children suffer and were gone by the morning.'

Harold Talbot, somewhat mellowed by taking food into his belly, nodded. 'By my guess, upwards of fifty of the younger men absconded,' he told Thaddeus. 'They promised to come back for their families when they'd found shelter elsewhere, but none ever has. It may be that this child belongs to one of them.'

Thaddeus ran his finger down the page. 'We're left with two. William Fulcher and Godfrey Lovell.'

Edmund raised his head. 'My grandfather was Godfrey Trueblood and my grandmother was Meg Lovell. That can't be chance, can it?'

Thaddeus turned back pages to find the births of Godfrey Lovell's parents and grandparents. Every so often, he saw surnames he recognised from Develish and he wondered how many of the demesne's daughters had married into Pedle Hinton. The stories of so many families were written in these simple inscriptions of births, marriages and deaths, and yet the knowledge was lost when there was no one to read them. With patient cross-referencing, he traced Godfrey Lovell's lineage to the birth of his grandfather, Robert Lovell, and from there, three pages earlier, learnt the name of Robert's older sister, Meg.

He gave a bark of satisfaction. 'I can tell you for certain when I've checked the Develish ledger,' he told Edmund, 'but it looks as if your grandmother was sister to this little fellow's grandfather. She must have moved to Develish on her marriage.' He read out the entries for both births. 'Godfrey Lovell is your cousin.'

ᘏᗅᘔ

Alice looked down from the gallery as the young men in My Lord of Athelstan's entourage untied the sheaves and dropped the hay in loose piles amongst the flock. They were very assured in what they were doing. Peter Catchpole turned a lame ewe on her back and used his knife to dig a stone from between the cloves of her hoof while the twins moved from sheep to sheep, running their fingers around faces and ears, searching for ticks. Through the open door of the kitchen, she saw Edmund and Joshua filling My Lord of Pedle Hinton's embossed metal piss-pots with snow before holding them over six-inch-wide candles to melt the crystals to water. She made a silent prayer that her father wasn't watching as they carried the costly vessels into the great hall and placed them in front of the animals as drinking troughs.

When she'd first seen the youths, she hadn't doubted their status was above hers. True, they looked younger than the fighting men she'd seen in the past, but their weapons, their manner of speech and their coats and liveries, though saturated, had given them the bearing of freemen. Seeing them now, dressed in tunics and britches and showing more knowledge of how to manage stock than any Pedle Hinton soldier ever had, she wasn't so sure. Certainly, her father believed them to be serfs, whispering constantly in her ear that Gyles Startout was as low-born as he.

She turned to watch Thaddeus sort through scrolls on the shelves in My Lord of Pedle Hinton's chamber. Most he returned to their places with only the briefest of glances, a few he placed on the floor at his feet. Feeling her gaze upon him, he looked towards her with a smile. 'What troubles you, mistress?'

A flush of embarrassment stained her cheeks. How churlish she would seem to question this man when his presence had brought so much hope and strength. And yet she was fearful. 'You must not think me ungrateful, sire. Two days ago, I could barely stand, and I wept to see little Godfrey fade when the last of the dried plums were gone. It filled me with happiness to hear him laugh this morning.' She searched his face, her own creased with anxiety.

'Say what is in your heart, Alice. The truth will not offend me.'

She took a breath to steady herself. 'My father tells me Gyles Startout is as base-born as we and that his sons can be no different, sire. To accept the food they give us will not serve for excuse when a new lord comes.'

Thaddeus interpreted her words as best he could. 'You think it better to say you took food from a noble?'

'We are obligated to obey the commands of those above us, sire.'

He studied her with amusement. 'You've come a long way, Alice. When we first met, you were afraid of God; now your mind is troubled only by the imagined arrival of a man who doesn't exist.' He nodded towards the burnt-out roof. 'Which lord is so foolish that he'll pay the taxes of inheritance to acquire a demesne without labourers? Who will repair this house and rebuild the village? Who will plough the fields and harvest the corn?'

Alice shook her head in bewilderment. Such thoughts had never occurred to her.

'No landowner in England will have the men to work his estates once the pestilence has passed,' Thaddeus went on, bending to lift a scroll from the floor. 'This letter was sent to My Lord of Pedle Hinton from a cousin in Normandy.' He unfurled the vellum. 'It's dated Christmas, 1347—some six months before the pestilence entered Melcombe—and speaks of towns and villages in France and Italy being laid waste by a killing disease. In his own estates, this man had already lost one-third of his serfs and expected to lose another third before summer. He finishes by saying he'll be reduced to penury if that happens.'

He watched Alice's expression move from bewilderment through shock to anger. 'We thought only Dorseteshire had sinned,' she said. 'My Lord of Pedle Hinton raged at us for bringing God's wrath to the county, and the priest ordered us to beg his forgiveness before we asked God for His. Neither said Normandy was afflicted.'

'Would it have made a difference if they had?'

'For certain, sire. It filled us with terror to think we were alone in our suffering. My poor husband died not knowing what wickedness Dorseteshire had committed.' She dashed a tear from her eye with the back of her hand. 'The master was cruel to berate us. If he knew that France had fallen to the sickness, he should have made plans to protect us, the same way My Lady of Develish did.'

'I doubt he had Lady Anne's courage, Alice. It takes strength and bravery to defy the Church. If Milady had believed what His Grace the bishop told her, the story of Develish would have been different.'

'Why did she not believe it, sire?'

Thaddeus answered honestly. 'She was raised by nuns who taught her to follow the teachings of Jesus. It makes her the kindest and most considerate of mistresses. Since she sees no fault in her people, she cannot accept that God does either, and strives to keep them safe because her faith tells her that this is what she must do.'

'Do her serfs follow the teachings of Jesus, sire?'

'They try, Alice.'

'Then that is why God has spared them, sire. They have more goodness than the rest of us.'

Thaddeus laughed as he dropped the scroll to the floor and took another from the shelf. 'I have high hopes of you, mistress,' he teased. 'A minute past, you were quibbling about taking food from Develish thieves, now you raise them to the level of saints. You'll be stealing yourself in another two days, if you believe the cause virtuous enough.'

The last day of February, 1349

Thaddeus has returned with yet more plundered sheep. He has put them to graze on the common land, which is bare of snow now that the thaw has come.

He and his companions surprised us by emerging from the woodland where the footpath from Pedle Hinton enters Develish. We had been searching the highway to the north and south for days, never expecting them to come along the track. They were herding the flock ahead of them, using Joshua's dogs to confine stragglers, and we heard the animals' plaintive bleating before we saw them. Gyles summoned me to watch as the column of sheep issued from the trees, followed by a motley army of women and children on horseback, and Thaddeus and his companions on foot.

Edmund Trueblood appeared first, bearing a tiny boy on his shoulders and leading his horse with 3 young maids in the saddle. The Startout twins, Peter Catchpole and Joshua Buckler followed, each with 2 or 3 frail-looking passengers on their mounts, while at the rear came Thaddeus, guiding a heavily laden pack pony with one hand and, with the other, his charger with a greybeard and woman upon its back. I counted 18 extra souls and asked Gyles where they could have come from. He guessed Pedle Hinton, for he recognised the greybeard as an elder who goes by the name of Harold Talbot.

And so it proved. Thaddeus called out their circumstances from across the moat and, with the agreement of my people, I have given permission for them to remain in Develish once they have served their fortnight's exclusion. Thaddeus believes some may have kinship with our serfs and has given me their names so that I may search our registers. Certainly, John and Clara Trueblood have no doubt that Edmund's small charge is part of their family, for he has the look of Edmund at the same age. They have pledged to raise the child as their own, and I don't doubt others will be as generous.

Thaddeus and his men (they are too well grown now to be called boys) have cleaned one end of the open-sided barn and strung fleeces in the gaps between the upright posts to provide shelter for the Pedle Hinton serfs. Our sheep still have use of the other end and will add warmth from their bodies at night. It is hardly the most inviting of welcomes to our demesne, but the 2-week exclusion has served us well until now. For themselves, Thaddeus and his men use the hut they built when Bourne was here.

I have sent clean clothes and warm broth across on the raft, and in return Thaddeus delivered our chest of gold and a coffer of scrolls from Pedle Hinton. In a private letter atop the documents, he drew my attention to the warnings Pedle Hinton received from France—but did not heed—about the progress of the pestilence. He urged me to study one vellum in particular, dated August, 1348, which he found with its seal intact. This suggested to Thaddeus, as it does to me, that My Lord and his steward never saw it, being dead before it arrived.

The letter was scribed by a French monk who charged himself with informing My Lord of Pedle Hinton that his cousin, a bishop of Normandy, had relinquished his life after days of intense suffering. I record the second paragraph here to remind myself that the rules we follow are wise:

'In his dying breath, His Grace implored that I request all in his family to protect themselves against this pestilence. His greatest fear was that none will survive and a proud name will be lost. Be comforted that you will do no wrong by closing your doors to sufferers since His Holiness, Pope Clement of Avignon, has granted remission of sins to all who die a painful death. Such benevolence will allow those you exclude to enjoy eternity. Nonetheless, His Grace's wish was that you embrace life, and he asked that you pray daily for his soul, avoid contact with the sick and pledge yourself to the service of God.'

There is much to read in the words of this unknown bishop, not least his belated realisation that it might be possible to survive the pestilence. I am left to wonder why he didn't come to this reasoning earlier and why His Holiness thought it kinder to remit sins—a fact which is known only to a handful of French clerics, I imagine—than offer wise advice on avoidance.

ଓଡ଼

The fourth day of March, 1349. Midnight

Thaddeus and his companions will leave again at dawn, and I am sad to have had only one chance to talk with my gentle giant. Clara allowed us the use of her kitchen for a snatched hour once all were asleep, but our meeting was bitter-sweet, being too short and taken up with business. We both issued warnings as often as we exchanged expressions of tenderness.

Thaddeus worries that Harold Talbot will cause disharmony when I allow him into our enclosure, and urges me to assist his daughter, Alice Bartram, in the management of him. The old man's mind has gone, causing him to dwell on the sins of others, and he makes his accusations with such force and anger that even Thaddeus's companions find them unsettling.

In return, I worry that My Lord of Blandeforde's steward will know Athelstan for an imposter. Thaddeus tells me his plan is to travel to Blandeforde in April, and I am already concerned for him and his companions. The steward's name is Jacques d'Amiens and I have never met a man so clever or so knowledgeable about his master's demesnes. In the time I've lived in Develish, he has come several times to oversee the collection of taxes, and I am deeply afraid he may have seen my dear friend performing *ad opus* work inside the moat. If he did, he will recognise him and know him for a serf. Thaddeus's appearance is too distinctive not to have been noticed.

Thaddeus pays little heed to these fears, for he has no understanding of how eyes are drawn to him because of the tallness of his frame, the darkness of his skin and the fineness of his features. I have begged him to avoid all contact with the steward but he refuses to humour me. He says, quite rightly, that he cannot secure a future for our people without talking to the person who controls My Lord of Blandeforde's affairs.

Thaddeus has written a long report of all that happened in Bourne, begging me to read it to our people once he and his companions have left. It seems the youths have lost their taste for storytelling, having learnt the last time that there is always a clamour for more. I wonder if they finally understand why Gyles was so reluctant to speak of his final journey with Sir Richard. After all, some things are best kept to oneself.

Thaddeus and his companions will ride first to Dorchester and Melcombe to discover how many still live in those towns. From there, they will travel to the west, charting the deserted demesnes along the way, and then to the east for the same purpose. They expect to arrive in Blandeforde in the second week of April, and Thaddeus hopes their knowledge of how south Dorseteshire fares, along with news of France and Italy from the Pedle Hinton letters, will stand them in good stead when they arrive.

This eve, the raft carried their newly laundered liveries, together with half the gold nobles from Eleanor's dowry. Our leather workers have created 6 separate saddle packs so that the weight of the coins can be spread evenly between 6 riders. The packs have been stitched in such a way that the coins stand in a series of columns inside them and the slimness of the design should allow them to escape notice beneath the bulkier packs above them. I pray this is so, for it will be a tragedy indeed if bandits believe they see something worth stealing.

Thaddeus is so determined to prove himself a worthy match for me by purchasing a demesne of his own, he's quite foolhardy enough to give his life in defence of gold.

Ten

Develish, Dorseteshire

CLARA TRUEBLOOD HAD WITNESSED MANY things in her kitchen but never a wild-haired old man pushing a young maid to the floor and raising her skirts to beat her naked buttocks with a wooden paddle. She thrust through the crowd of startled servants and seized Harold Talbot's wrist before he could land another blow. 'What is the meaning of this?' she demanded.

He turned his fury on her. 'You dare lay hands on an elder?'

'I dare and I will. You have no authority here, Master Talbot. By what right do you chastise one of my helpers?'

'By God's right. She profaned against one superior to her.'

Clara nodded to the girl to stand up. She was half-sister to Thaddeus and had yet to turn eleven. 'Is this true, May? Did you speak ill of Lady Anne?'

The girl shook her head.

'Who then?'

She wriggled her shoulders. 'Father Anselm . . . but I said only what others say.'

'Which is?'

'No one wants to clean his chamber because he lives like a pig.'

Clara turned her face so that Harold Talbot wouldn't see the smile that twitched at the corners of her mouth. She received more complaints about the drunken priest's dirty habits than anything else, and had heard rather worse slurs than 'pig' used to describe him. Some days, when she was feeling kind, she left the kitchen in another's charge and did the job of cleaning his quarters herself, if only to give some respite to the younger servants. It was one thing to empty the old brute's semen-filled piss-pot, quite another to run the gauntlet of his groping fingers. She had a sense that Harold Talbot was cut from the same cloth, since he had been overly keen to raise little May's skirts in order to give her a beating.

She resisted his attempts to free himself. 'Calm yourself, sir. This is my kitchen and you are an uninvited guest.'

He slapped her face. 'Where is your respect? I don't take orders from women.'

Clara, bigger and stronger than he was, caught his other wrist and twisted both arms behind him. 'You are in Develish, sir, where customs are different from Pedle Hinton.' She picked out thirteen-year-old Isabella Startout, who was standing near the doorway to the great hall. 'Oblige me by fetching Milady, Isabella. She will know better than I how to judge the rights and wrongs of this. Be sure to explain the situation to her. I wouldn't want her to be unprepared for what she finds.'

Isabella gave a nod of understanding before darting from the room. It was minutes only before she returned with Lady Anne, and Clara was relieved to see that her mistress seemed fully aware of why she had Harold Talbot under restraint. She spoke gently to him, but her words were intended for everyone.

'Do you know me, sir? We met two days ago when I welcomed you to Develish as your new liege lord.'

The old man spat on the floor. 'My Lord has been dead these many months. His wife also.'

'Indeed. Pedle Hinton suffered cruelly from the pestilence. Only you and a handful of women and children remain from the hundreds who once lived there.'

He stared at the faces around him. 'I see many in this room alone.'

'But all are strangers to you, Master Talbot, for this is Develish and not Pedle Hinton. Will you allow me to take you to your daughter, so that she can tell you again why you are here? I believe weariness has caused you to forget the journey you made to reach us.'

He frowned in confusion. 'My daughters are lost to me.'

'Not all, sir. One still lives. Her name is Alice. You will know her when you see her.'

He gave a baffled nod, and Lady Anne signed to Clara to release him. The woman did so, but remained ready to seize him again if he raised his hand to her mistress. She had more knowledge than most of the anger that accompanied the scrambled wits of age, for her grandmother had suffered the same debility.

'Shall I come with you, milady?' she asked.

'I believe we can manage on our own,' Lady Anne answered, putting her hand beneath Harold's elbow. 'It's but a few steps to the great hall, where Alice awaits us. It would be a kindness to make Master Talbot a bowl of chamomile tea with an infusion of valerian. He is much in need of rest, I think.'

'Isabella will bring it to you promptly, milady.'

Clara watched them make their way through the door and then took a jar of dried chamomile and a vial of valerian tincture from a high shelf on the wall behind her. 'You've nothing to feel anxious about,' she told May Thurkell as she spooned petals into an earthenware bowl and added a ladleful of water from the boiling cauldron on the fire. 'Milady finds no fault in you.'

'Are you sure, Mistress Trueblood?' the girl asked tearfully. 'I thought her kinder to Master Talbot than to me.'

'He's old and his mind has wandered. She sought to lessen his rage not provoke it further.' Clara strained the liquid into a second bowl and poured in the vial of valerian. 'He'll give us no more trouble today, as this tea will send him to sleep, but you must take care to avoid him tomorrow.' She beckoned Isabella forward. 'You also,' she said, handing her the dish. 'He's not so confused that he won't remember the prettiness of both your faces.'

Isabella knew Clara was right when she saw how the old man leered at her as she entered the hall. His daughter stood beside him and he seemed less confused than in the kitchen. He was telling Lady Anne he'd been a man of importance in Pedle Hinton.

Milady smiled as she took the bowl from Isabella. 'We must find you some quarters suitable to your status, sir. It's not fitting for an elder to sleep in this hall with children and servants.'

'I had a fine house in Pedle Hinton.'

'And you shall have the same in Develish. Alice tells me you're a man of devotion and, from recollection, we have an empty dwelling on the path to the church. You will be neighbour to one of my leading advisers and able to make confession at times of your own choosing.' She turned to Isabella. 'Will you ask your mother to help you make the hut comfortable, child? Master Talbot will sleep more soundly on a good bed of rushes. A handful from each of the rolls in my chamber should suffice.'

⁂

Martha Startout tut-tutted loudly as she and Isabella swept dusty remains from the empty shelter and laid new straw on the floor. 'The women will resent having their mattresses depleted for the sake of a vicious old man.'

'They'll complain more if he pulls up their daughters' skirts in the middle of the night,' said Isabella.

Martha straightened the rushes and stood back. 'Thaddeus was wrong to bring him here. Not one of the Pedle Hinton women can control him—certainly not Alice, who flinches every time he approaches her.'

'It's not her fault, Mama. She has told me some of her story and it makes me glad I wasn't born in Pedle Hinton. It sounds a cruel place.'

'How so?'

'Girls and women were treated as slaves. All Alice has ever been shown is that men are above her.'

'Develish was no different before Milady came.'

'That doesn't make it right, Mama.'

'I don't say it does, but pity won't help them. The best lesson Lady Anne taught me was to learn to speak up for myself. She was a year older than you when she married Sir Richard, but she refused to back down before any man.' A smile lit her eyes. 'She took your father to task in a way I would never have dared, never mind he was more than twice her age.'

Isabella eyed her curiously. 'What had he done?'

'Demanded food after eighteen hours' toil in the fields.'

'And that was wrong?'

Martha laughed. 'Milady thought so. She pointed to the cauldron of meat she'd prepared and instructed him to serve himself, saying that only the most selfish and uncaring of men would expect the mother of newborn twins to act as his slave.' She shook her head, remembering. 'It was but a month since the boys had been delivered, and your sister Abigail was yet to reach her second birthday. I had scarce enough milk to feed one baby, let alone two, and without Lady Anne's help, I could not have managed. She came each day to care for the babies while I worked in the kitchen, and even persuaded other women still in milk to act as wet nurses at the end of their long days.' She touched her finger to Isabella's chin. 'Best of all, by staying late that eve, she showed me your father wasn't the monster I thought he was.'

Isabella struggled to believe Martha had ever seen Gyles in such a light. 'How?'

'He begged her to tell him what else he could do to ensure his wife and his children's welfare and, such was her understanding of his position, she insisted on speaking to him outside so that all in the village would hear.' She saw her daughter's puzzlement. 'He was a man,' she explained. 'His duties were to honour his oath to his lord, plant and grow crops, and govern his household according to custom and law. To tend one twin while the other fed at my breast or prepare a meal to give me time to sleep were tasks reserved to women. Milady attracted much criticism for forcing a proud man to demean himself, but she freed Gyles of blame.'

'Did Father feel demeaned?'

Martha shook her head. 'It made good sense to him that a husband should tend his wife and children as carefully as he tended his master's stock. Your brothers were the first set of twins ever to live beyond six months in Develish and Gyles has sung Milady's praises ever since.' She gestured towards the door. 'We should go. There'll be no advantage to anyone if Master Talbot falls asleep in the house.'

Isabella followed. 'Develish is lucky Milady passed her wisdom to Father,' she remarked thoughtfully. 'If she'd chastised a man like Master Talbot, he'd have turned the demesne against her.'

'He still might,' said Martha sourly. 'There'll be no keeping him in that hut unless she orders John Trueblood to padlock the door.'

ℰℐ

Father Anselm made no attempt to hide his suspicion as Lady Anne closed the church door and joined him at the altar where he was lighting candles for Vespers. There was too much distrust between them for her to have an amiable reason to seek him out. He gave a token nod of his head. 'Milady.'

'Father,' she answered courteously.

He waited for her to state her business but, as ever, she teased him with silence. 'Is there some service I can perform for you?' he asked.

'I've come in that hope, sir.' She watched him offer a spill to a wick but his hand trembled so much that the two never met. She took the spill from him and held the flame to the wick herself. 'Clara tells me you're out of mead. Is she right?'

He made no answer.

'We have a goodly store of wine at the house which has remained untouched since Sir Richard's death. I'll have some sent to you. My husband's tremors were never so bad as when he was forced to abstain from drinking because the carter was late in bringing fresh supplies.' She lit the remaining candles and then blew out the taper.

The priest put need before pride. 'Milady is kind.'

She pulled a wry smile. 'Don't be too keen to thank me, Father. You have yet to hear my request.'

He cursed himself for not guessing she would set a trap. 'Does the wine depend on my agreement, milady?'

She shook her head. 'I give you that with the same willingness I have given you tinctures in the past to cure the aches in your bones. I have no wish to see you suffer. The disputes between us have been over matters of conscience, never medicine.'

Father Anselm doubted heresy could be dismissed so easily, but he was willing to accept that wine was a medicine. 'I have always recognised that your skill in healing is superior to mine. I told Sir Richard of it many times.'

Lady Anne answered with a laugh. 'For which I had little reason to thank you. My husband found a new ailment each day to bring to my attention. Had he been less ready to accept a vial of tinted water as a cure, I might have encouraged him to bedevil with you with even more requests for confession and absolution.'

The priest bridled. 'And I would have offered both gladly as my duty demanded,' he snapped. 'You will not deny, I hope, that in matters concerning the rites and rituals of the Church I have superiority.'

'I will not, sir. You stand alone in your knowledge of procedure.'

Strangely, her words seemed to trouble him. He turned to the altar and fluttered a finger to his forehead to make the sign of the cross. 'So Thurkell would have us believe. I pray hourly that he is mistaken.'

It was a moment before Lady Anne understood his meaning, and she reached out an instinctive hand in sympathy. 'Forgive me,' she said. 'I should have asked myself long since how Thaddeus's talk of priests and monks dying might affect you. You're so much a part of Develish's community that I forget you belong to the wider one of the Church. It must have distressed you greatly to hear of the deaths of your brothers.'

He seemed glad to take her hand. 'I am more afraid than distressed, milady.'

She studied him with surprise, as much for the tight, needy grasp of his fingers as for the dread in his voice. 'What is it you fear?' she asked.

'That I shall be the only priest to survive. I haven't the ability to carry so much responsibility alone.'

Lady Anne wondered that so bleak a vision of the future had never occurred to her. She had little trouble imagining the sense of isolation and loneliness he must be feeling, because she felt it herself. She sought for an answer that would comfort. 'God never tests us so hard that we fail, Father. Perhaps His purpose for you—and for everyone who survives the pestilence—is to be a witness for those who have died. Their names will be written out of history if we allow ourselves to forget.'

Her words seemed to alarm him more. 'I've witnessed nothing,' he cried, snatching his hand away to tremble through another sign of the cross. 'You've kept all suffering from Develish's door . . . even your husband's.'

'But isn't that something to celebrate?' she asked in perplexity. 'I could wish all demesnes had done the same. The lives of so many have been lost unnecessarily for want of a little thought.'

The priest rounded on her angrily. 'It's not for you to decide which death is necessary and which is not. You raise yourself above God when you make such statements.'

Lady Anne gave a weary shake of her head. 'That was not my intention,' she answered quietly. 'If I have offended you, I am sorry.'

'Your offence is against God.'

'Then I beg His pardon even more humbly than I beg yours. He watches over us with more kindness than we deserve. Are you able to bear witness to that at least?'

The old man's mouth worked in furious denial. 'I am not. God has been absent from this place since you came here. Master de Courtesmain saw it and so do I.' Spittle formed along his lips. 'You have encouraged your people to break every commandment, and so infected are they by your profanity that none sees the need for confession or absolution. Would you have me speak of that? Or *worse*—' his spittle sprayed the air—'describe how your lover, a slave, parades as a noble, steals at will, and even brings demons into our midst in the shape of cats?'

Lady Anne turned away, unwilling to be drawn into any more argument. 'You must state the truth as you understand it, Father,' she said. 'That's all any of us can do. I'll have the wine sent to you shortly but be wise in how much you consume each night. The supply is limited.'

He watched her small figure disappear into the shadows beyond the candlelight. 'You had a request of me.'

There was a pause in her steps. 'It's of no matter. You gave me your answer when you spoke of your knowledge of rite and ritual.'

He heard the sound of the latch being raised and Lady Anne's voice speaking softly to people outside. She must have given them leave to enter, for her words were followed by the whisper of feet across the rush-strewn floor. He recognised the faces of the Pedle Hinton serfs, whom he'd watched cross the moat, and frowned from one to the other in puzzlement. 'What brings you here?' he asked.

'Vespers, Father,' said Alice Bartram. 'It's six months and more since we've attended a service.'

'Or seen a priest,' said another woman, dropping to her knees and reaching for Father Anselm's hands. 'We beg you most earnestly to hear our confessions.'

Harold Talbot stepped from their midst and searched Father Anselm's face. 'I don't know this man,' he said, turning to his daughter. 'Where is Father Jean?'

'He died of the pestilence and is buried in Pedle Hinton,' said Alice. 'We are in Develish now and this is their priest.' She made a gesture of pleading to Father Anselm. 'He will take solace from your chanting of the psalms, sir. Please begin—and pay no mind if he interrupts. He is excitable from having spent the day in sleep. He means no offence by it.'

Offence. The word rang like a condemnation in Father Anselm's ears, and he wondered if he'd been wrong to distrust Lady Anne's motives. 'Why did you wait outside?' he asked.

'Milady advised us that your custom is to use Vespers for private communion between yourself and God, sir. She wanted to be sure you were happy to include us. My father knows all the psalms, having learnt them word by word from Father Jean. He will assist in their recitation if you allow it.'

Father Anselm retreated to the altar to support himself. In drink he had some memory of the Vespers' chants, but sober he had none. He ran a trembling hand over the surface of the table as if a miracle might suddenly produce his Bible and catechism, for he had no recollection of where they were or when he had last used them. He felt the brush of a cloak against his arm.

'You will do Master Talbot a great kindness if you allow him to lead the service, Father,' said Lady Anne. 'He asks for understanding of mistakes, being less proficient in the language of the Church than you.' Under cover of her cloak, she took her own Bible from the pocket of her kirtle and slipped it onto the altar. 'He wishes to begin with Psalm One Hundred and Nine.' She opened the book at a marked page and read aloud in Latin: *'My God, whom I praise, do not remain silent, for people who are wicked and deceitful have opened their mouths against me.'*

From behind them, the old man took up the verse in the same language. *'They have spoken against me with lying tongues and surround me with hatred. They attack me without cause and repay my friendship with loathing. I am a man of prayer, my God. Appoint someone evil to oppose my enemy. Let an accuser stand at his right hand. When he is tried, let him be found guilty. Let his days be few. Let his wife become a widow, and his children wandering beggars, driven from their ruined homes.'*

When Father Anselm failed to respond, Lady Anne placed a finger beside the text to show him where they were. *'May no one extend kindness to my enemy or take pity on his fatherless children,'* he read in tremulous tones. *'May his descendants be cut off, their names blotted out from the next generation. May the sins of his mother never be forgiven. May knowledge of his family be erased from the earth . . .'*

He faltered to a halt and, in the silence that followed, Harold drew breath to start again. With a sigh, Father Anselm turned towards him. 'Do you have any understanding of what you are saying, my son? Did your priest in Pedle Hinton ever give you these words in English?'

'He did.'

'Do you take comfort from them?'

Harold studied Father Anselm with suspicion. 'All men of prayer do. We imperil our souls when we forget that God should be feared. His wrath is terrible against the unrighteous.'

This time Father Anselm's hesitation went on so long that Lady Anne found herself regretting his sobriety. If she'd had the foresight to send a flagon of wine an hour before Vespers, he would be looking on Harold as a man of virtue and reciting Psalm 109 without a qualm. As it was, he seemed lost in indecision. She lifted the Bible from the altar and stepped forward to read for him, but he stayed her with a surprisingly firm hand.

'There's no fear of God in Develish and no place for this psalm in our church,' he told Harold. 'The Lord blesses us with love and kindness and we do our best to repay Him by sharing what we have with each other. Milady urges her people to entreat that all men are spared, be they God-fearing or not, for we have no wish that anyone should suffer death and misery. Were you so surrounded by enemies in Pedle Hinton that you like to be reminded of their suffering through these bitter words of hatred?'

'It's God's choice if I am. The words are His.'

Father Anselm shook his head. 'They are a man's, spoken in malice against those who disagree with him. Do you repeat them because your own heart is full of malice?'

Anger flared in Harold's eyes. 'The Bible is the word of God. What manner of priest are you that you don't know that?'

'A poor one, my son, for I am ignorant of how God answered this man's demands for retribution. Was it Father Jean's belief that rage and resentment are rewarded? For myself, I know only that God sent His son to take our sins upon His shoulders and teach us to forgive one another—and that simple message of love couldn't be more distant from the brutal vengeance requested in this psalm.'

Harold seemed so baffled by the question that Alice answered for him. 'The bishop sent word that the pestilence was a punishment for ungodliness, sir, and My Lord of Pedle Hinton ordered Father Jean to read the psalm each Vespers as warning that everything predicted in it would come to pass if we forgot our prayers and strayed from the path of righteousness. We thought him correct until we came to Develish.' She glanced shyly at Lady Anne. 'Now we're unsure what to believe except that the people here are blessed in their mistress.'

Perhaps Father Anselm was as confused as Harold, for he sank to his knees before the altar and buried his head in his hands.

EASTER, 1349

Eleven

Blandeforde, Dorseteshire

THADDEUS SAT ASTRIDE KILLER ON the ridge of a small hill and gazed down on Blandeforde. Gyles had described this place as a busy market town which drew its importance from standing at a bridge across the River Stour, but while the settlement was larger than many Thaddeus and his companions had seen, there was no greater evidence of people. They could see handfuls lingering at corners or moving about the streets, but not enough to indicate a once-thriving community. As ever, Thaddeus was struck by their lethargy. Even those who appeared to be walking with purpose lacked urgency, as if they had long since accepted that the struggle for life was more trouble than it was worth.

Ian adjusted his reins as his horse sidled sideways out of boredom at being forced to stand still for so long. 'Do you suppose they know tomorrow's a feast day?' he asked. 'Perhaps all their priests have perished and they think we're still in Lent?'

Thaddeus shook his head. 'There's not a man or woman in England who doesn't know that Easter falls on the Sunday after the first full moon of spring. The skies have been clear this last week. They'll have seen it shining in the heavens just as we did.'

The swelling moon had been their signal to ride north, for Thaddeus had hoped their arrival would spark less interest amidst the joy and celebration of Christ's resurrection. Easter was a day for parades and hearty eating after six long weeks of fasting, and he had expected to find Blandeforde readying itself for the festivities. In Develish, the Saturday eve was taken up with the slaughter of lambs for roasting and the final stitching of new apparel for the parade. But there was no such industry here.

'They'll be like the survivors in Melcombe,' said Peter. 'We didn't find one who thought there was cause to rejoice.'

'Nor anywhere else,' added Joshua. 'They're all just waiting for death.'

Thaddeus couldn't disagree with either statement. They had travelled the coastline for a month, seeking knowledge, but they could have ended their journey in Melcombe had they realised the people's sense of despair there was shared by everyone else. By night they had camped outside the port; by day they had ridden the streets to gain what information they could. It was hard to come by. The pestilence had so overwhelmed the town that no one could say how many had died. Even when they were directed to a town elder, a man of authority, he proved as ignorant as the beggars who inhabited the gutters. So many had fled when the pestilence first struck, there was no knowing who had perished and who had survived.

From Melcombe they had headed west along the coast to Lyme Regis, riding through deserted or barely inhabited demesnes along the way. Thaddeus spoke to all he met, offering what help and advice he could, but he had no answers to the three questions he was most commonly asked. Does God punish us by keeping us alive? Will our liege lord ever return? Does the King know of our troubles? All he could say with certainty was that, whether through flight or death, Dorseteshire was almost empty of people.

The truth of this statement was driven home to them when they returned along the highway to Dorchester—once the most prosperous market town in south Dorseteshire. They found it all but deserted, with shops and taverns closed, doors daubed with crosses and only the odd movement at windows to suggest that anyone still lived there. Thaddeus would have turned north towards Blandeforde then had the sea held less fascination for him. He told his companions he wanted to discover if there was another port to the east, but he showed no hurry to find it, choosing bridleways that hugged the crooked coastline as often as he returned to the straighter highway that ran inland.

The youths had no complaints. A man could believe he was free indeed when he stood on a rocky height and stared across an ocean. Some days the water was a turgid grey, but on clear afternoons, when a spring sun shone in the heavens, it mirrored the blueness above and there was no saying where the water ended and the sky began. Their favourite camping spots were on pebble beaches where small rivers had cut through the cliffs to empty into the sea. Driftwood made easy fires and the rhythmic sound of the waves lapping along the shore brought a deep and restful sleep.

They grew accustomed to the mournful cries of seagulls but never to the numbers and size of the birds. As big as buzzards, they ruled the sea and the shore, watching the travellers from pale eyes. Thaddeus thought they must live on fish, but Joshua said he'd seen a dozen pecking flesh off a dead sheep outside Melcombe.

Only Peter had any liking for them, mimicking their calls with the same ease he mimicked blackbirds and larks.

They took most pleasure from discovering a stretch of golden sand which ended in a mighty bay, dotted with tree-covered islands. Because the entrance was narrow—a quarter-mile cleft between two arms of land—the waters of the bay were as calm as an inland lake and the youths shook their heads in wonder at the beauty of the scene. How dreary Develish seemed by comparison. Half-a-dozen sailing ships rode at anchor down the centre, but all seemed as carelessly forgotten as the fishing boats that lay tilted on their sides along the banks. Edmund's long sight picked out a settlement far away on the other side, but Thaddeus guessed the only way to reach it was by the highway. There were too many marshy inlets where brooks and rivers were feeding into the bay for horses to find an easy path around the shoreline.

He gladly gave in to his companions' pleas to spend the night on the beach, being as entranced as they by the softness of the sand and the white-frothed spume that rolled across it. They returned the way they'd come, looking for a sheltered spot amongst the trees that grew along the promontory. Thaddeus chose to remove his boots and lead Killer through the shallow waves. He was fascinated by the pull of sand beneath his feet each time the water receded and only became aware that a fishing boat was drifting towards the shore behind him when Ian called a warning.

He turned to watch a greybeard and a youngster using their oars to try to push the vessel back into deeper water. He called out to them, asking where they were headed, and the greybeard pointed back to the mouth of the bay, saying the current had carried them past it. The craft was too heavy for a tired old man and his grandson to handle alone when all their effort had gone into hauling in nets full of fish. Without thought for whether either had fleas, and pausing only to remove his coat and jerkin, Thaddeus released Killer and waded towards them, putting his shoulder to the planking at the bow. As the boat began to turn, he moved to the stern to push it into deeper water and then called for a rope.

'The water's shallow enough for me to tow you to the end of the headland, but from there you must manage on your own.'

The greybeard had no doubts that his finely apparelled rescuer was a man of status and he expressed his gratitude humbly, promising My Lord a parcel of mackerel as reward for his help. Thaddeus said he would be as happy with information, and the talkative old man gave him all he required. Thaddeus learnt that the settlement on the far side of the bay was called Poole, with another to the west named Warham, which stood between the mouths of the River Pedle and the River Frome. More than half the inhabitants of both towns had died or fled, and fishing had become harder with only the weakest left to handle the boats and nets.

'The boy and I have done well this day, but our catch would have become food for gulls if the tide had stranded us on the beach. God was kind to send us a man so tall to push us clear. Do you not fear drowning, sire?'

Thaddeus laughed as the waves lapped around his chest. 'Not yet, my friend. Tell me about these fish you've caught. Do they taste the same as river fish?'

'Better. The salt water gives them flavour.'

'And they're called mackerel?'

'They are.'

'And the birds are gulls? I've not encountered them before either.'

The greybeard found that hard to believe. 'You have the look of a foreigner, sire. How did you come here if not by sea?'

Thaddeus made a mental note to watch his words more carefully when he spoke with Blandeforde's steward. 'I came as an infant and have no memory of the journey,' he lied. 'Since then I've lived in the north.' He ran some of the rope through his fingers to allow the craft to move farther from the shore as the end of the headland approached. 'Do many foreigners come to this bay?'

'They used to, but we've seen none since September. Word has it that all Europe has perished.'

'Not all. There'll be some like you who've survived. They'll take to their ships again once the pestilence passes.'

He was answered with a hollow laugh. 'There's few here believe it will, sire. If we don't die today, we'll die tomorrow. What makes you think differently?'

'Common sense. When did the last person succumb to it in Poole?'

'I've not heard of any deaths since Christmas.'

'Then, God willing, the towns along the coast have seen the end of it already, for we've been told the same story in Melcombe and Lyme Regis.' Thaddeus halted. 'You must make ready to take the rope and begin rowing, my friend. I cannot take you beyond this point.'

'A moment longer, My Lord. The boy wraps fish in sacking and will throw them when you've tossed the rope.' The old man's eyes regarded Thaddeus thoughtfully. 'You seem more trusting than most that you'll survive, sire. What practices do you follow to avoid it?'

Thaddeus recalled Ian's injunctions to avoid talk of rats and fleas. It was one thing to give people hope that the pestilence had run its course but quite another to invite derision. 'I come from a country where cleanliness is valued,' he said instead. 'We bury our waste and do not tolerate vermin or parasites in our houses or on our persons. Such customs keep us healthy.'

'Would that be one of the Moorish lands of Africa, sire? We've had ships from there in the past and all the sailors have your height and dark skin. They have more kindness and courtesy than most and are a goodly sight cleaner. Many's the time I've watched them cover their mouths and noses to protect themselves from English stink.'

Africa . . . 'Do you know the names of these lands?'

'Only Egypt.'

'Because her people visit here or because your priest has taught you about Moses?'

'Both. Their ships sail from a town called Alexandria. It's said to be very fine.'

Thaddeus nodded to the youngster, who was showing him that the parcel of fish was ready. He coiled the end of the rope and threw it towards the greybeard before catching the sacking bundle in return. 'Stay well,' he said, raising his hand in farewell.

The old man chuckled. 'If you were from a land in Africa, you would do this,' he said, leaning his head forward and touching the fingers of his right hand to his forehead.

Thaddeus mimicked the gesture. 'I thank you for the fish.'

The old man took up his oar. 'And you for your help, sire. Thanks be to God, we'll all eat well tonight.'

Thaddeus retreated to the shore and watched them angle into the bay before returning along the sand to where Ian was holding Killer. His teeth chattered uncontrollably as he stripped off his dripping clothes and pulled spare ones from his saddle pack, but his eyes were alight with good humour as he did it.

'What did the fishermen say to make you so cheerful?' asked Ian.

'He told me something I didn't know.' Thaddeus re-dressed himself and knelt to undo the sacking. 'These are called mackerel,' he said, revealing twelve silvery-blue fish. 'They'll make a welcome change from mutton.'

There was never any shortage of sheep. Everywhere they went, flocks were multiplying as ewes gave birth to spring lambs and pastures recovered from the frosts of winter. But these days only Joshua's dogs showed excitement to see yet another carcass being butchered. Despite the height and bulk that plentiful meat had added to the previously slender frames of Thaddeus's companions, they grumbled endlessly about the boredom of their diet. Even so, faced with only two mackerel apiece after a long day's riding, the ram Joshua had been carrying across his horse's withers was turned into stew anyway.

They made a fire in the sand, using driftwood and fallen branches from the woodland, and watched the sun turn brilliant red as it dipped towards the horizon and sent a blazing trail across the sea. The mackerel was roasted on a woven lattice of pliable green saplings and the scent from the bubbling skin was irresistible, as was the tender oily flesh when they came to pick it from the bones. Ian licked his fingers after swallowing the last morsel.

'What else did the greybeard tell you?' he asked Thaddeus. 'I don't say the taste of mackerel isn't enough to make any man smile but just learning its name wouldn't.'

Thaddeus pondered for a moment, wondering how much to reveal about himself and the questions that had plagued him most of his life. 'He told me something about the man who sired me. I've never been able to picture him before.'

'How do you see him now?' asked Peter.

'As a clean, courteous, dark-skinned Moor from a land in Africa . . . perhaps even a town called Alexandria in Egypt.' A small laugh escaped his mouth. 'I have no idea what or where Africa is, but a father from there sounds sweeter to my ears than "passing gypsy".'

'He'll be a man of importance, whoever he is,' said Joshua. 'You're too clever to have a dunce for a sire.'

Peter nodded. 'My guess would be a wealthy merchant who journeyed to England to sell silks and tapestries.'

'Or a lord,' countered Edmund. 'Why settle for less if you can have more?'

Thaddeus shook his head. 'It's a private comfort only and not something any of us should dwell upon,' he warned. 'If I'm to pass for Athelstan, my title must have come from my father and my Moorish blood from my mother. Take care to remember that in Blandeforde and never mention Eva. We'll none of us fare well if my imposture is discovered.'

✺

Ian recalled those words as they looked down on the town. The prospect of entering it had been such a distant idea when they set out, and so easily put from mind during their travels along the coastline, that he'd given no heed to whether or not he was ready. Thaddeus might feel confident about being questioned by the steward, but the same wasn't true of his companions. To pass as a fighting man before a fisherman was very different from upholding the pretence before My Lord of Blandeforde's proctor. Nor, in truth, did any of them understand why it was necessary. What did Thaddeus hope to learn from the steward that he couldn't as easily discover from the townsfolk?

Olyver, picking up on his twin's thoughts, shifted in his saddle. 'Why is it so important to go there?' he asked Thaddeus. 'Can't you tell just by looking that we'll hear nothing new?'

'I doubt we'll be allowed in,' said Edmund, pointing to the far end of the bridge. 'I see a group of men in livery who look like guards. I'd guess they're there to turn back all who come from this direction.'

Thaddeus nodded. He, too, had seen the men. 'We might be able to use them to our advantage,' he said thoughtfully.

'How?'

'By persuading them to fetch the steward to us. He'll be less alarming out here than inside Blandeforde.'

'What is it you want from him anyway?' asked Peter. 'And don't say "news", because that's the excuse you give for everyone you speak to.'

Thaddeus thought it only fair to answer honestly, since his companions would take the consequences alongside him if he failed. 'I want his agreement to Athelstan's purchase of Pedle Hinton for two hundred nobles. Unless the steward's a fool, he'll jump at the chance to replenish his master's coffers in return for a derelict demesne and a half-ruined house.'

'Are you serious?'

'Very serious.'

'How will it help Develish to buy another demesne? You've always said our future will be in a town where we can earn our living as freemen.'

'But not lawfully. Wouldn't you rather gain your liberty in Develish first and then choose the future you want?' He smiled at Peter's puzzlement. 'Milady and I look to turn Develish into a demesne like Holcombe, where every man is free to earn his living as he chooses. His rent will be in coin from the trade he pursues, and a proportion will be rendered as taxes to Blandeforde.'

'What does Pedle Hinton have to do with that?' Edmund asked.

'If Athelstan is granted title to a derelict demesne, and succeeds in remitting taxes at the required time, Milady believes Blandeforde will look more favourably on his request to partner Pedle Hinton with Develish. Once both demesnes are under Athelstan's governance, all serfs will have the right to buy themselves out of bondage—as long as they have the money.'

Olyver grinned. 'Is that why we've been stealing dead men's gold these last few weeks?'

'It is.'

'Does Milady know?'

Thaddeus shook his head. 'She's too honest to do what Bourne did. Fortunately for you and your families, I am not.'

'But why not just offer for Develish?' asked Joshua.

'Because it was in Blandeforde that Bourne heard rumours of everyone still being alive there, and if he picked up on those stories, then be sure the steward has also. He'll be wary of granting anyone title to a lucrative demesne, let alone an unknown noble whose lineage shows he's related to Sir Richard's widow. I look to allay his suspicions not raise them.'

Peter groaned. 'It won't work. He'll know us for imposters.'

'Only if you show timidity. Play the part of a fighting man and you'll be taken for one. Even stewards believe what their eyes tell them.'

'Why didn't you explain all this before?' asked Ian.

Thaddeus's dark face split in smile. 'Because you'd have bedevilled me with your doubts these last few weeks.' He nodded to a large stone building which stood on pastureland inside the western loop of the river, some five hundred paces from the nearest habitation. 'Is that a house or a monastery?' he asked Edmund.

'What's the difference?'

'Does it have a belltower?'

Edmund shook his head. 'There's a church behind that does, but not the house.'

'Are you thinking it's where My Lord of Blandeforde lives?' asked Ian.

'When he's at home.' Thaddeus cast a last glance across the town. 'There's nowhere else imposing enough for a man of his wealth.' He shortened his reins and touched his heels to Killer's flanks to set him back on the highway. 'Let's see if the guards let us pass.'

They descended the slope into the valley at a walk, with Joshua and his dogs at Thaddeus's side and the others riding two by two behind. The white-and-gold crest of Athelstan, stitched by Lady Anne and her seamstresses onto the cloth beneath Killer's saddle and the breasts of the youths' crimson tabards, showed up well in the late-afternoon light, but it was greeted with blank looks from the men at the northern end of the bridge. They knew every lord's emblem for miles around but this wasn't one they recognised.

Thaddeus brought Killer to a halt when he was halfway across the cobbled bridge and leant his arms on the pommel of his saddle to study the five men who guarded the exit. He made an impressive figure with his great height, his jet-black charger and seven large hunting dogs quivering at his side. 'I come to speak with Blandeforde,' he called in French. 'Lord Bourne of Wiltshire said I'd receive a warm welcome here. Was he wrong?'

Their leader answered in the same language. 'Wiltshire's to the north. Why do you approach from the south?'

'Eight weeks have passed since I was in Bourne. In that time, I've journeyed through Dorseteshire to discover if there's any truth to the reports that all in the south have perished.'

'What have you found?'

'Nothing that I choose to share with you. Is your lord in residence?'

'He left for his estates in the west last summer. The steward governs in his place.'

'Is he as ill-mannered as the men he commands?'

'We are here to prevent strangers crossing the bridge. There's no requirement to pretend a welcome that doesn't exist.'

Thaddeus looked to his left and picked out a stretch of woodland some half-mile to the west across cleared land. 'My men and I will camp there overnight. You may tell the steward that Athelstan has news of Blandeforde's vassal demesnes. If he wishes to hear it, he must seek us out before the light fades. I take no responsibility for my dogs once darkness falls.'

He nudged Killer into a turn, instructing Ian to lead them out across the cleared land. The guard shouted that he hadn't meant to be disrespectful. The town had seen all sorts, demanding refuge and bringing the pestilence with them. Had he known he was speaking to My Lord of Athelstan, he would have sent a runner to fetch the steward. He would do so now if My Lord was willing to wait. The sun was a bare two hours from setting and it made better sense to converse at the bridge. Thaddeus ignored him.

'Why didn't you answer?' asked Joshua when they were clear of the cobbles.

'Because leaving makes the point better. Stewards wait on lords not lords on stewards.'

'He only showed interest when you said you were Athelstan.'

Thaddeus nodded. 'I noticed.'

'Do you think the steward will come to the camp?'

'Not in person, but I'll wager he'll be curious enough to send spies.'

༼༽

They came when the soft grey of twilight had drained colour from the grass and trees, and the flames of the fire shone bright in the gathering gloom. The dogs heard them long before Thaddeus and his companions did, leaping to their feet with throaty growls and pointing their muzzles along the line of trees that bordered the cleared land between the camp and the highway. With an encouraging smile, and certain that his voice would carry in the stillness of the night, Thaddeus ordered his men to arm themselves.

'But keep the pack close until we know who these visitors are, Buckler. The steward won't thank us if his envoys are mauled in mistake for bandits.'

For himself, he remained where he was, seated on a bed of bracken with his back supported by his saddle and his legs stretched out in front of him. On his lap was a slim wooden box crafted by John Trueblood, which, when closed, contained vellum and writing implements, and when open served as a desk. As he'd been doing for the last hour, he continued to write on the page in front of him, dipping his quill into the inkwell at his side and forming his letters by the light of the fire.

'Three men have walked from the woodland, sire,' called Ian. 'They're still some fifty paces away but they're not wearing livery. What is your command?'

'Hold your bows level until they prove themselves. No one of good intent creeps through trees when he can more easily approach across pastureland.'

'They hold their hands high to show they're unarmed, sire.'

'Ask their names and what service they perform for My Lord of Blandeforde. I'll not accept beard-trimmers, cooks or pot-emptiers.'

'We are Joseph Spend of the guild of wheelwrights, Paul Cooper of the guild of barrel makers and Andrew Tench of the guild of wool merchants,' cried one. 'We come at the request of My Lord of Blandeforde's steward.'

Thaddeus lodged his quill in the inkwell and raised his head to look at them. 'Take ten paces away from the trees and thirty towards me,' he instructed. 'My soldiers will range themselves in front of you while my dogs search the woodland for others who may be hiding.' He gave a nod to Joshua. 'Wait until they reach their places and then send the hounds about their business.'

The men, trembling visibly, advanced a bare three steps before a shadowy figure stepped from between the trees some twenty paces away. He made a small bow. 'I am Jacques d'Amiens, steward to My Lord of Blandeforde, sire,' he said in French. 'There are no others. These three men and I came alone.'

Thaddeus studied him with interest. He was somewhat as Lady Anne had described him, of middle height and middle build, but there was no sign of the birthmark—a port-wine stain on his nose and right cheek—that Lady Anne had said was his most distinguishing feature. Whoever this man was, he was not who he was claiming to be.

Nevertheless, Thaddeus gave a small nod of acknowledgement before telling Joshua that his instructions for the dogs remained unchanged. 'You must forgive my suspicious nature, Master d'Amiens,' he answered in the same language, 'but it's an unusual Norman who chooses unarmed Englishmen to protect him when he could as easily have brought the guards from the bridge. You still have time to order them from the trees. My men and I wish them no harm but I can't say the same for my mastiffs.'

Whatever command the man gave was too low for Thaddeus to hear, but four armed soldiers appeared from the trees behind him. 'We live in difficult times, My Lord. All men are wise to be wary of strangers.'

'Indeed.' Thaddeus turned to watch the guildsmen's hesitant approach. 'These poor fellows look ready to die of fright,' he murmured. 'Are they here of their own free will or under threat?'

'Your dogs unsettle them, My Lord.'

Thaddeus ordered Joshua to take the pack twenty paces onto the pastureland before beckoning the guildsmen closer. 'We'll do well to keep the fire between us,' he told them. 'You don't look as if you're carrying the pestilence but I'm reluctant to risk my life on it.'

'Does God not protect you, My Lord?'

'Without doubt, but I do my best to assist Him.' He pointed to a pile of saddle packs. 'Bring forward three of those if you care to sit. Do you find French easy to understand or would you prefer that we speak in English?'

It seemed they needed the imposter's permission both to seat themselves and express a preference for English, and Thaddeus wondered who the man was and what his purpose was in bringing them. The guildsmen's anxiety remained strong even with the dogs at a distance, and he sensed they'd been given a task they didn't want to perform. The imposter elected to stand apart with his guards, watching without comment as Ian positioned himself and his remaining men behind Thaddeus. None held weapons in their hands but Ian took quiet satisfaction from the unease in the faces of the two younger soldiers.

The only change Thaddeus made to his position was to sit a little straighter by easing his saddle more firmly into the small of his back. He asked the guildsmen to repeat their names and tell him about their families, showing sympathy when they listed their numbers of dead.

'Our guilds are as badly affected, My Lord,' said Joseph Spend. 'I am one of but two wheelwrights who remain, and Master Cooper and Master Tench are the only barrel maker and wool merchant left in Blandeforde.'

'How many departed before the pestilence arrived?'

'We don't know, sire. The town was so filled with people heading north there's no saying how many of our own went with them. Will they have found safety? Is the north more favoured by God than the south?'

'I've seen nothing on my travels to tell me so. Wiltshire's as badly affected as Dorseteshire, and as long ago as last September, we heard that the sickness had reached Oxford. I fear all England will have fallen to it before the year is out.'

'Is there good news, My Lord?'

'Some first glimmerings, perhaps.' Thaddeus selected a parchment from a small stack at his side and held it up for them to see. 'These are the towns and villages along the coast of Dorseteshire where my men and I found people still living. In each place, we were told that no one has died since Christmas. Does Blandeforde fare the same or worse?'

There was a short silence before the barrel maker spoke. 'The last burial was eight weeks ago, sire. Should we take that as a sign of hope?'

Thaddeus wondered why the man found it so hard to meet his eye. 'I can think of no reason not to, Master Cooper. A full season without death in those communities first afflicted suggests to me that the pestilence may have run its course. It's surely something to celebrate that the same seems to be happening here.'

The imposter stirred. 'You speak as if the pestilence is no different from the pox or the ague, My Lord. Is that your belief?'

Thaddeus watched Andrew Tench, the wool merchant, give the faintest shake of his head. He took it for a warning, though why a Blandeforde freeman should side with a stranger against the man who had brought him here, he didn't know.

'There's no likeness at all between the pestilence and the pox, Master d'Amiens,' he answered. 'The one gives rise to virulent boils which kill in three days, and the other to a red rash that fades after two weeks. Have you not seen sufferers yourself?'

'My apologies, sire. I should have made my meaning clearer. We live in ignorance here in Blandeforde and any information you can give us about the pestilence would be welcome. To describe it as an infection that must inevitably run its course is to suggest it's a disease like the common pox. I'd be interested to hear what led you to that belief.'

If Thaddeus believed anything, it was that knowledge shared was knowledge gained, but he hardly needed the clear alarm in Tench's face to avoid an honest answer. 'You're asking if I know God's mind, sir, but I'm as ignorant of His plan for us as you are. I take comfort from the knowledge that no one has died in Melcombe in the last four months, but I can't give a reason for it. Only priests know why some are more deserving of life than others.'

'Did you consult with the clergy in Melcombe?'

'There were none to be found. An elder told us the last to die was a Franciscan monk who tended sufferers into autumn and then fell to the sickness himself. The same was true everywhere we went.'

'Here too. All the clergy in the town have been taken, and there are many who question why—these three guildsmen amongst them. They came in the hope you'd have answers, My Lord.'

Thaddeus ran a thoughtful hand around his beard. 'Can your own priest not help them? I presume he still lives since you spoke only of those in the town dying.'

'His duties to the household keep him occupied.'

Thaddeus smiled slightly. 'Then you and My Lord of Blandeforde's servants are more fortunate than your fellows in the town.' He shifted his attention to Tench. 'Does the household fare better than you and your neighbours?' he asked.

'We believe so, sire, but it's a long time since we saw any of the servants. We've heard of only four dying since the pestilence came.'

Thaddeus allowed his surprise to show. 'Out of how many?'

'Above one hundred, sire. Father Aristide hears the confessions of all and recites the liturgy of the hours from Matins to Compline so that the house is sanctified by prayer and absolution. The town accepts that this is why so few have succumbed.'

But not you and your friends, thought Thaddeus, while pondering Tench's use of the word 'accept'. Had he chosen it deliberately? 'Truths have to be explained before people can believe them. Why do you not seek answers from whomever told you of Father Aristide's cleansing rituals?'

'It was a young maid, sire. She was sent from the house to seek solace from her mother and father, and was in great despair to find they had perished. She had the early signs of the pestilence and died some five days later. Her anguish at being judged more wicked than the rest of the household was matched by her despair to find that every member of her family was dead.'

Thaddeus leant forward to stare into the fire as an excuse to lower his gaze. The man posing as d'Amiens was ignorant of the expressions on the guildsmen's faces because their backs were towards him, but for Thaddeus to respond to their intense stares with even a nod to show he fully understood what he was hearing would be to reveal the same to the imposter. There were too many conflicting tensions at play, and Thaddeus had little grasp of any of them. Had d'Amiens died and this man seized control? Did the guards on the bridge serve some purpose other than to keep the pestilence out?

The only thing he was sure of was that the imposter was inviting him to challenge the Church's position on the pestilence. But why? What possible reason could he have to suspect a lord he had never met of dissent? And why accuse Athelstan of a heresy he clearly shared? There was surely only one interpretation of the maid's tale: that My Lord of Blandeforde's household had isolated itself from the rest of the town, expelling any who showed signs of fever, while claiming to be protected by prayers and absolution.

Thaddeus took a slender branch from a stack at his side and fed the tip into the fire. 'Word has come from France that Pope Clement grants absolution to all who die of the pestilence,' he told the guildsmen. 'Had the young servant known that, her anguish for herself and her family would have been lessened.' He raised his head. 'Does the closure of the bridge prevent such news reaching you?' he asked Spend.

Spend shook his head. 'There have been no messengers in months, My Lord. The guards make no difference.'

'How long have they been there?'

'A matter of days only, sire. The steward looks to deter thieves from entering the town while the Easter festivities take place. Pickings will be easy while all attention is on the parade.'

A faint smile curved Thaddeus's mouth. 'You have reason to thank him. Only the pestilence is less welcome than a thief.'

Twelve

IAN HAD BLESSED THADDEUS EACH time he'd answered a question wisely but now, hearing the edge to his friend's voice, he became nervous that Thaddeus's patience was wearing thin. In his mind, he begged him not to abandon restraint. There was too much strangeness in the air and Ian, with no reason to doubt that the steward was who he said he was, had even less understanding of why that should be than Thaddeus.

Perhaps Thaddeus picked up on Ian's silent urgings because he took up his quill and wrote the signature of Athelstan at the bottom of the parchment page before raising his head to look at the imposter. 'I've documented what my men and I discovered in the demesnes we believe to be Blandeforde's, Master d'Amiens. Some are abandoned and derelict. Some retain small groups of serfs and servants whom God has chosen to spare. They are without guidance because their lords, priests and stewards have died or fled.' He retrieved the branch from the fire and used its smouldering tip to melt sealing wax on to the page beneath his signature before pressing his ring into the soft surface. 'If

Blandeforde returns, I suggest you prepare him for the news that there'll be no tax receipts this year. If he does not, you must account to the King yourself.'

The man seemed amused. 'You expect me to take your word on this, My Lord? You and I are strangers to each other. What assurances can you give me that what you say is true?'

Thaddeus rolled the parchment between his hands and then secured the edge with a second seal. 'None. The choice of whether to believe me is yours. I tasked myself only with passing on what I've learnt. Tomorrow we ride for Sarum so that I can render the same service to His Grace the Lord Bishop. He may not be aware how many of his clergy have died or that tithes will go unpaid.'

There was a brief hesitation. 'Is His Grace expecting you?'

Thaddeus shook his head. 'No more than you were.'

'Why should he grant you an audience?'

'For the same reason you've chosen to speak to me, Master d'Amiens. I'm the messenger who gives information to those who want to hear it.'

'On whose authority do you act?'

Thaddeus smiled. 'God's . . . as do we all.' He tossed the scroll across the fire to Andrew Tench and settled back against the saddle. 'Be good enough to hand the parchment to the steward as you leave, Master Tench,' he murmured, closing his eyes. 'I believe our business is concluded.'

The guildsmen rose to their feet immediately but the imposter clenched his hands in irritation. 'I have more questions, sire.'

'I'm sure you do, Master d'Amiens,' came the lazy response. 'Every person we meet has questions. Put them to your priest. I don't doubt he'll be able to answer them better than I can.' He made a gesture of dismissal. 'Take the path across the cleared land. My soldiers can shield you from the pack in the open, but not if you're hidden by trees.'

Ian, recognising that these words were as much for him as d'Amiens, called to Buckler that the visitors were leaving under escort. 'My Lord asks that you hold the hounds steady until we've passed. Once we're clear, send them to search the woodland.' He stepped around the fire and motioned to the steward and his guards to join the guildsmen. 'My men and I will accompany you the first two hundred paces, sir. I suggest you make speed in order to reach the bridge before the light goes.'

Edmund, Peter and Olyver moved to join him and together they shepherded the eight men away from the fire. Thaddeus remained where he was, pretending sleep, but from beneath his apparently closed lids he was watching for movement in the darkened woodland. It may have been imagination but he fancied he saw a shift in the shadows amongst the trees. But were they retreating or coming forward?

Unhurriedly, he rose to his feet, stretching to his full height before stooping to take a torch from beside the pile of parchments. He heard Joshua approach with the dogs as he held the resin-soaked hemp to the flames of the fire. 'We'll be following the pack, Buckler. The steward brought more men than he admitted to. I want to know why.'

Joshua searched his face for guidance. 'I can't believe the steward would lie, My Lord.'

'He's done nothing else since he arrived.' Thaddeus raised the torch in his left hand and drew his sword from his sheath with his right. 'Come,' he said, crossing the space to the trees. 'Let's see what the dogs unearth.'

Joshua couldn't tell what Thaddeus's expectations were, but if he hoped to flush men from the woodland with words, he was disappointed. Nothing stirred. Joshua watched him advance through the trees, swinging the torch slowly from side to side until the beam settled on a well-trodden path, running east to west. He nodded understanding when Thaddeus levelled the tip of his sword towards it. On quiet feet, he led the pack across leaf mulch to the impacted track and knelt to point the muzzle of his best wolfhound in the direction of the highway.

The animal set off at a rapid pace with the others falling in behind, and Joshua muttered that they were probably following a deer's scent. But Thaddeus shook his head. In the flames of the torch, he could see where boots had trampled over clusters of the bluebells which grew in profusion beside the track, flattening leaves and breaking stems. Beckoning to Joshua to keep up, he strode fast behind the dogs, holding the torch high to light the gloom.

They were almost at the highway when a discordance of barks and throaty growls split the air. Joshua made a vain attempt to catch at the skirts of Thaddeus's coat in the hope of encouraging caution, but the black-haired giant was beyond his reach. Without even the briefest break of stride, Thaddeus stepped boldly onto the road, showing neither care nor fear of what might be waiting for him.

❧

At two hundred paces, Ian ordered his companions to halt and allow the eight Blandeforde men to continue alone. 'My respects, sirs,' he said in French. 'We wish your town a joyful Easter and pray that you will have good fortune in the coming months.'

The imposter gave a dry laugh. 'Your lord has taught you well. *Too* well. I've yet to meet a Norman soldier who speaks so eloquently. Is your twin as fluent?'

Ian held his gaze for a moment before turning to the guildsmen and speaking in English. 'May God go with you, sirs. We will wait here until you're safely across the river.'

Peter, Edmund and Olyver formed a line beside him and stood in silence as the column moved away. By then the light was so dim that it wasn't long before all eight were swallowed by darkness. 'Maybe we should have accompanied them to the bridge,' Edmund muttered in an undertone. 'There's nothing to stop them doubling back along the highway.'

'They'll do that anyway if they have a mind to it,' said Peter reasonably. 'Watching them cross won't prevent it. They'll wait an hour or two on the other side and then creep over again.'

Olyver stood with his arms folded, trying to pick out the fleece collar on Andrew Tench's cloak, but even that was invisible. 'What did the steward say that troubled you?' he asked Ian. 'I felt your worry.'

'He spoke of my twin.'

'So?'

'How did he know I had one? It was dusk when he arrived and you and I look less alike now than we've ever done. He might have taken us for brothers, but never twins.'

Pensively, Olyver scratched at the stubble around his jaw. From a young age he and his brother had sought to look different. Since riding with Thaddeus, however, they had turned their quest for difference into a sport to amuse their companions. The longer Ian's hair grew in the manner of Thaddeus's, the shorter Olyver cut his to resemble the shaven look of their father. The more Olyver nurtured and darkened his beard and moustache with charcoal, the sharper Ian kept his knife in order to scrape his face clean. Close to in daylight, a stranger might see the identical shape and colour of their eyes. But at night? And at ten paces distant?

'It must have been a guess,' he said slowly. 'Who could have told him? The only people who know about us are in Develish.'

'You're forgetting Bourne,' murmured Peter. 'There wasn't a person in the demesne who didn't know you were twins. The girls kept asking you to stand together because they'd never seen grown ones before.' He paused. 'It can't be far from here. I remember the elder in Melcombe telling Thaddeus that Blandeforde was only half a day's ride from the Wiltshire border.'

Ian would have answered that it was My Lord who'd been most intrigued by their twinship, but he was distracted by the distant barking of dogs. The sound seemed to be coming from the highway and he turned to look in that direction. As he listened, the barking turned to whimpering and, with a sense of terrible foreboding, he drew his sword and began to run.

ॐ

Joshua remained hidden inside the tree line, frozen by fear and indecision when he saw that there were other lights than Thaddeus's. Even as he watched, more sprang to life and his dogs whimpered and cringed as burning flames were thrust into their faces. It seemed to Joshua that soldiers were everywhere. Some six stood abreast across the highway to bar escape to the south and a dozen more lined the verges on either side. All had their swords drawn with the tips pointing at Thaddeus, who had walked so carelessly into their trap.

If the big man was aware of the danger he was in, he didn't show it. Sheathing his own sword, he knelt to quench his torch in the dust of the road and then drew the dogs to him with a click of his fingers. As he ran his hands around their muzzles to calm them, he was looking at a cloaked figure in the centre of the highway some fifteen paces distant. Joshua followed his gaze and felt a thrill of horror as the man lowered his hood to reveal a disfiguring stain across his nose and right cheek. So pale was the rest of his skin that the splash of livid colour appeared black, and Joshua's immediate thought was that he must have the pestilence.

Thaddeus gave a nod of acknowledgement. 'My respects, Master d'Amiens,' he said in French.

'Sir.'

With a smile, Thaddeus rose to his feet and gestured to the soldiers. 'Whom do I have to thank for this honour guard?'

'Yourself. I thought you'd have more sense than to pursue me.'

'You pay me too much credit, Master d'Amiens. I'm not so sharp-sighted that I knew it was you I was following. I took you for a thief.' He tapped a finger against his cheek. 'I only know you now because of your birthmark.'

'Who told you of it?'

'My Lord of Bourne. He passed through Blandeforde some months ago.'

D'Amiens gave an indifferent shrug. 'We've had a hundred lords use our town as a staging post these last two seasons. What marks Bourne out that I should recall him?'

'Nothing at all,' said Thaddeus with amusement. 'Dressed in tunic and britches, he could easily pass for a serf. Few have the good and bad fortune to be as recognisable as you, Master d'Amiens.'

The man's lips thinned in a sardonic smile. 'Or *you*, Master Thurkell. We are both known by the unusual colour of our skins.'

Terrified, Joshua shrank deeper into shadow. He had feared this moment from the day Thaddeus had ridden into Woodoak and allowed a handful of serfs to believe he was a lord. Thaddeus broke every law by doing so—not least the laws of treason against the King—and Joshua cursed him for ever believing that Lady Anne's invented lineage and My Lord of Bourne's letter of accreditation could provide protection. He watched in anguish as the steward instructed Thurkell to step away from the dogs and surrender his weapon.

Thaddeus answered with a laugh. 'How long have you believed yourself the equal of lords, Master d'Amiens?'

'You're no lord, sir. You're a slave posing as one.'

'Then show me the warrant that accuses me of such. I would know who signed it and what his status is. You can't be so ignorant of the law that you'd arrest Athelstan on your own recognisance.' He shook his head scornfully when d'Amiens made no answer. 'You're a fool, sir. Acting for your absent lord doesn't give you licence to behave without due process.' He glanced towards the soldiers. 'Which of you is captain of arms?'

'I am, sire,' said one, stepping forward.

'Then escort me back to my camp before Master d'Amiens' hubris leads you and your men to further sedition. Your duty to your lord is to uphold the King's justice not traduce it on the twisted fancies of an ambitious steward.'

Without pausing to see if the captain would obey, he approached the two soldiers who were guarding the entrance to the track and instructed them to lower their swords and move aside. They did so, but whether out of fear of a man whose height was so much greater than theirs or because the captain gave a curt nod, Joshua couldn't tell. He watched in relief as the dogs responded to the clicking of Thaddeus's fingers, but he was at a loss as to whether to show himself when the captain followed behind with a torch. Was it better or worse that these people believed Thaddeus was alone?

His indecision meant he heard d'Amiens' muttered instruction to the two soldiers nearest to him.

'Find the priest's guest and bring him to me. He's a wretched creature but I don't doubt he's telling the truth.'

ᘒᘔ

Ian, who had crossed the cleared land at an angle to reach the highway where the woodland began, saw a glow of light through the tree trunks. He came to an abrupt halt, dropping to one knee and placing his hand over his mouth to mute his laboured breathing. Close behind, Edmund did the same.

They could tell from the way the flames moved from side to side that they were looking at torches but neither could judge how distant they were. Ian counted eight, Edmund ten, and both knew there must be a throng of men on the road. To draw closer in order to see if Thaddeus and Joshua were amongst them, Ian pointed towards the tree line and then flattened and lowered his hand to urge Edmund to keep low, but he'd barely given the signal when they heard the sound of running feet on the road. Together, they dropped to the ground, faces pressed to the grass, and through half-closed lids watched two liveried soldiers, the foremost bearing a torch, hasten past them towards the bridge. Ian turned his head to the left to watch their progress, Edmund looked to his right, where he thought he'd glimpsed the intermittent flicker of a light inside the woodland.

It took only a second or two of searching to find it again. It was a single flame, and he couldn't see who carried it, but he was ready to wager that soldiers were involved. He pulled himself forward on his elbows and pressed his mouth to Ian's ear. 'Someone's heading towards our camp,' he said. 'Perhaps several. If they're armed, we should go back to help Peter and Olyver defend it.'

'Where are they?'

'Behind you to your right.' Edmund drew away and pushed himself into a crouch, raising his arm to show the direction. 'There,' he whispered. 'Do you see the flame?'

Ian nodded. 'They're too far ahead. We'll not reach the camp before them.'

'Then let's cut through the trees and follow. They'll not be expecting an attack from behind.'

A stream of quiet curses issued from Ian's mouth as he rose to his feet. 'I *knew* it was a bad idea to come here,' he muttered.

℘

Joshua was thinking the same as he slipped through the trees behind Thaddeus and the men who accompanied him. The captain had instructed another three to fall in behind as he followed Thaddeus onto the path, and not one had sheathed his sword. Joshua kept close enough for the torchlight to show him the silhouettes of trunks but not so close that the dogs would detect his presence. While they remained at Thaddeus's heels, the soldiers hung back, but Joshua trembled at what might happen if the pack deserted him. He appeared quite blind to the danger he was in, engaging in light-hearted chitchat with seemingly little concern for his safety.

With no wind inside the woodland to carry Thaddeus's words away, Joshua heard them easily. He asked the soldiers their names, where they came from and how long they'd been in My Lord of Blandeforde's service but, receiving no answers, he glanced over his shoulder to address the captain directly, allowing a note of sympathy to enter his voice.

'You must worry for your family in France, captain. I've met many mercenaries who long for news that never comes. All fear they'll die in England without ever knowing the fate of those they love. Is it a wife or a mother who holds a place in your heart?'

Perhaps it was surprise that this man understood another's anguish that prompted the captain to reply. 'A mother and two sisters, sire. I haven't seen or heard from them in over a year.'

'I feel for you, my friend, but it's truly said that while there's life there's hope. Keep faith that God blesses your women as surely as He blesses you.'

'I try, sire—we all do—but it's not easy.'

'At least you're fortunate in your priest. His understanding of God seems greater than his brothers' in the town, since he is alive and they are dead.'

'The town priests gave their time to tending the sick, sire. Father Aristide gives his to prayer and absolution. By such means he keeps the household alive.'

'He deserves much praise for it. It's an onerous task to hear a hundred confessions each day while finding time to recite the liturgy of the hours.'

'I doubt any man could do so much, sire. We are summoned to the great hall each morning so that Father Aristide can absolve us with a blessing. His Holiness the Pope sent word last autumn that sins can be pardoned without the need for confession.'

Thaddeus slowed. 'Were the town priests dead when this news came? I wonder they took such care of the sick if they knew that general absolution was all that was needed to keep the pestilence at bay.'

'There's more sin in the town than in My Lord's household, sire. Thieving and fornication are rife, and merchants worship money more than they do God. A priest can only protect the pure of heart.'

Joshua prayed most earnestly that Thaddeus would let these statements pass. To challenge the Church's teachings in front of men carrying swords would be madness.

'Indeed. Some transgressions demand a more profound penance than can be gained from a blessing. Was the little maid who was forced from the house a thief and a fornicator? Her depravity must have been great to merit such a punishment.'

There was a long pause before the captain answered. 'The punishment was God's, sire.'

'How so?'

'He afflicted her with the pestilence.'

'What age was she?'

'A child still. Perhaps ten or eleven.'

'Were you acquainted with her?'

'She came with the women who brought food each night to our barracks. We called her Little Sparrow because she was timid and shy, but we were greatly deceived by her. Satan uses many guises to lure men from the path of righteousness.'

Thaddeus came to an abrupt halt and turned to look at the captain. 'Then she was wicked indeed,' he said with such sarcasm that Joshua couldn't believe all four of the fighting men didn't hear it. 'What vile sins did she persuade you to commit? Was her timidity enough to lure you into bedding her?'

The three soldiers drew level with their captain and one raised his sword. The tip was only a wrist's length from Thaddeus's throat. 'If you're the slave the steward says you are, I'll have your hide for that. There's not a man here would have tarnished the maid. You malign *her* when you malign us.'

Thaddeus's reach was so long and his reactions so fast that he'd seized the blade in a gauntleted fist and snapped it across his knee even before the other was aware it was gone. 'Your anger's misplaced,' he said, tossing the pieces into the undergrowth at the side of the track. 'Blame your captain for saying she was touched by Satan before you blame me for asking how Satan manifested Himself.'

'He repeats only what the priest said when he ordered her expulsion.'

'Who was tasked with it?'

'We were.'

'Did she resist?'

The man shook his head. 'She accepted that she was damned.'

A look of contempt crossed Thaddeus's face. 'Then take responsibility for the guilt you feel,' he said coldly, 'and be grateful to the thieves and fornicators in the town who took her in and cared for her. She died in wretchedness because she believed herself too wicked to live, but at least she knew kindness at the end.' He turned to the captain. 'Keep your men under better control. I'll do more than break the weapon of the next to threaten me.'

'Philippe was provoked by what you said, sire. He had a great fondness for Little Sparrow, who reminded him of his sister.' The captain gestured to the other two soldiers to sheathe their swords. 'Why do you say in one moment that we are fortunate in our priest and then judge us harshly for obeying his orders?'

'I make no judgement on your obedience. You and the rest of the household stay alive by following his instructions, do you not? It's your willingness to accept his reasons that angers me.'

'I don't understand, sire.'

With a shrug, Thaddeus began walking again. 'It's an offence against God to call an innocent ten-year-old a creature of Satan.'

ഓ

Ian put an arm around Joshua's chest and clamped a hand across his mouth to keep him from shouting out. Their paths had converged some fifty paces from the camp, and Joshua, intent on listening to Thaddeus's dangerously honest answers to the soldiers, had neither seen nor heard Ian and Edmund's approach. He ceased struggling when he heard Ian's voice in his ear. 'Is Thaddeus their prisoner?'

'Not yet,' he whispered when Ian removed his hand. 'He's looking to win them to his side.'

'How?'

'In the worst way possible. He's telling them their priest's a liar and a fraud.'

ഓ

Olyver and Peter fed arrows onto their strings, raised their bows and sighted along the shafts. They stood before the fire, their left shoulders towards the woodland, their right hands holding steady against their cheeks. The only movement either of them made was a fractional adjustment of their bows to the left when the sound of voices amongst the trees seemed to shift direction.

Thaddeus was the first to emerge and he nodded approval when he saw their readiness. Briefly, his gaze roamed around the rest of the campsite, looking for Ian, Edmund and Joshua, but he made no comment when he didn't find them. He moved to stand beside Olyver, clicking his fingers to persuade the dogs to follow him, and raised a hand in acknowledgement to the captain and three soldiers who remained within the trees.

'I thank you for your safe escort, captain, and wish you and your men well.'

'The steward will expect us to stay with you, sire. Will you ask your soldiers to lower their weapons?'

Thaddeus shook his head. 'The steward is your master not mine, my friend. He has no authority here. You may go of your own free will or I will ask my men to accompany you.'

'We are four and they are two, sire. The odds are not in your favour.'

Ian's voice spoke from behind them. 'You're in error, sir. The odds have always been in My Lord's favour. Had he given the signal we would have felled you in the woods.'

 exo

Thaddeus listened to Joshua and Ian's stories as he knelt to replace the parchments and writing implements in his travel desk, but he didn't need Ian's account of the imposter's mention of twins or Joshua's repeating of d'Amiens' reference to the priest's guest to tell him it was time to leave. He'd guessed from the moment the guards on the bridge responded to the name of Athelstan that he was testing his luck, but he'd known it for certain when the guildsmen signalled their unease.

He refused to waste time, debating over who had betrayed them, and shook his head when Peter asked if he should stamp out the fire. 'We'll build it up. The steward will see its glow from the highway and the longer it burns the better start we'll get.'

'But in which direction?' asked Olyver. 'We'll not find a path to the south through these woods in the dark—and even if we do, there's no knowing where we'll come out. What if the steward's set a second block on the road a mile farther down? We'll ride straight into it.'

Thaddeus nodded. With the bridge to the north and the highway to the east and south, their only way out was to the west. But at night in the forest they were as likely to veer south as maintain the direction they wanted. He pictured the loop of river that he'd studied earlier that day, recalling how it had run west from the bridge for some five hundred paces before curving towards the north.

'We'll hug this tree line to the river,' he said, 'and then make our way along the bank. Providing we follow the water course, we'll come to another highway eventually. This bridge can't be the only crossing.'

'It could be miles away,' said Edmund.

'It could,' Thaddeus agreed, 'and we'll be doing it on foot. We need to move quietly. Lead your horses on rope halters and store your reins and stirrups in your saddle packs. The night's so still, the rattle of harness will give us away.'

'Who's to hear us?' asked Joshua.

'Anyone with the wit to work out which way we've headed.' Thaddeus rose to his feet with a sigh. 'I've led you into a trap and for that I am deeply sorry. If we're fortunate, the flames of the fire will persuade the steward we're still here; otherwise, he'll send men who know the forest paths to cut us off somewhere along the riverbank.' He glanced from one anxious face to the other. 'Should that happen, I want your promise that you'll leave me to deal with the threat alone.'

'None of us can promise that,' said Ian.

'You can and you will, for we carry the fate of Develish in our hands as well our own.' He held out his palm. 'Give me your pledges. Free of restraint, you have a better chance of helping me than if I'm forced to watch as each of you is broken on the wheel.'

Easter Day, 1349

Harold Talbot lost his temper again today. This time his wrath was directed at our parade from the church as Father Anselm led us through the vegetable garden and orchard before shepherding us into the great hall for our Easter banquet. Before the pestilence, women and maids would spend weeks stitching new apparel for themselves and their families in honour of Christ's rising, but with fabric in short supply they chose instead to bedeck old clothes with brightly coloured woollen sashes and tassels. The children hopped and skipped to set their ribbons fluttering and the sight was pleasing to all except Harold.

I've never known a man so keen to embrace misery. If he'd had his way, every person in Develish would have worn hair shirts and beaten themselves with flagellants' whips as penance for Christ's crucifixion instead of walking together in celebration of His resurrection. Alice tells me his temper has grown worse since age scrambled his wits, but in truth I suspect he's always been angry. On the rare occasions when his mind is untroubled, he shows himself to be a person of intelligence, and I can't help feeling his frustrations would have been lessened if he'd received an education.

As ever, it was Eva Thurkell who soothed him. There's no accounting for why he responds so readily to her voice and touch, but she wins our admiration each time she succeeds in quieting him. Alice says Eva's fair prettiness reminds him of his youngest daughter, but I wonder if it wasn't Eva's staying of Will's hand when he sought to punish Harold for raising little May's skirt that won the old man's heart. Whatever the reason, it pleases me that Eva has gained in confidence from being able to do something that no one else can.

I thought my eyes deceived me yesterday when I watched her inscribe her name on a slate with Isabella's help. She took so much satisfaction from the task that her face was wreathed in smiles, and for once they didn't disappear when she became aware of my presence. She tells me she is determined to master the names of all her family before Thaddeus returns, and I wonder whether her previous resistance to acquiring new skills was driven by fear of mockery if she failed.

She asked if I thought Thaddeus and his companions were safe, and I said I was sure they were. But it wasn't an honest answer. This last week my nights have been troubled by dreams of Jacques d'Amiens. It may only be because Thaddeus said he would enter Blandeforde during the Easter celebrations, but my sense of foreboding is very great.

Thirteen

Develish, Dorseteshire

GYLES HAD REASON TO BLESS the Easter festivities as he released the raft from its moorings and let it drift on long ropes towards the centre of the moat. By Lady Anne's command, the day of revelry, sport and feasting had ended with watered wine being shared by all as the sun began to set; and now, at close to midnight, every person in Develish was deeply asleep, except for the men who stood on the guard steps.

The bank was narrow beneath the defensive wall that surrounded the manor house enclosure but, even in the miserly light of a shrouded moon, Gyles was sure-footed enough to keep his balance. The raft moved with the current from Devil's Brook and needed little effort to assist it on its way. He heard Adam Catchpole's whispered acknowledgement as he passed beneath the western guard step and then, five hundred paces later, felt the touch of his brother Alleyn's hand on his shoulder to tell him he'd reached the southern step behind the church.

Neither he nor Alleyn spoke, for fear of alerting Father Anselm to their presence. This part of the moat was the least visible to anyone inside the enclosure, but they had no wish to make the irascible priest a witness to what they were doing. Gyles dug his heels into the moist grass of the bank and pulled on the ropes to draw the raft in, allowing the hemp to drop in coils at his feet. He heard the soft thud as John Trueblood eased himself over the wall and dropped to the ground beside him and then the rub of cloak against homespun kirtle as Alleyn swung Lady Anne across the parapet and lowered her into John's waiting arms.

Without a word, Gyles took the heavy leather bag that his brother handed down to him. He placed it on the raft and assisted John and Milady aboard before running the ropes through his hands to allow the vessel to drift towards the far bank. He watched a shadowy figure step from behind a clump of alders to catch the coils which John threw from the front and then raised his hand in acknowledgement when Edmund turned to signal that the raft was firmly moored to one of the alder's trunks. He forgave John's intemperate clasping of his son to his chest as soon as he stepped ashore—he would have done the same had one of his twins returned—but he prayed most earnestly that Edmund was free of the pestilence.

The boy had shown himself to James Buckler some hour after the sun had passed its zenith. James, standing guard on the southern step, had been staring towards the woodland that bordered the cleared land to the south when the edge of his vision caught movement amongst the dried brown stems of vetch on a peasant strip some fifty paces from the moat. He thought it was a fox until he shifted his gaze towards the rustling plants and saw that it was a man. He lay flat on the ground, his britches and tunic so close in colour to the dead vetch that it would have been hard to make him out were his head not raised and his face visible. When he was sure he had James's attention, the man placed a finger to his lips to urge silence and then rose to his knees. It was arguable which surprised James more—that the 'man' was fifteen-year-old Edmund Trueblood or that he had made his way across a quarter-mile of open land without being seen.

James needed no prompting to hoist himself across the wall and slither down to the bank below. The mere fact that Edmund was alone suggested he had bad news to impart, and the fewer who heard it the better. He beckoned the boy to approach the far bank and urged him to keep his voice low. The Easter feast had yet to end but there would be some, already replete, who preferred to walk outside than stay in the great hall. Edmund, seemingly more aware than James of how his unexpected arrival might impact on Develish, positioned himself beside a small copse of alders, scanning above the wall for listeners and ready to duck out of sight should he see one. He spoke in short, clear sentences to be sure he was understood.

Thaddeus had been taken prisoner outside Blandeforde the previous night by the steward, Master d'Amiens. His companions had escaped by following the River Stour, and were safe. They had camped overnight at a distance from Blandeforde, and Edmund had ridden south at dawn to consult with Lady Anne. She was the only person clever enough to advise them on how best to help Thaddeus. Should Edmund fail to return by noon tomorrow, his friends would act as they saw fit. Would Lady Anne come to the moat so that Edmund could speak with her? It would be wiser if she came after dark so that they could talk freely. He would wait amongst the alders for her answer.

Despite the grimness of the message, James's first emotion was admiration for Edmund's courage and good sense. The lad must have ridden hard to reach Develish so soon, yet rather than cause alarm, he'd taken the time to leave the highway and circle around the valley from the north in order to approach the only guard step that wasn't in constant view of the house. Such a feat was beyond most men. He raised a hand in agreement, motioning Edmund to take some rest inside the copse, then pulled himself back over the wall and went in search of Gyles. Together they sought out Lady Anne.

They found her in the steward's office, taking time for herself while the great hall was cleared of the feast before being made ready for skittles and horseshoe throwing. She was writing in her journal and looked up with a smile when Gyles and James entered, but the smile died when she heard what they had to say. Nevertheless, they were surprised at how calmly she took the news, showing more concern for Edmund than for Thaddeus. Was the boy frightened? she asked James. Did he look in need of food? Should she come now to speak with him?

James shook his head to all the questions, describing Edmund's demeanour as composed and strong. 'He's a credit to Thaddeus's teaching, milady. He'll wait as long as he must to hear your advice—though I'm sure he'll be glad of something to eat if we can find a way to send it across.'

Lady Anne glanced again at what she'd been writing. 'Did he say why the imposture failed?'

'No, milady. Only what I've already told you. Shall I tell him you'll speak to him?'

She hesitated for several long seconds. 'I've long feared this moment would come, and I've made a hundred plans for how to respond when it did. Yet even at my most hopeful, I didn't expect to hear within hours that Thaddeus was arrested. At best,

I thought a month would pass before we learnt of it. At worst a year.' She turned to Gyles. 'Is it possible to float the raft to the southern step once darkness has fallen?'

'I see no reason why not, milady. What do you have in mind?'

⚬⚬⚬

The ghostly shapes on the other side of the moat were quickly swallowed by darkness as they moved out onto the peasant strips, and with a sigh Gyles bound the ropes about his waist and hunkered down for a long vigil. Every so often, he heard the shuffle of boots on stone above him as his brother shifted position, but otherwise the only sound to accompany his thoughts was the soft ripple of water through the grass at the edge of the bank.

Who was to say that Lady Anne's decision was wrong? Certainly not he. He couldn't remember a time when he'd had reason to think her ideas misguided or foolish. His fellows on her council had urged him strongly to use his influence to make her think again, for they all knew she was acting with her heart and not her head, but Gyles had refused. He couldn't agree that Thaddeus's life was worth sacrificing for the good of all; and nor, he believed, would his sons or their friends. Nonetheless, he had raised no objections to one or all of the other fathers arguing their case.

He heard John's quiet call from the far bank sooner than he expected. 'Make ready, Gyles. I've freed the moorings on this side.'

Gyles rose to his feet and pulled on the sodden ropes to draw the raft back. 'I'm sorry, my friend,' he said with sincerity, as he reached out a hand to help the other ashore.

John gave a dispirited shrug. 'You were right and I was wrong. Neither listened to reason.'

'Did Milady honour her promise to order the boys home?'

'She did, and more forcefully than I thought she would. Edmund seemed taken aback that she would even issue such a command. He told her he'd come for advice, not to be ordered to forsake his leader.'

'How did Milady reply?'

'She asked him to hear my arguments before he heard hers, but Edmund said he and his friends would rather suffer the same fate as Thaddeus than play the part of traitors.'

'It's a fine impulse, John.'

'Maybe so, but you know as well as I that Lady Anne is allowing her feelings for Thaddeus to cloud her judgement.'

Gyles handed him one of the ropes. 'I'll need your help to tow the raft back to its mooring position beneath the northern step. We'll be going against the current.'

John stared at him in frustration. 'Why does her foolishness not concern you? There'll be no future for Develish without her.'

Gyles lifted the sodden hemp to his shoulder and prepared to take up the slack. 'She'll be lost to us anyway if Thaddeus denounces her. Which he will. No man's strong enough to stay silent while his legs and arms are broken on the wheel. Pray God Milady reaches Blandeforde before that happens. All Develish will be condemned otherwise.'

ɝꙮ

Edmund led Lady Anne through the peasant strips to where he'd left the horses in a grassy clearing amongst the trees that bordered Devil's Brook. To assist her across the rough ground, he held his right forearm rigid so that she could rest her palm on it while in his left hand he carried the heavy leather bag. He spoke only to warn her of ruts and tangled vetch, being too shy to voice his opinions on anything else, and she blessed his silence because it allowed her to fix her mind on staying upright in the darkness. It wasn't part of her plan to make the poor boy regret her company even before they'd started.

He launched into words when the hobbled horses snickered at their approach, apologising for only being able to give her Killer to ride. 'The twins thought you might permit their father to help us, milady. If we'd thought you'd make the journey, I'd have brought one of the ponies.'

She smiled. 'I'm grateful you had the foresight to bring any mount at all, Edmund. I don't say you won't have to lead me— and that I shan't complain royally of soreness before we ever reach Blandeforde—but I'm sure Killer will make the journey less wearisome than if I had to do it on foot.'

'I can lift you into the saddle so that you can sit sideways, milady. If you hold hard to the pommel, you'll find Killer's gait smooth enough at a walk.'

She shook her head. 'We need to travel faster than that, Edmund, at least when daylight comes. I shall ride astride.'

'Do you know how, milady?'

'My father taught me when I was very young.'

She asked him to place the leather bag on the ground and knelt to undo the straps. 'I've brought food for you. James Buckler tells me you must have been on the road since dawn.' She handed him a package of bread and cold meat left over from the Easter banquet. 'It was thoughtful of you to make your way around the valley to approach from the south, Edmund. A lesser man would have caused panic by riding at full tilt down the road from the village.'

Had it not been so dark, she would have seen that her compliment caused a flush of pleasure to colour his cheeks. 'It wouldn't have helped Thaddeus to spread panic, milady,' he said gruffly, tearing at the meat with his teeth. 'He told us to keep cool heads before he ordered us to abandon him.'

'When did that happen?'

'Around midnight, milady.' He described the events leading up to Thaddeus's capture and the pledge they'd given him to avoid being taken themselves. 'He handed me Killer's reins when Joshua's dogs became restless. Shortly afterwards we saw torches moving along the riverbank towards us. Thaddeus sent us into the forest, and he went on alone to meet the guards.'

Lady Anne laid some folded garments on the ground beside her. 'Did you see him being taken?'

Edmund nodded. 'They surrounded him the same way they did on the highway. He gave them his sword, and the captain asked where his men were. He said we were with the horses at the camp, looking to keep the steward's attention while he escaped along the river.'

She drew a sash from the bag. 'And they believed him?'

'They must have done. No one came looking for us in the wood, though they'll know he lied if they raided the camp later.'

'What happened next?'

'The guards took Thaddeus back the way they'd come and we continued to follow the river. We came to a ford after about five hours. We waited there for dawn to break, and I left as soon as it was light enough to see the road.'

Lady Anne replaced all the garments in the bag except for the sash and one folded item of clothing. 'Did you know where you were?'

'Only when I saw the first milestone, milady. It told me I was on the highway from Shafbury to Dorchester—the same one

Develish is on. I couldn't believe my luck. Do you think it means God doesn't want Thaddeus to die?'

She stood with a smile. 'I'm sure it does. Will you be so kind as to turn your back so that I can pull on these britches and tie the hem of my kirtle about my waist? We'll make better progress if I'm not hampered by skirts.'

ଔଓ

Confident that the night was dark enough for them not to be seen from the house, Edmund led Lady Anne through Devil's Brook and across the pastureland to the highway north. He chose to go on foot, leading both horses, and she seemed happy to accept that their pace must be careful and slow while the moon was obscured. He was glad to see that she sat straight in her saddle once he'd adjusted the stirrups, but his doubts about taking her with him were very great.

His companions expected to see Gyles Startout, and he knew they'd react as he'd done to having Milady wished upon them instead. Edmund had hidden his own disappointment well to her face, but it swelled and grew in his heart as he walked ahead of her. What good was a woman when they needed an experienced fighting man? How much time would they waste attending to her needs? How uncomfortable would she make them feel when she discovered how rough and hard it was to live in the open air and learnt that men behaved coarsely when they were alone?

From disappointment, he moved to anger, for he felt he'd been given no choice but to assume responsibility for her after she'd announced her intention of accompanying him. He should have been able to appeal to his father, but John had been too intent on persuading him to obey her first command to bring his companions home. He'd lectured his son about common sense and obligation to Develish, and the right moment never came for Edmund to say that he and his friends wanted Gyles and not Lady Anne.

Perhaps Lady Anne guessed at his conflict, for she spoke once they'd breasted the hill out of Develish valley. 'Did Thaddeus suggest how you might rescue him, Edmund?'

'No, milady, but we made some plans of our own while we waited for daylight.'

'Bold ones, I'm sure.'

'Bold enough, milady.'

A smile entered her voice. 'Your fathers feared as much. They know how courageous you are. Thaddeus also. Tell me how he persuaded you to give him your pledge when your more natural instinct was to remain at his side.'

'He said we'd have a better chance of helping him if we were free, milady, though, in truth, I think he was more worried about what the steward might do to us.'

'With good reason,' she answered. 'There's no quicker way to force the truth from a man than to put his friends to the torture in front of him.'

'We'd not have confessed to anything easily, milady . . . and nor will Thaddeus.'

'I know that.'

He waited for her to say more and, when she didn't, he spoke more curtly than he should. 'What plans do *you* have to rescue him, milady?'

'Only one, Edmund. To enter Blandeforde this day and demand that he's tried for the crimes he's said to have committed.'

൦ᕳᎧ

They made faster progress once the sun was above the horizon. Better able to see the road ahead, Edmund mounted his own horse and led Killer at a fast trot. He called to Lady Anne to relax into the saddle and allow herself to rise and fall with the charger's extended gait, but the strain in her face when they were within a half-mile of the ford told him the ride had been an uncomfortable one. He slowed to a walk.

'We're nearly there, milady. Would you like time to compose yourself?'

She summoned a smile. 'Will your friends think less of me if I arrive on foot?'

'I'm afraid they might, milady. They're hoping to see the twins' father.'

'Then I must endeavour to play the part of an experienced horsewoman. Will you be so kind as to pass me the reins, Edmund? I shall be greatly obliged if you stay at my side and keep Killer from bolting. I shall look very undignified if he throws me by the wayside.'

Edmund could only admire her fortitude when they reached the ford and his companions emerged from the woodland to greet them. He well remembered his own blisters and bruises the first time he rode any distance, and he wondered that Milady was so able to dismiss hers. She accepted his help in dismounting and took his arm gratefully as he led her towards where his fellows had made their camp; but not once did she stumble or show distress at the looks of despair on the faces that greeted her.

൦ᕳᎧ

The sun had been up a bare hour when the peace of Develish was rent by high-pitched screams. Clara Trueblood, organising work in the kitchen, clapped a hand to her chest in shock. 'Mercy me!' she cried to the other servants. 'What in heaven's name is going on?'

'It'll be Harold Talbot up to his tricks again,' said one of the women.

Clara looked for Eva Thurkell. 'Come,' she said, hurrying her through the door to the great hall. 'You're all that stands between him and instant death. I'll smother the old brute myself if we find him molesting a child.'

But whatever the trouble was, it was happening elsewhere, for they were greeted with looks of puzzlement from the serfs in the hall. Most were tying their rush mattresses into neat rolls, making them ready to stack along the walls, and all had paused to listen to the screams. Some crossed themselves for fear the Devil was nigh; others looked towards the stairs which led to the upper storey, as if to say the sound was coming from above.

This was proved true when the screams gave way to thumps that drummed on the wooden ceiling. Seizing Eva's hand, Clara shouldered her way through the crowd, instructing mothers to take their children outside and men to follow her to the stairs. She had no idea what the confusion of sounds represented, but they spoke of violence and seemed to be coming from Lady Anne's chamber. Her first instinct was that Harold Talbot had lost complete leave of his senses and was attacking Eleanor; her second that Eleanor had lost leave of hers and was venting her rage on Milady. In either case, she didn't doubt that murder was being done.

She and Eva were halfway up the stone steps when the thudding ceased and a great hush fell on the hall. They heard the sound of running feet along the walled-in corridor that linked the rooms, and even Clara's stout heart quailed at the thought of who might appear. None expected to see Isabella Startout.

She cried out in relief when she saw Clara. 'Oh, Mistress Trueblood, Lady Eleanor is much in need of help and I don't know what to do for her. I fear she's dying.'

'Is Lady Anne with her?'

Isabella shook her head. 'She must be in the church, but it'll take too long for her to come.' She descended the steps and tugged at Clara's free hand. 'Please make haste. Lady Eleanor will perish for certain if we do nothing.'

Clara paused only to send one of the men in search of Lady Anne and then, together with Eva, ran with Isabella to the chamber. They found Eleanor, pale and limp upon the ground, blood and froth oozing from the side of her mouth. There was no one else in the room.

Clara knelt to place her palm on the girl's chest. 'She's still breathing,' she said, 'and I can feel the beat of her heart. What caused this foam and blood to come from her mouth? Did you strike her, Isabella? We heard screams and then a terrible thudding on the floor.'

'It was none of my doing, Mistress Trueblood. I was in the spinning room when the cries began and I was sorely afraid the voice was Milady's. I crept to this door and pushed it wide but all I could see was Lady Eleanor flinging herself about the floor and banging her head and heels on the planks. She's so pale. What should we do for her?'

Eva Thurkell knelt on Eleanor's other side and used the hem of her kirtle to wipe the blood and foam from the girl's mouth. 'Nothing,' she said. 'She has bitten her tongue is all and the pallor comes from her swoon. It won't last long. There was a boy on my last demesne who suffered the same.'

'What made him do it?' asked Clara.

'The priest said it was heat in his brain. He was an excitable child—keen to dance and play one moment, angry the next. He fell and twitched most often when he was thwarted. He always slept afterwards. Lady Eleanor will do the same.'

'Was he able to speak when he came out of the swoon?'

Eva nodded. 'It was as if it had never happened. See? Lady Eleanor's lids are beginning to flutter. I expect she'll ask us why she's on the floor and what we're doing here.'

Clara answered as well as she could when Eleanor did precisely that. 'You swooned, milady. Isabella summoned us to help you. I've sent for your mother. She'll be with us shortly.'

Eleanor stared at her in confusion. 'Where is she?'

'In the church, milady.'

'Is she in her coffin?'

Clara's surprise was obvious. 'Of course not. Whatever made you think such a thing?'

Eleanor turned on her side, unable to fight sleep. 'Her silk gown is gone,' she slurred. 'I thought she must have died . . .'

As her voice faded to nothing, Clara turned to Isabella with an enquiring frown. 'What did she mean?'

Isabella was equally puzzled until she saw that the lid of a small chest in the corner was open. She walked across to look inside. 'It's quite empty,' she said.

Clara motioned to Eva to lift Eleanor's legs while she placed her hands beneath the girl's arms. 'What did you expect to find?'

With an anxious expression, Isabella watched them carry the inert body to the bed. 'The embroidered blue gown that Lady Anne stitched for her wedding day. It's her finest and most beautiful. Lady Eleanor has tried many times to persuade her to wear it but she always refuses. She says it would be a shame to reduce it to tatters before it's needed.'

'You're talking in riddles,' Clara declared bluntly, as she placed a feather pillow beneath Eleanor's head. 'What does a missing gown have to do with death?'

Isabella clasped her hands together. 'Everything,' she said. 'Milady told Lady Eleanor she was keeping it for her burial.'

∾

Eleanor watched Isabella through half-closed lids for several minutes. She thought it was Lady Anne perched on a stool before the tapestry frame, making tiny French knots in a pattern of fleurs-de-lis, because the maid sat in silhouette against the bright spring sun which shone through the latticed windows. Her soft brown curls were tumbled about her face as she leant over her work, just as Lady Anne did, and Eleanor felt a surge of relief that her earlier anguish had been misplaced.

Her last clear memory was of screaming in terror when she believed her mother dead, but she realised now that she must have been mistaken. There was some other reason for Lady Anne's possessions to be missing and her bed not to have been slept in. Eleanor had no recollection of how she came to be in the bed herself, or when Lady Anne had returned to the chamber, but she took comfort from her presence. Her grief at the thought of losing her had been very great.

She had so many apologies still to make to Lady Anne, but anxiety had kept her mute, for she feared seeing reproach in Lady Anne's eyes if she talked of things best forgotten. Eleanor's greatest shame was that she'd believed her father's lies about Milady. Robert said it wasn't her fault—Sir Richard had twisted her mind for his own purposes—but Eleanor guessed the boy only said this to lessen her feelings of guilt. Robert would never accept another's judgement on a person without questioning whether it was true. He proved it every day through his continued friendship with her, despite being told by others that he should open his eyes and remember that the acorn didn't fall far from the tree. Eleanor was Sir Richard's daughter and no amount of teaching could change her vicious nature.

Eleanor took comfort from Robert's scornful rejection of such ideas. Even the numbskulls who mouthed them were capable of learning from their mistakes, and the same was true of Eleanor. Look how far she'd come already through learning her letters with his and Lady Anne's help. Before Sir Richard's death, she had thought reading and writing beneath her; now she was striving hard to become as proficient as Robert. And what of the cats? Her father would have ordered them killed but Eleanor preferred to love and nurture them. Did these choices not suggest she was more like Lady Anne than Sir Richard? All Eleanor needed was the courage to embrace her mother and trust that nothing she confessed would be betrayed or greeted with disapproval.

Sleep might have taken her again had Isabella not turned to look at her. This time there was no mistaking the girl for the woman, and Eleanor's eyes widened in shock. Fearing more screams, Isabella rose from her stool and came to kneel beside her. 'Try to be calm, Lady Eleanor. You will bring on another swoon if you allow yourself to fret.' She took a cloth from a bowl of water and wrung it out to press the cool fabric against Eleanor's brow.

'Your tongue may hurt where you bit it but, when you're able to sit up, I have medicine that will soothe the pain.'

Her words made no sense to Eleanor until she tried to form a response. Her lacerated tongue rubbed against her teeth and the pain was such that her shock gave way to tears. With a sigh of concern, Isabella replaced the cloth in the bowl and reached her hands beneath Eleanor's arms to pull her upright. She plumped the pillow and urged Eleanor to shuffle backwards while she tucked the coverlet about her legs.

'The medicine is salt, Lady Eleanor. I will add it to a beaker of water and you must keep the brine in your mouth for as long as you are able before spitting it out. If you swallow it, you will be sick. Do you understand?' Receiving a nod, she took a spoonful of salt from a wooden box on the table beside the bed, stirred it into some warm water and then held the beaker to Eleanor's lips. 'The longer you hold it, the more easily you will be able to speak afterwards,' she said, placing a clay bowl in Eleanor's lap for the spit. 'When you're ready, you may ask as many questions as you like. I will answer each as best I can.'

Eleanor did as she was bid but it took three doses of brine before the stinging was numbed enough for her to speak. All the while she felt Isabella's strength and wondered how the girl had grown so much in half a year. Gone was the timid maid who been the victim of Eleanor's tantrums since she was eight years old, and in her place stood a composed and confident young woman who seemed as adept as Lady Anne at alleviating suffering. Her prettiness was startling yet, far from feeling jealousy, Eleanor knew only regret for the careless disregard she'd had for Isabella in the past.

She spat the last of the brine into the bowl. 'You shouldn't be alone with me,' she managed. 'Lady Anne made me promise to keep ten paces between us at all times.'

'And so you have, milady. I choose to be here, which is what I shall tell your mother if she asks.'

'Do you still think of her as my mother?'

'I find it hard not to, milady. She's always loved you as a daughter and treated you as such.' Isabella took the bowl from Eleanor's lap and placed it on the table. 'Would it please you better if I called her your guardian?'

Eleanor shook her head. 'I have no wish to deny her a second time.' She stared at her hands. 'I remember being frightened to discover that her gown was gone . . . also her comb and her hand mirror . . . but I don't recall anything else. Why did I bite my tongue? And who put me in this bed?'

Isabella pulled forward her stool and described the seizure Eleanor had suffered. 'Eva Thurkell says it's nothing to worry about, milady. It was just a faint. She says fear for your mother made your brain overheat.'

'You said I was throwing myself about the floor.'

'A boy on Mistress Thurkell's last demesne did the same, which is how she knows so much about it. He always recovered afterwards.'

'How often did it happen to him?'

'Hardly at all,' Isabella lied, 'and only when he became overexcited. He was very young and liked to dance and shout.'

'I remember screaming.'

Isabella nodded. 'That will have been the cause, milady.'

When Eleanor made no response, Isabella wondered if she believed this excuse or was looking to blame others for her strange condition. In truth, it was hardly a convincing explanation. Isabella couldn't count the number of times Eleanor had thrown tantrums and screaming rages in the past without ever dropping in a swoon afterwards.

Eleanor reached for Isabella's hand and raised it to her cheek. 'I was afraid,' she whispered. 'My mother gives me an hour each morning to teach me my letters, but when I awoke at dawn she wasn't here. I listened to the sounds of people rising in the house, thinking she'd been called away, but when the sun had been up for some time and she hadn't returned, I decided to read our book alone to show her how much I've improved. It's the record she makes of Develish's history. She brings it to this chamber at the end of each day and places it beside her pillow—but I couldn't see it, and nor did her pillow look as if it had been used.'

'And that frightened you, milady?'

'Not so much as finding that everything personal to her was missing. Her washing cloth, her comb, even the small jar of rouge that she kept for when my father had guests. I became truly frightened when I opened the chest that holds her wedding gown and slippers. I have such dread of her dying, for she is all I have left in the world.'

Isabella's warm heart was moved. She understood now why Eleanor had thought Lady Anne had passed to the next life. Everything she'd mentioned spoke of preparation for the coffin. A cloth to wash the body. A comb to draw the hair about the face. Rouge to give colour to dead skin. A gown to be worn for burial.

She took both of Eleanor's hands in her own to warm them. 'She's not dead, milady. She rides to Blandeforde with Edmund Trueblood in the hope of freeing Thaddeus Thurkell from imprisonment. If she fails, he will likely be hanged for imposture.'

Fourteen

Blandeforde, Dorseteshire

THADDEUS SNAPPED AWAKE WHEN THE first grey fingers of dawn
lifted the gloom inside his prison. He looked to see where the
light was entering and saw an unglazed slit in the wall to his
right. He guessed he was in a storeroom for ale because the air
smelt strongly of fermented grain and yeast, yet his brief glimpse
of the chamber in the flames from his guards' torches the night
before had shown it to be empty of barrels. The only piece of
furniture had been a narrow bench against one wall, and when the
door slammed shut, plunging him into darkness, he had stretched
himself along it, preferring the discomfort of unforgiving wood to
the risk of disturbing rats amongst the litter of straw on the floor.

He'd been confined the first night to a six-foot-square cell
in the soldiers' barracks outside. Shackled and chained to a bar
on the wall, he'd been able to squat on the floor, but not lie down,
and he viewed the bench as an improvement. He still wore the
shackles on his wrists but, since they weren't tethered to anything,
he could tolerate their discomfort more easily. No explanation had

been offered for his removal from the barracks, but he guessed his guards' increasing friendliness had had something to do with it.

The steward could have wished for a better day to incarcerate a felon than Easter Sunday, for the Church banned the meting out of punishment on the anniversary of Christ's resurrection. It was a time of giving, and in that spirit, Thaddeus's guards had taken him into the main chamber of the barracks and allowed him food and water and the use of their piss-pot. He'd had little trouble engaging with them. His ease of manner, fluency in their language and genuine gratitude for their charity won him sympathetic ears. He listened to their histories and told them some of his own—his descent from Godwin of Wessex, the marriage of his grandfather to a Moorish princess and his rearing in Spain—and, by evening, many were questioning whether the steward had been right to arrest him. Given more time, he had hoped to induce the captain to accept his parole and remove his shackles, but his abrupt transfer to the house had put an end to familiarity.

His sleep on the wooden bench had been restful. In childhood, he'd passed many a wakeful night worrying about the morrow but, as he grew, he'd come to understand the futility of so much squandered energy. The blows of Will Thurkell's cudgel across his shoulders were no less raw for imagining them in advance. The trick of closing down his thoughts had been hard to master but, once learnt, it had stood him in good stead. Even pain became bearable when the mind was able to free itself from the body.

This wasn't to say he hadn't dwelt for some time on Hugh de Courtesmain. The Frenchman had been in the great hall when Thaddeus had been brought through the imposing entranceway the previous night. The signs of Easter Sunday's festivity lingered in the air—the redolent scent of roasted lamb, the sourer smell of ale and wine—but none of the household was in evidence. Jacques d'Amiens had sat alone at the head of a long table, the livid stain across his nose and cheek enhanced by the light of torches in sconces around the walls, his fingers playing with a garland of spring flowers on the surface in front of him.

He had made Thaddeus a mocking bow and then summoned de Courtesmain from the shadows behind a pillar. The shock in the Frenchman's eyes to be forced to confront the man he'd accused was very great, and Thaddeus had felt a small pity for him. It was one thing to traduce an enemy in his absence, quite another to do it to his face. For himself, he showed only indifference when de Courtesmain confirmed him as Thurkell, but in truth his relief had been huge to discover that his betrayer was the duplicitous Frenchman and not Bourne. It would have been harder to brand a peer of the realm as a liar, particularly one for whom he had developed a liking, than a hired steward who seemed unable to remain in post.

As the light strengthened outside, Thaddeus rose from the bench and moved to the window. His view was restricted by the narrowness of the slit, but he could tell he was on the northern façade of the house because he could see the roofs of the town in the distance. He had a clear picture of the lie of the building, thanks to his study of it from the hillside two days before, and knew the entranceway opened on to a forecourt on the southern-facing side. If he wanted to escape, that would be the easiest exit to find, but the idea wasn't a serious one and he didn't linger on it. He knew from his counting of the guards in the soldiers' barracks that d'Amiens had in excess of fifty armed men guarding his lord's estate, and to attempt to evade them all would be fruitless.

The air was filled with the sound of the dawn chorus and Thaddeus's gaze was drawn to a group of sparrows pecking for seeds in the grass beyond the window. There was no telling them apart, and he wondered what it was about the human face that made each so recognisable. All had eyes, noses, mouths and hair, and the position of these features never varied, yet no one who had acquaintanceship with a person mistook him for another.

Would he be believed if he denied he'd ever met Hugh de Courtesmain?

⊘⊘

Only Edmund, who'd had time to think about it, listened with any enthusiasm to Lady Anne's plan to rescue Thaddeus. The others stared despondently at their hands and questioned how entering the lion's den could achieve anything but their own and Lady Anne's arrest. She placed too much trust in Master d'Amiens' willingness to obey the law and even more in her belief that Thaddeus would never admit that his claim to the title of Athelstan was fraudulent.

She sat cross-legged on a bracken bed, sharing the cold remains of some mutton stew with Edmund, attending patiently while the youths explained that her idea wouldn't work. Each in turn tried to persuade her that she would risk her own safety if she presented herself as Thaddeus's advocate and demanded he be tried according to law.

Ian Startout spoke for them all. 'You'll be condemned as a perjurer alongside him, milady, and he won't want that. He has too much regard for you to see you suffer the same fate as him.'

She had heard the same arguments from their fathers. 'I can only be accused of perjury if he denies being Athelstan before we arrive,' she said lightly. 'Do you have so little faith in him that you believe he might?'

'If he thinks it will help Develish, he will, milady.'

She laid aside her plate. 'Then we have nothing to worry about, for he knows it won't. Every serf on the demesne will be punished if the steward believes they knew of the deceit.'

'You more than anyone, milady.'

She shook her head. 'Master d'Amiens' authority extends only to the serfs and tenants on his lord's estates. He may convict a base-born man of criminality in Blandeforde's absence but not a person of noble birth.' She rested her soft gaze on their anxious faces. 'Thaddeus is as knowledgeable of the law as Master d'Amiens. As long as he insists on his right to be tried by his peers, the steward cannot act against him.'

'But what if it's My Lord of Bourne who accuses him, milady?'

Lady Anne leant forward to unbuckle the leather bag that Edmund had placed in front of her. 'He'll wish he'd held his tongue,' she said, showing them the letters from Dorset widows. 'I'll not spare him if he's broken the pledge he made to me in Develish.'

⚬⚬

Thaddeus's prison was the last chamber at the end of a long corridor. The five guards who escorted him from it blocked his view of the other rooms they passed, but he guessed that, like his, they were used for storage. Ahead was a kitchen. The door stood slightly ajar and Thaddeus heard the clatter of pots and crockery before he was shepherded to the right and through an archway into the great hall. The room was quite empty. If servants slept in it, they had long since risen and placed their bedding rolls out of sight.

Thaddeus wondered if he was being kept from their sight when the guards marched him to the front entranceway and took him outside. Were this Develish, the hall and forecourt would be humming with industry, but here there was none. The house and grounds seemed deserted, and he began to think it was by design that the only people he'd seen since his arrival were Norman fighting men. Yet why? What had the steward to fear from his English servants? And why had it taken the man so long to decide on what to do with him? By the sun, which was casting the shadows of trees across the forecourt, he estimated the time to be some four hours after dawn.

They turned right out of the doorway, and the captain of the guard ordered him to relieve himself in a sewage channel which ran from the western end of the house to the river. Thaddeus made a play of viewing it with disgust, even though he recalled being taken over it twice in darkness. His nose had told him it was there even if the night had obscured it. 'Is cleanliness unknown in this godforsaken place that you ask a guest to soil his boots on other men's excrement?'

'It's this or nothing, sire. Be grateful for the chance. You'll take a flogging from the priest if you foul yourself inside his church.'

Thaddeus had already noticed the tower, sheltering amongst trees some two hundred paces farther to the west. He could also see a nearer building, which he guessed was the guard house where he'd spent the previous day. He could have wished to return to it, since he doubted the priest's company would be as congenial as the soldiers'. 'He should worry more about the filth you trample on his floor. God asks more of men than that they behave like pigs.' He nodded to a small, planked bridge which carried a path across the channel. 'Is that the route we'll take?'

'It is.'

'Then allow me to stop on it and perform the function there. I have more respect for my Maker than to carry the stench of this place into his house.'

It was hard to say what the younger guards made of him. He was a full head taller than they were and, though his age was no greater than theirs, his thick black beard made him look closer to thirty than twenty. They'd abandoned any thought of trying to restrain him after he'd prised the captain's fingers off his arm in the chamber. He was willing to accompany them, he said, if only to find out why he'd been confined all night in a stinking storeroom, but he had an aversion to being touched. The pain on the captain's face as the bones of his palm were crushed in a giant fist persuaded the others to keep their distance.

'Your lord and priest lack education,' he murmured as he rebuttoned himself and stepped from the bridge, gathering the chain into his hands again. 'It's the habit of animals to pollute their ground and water in this way. I expect to find such foolishness in towns where land is limited, but not in a demesne like this.'

One soldier eyed him curiously. 'What other method is there?'

'The Bible tells us to bury our excrement.' Thaddeus gestured to the grassland around them. 'In a single day, a dozen men could dig a large enough pit to take the waste of the whole household for a year. Open sewers attract vermin. Do you enjoy the thought of your food being defiled by rats which carry other men's faeces on their fur?'

The soldier shrugged. 'We don't see many. The steward has a hatred of them and orders their nests destroyed. Rumour has it he found rats in his bed when he was a child and has had a fear of them ever since. The same with mice.'

'His instincts serve him well,' said Thaddeus mildly. 'You'd be wise to follow his example.' He glanced along the channel towards the river. 'He should worry as much about polluted water. To bathe in sewage is worse than not bathing at all.'

'We do neither.'

Thaddeus gave a grunt of amusement. 'Indeed. The reek of sour sweat blowing off your clothes would fell an ox.' He continued along the path. 'Come. I'm interested in meeting your priest. It's an unchristian nature that condemns a shy little sparrow to Hell because she had the misfortune to fall ill of the pestilence.'

∞

The church was twice the size of Develish's, and it was a moment before Thaddeus's eyes were well enough adjusted to the gloom to see the figure of a man before the unlit altar. He wore a long black vestment with a cowl pulled over his head and he seemed to be struggling to set fire to the char in a tinderbox. The impatient click of flint on fire-steel echoed loudly in the vaulted chamber. He half turned at the sound of approaching steps.

'Are you practised in the use of a tinderbox, Thurkell? I seem unable to strike a spark this morning.'

The voice was the imposter's, and his question so blatant a trick that it would have brought a smile to Thaddeus's face had he been a mere observer to this piece of mummery. Instead, he looked about the church, showing more interest in the murals on the wall than the man at the altar. He understood now why the guildsmen had been so uneasy two nights before. They'd been brave to voice any thoughts at all in front of a priest who condemned townsfolk as fornicators and thieves, let alone caution Thaddeus to be wary of him.

The captain stepped in front of him to catch his attention. 'Father Aristide addresses you, sire,' he said.

Thaddeus frowned. 'He does? Then I'm confused. Do names count for nothing in Blandeforde? Is this not the person who told me he was Jacques d'Amiens? Was he lying to me then or do you lie to me now?' When he received no answer, he raised a manacled wrist to point at a silk-robed depiction of St Nicholas, carrying the Christ child across a river upon his shoulder. 'Would that be the face of Lord Blandeforde? I see the shadow of an older image behind it, so the figure must have been painted recently. Is the likeness a true one?'

'It is, sire.'

'How strange. For myself, I would hesitate to display my arrogance so openly.' He turned to address the priest. 'I came for explanations. Begin with why I've been brought to this church under restraint.'

'You know the reason.'

'I do not, unless Blandeforde treats all his guests in the same way. Is he touched in the mind that he imagines himself to be a richly robed saint while demanding penance from visitors?'

'It's God who demands penance from you.'

'Perhaps so, but only He knows how much.'

The priest stared at him for a moment before instructing the captain to take his men outside. When the door had closed behind them, he pushed back his cowl and beckoned Thaddeus to approach the altar. 'Let's be done with pretence,' he encouraged. 'There's no escape from the trials that await you. The steward is set on punishing you as an example to others. He fears rebellion across his master's vassal demesnes if every base-born serf thinks he can feign nobility.'

Thaddeus took the flint and the fire-steel from the altar. 'If you speak of your pretence at being a priest, then I agree,' he said, striking sparks onto the char cloth and blowing on the embers to encourage a flame. 'On my reckoning, you've missed the hour of Terce by sixty minutes.' He held a splint to the flame.

'You're foolish to mock. Be grateful for this chance to purge your sins while you can still speak.'

Thaddeus lit each candle in turn. 'Who offers me this chance?'

'I do.'

Thaddeus pinched the end of the splint between his fingers and studied the man's face through the drift of smoke that rose from it. 'Any deceiver can don a priest's vestments. Who vouches for you? Certainly not the guildsmen who referred to you as the steward two nights ago.'

'You heard the captain address me by name five minutes ago.'

'I've no more reason to believe him than I have you. Why would God have spared Father Aristide when every other priest in Blandeforde is dead? What marks him out for saintliness? Does he honour his vows to comfort the dying with more sincerity than his fellows?'

He was surprised at how easily the other was provoked when he saw a flush of anger rise in Aristide's cheeks. Or was it shame? Whichever, Thaddeus took heart from the display of emotion, since he didn't doubt the priest had been tasked with teasing a confession from him. A man who couldn't be riled would be harder to manage than one who rose to every bait, yet he questioned why a confession was necessary if Hugh de Courtesmain's allegations of imposture were believed.

'You accuse Blandeforde of arrogance but yours is worse,' Aristide snapped. 'Pride will be your downfall. You think you can speak and act with impunity, but your crimes are so numerous God will have His vengeance—if not in this life, then in the next.'

Thaddeus shifted his gaze to the south-facing chancel window. Through the panes he could see the graveyard, and beyond, the river. He wondered what his chances were of shaking off the guards and swimming to the far bank. Since none bathed, he doubted they'd learnt the skill of staying afloat, but he knew he'd fare no better, dressed as he was in the full regalia of a lord and carrying the weight of shackles. 'What crimes do you say I've committed?' he asked.

'Murder . . . thievery . . . imposture . . . heresy. You embraced Satan when you denied the authority of the Church.'

Thaddeus gave an involuntary laugh. 'Then it's a mystery I've avoided God's vengeance for so long.' He glanced back when the priest made no answer. 'What crimes did the young maid commit to warrant His wrath? The fighting men called her Little Sparrow because of her shyness, but I find it hard to imagine that a timid, illiterate child was guilty of anything as venal as heresy.'

'She judged herself to be wicked when the signs of the pestilence first appeared on her neck.'

The guards had told a different story but Thaddeus let the falsehood pass. 'Did Father Aristide offer comfort and absolution? He will have known from her confessions that her view of herself was flawed.'

'No priest can decide a person's worth. Only God sees into our hearts.'

'Indeed . . . yet it's hard to understand why He found so little worth in the clergy of Blandeforde that He allowed them to perish along with those they tended. Is that not the puzzle the guildsmen wanted explaining?' A glint of irony appeared in Thaddeus's dark eyes. 'How would Father Aristide have answered them had he been there?'

This time there was no mistaking anger for shame. The priest slammed his fist upon the altar, causing the candle flames to flicker. 'You're a slave . . . the bastard son of a harlot . . . incubus to a black-hearted woman who stole her husband's demesne by denying him access to it. And you dare accuse *Aristide* of perfidy?'

Perfidy . . . It was an interesting choice of word. 'I imagine he accuses himself,' Thaddeus murmured, placing his hand on the wooden cross at the centre of the altar to steady it. 'There are kinder ways to separate the sick from the healthy than to persuade an innocent maid she's too evil to live amongst righteous people.'

'She left of her own free will.'

'I doubt that.' He repeated the thoughts he'd shared with the soldiers in the woodland. 'A ten-year-old would have been fearful even to seek solace from her family after being told the town was full of thieves and fornicators. God was merciful to allow her to live long enough to learn she'd been sold a bag of lies. She received more kindness and charity in five days from sinners than she ever did here.'

'You speak from ignorance.'

'Maybe so, but her story's no different from others I've heard. Do you think you're alone in shunning those you suspect of having the pestilence? Or that sufferers don't feel anguish to die in wretched abandonment?'

Aristide's face darkened. 'You must know this better than I, for you condemned your sworn lord to die in such a way.'

Thaddeus allowed a frown of puzzlement to crease his brow. 'Now *you* speak from ignorance. What is it you fear? That your lies about absolution and cleansing rituals will be exposed?' He turned back to the window when the priest made no answer. 'The steward should have ordered a hospital built on the cleared land beyond the river,' he said, nodding to the trees on the other side. 'More of the townsfolk might have survived had the sick been given care away from their families and neighbours. It won't please Blandeforde to find that his paying tenants have perished while his unproductive household lives. What use will a hundred servants be to him when the King demands his taxes and the Church her tithes?'

'God will provide.'

'I pray you're right,' Thaddeus responded dryly, 'for I doubt many cooks know how to drive a furrow through compacted earth.'

Behind him, he heard the sound of the door to the priest's chamber creak open, followed by the scuff of boots across the rushes on the church floor. He made out two sets of steps—the first determined and strong, the second faltering—and it didn't require much guesswork to tell him the bolder tread was Jacques d'Amiens' and the weaker Hugh de Courtesmain's.

If this was to be his trial, he thought, his chances of escaping justice were slim. It wouldn't matter how cleverly he tied Hugh de Courtesmain in knots, or how poorly the Frenchman gave his evidence, the zealous steward and self-righteous priest would find Athelstan guilty.

ᐁᐊ

Ian explained to Lady Anne that there were only two ways to Blandeforde: to return along the riverbank, or to ride down the Shafbury to Dorchester highway in the hope Edumund was right that a crossroad he'd seen some mile to the south would take them to the Blandeforde road. The riverbank, being completely encroached by forest, would have to be walked and might take upwards of five hours; the highway could be done on horseback at greater speed, making their arrival earlier. Lady Anne chose horseback.

'If we had time to spare, I would prefer to go on foot,' she said with a wry smile, 'but since we do not, I beg you to ignore my groans and sighs. I had forgotten how painful it is to sit astride a horse.'

'There's no shame in groaning, milady,' said Peter. 'We all cursed mightily the first time we rode any distance.'

Ian looked towards the saddlebags which were piled beneath a tree. 'You might be more comfortable if you're willing to sit across one of our laps, milady,' he said. 'We can fashion a cushion out of Thaddeus's clothes to give you a softer seat, and as long as you hold tight to the horse's mane, you'll not slide so much.'

'I'd hate to be a trouble, Ian.'

'You won't be, milady,' he answered gruffly. 'In any case, Thaddeus will have our hides if he thinks we haven't looked after you properly.'

'Not to mention that you'll be too weary argue his case if you're as sore as we were the day we left Develish,' Peter said. He clapped Edmund on the back. 'You should choose this fellow. He's the strongest of us all except Thaddeus.'

Joshua nodded agreement. 'And the most accomplished rider, milady. He'll give you more support than we can.'

'And see the ruts in the road sooner,' added Olyver. 'It wasn't by accident that we chose him to bring the news of Thaddeus's arrest to you.'

Lady Anne had to take a breath to quell the sudden emotion that rose in her throat. It was one thing to dream of giving her people the chance of freedom, quite another to have the worth of the idea proved through results. These five conducted themselves so well they were quite unrecognisable as the unformed serf boys who'd departed Develish with Thaddeus the previous summer. 'It would be a great kindness if you felt able to oblige me, Edmund.'

Edmund ducked his head in a bow. 'It will be my pleasure, milady. If I had half Ian's cleverness, I'd have thought of it myself before we left the demesne.'

Lady Anne expressed confidence in Ian's saddle-pack cushion, though in truth she viewed it with considerable alarm, since there was no way of attaching it to Edmund's saddle. Both youths seemed to think it was enough to empty one bag, fill the other with soft, woollen clothes, and then lay the central strap and flattened bag along the saddle. Edmund mounted to sit astride the strap, settling the cushion over the pommel and into his lap and then invited Ian to jump Milady backwards into his arms. She was so small and slight that he caught her with ease and placed her to sit sideways in front of him with her legs across his thigh.

'You'll feel more secure if you hold the horse's mane in your right hand and grip my belt at the back with your left,' he said, steering her arm around his waist. 'It's the way your husband used to take Lady Eleanor around the demesne when she was younger.'

'I'd forgotten,' she answered, forbearing to add: *but only at a slow walk*. Sir Richard's riding skills had been so poor, and his fear of Eleanor wriggling so great, that he'd been afraid of falling himself. And for once Lady Anne had sympathy with him. 'What of my bag?' she asked, closing her mind to the dangers of being tossed to the ground at speed.

Ian lifted the packs of gold from behind Edmund's saddle to lighten his mount's load. 'I'll attach it with this and Thaddeus's writing desk to Killer's back, milady,' he said, stepping aside and instructing Edmund to set off. 'We'll follow when we've struck camp. Wait for us at the crossroad if we don't catch up with you sooner.'

Was there ever such a ride? It was surely sinful for a woman of Lady Anne's years to experience such excitement in the arms of a boy half her age. Even more sinful to wish that the arms had been Thaddeus's. Yet she felt every exhilarating moment as Edmund spurred his mount from walk to trot to canter. He steered one-handed, wrapping his left arm about her waist to hold her tight against him, and as her fear of falling lessened, she gave way to the thrill of moving at speed.

She recalled something Thaddeus had written in one of his accounts about his first journey out of Develish. It was a description of the fear and elation he'd felt at riding a bolting horse with ravening hounds at its heels.

It's good to be afraid. In that quarter-hour dash, I felt more alive than I'd done in the twenty years that went before.

ᐁᔓ

Thaddeus acknowledged Hugh de Courtesmain with a nod, running his gaze over the other's peasant clothes. 'You seem much diminished from the last time I saw you, sir. I thought you set for life as steward at Bourne.'

Hugh cast a look of triumph towards the priest, as if to say Thurkell's acknowledgement of him proved his accusations. 'It's you who wears shackles. Not I.'

'Indeed. God tests us all. I pray Bourne and his people are well, and that it's not through fear of the pestilence returning that you left your post.'

'They are well.'

'I'm glad to hear it. Did you ignore my advice to work with My Lord and not against him?'

'I was unable to work with him at all. He found his serfs' company more congenial than mine and refused to listen to anything I said.'

A gleam of humour sparked in Thaddeus's dark eyes. 'You should have been more careful, Master de Courtesmain. Ambition is never served well by the spreading of falsehoods. Have you not learnt that by now?'

D'Amiens stirred impatiently. 'Enough. It's your deceit that's in question not this man's.' He moved to the altar and placed several rolls of parchment in front of the cross, selecting one to read before handing it to Thaddeus. 'Do you recognise this letter? De Courtesmain tells me you left it for him to find when you departed Bourne. It's signed Thaddeus Thurkell. How so when you're now calling yourself My Lord of Athelstan?'

Thaddeus scanned the words to remind himself of what he'd written. 'I remember it well,' he agreed. 'I wrote it in friendship to try to help de Courtesmain keep his position. I doubted he had the ability to stay long in Bourne's good graces—' he replaced the scroll on the altar—'and I was right.'

'Why is it signed Thaddeus Thurkell?'

Thaddeus shrugged. 'It's the name by which de Courtesmain knew me when he first came to Develish. He grew embittered when he learnt my true status. I thought he'd take Thurkell's advice more readily than Athelstan's.'

'You call the preaching of heresy and insurrection "advice"?'

'I was merely repeating what Bourne believes,' Thaddeus answered. 'Blandeforde too, in all probability. There won't be a landowner anywhere who isn't counting the cost of the pestilence to his revenues and working out how best to manage the serfs who remain to him. Bourne chose to bring his together on one demesne and offer them rewards for increased production. Will you accuse *him* of heresy and insurrection? He seeks only to protect the land the King gave him, and the position and responsibilities bestowed on him by God.'

D'Amiens eyed him thoughtfully. 'Explain why you went by a different name in Develish from the one you're claiming now.'

Thaddeus nodded to the priest. 'For the same reason this man called himself Jacques d'Amiens when he came to my camp. It suited my purpose for the brief time I was there.'

The answer seemed to throw d'Amiens. He turned to Hugh de Courtesmain with a frown. 'You said Thurkell was born in Develish.'

'He was . . . to a harlot called Eva. She was already with child when she arrived in Develish and looked to pass the infant off as her husband's once they were wed. I heard the story from Lady Eleanor who had no reason to lie.'

'How do you answer that?' d'Amiens asked Thaddeus.

'With the contempt it deserves. De Courtesmain's stay in Develish was briefer than mine and he was greatly disliked. Every person in Develish had reason to lie to him.'

'Not Lady Eleanor,' Hugh cried. 'She took me as her confidant and begged me to escort her from the demesne after Sir Richard died.'

'Only because her mother told her you'd refuse. Lady Eleanor wanted to see for herself how far your hypocrisy went. You changed your loyalties so quickly it was hard to keep up with them.'

Hugh turned a haggard gaze on the steward. 'He twists the girl's feelings as falsely as he twists my words. Her hatred for her mother and the Develish serfs was nothing compared to the hatred she had for this—' he pointed a trembling finger at Thaddeus—'*slave.*'

'You surprise me,' d'Amiens said dryly. 'If Lady Eleanor is like other young women, I would have thought the opposite to be true. Whoever this man is, he is not without charm.' He ran the back of his thumb down the stain on his nose as if to point up his own deficiencies. 'What purpose took you to Develish?' he asked Thaddeus.

'I can't tell you that. I gave my pledge never to speak of it.'

'You will make me doubt you if you don't.'

'Then do so. The matter was a private one. Would you have me betray a confidence because a duplicitous steward puts ambition before allegiance to those who employ him?'

'Who can release you from the pledge?'

'My cousin, Lady Anne of Develish.'

'He lies,' protested Hugh. 'There's no familial relationship between them. He took the woman for his whore on her husband's death.'

With a sigh, Thaddeus slammed his elbow into the Frenchman's throat. 'Next time you slur Milady so vilely, I'll have your liver,' he murmured, watching in idle curiosity as de Courtesmain toppled backwards to the floor, gasping for breath. 'You were never deserving of the kindness she showed you.'

Fifteen

Develish, Dorseteshire

ISABELLA SOUGHT OUT HER FATHER and begged him to come to Lady Anne's chamber to speak with Lady Eleanor. 'She's in great distress, Papa, and through my fault. I told her of Thaddeus's arrest and now she fears her mother will be condemned alongside him. I've tried to explain that Milady's in no danger from the Blandeforde steward but she doesn't believe me. She may understand it better if it comes from you.'

Gyles was on the forecourt, having just made his rounds of the boundary wall. 'I'm not the person to do it,' he said. 'You must ask John Trueblood. We all agreed he should govern the demesne in Milady's absence.'

She caught his hand. 'But you told me he tried to stop Milady leaving, Papa, and I fear it will make Lady Eleanor's distress worse if Master Trueblood agrees Milady should never have gone.'

Gyles squeezed her fingers by way of comfort. 'How real is her concern? Is it truly for her mother . . . or only for herself?'

'It seems real to me, Papa. She talked about Lady Anne leaving a letter but she was crying so much I didn't really understand her meaning. I think it has something to do with Master de Courtesmain. She believes her mother will be burnt because Master de Courtesmain was in the great hall when she accused her of heresy.'

Gyles made what he could of these confused ideas. 'Come,' he said, drawing her towards the house. 'We'll talk to the girl together. I'm sure I can persuade her that she worries unnecessarily. It's My Lord of Blandeforde's steward Milady expects to confront, not de Courtesmain.'

But he wondered if he was right after he'd heard what Eleanor had to say. They found her standing at the window of Lady Anne's chamber with a parchment in her hands. Through tears, she told Gyles her mother had written it the afternoon before. 'She placed it atop the gowns in my coffer and I asked her what it was and why she had put it there. She said it was a letter to me which I would be able to read for myself when I was practised enough.'

'She teased Isabella in the same way, milady,' Gyles said gently. 'It's her way of persuading her pupils to work harder at their alphabets. Can you make sense of it?'

Eleanor shook her head. 'There are too many words I've never seen before though she taught me to know the name de Courtesmain, and I see that here.' She stared down at the script. 'I think she wrote it this way so that I wouldn't know what it said before she left.'

Gyles was sure she was right and wondered if Lady Anne had hoped Eleanor would ask for help in deciphering it. 'Will you permit Isabella to read it to you, milady? I'll wait outside while she does. You can be sure she'll not repeat the contents to anyone else unless you give her leave.'

The girl raised anguished eyes. 'What if Mother blames me?'

'For what, milady?'

'Revealing so much to Master de Courtesmain. I said many cruel things about her and he'll remember them all.'

Gyles shook his head. 'She'll not blame you for that, Lady Eleanor. Herself, perhaps, because she knew he wasn't to be trusted, but never you. The words will be kind. Let Isabella read them to you.'

෨෬

My Dear Eleanor,

I worry that my departure will frighten you but beg that you put your trust and faith in our people. They accept you fully as my daughter and will protect you until my return. Have confidence that you will see me again before the week is out.

You have asked me several times about the dreams that have disturbed my sleep this past week. I did not give you an answer, for I knew it would trouble you to learn about them, but I do so now. The images I see are of My Lord of Blandeforde's steward and Hugh de Courtesmain. The steward sits in judgement while de Courtesmain accuses every man, woman and child in Develish of treason and heresy.

I know not if these visions were God-sent, Eleanor, but I do believe I would be wrong to ignore them since hearing of Thaddeus's arrest. It seems his imposture was discovered even before he entered Blandeforde, and that speaks to betrayal by one who carries deep resentments against both him and Develish.

Dear Daughter, only Master de Courtesmain fits that description. Can you understand why I must try to prevent him speaking against Thaddeus and our people? There will be no future for anyone in Develish, yourself included, if all are punished for decisions that I—and I alone—have made.

Be strong and brave, and know that I love you.

Your Affectionate Mother,
Anne

෫ɤට

The sun was still an hour from noon when the column of horses neared the hill from where Thaddeus and his companions had looked down on Blandeforde two days before. Ian, at the head, slowed to a walk to allow the others to draw level with him. 'We're almost there, milady,' he said, signalling a halt. 'When we top that crest, we'll be in sight of the bridge. You said there were preparations you needed to make before we present ourselves.'

She glanced towards the woodland on their left. 'Which can be done inside the privacy of those trees if one of you is kind enough to carry my bag and give me a goatskin of water.'

Ian performed the service for her and, when he returned, he instructed his companions to brush the dust of the road from their liveries and hair and use their own goatskins of water to moisten their cloths and wash their faces. 'We'll let Milady down if we look like paupers,' he told them.

'What's she doing?' asked Peter.

'You'll see.'

It was a quarter-hour before Lady Anne emerged again from the trees and asked Ian to be kind enough to retrieve the bag. She smiled at the look of astonishment on the youth's faces. 'The guards on the bridge won't give us passage if they think me a peasant,' she said.

'You look like a queen, milady,' said Joshua.

'Thank you, Joshua, but a real queen would have a carriage. Can you think of a way to convey me to Blandeforde in a fitting manner? Much as I've enjoyed riding with Edmund, it's hardly seemly for a liege lady to sit across a soldier's lap.'

ဢ

Ian could only guess at what the guards on the bridge made of their approach. Even when My Lord of Bourne was in Develish, she had never been so finely adorned as she was now, sitting sideways on Killer's saddle. To see her arrayed in blue silk, with gold around her neck and on her fingers, was to be reminded of how high her status really was. Even so, he worried that appearance alone wouldn't be enough to convince the guards to let them pass. Thaddeus had looked every inch a lord and had been denied.

Their progress down the hill was necessarily slow, for Lady Anne's position was too precarious for anything faster than a walk. Ian and Olyver rode at her side, controlling Killer with thin rope halters through the metal loops of his bit strap, while Edmund and Peter followed close behind. At the rear, some ten paces back, came Joshua with the dogs and the pack horses, giving a sense of greater numbers than there were. By the time they reached the bridge, Ian took some relief from the fact that the attention of every guard was fixed on Lady Anne.

He was conscious that the crests on his and his companions' tabards were Athelstan's when they should have been Develish's. Conscious, too, that, even if the guards were different from those two days ago, they would know from what their fellows had told them that Lady Anne's entourage was the same as Thaddeus's. He'd worried about embroiling her in trouble before she ever reached the steward; but when he'd voiced his concerns, she had begged him not to worry, saying her peril would be greater if she rode alone.

Ian discovered the truth of this when they were some two-thirds across the bridge and he could see the way the guards were leering at her. One was moving the circled forefinger and thumb of his right hand up and down the middle finger of his left, another was rubbing his rod within his britches. Perhaps Lady Anne felt his anger for she urged him in a whisper to pay no heed, but he was offended enough on her behalf to act on impulse. The men were ranged at the end of the bridge some fifteen yards distant and, with a command to Olyver to hold fast to Killer, he let drop his rope and spurred his mount from a walk to a canter. The charge was so rapid and unexpected that the line of guards fragmented without a sword or bow being drawn.

Olyver watched his twin wrestle the animal to a halt on the road as the soldiers scattered in disarray towards the riverbank. 'By rights he should be flat on his back on the ground,' he murmured, clicking his tongue to set Killer moving again. 'Only a mad man rides his horse at speed over cobbles.'

'Or a brave one,' Lady Anne said.

Olyver grinned. 'Thaddeus would tell you they're one and the same, milady.'

૭૪૭

The steward took another parchment from the altar and handed it to Thaddeus. 'What is this, if not further evidence of imposture?'

Thaddeus unrolled it and recognised it immediately as a page from the Develish parish register. It was a record of births and deaths in 1328 and towards the bottom he saw his own name. *A sun, Thades, was bor this 2 week of June, 1328, to Wil and Ev Thkell.* The script was poorly formed and the words ill-spelt, and he knew them to be Father Anselm's because it wasn't until Sir Richard's violation of Abigail Startout some decade later that Lady Anne had taken charge of the register. Her anger against the priest for supporting Sir Richard's claim that an unformed maid, yet to reach her eleventh year, was above fourteen and known to have experience of men was so great that she had forbade him from ever recording the lives of her serfs again.

Each page of parchment was held inside the wooden covers of the ledger by leather thongs, threaded through holes on the left-hand side, and he saw the careful snips de Courtesmain had made to allow him to withdraw this page without its removal being obvious. Such planning spoke of the Frenchman's intent to unmask Thaddeus, and by entanglement Lady Anne, even before he knew he would be going to Bourne. There hadn't been time between Lady Anne giving him permission to leave, and his departure three hours later, to extract and hide documents in the chest of clothes he took with him.

Thaddeus scanned the scroll. 'Why should a list of names and dates in a hand I don't recognise suggest imposture? The letters are so poorly drawn and the words so illiterate I would hazard a guess the scribe sought to disguise his own style. Where do you say it comes from?'

D'Amiens watched Hugh de Courtesmain struggle to his feet. 'From the Develish parish record, if this man is to be believed.'

'I've seen that record. It's a detailed history, kept by Lady Anne. She was taught the art of inscription by nuns and has a fine hand which looks nothing like this.'

'It's rare for a lady to have such a skill.'

'Milady is a rare woman, Master d'Amiens. As you should know since you've met her.'

'You credit me with too much knowledge. I've never had the pleasure of speaking with her. She always stood in the shadow of her husband, ready to prompt him with answers that would satisfy me.' D'Amiens turned to Hugh. 'Explain why the document is so flawed.'

'At the time of Thurkell's birth, the scribe was Father Anselm,' muttered Hugh. 'Lady Anne discharged him from the responsibility some ten years ago. The reason why is unknown to me, but she holds the priest in great animosity . . . and he her.'

With a shrug, Thaddeus handed the page back to d'Amiens. 'Anselm must have lived well beyond his natural span for his hand to have been trembling so badly more than two decades ago. What age does de Courtesmain say he's claiming?'

Hugh stared at him with loathing. 'You know the cause as well as I,' he snapped. 'The priest is an inebriate. His office weighs heavily on him because of his mistress's rejection of the Church and the heretical beliefs she teaches her people.'

Thaddeus's eyes creased with amusement. 'You should rehearse your history before you assign yet more villainy to Lady Anne, Master de Courtesmain. Whatever ailed Father Anselm when he was appointed to the benefice of Develish could not have originated with her. He was in position a good eight years before Sir Richard brought her to the demesne as a bride of fourteen.'

There was a lengthy silence which was finally broken by Father Aristide. 'This man offers other documents to prove you're a base-born serf. Will you deny them all?'

It was a foolish question. 'What else would you have me do? Admit de Courtesmain tells the truth? At least acknowledge that my age alone rules me out of being a serf called Thurkell. My years are thirty but, if this man lives, he has yet to pass twenty-one.'

The priest gave an uneasy shrug. 'De Courtesmain has less reason to lie than you. He gains nothing by what he does.'

Thaddeus smiled slightly. 'I doubt you're wise to disappoint him so early, Father. Treachery looks more enticing when it's rewarded with thirty pieces of silver.'

ↀↀ

Ian hadn't counted on people leaving their houses to watch Lady Anne's passage. He was used to riding through towns which seemed deserted, with only the odd glimpse of faces at open doors and unshuttered windows to show that anyone had survived. To say the streets of Blandeforde were thronged would be an exaggeration, but enough were drawn by the sight of a richly gowned lady to give a sense of numbers.

For Lady Anne, it was her first experience of the despair most felt to still be alive. She saw the early signs of starvation in the hollow eyes of children who had been left to fend for themselves on the deaths of their parents, and the seeming lack of purpose in men who stood listlessly at corners, barely speaking with each other. More particularly, she was struck by the empty expressions of widows who stood alone and bereft before houses that had once been filled with laughter. It was as if the women had turned in on themselves, so consumed by their own woes that they barely noticed the trials and tribulations of others. She asked Ian why this should be. Would they not benefit from taking the orphans into their homes?

'You would think so,' he answered, 'but we see the same everywhere we go. Thaddeus says it's because their priests are dead and there's no one to guide them. When men are without answers—worse, believe the pestilence will take us all in the end—women lose their resolve. It's hard to make decisions for yourself when your life has been lived in obedience to others.'

Lady Anne looked ahead to where a cluster of men was gathered outside a church. 'What of the three guildsmen who were at your camp two nights ago?' she asked Ian. 'Are they not leaders here?'

He shook his head to say he didn't know.

'Do you remember their names?'

'The one who talked the most was called Andrew Tench, milady. He said he was a wool merchant.'

She nodded to the group by the church. 'Will you halt us there and ask for him to be brought to me? It's surely right to offer hope if we can.'

Ian kept to himself that Thaddeus had tried the same many times and had learnt that it took days of persuasion to convince survivors to embrace life. A person on his own, such as the fisherman or Robin Pikeman might listen to a quarter-hour of reasoned sense, but a company of more than two rarely did. It was as if their minds were so firmly set on death that resistance to hearing good news was strengthened in proportion to their numbers.

He was surprised, therefore, when his request that Master Tench be summoned to speak with Lady Anne of Develish was greeted with warmth. A young urchin was dispatched and an old man dropped to one knee. 'We've heard stories of Develish from travellers who've passed through our town, milady. They say the village is deserted but a multitude of men and women in peasant clothing are alive inside the moat. It leads us to wonder if their lord seeks to protect his serfs from the pestilence.'

Ian answered when Lady Anne hesitated. 'The lord of Develish is this lady,' he said. 'The responsibility for her husband's demesne fell to her when Sir Richard died away from home, and, yes, she has sought from the beginning to protect all her people—be they nobles, freemen or serfs.'

'We could wish our own lord as generous.'

'Is he here?' asked Lady Anne, wondering if Bourne's captain of arms had led her false the previous autumn by saying Blandeforde had left for his estates in the west.

'He is not, milady. He abandoned us when news of the pestilence first arrived.'

'Who acts on his behalf?'

'The steward, Master d'Amiens, who takes his instructions from the priest.'

Lady Anne saw discomfort in the faces of the younger men around him, as if they felt he'd been more honest than he should. 'Would that be My Lord of Blandeforde's confessor? Why did he leave him behind?'

The greybeard made to spit on the ground but thought better of it when the hand of one of his companions gripped his shoulder. 'Father Aristide would make any journey burdensome, milady.'

There was a bustle of movement behind him as a man of middle years with a sheepskin collar about his cloak pushed through the small crowd and presented himself to Lady Anne with a bow. 'You summoned me, milady. I am your obedient servant, Andrew Tench. How may I be of service to you?'

He had a pleasant, if careworn, face and she dipped her own head in acknowledgement. 'I sought rather to be of service to you and the people of your town, sir. I see children looking hungry, men without purpose standing at corners, and women, alone and sad, in doorways. Is there a reason why all feel so lost and desolate?'

'Each one of us has had to watch our families die before our eyes, milady.'

'And for that I am deeply sorry, Master Tench. The pestilence is a cruel disease.' She glanced from one man to the next. 'God cries out in pain each time another innocent dies . . . as all of you will have done to see your beloved wives and children perish. But is that cause to turn your backs on the widows and orphans of your neighbours?'

They shuffled their feet as if the question had been put to them before. 'Master Tench has argued the same, milady, as have I,' said the greybeard, pushing himself upright, 'but these fellows—' he gestured towards the crowd—'would rather debate issues of property than the welfare of women and children.'

Tench placed a calming hand on the older man's arm. 'Many of us would willingly take the needy into our homes, milady— God knows we are all in want of companionship—but none can agree on how to do it. The man who offers his home to a widow, rich in property, will double his wealth overnight if she agrees to tie her assets to his. Orphaned sons of successful merchants are as prized.'

Lady Anne nodded understanding. 'For the value of their inheritances.'

'Yes, milady.'

'It's a great problem,' she said thoughtfully.

Tench nodded. 'Master Slater and I—' he indicated the greybeard—'have proposed drawing lots, but most resist the idea for fear of picking badly. Concern about the pestilence remains strong and few wish to invite it into their homes through ill chance. It's but eight weeks since the last sufferer was buried.'

Lady Anne had heard this from Edmund when she'd asked him to repeat as much as he could remember of Thaddeus's conversation with the guildsmen. 'Eight weeks is a long time, Master Tench. Did my cousin Athelstan not tell you that towns to the south have been without deaths since Christmas? God willing, we can dare to hope that Dorseteshire's suffering is almost over.'

He looked startled. 'My Lord is your cousin, milady?'

'He is, sir, and has travelled the land, seeking and dispersing news so that all who survive may know they're not alone. I trust he gave you reasons to believe in a future free of the pestilence. His men tell me you spoke with him two nights ago.'

Tench stared at her in horror. 'We did our best to warn him, milady.'

Her kind eyes smiled into his. 'About what, Master Tench?'

'The fate that awaited him, milady.'

The greybeard gave a grunt of impatience. 'There's no sense mouthing riddles,' he said. 'Milady wouldn't be here if she didn't know of the arrest.' He raised his gaze to Lady Anne's. 'If it's information you seek, I can tell you the little we know. The steward's guards brought your cousin through the town in chains two nights ago after three of our people were ordered to meet him. The priest told them he was an absconding serf, looking to pass for a lord, and tasked them with unmasking him. He thought an English peasant would speak more openly with men of his own kind.'

Lady Anne pretended surprise. 'How strange. Whatever gave the priest such ideas?'

The greybeard shook his head to say he didn't know.

She turned to Tench. 'Was my cousin easily mistaken for a serf?'

'Not at all, milady. I doubt I've ever seen so fine a noble. Father Aristide feigned the role of steward in order to question him on matters of heresy, but I heard nothing untoward in what My Lord said.'

'Then why does the Father accuse him of imposture?'

'We don't know, milady, unless the allegation was made by the Frenchman who entered the town from the north some dozen days ago. He demanded to be taken to Master d'Amiens, claiming to be a messenger, but since none is allowed to approach My Lord's house, we could only point out the direction he should take.'

'Was he on horseback?'

'No, milady, he came on foot. Had he not declared himself a messenger, we would not have taken him for one. He shrank from us, calling us filthy and unclean, and jumped at every shadow, believing they were rats.'

The greybeard gave a grunt of contempt. 'I've never seen such a pitiful creature. Mind, he must have had a good tale to tell, because the steward stationed guards on the bridge after speaking with him.' He glanced towards the river. 'It's a pity he didn't have the sense to do it months ago. More might have survived if the bridge had been closed when news of the pestilence first reached us.'

Once again, Lady Anne saw disquiet in the faces of those around him, as if they feared his intemperate speech would reach d'Amiens' ears. 'Was the messenger of small stature with dark hair and thin features . . . aged some thirty years?'

'He was, milady.'

She gave silent thanks to God for her dreams. 'Then all is explained,' she said. 'I know this man and he is not to be trusted. He uses deceit to win positions of favour, and I don't doubt he hopes to do the same here.' She glanced from one face to another in the group. 'Good sirs, am I right to understand from Master Tench's words that there is little communication between you and your lord's household?'

'You are, milady,' called a man from the back. 'The steward looks to the priest to keep the house cleansed of sin and has barred entry to the townsfolk for fear they'll bring their wickedness with them.'

Andrew Tench pointed to the church behind him, where several parchments were nailed to the door. 'Guards come from time to time to post these writs, milady, but we see no one else.'

'What sort of writs?'

'Reminders of when our rents and taxes are due, milady. Most were able to pay last quarter day but, without commerce, none will have the wherewithal on the next. The town tax is the most onerous, for it remains unchanged despite there being fewer to pay it. We've tried to send warning of this to the steward but have had no reply. He reserves his care for My Lord's servants.'

Lady Anne doubted that. She thought it more likely d'Amiens' care was for himself, since he had a better chance of saving his own skin if he kept the household free of the pestilence. She asked to see the most recent writ, and it was torn from the door and passed forward to Master Tench, who prepared to read the words aloud. She would have allowed him to do so had Olyver not seen benefit in earning the crowd's respect. With a smile, he leant down and took the parchment from Tench's hands, saying Lady Anne would prefer to read it for herself.

She did so, and her expression when she'd finished was pensive. 'Do you commonly pay taxes in grain and foodstuffs?' she asked Tench. 'It's the practice on demesnes, but I would have thought coinage or silver a more normal currency in towns.'

'We pay in any way we can, milady. Some were grateful that the guards were ordered to seize grain from the communal store in lieu of silver last quarter day.'

'We think the steward uses it to feed the household,' said the greybeard. 'If so, he's stealing from us. We keep the grain for selling not for eating.'

'There's no one to buy it,' called the man at the back. 'You know this, Master Slater. It's months since merchants came from outside. Better we keep our silver than grain we can't use.'

The greybeard gave a grunt of impatience. 'It's time you took thought for the future, Miller. You'll change your mind when your own stores run out. Not one of us will be greedy for silver when we've nothing to eat.'

Andrew Tench nodded. 'It's these concerns we wish to raise with the steward, milady.'

She placed the writ on her lap. 'I will do my best on your behalf when I speak with him,' she said, 'though I fear he'll pay as little heed to me as to you. Men who close their eyes to the troubles of others usually close their ears as firmly.'

A wry expression crossed Tench's face. 'Do you accuse us of the same thing, milady?'

'I do, sir. The town needs leadership but you waste your time squabbling.'

The man at the back raised his voice again. 'The last of our council died before Christmas. Since then we've been without elders because none can agree on who should take the authority.'

Lady Anne smiled slightly. 'Then I despair of you, Master Miller. Do you think Develish could have survived the pestilence if my people were as mean-spirited as the men of Blandeforde? It takes courage and generosity to keep a community alive. Are those qualities absent here?'

'We ask only for a fair distribution of property,' he answered irritably. 'If you know of a way to achieve that, then tell us.'

He reminded Lady Anne of Will Thurkell, who was always first to complain that his share of food was smaller than his neighbour's. Yet the looks of approval on the faces of those around him whenever he spoke suggested he had a following. 'Explain what you mean by fair, sir, and I will do my best to oblige you.'

'Wealthy widows should go to poor men, impoverished widows to the rich. By such methods, all will be equal.'

'And what do the widows say? Does the woman who's worked hard to help grow her dead husband's wealth agree that it should go to a man too lazy and profligate to accumulate anything?'

Her words were greeted with a scowl. 'Do you accuse me of laziness?'

'I accuse you of nothing, sir, for I don't know you.' She paused. 'I merely question your interpretation of fairness. Where's the justice in bartering women and children like cattle so that envious men can feel the equal of their more successful neighbours?'

Miller shrugged. 'I can barely sustain myself. How do you expect me to feed more mouths on the little I have?'

'I don't,' Lady Anne answered lightly. 'If what you tell me is true, you're in no position to welcome anyone into your house. My advice would be that only the men who can afford to be generous should put their names forward.'

'Thereby enriching themselves further. How is that fair?'

'You're as free as any man here to do the same, sir. In Develish even those with the least share what they have with others.' She dropped her gaze to his midriff. 'You have a handsome girth, so could it be you have more in your cupboards than you pretend?' A ripple of amusement ran through the crowd and she shifted her gaze back to Tench and the greybeard. 'Your idea of drawing lots is a good one, but I would urge you to ask the widows and orphans to make the pick. Since God will be guiding their hands, no one can begrudge the choices they make.'

There was a short silence before the greybeard gave a throaty chuckle. 'You have a fine way of solving problems, milady. Now tell us how to choose leaders. I warrant you'll not find that as easy.'

She laughed. 'I warrant you're right, Master Slater, since you all seem more intent on fighting than advancing the cause of your people.'

'That's the truth of it,' he agreed. 'Even so, there are some amongst us who would appreciate your thoughts. You've spoken more sense in a quarter-hour than I've heard in months. What would you advise?'

She looked around the group, which had more than doubled in size since she and her companions had first halted. 'Choose one man and task him with picking the rest. You will argue less over a single name than you do over several.'

'Many will vie for such authority,' called Miller.

'Then be wise in whom you select. For myself, I would want the man who finds most fault in the steward and the priest, for it would give me confidence that his loyalty lies with the town and not the house.'

'There's only one who fits that description,' he answered. 'You'd choose Jeremiah Slater, never mind he loves to berate us for our failings.'

Lady Anne nodded to Ian that it was time to leave. 'I would, sir . . . and afterwards, were I Master Slater, I would choose you. You have a good mind and a loud voice and, if you're willing to lay your grievances aside, you'll make a fine leader. There are other ways for men to prove themselves than by swelling their coffers with widows' gold.'

'But none so tempting.' He stared hard at her for a moment and then, as if his mind was suddenly made up, he shouldered his way forward to stand beside Tench and the greybeard. 'Come,' he called to the crowd. 'If Milady is willing to express our concerns to the steward then the least we can do is walk with her to the gates of the house.'

I, Hugh de Courtesmain, steward to Lady Anne of Develish, swear by Our Lord Jesus Christ that everything written here is true. Should I die of the pestilence—and this vellum be found—I beg that whoever reads it will take it to My Lord of Blandeforde or His Grace the Bishop of Sarum and ask that prayers be said for my soul. Be confident that Hugh de Courtesmain is innocent of all wrongdoing and stands alone amongst the inhabitants of Develish in remaining true to the Church and the King.

I write this record without Lady Anne's knowledge or permission, for it is she who must answer for what has been done here when the pestilence has passed. Her heresies are numerous and she infects her people with them, inciting serfs to break their oaths of allegiance and conduct themselves as freemen. Even the priest fails to discharge his duties as he should, cowering inside his room through fear of the evil that surrounds him.

The King's taxes and the Church's tithes have been squandered on feeding a multitude of base-born men and women who have taken refuge in their lord's house. They treat it as their own and assume entitlement to everything inside.

My unhappy situation—being bound to Develish through promises I made to Sir Richard before his death—forces me to hold my tongue over each new sacrilege committed, but the truth of what my pen writes cannot be silenced.

Develish is well named. If God be present here, I do not see Him.

The worst of men goes by the name of Thaddeus Thurkell. He was born a slave and is shameless in his overturning of God's social order, taking powers to himself by virtue of the unnatural favours the widow of his liege lord bestows on him. Lady Anne debases herself and her class by making herself his whore.

Thurkell is a common thief and bandit, acting outside the laws of the Church and the King. In early September, he roamed the countryside with five companions, destroying villages at will and stealing whatever he could find. There is no sin or crime this man will not commit in service to himself and the woman he calls Mistress. He is a confessed thief and liar and, unless I miss my guess, a murderer also. It is beyond comprehension that all in the villages he has burnt were dead, yet neither he nor his companions show repentance. Instead they boast of their exploits, looking to receive admiration from the people who crowd about them wherever they go.

Along with 200 sheep and a wagon full of grain, he has delivered a Norman hostage, My Lord of Bourne, to Develish.

My Lord's age and infirmity make him quite unable to withstand the many terrors inflicted upon him by Thurkell. In return for his life and freedom, he has agreed to falsify a letter of accreditation, naming the man who bears it as My Lord of Athelstan.

Thurkell and his band plan to leave Develish on the first day of 1349, arrayed in finery once belonging to Sir Richard. Milady makes no secret of her approval of these men, labouring long hours with her seamstresses to stitch fine apparel for them. Since everything they wear or carry will be embossed with the crest of Athelstan, it is clear that Thurkell's intention is to pretend nobility in order to steal more easily from the unfortunates he and his men encounter.

Every person in Develish is complicit in the deceit—even the children. The intent of all is to free themselves from bondage, and Thurkell goes with their blessing to find the means to achieve this ambition. My guess is he plans to win the confidence of lords and freemen in order to cheat them out of their gold.

The crest and title have been bestowed on him by Lady Anne of Develish, who claims descent from Godwin of Wessex, father to the usurper Harold who was defeated in battle by the rightful King, William of Normandy. In wickedness and complicity in his crimes, she has permitted a base-born slave to claim royal English blood through a designation lost when her maternal grandfather died without male issue.

Let these words of mine be shouted across the country if I am not alive to testify to them when the pestilence has passed.

The man who calls himself Athelstan was born Thaddeus Thurkell, the bastard son of a Develish harlot, reared in bondage without land or property to call his own. He may be recognised through the quickness of his mind, the tallness of his build, the darkness of his skin, the blackness of his hair and the heresy in his heart. He is twenty years of age but has the look of a man ten years older. He is well educated, and reads and writes as fluently as any scribe.

In nomine Patris et Filii et Spiritus Sancti

Sixteen

THE SEVEN REMAINING SCROLLS CONTAINED de Courtesmain's record of his stay in Develish. D'Amiens took them one by one from the altar and allowed Thaddeus time to read them, and since Thaddeus saw merit in stalling for as long as he could, he lingered long over each parchment. In themselves they proved nothing, since they were written in de Courtesmain's own hand, but they made compelling reading. The angriest, denouncing Thaddeus as a thief and a murderer, had clearly been written in Develish; but from the differences of ink and vellum, Thaddeus guessed the others had been composed in Bourne.

It was hard to say what de Courtesmain's purpose had been in writing them because their tone was so bitter and vengeful they read more like a rambling reassurance to the writer that he was a good man amongst heathens than a well-constructed accusation. He painted himself throughout as an honest, God-fearing innocent, obliged to live amongst heretics for half a year, and called on God to witness his innocence as often as he condemned Lady Anne and Thurkell for their guilt. Indeed, so strong were his protestations of continued dedication to the Church that Thaddeus wondered if, in truth, he hadn't been trying to quell a voice of dissent in his own head.

He couldn't fault the Frenchman's memory. Every Develish secret was laid bare—from Lady Anne's encouragement to her serfs to bid for freedom through to Eleanor's revelation that Milady was not her mother—and, though Thaddeus toyed with dismissing it all as the workings of an imaginative mind, he knew the steward and priest would not believe him. No one could invent so elaborate a story and transcribe it in such detail to the page.

Thaddeus passed the last scroll back to d'Amiens without comment.

'Well?' the steward demanded. 'Is all this true?'

'As true as your priest's claim that he keeps the household free of the pestilence through the cleansing of sin.'

'What other truth is there?'

'That you and he are using the same methods Lady Anne employs. First, strive to keep the pestilence out by closing your gates, and then be ready to remove any who succumb. Milady would have taken Develish sufferers outside the moat and cared for them herself, but you and this man—' he glanced towards the priest—'chose to banish yours for wickedness.' He smiled cynically. 'Which truth do you prefer, Master d'Amiens?'

'It's not a case of preference. If the Church cites wickedness as the cause of the pestilence, who am I to argue differently?' The steward placed the scroll with the others on the altar. 'Tell me how Master de Courtesmain's account is flawed.'

Thaddeus glanced towards the Frenchman. His only recourse was to keep discrediting him. 'In his depiction of himself. Had he mentioned his many deceits, you would struggle to believe anything he said.'

'Name one.'

'His constant switching of allegiance. It was hard to know from one day to the next where his loyalties lay. It made him greatly distrusted by the people.'

De Courtesmain appealed to the steward. 'They had a hatred of Normans,' he cried. 'Sir Richard and Lady Eleanor felt their dislike as much as I did.'

Thaddeus gave an involuntary laugh. 'You're an ungrateful fellow,' he said. 'You were given the chance to leave after Sir Richard died. Why didn't you take it, if Develish was the Hell you portray in your writings?'

'The pestilence was at the gates.'

'You know it was not. We saw people moving north for several weeks afterwards. You were free to go whenever you wanted, yet you describe yourself as a prisoner.' Thaddeus looked back to the steward. 'He had more faith in Milady's ability to keep the pestilence at bay than he did in God's mercy. He's greatly afeared his sins will find him out.'

'Isn't the same true of all men?' asked d'Amiens.

'You tell me, sir. Do you not have confidence in Father Aristide's cleansing rituals?' His lips twitched into another cynical smile. 'I can't blame you if you don't. His inability to strike a spark suggests it's a long time since these altar candles were lit.' He caught the priest's hand as the man made to slap him. 'You and Master de Courtesmain are two of a kind,' he murmured. 'You both look to save your own lives at the expense of others. Do you fear becoming as low as he when your deceits are revealed?'

With relentless pressure, he twisted the priest's arm behind his back and forced him to his knees. The steward moved to intervene but Thaddeus shook his head in warning. 'Nothing would please me more than to wrap my chains around your neck, Master d'Amiens. Be sure de Courtesmain won't come to your assistance. He's more frightened of my anger than he is of yours. He knows I have little patience with hypocrites.'

'You'll compel me to summon the guards.'

'Oblige me by doing so. I'd rather deal with honest men than cowardly liars who pretend a piety they don't have.'

It seemed d'Amiens was as easily provoked as the priest. 'You'd be in your shroud if I had some recollection of you,' he snapped. 'De Courtesmain tells me you've been doing *ad opus* work in Develish for more than a decade, but I have no memory of seeing you there. Be grateful for that. Were it otherwise, I'd have known you for a common serf and ordered the skin flayed from your bones.'

With feigned impatience, Thaddeus released the priest's hand and thrust him away. 'I'm wearied of this nonsense. If it's the truth you want, put de Courtesmain to the question. He'll refute his claims on the mere threat of pain.' He cast a scornful look at the Frenchman. 'He can barely stand for trembling at the lies he's told.'

The sudden thoughtfulness in the steward's expression suggested this ploy might work, but the creak of the church door distracted him. He narrowed his eyes at the captain of the guard who eased through the opening. 'What do you want?' he demanded.

'Lady Anne of Develish is at the gate, sir. She's accompanied by men from the town and is requesting entry. I need your orders.'

A slow smile spread across d'Amiens' face as the captain's words registered with him. 'How fortuitous,' he murmured, turning to

Thaddeus. 'God must be as eager as I to see you released from your pledge. Will Milady's story be the same as yours, I wonder?'

ல்

Ian felt his twin's nervousness as they approached to within a hundred yards of My Lord of Blandeforde's walled enclosure. *This was madness.* On horseback, they could see above the gates, and both were intimidated by the extent of the enclosed land. A bend in the long driveway hid most of the house from their view, but enough of the eastern wall and roof was visible to suggest immense grandeur.

The trembling of Lady Anne's hands on the reins told Ian she was as nervous and he asked her in a whisper if she would like him to bring the column to a halt. She shook her head and answered from a dry mouth that the men of Blandeforde would withdraw their support if they thought her afraid. Ian knew this to be true because the closer they came to the gates, the more the crowd began to drag its heels. Even Master Slater's brow creased with uncertainty at the sight of archers with raised bows on the steps to either side of the barred entrance.

What to do?

Out of the corner of his eye, Ian watched Olyver remove a wooden beaker from the pack that was slung across the saddle in front of him and fill it from the goatskin of water that hung on the other side. He used movements so small they might have been taken for a need to adjust his horse's breast collar, and when he passed the cup quietly to Lady Anne no one noticed. As she sipped from it gratefully, Ian turned in his saddle to beckon Edmund, Peter and Joshua forward.

'Milady asks that we range ourselves in front of these brave townsmen to give them protection,' he called. 'Buckler, ride beside me with the dogs and pack horses. Trueblood and Catchpole, take up positions on the other side. As far as she is able, Milady promises to shield and safeguard all who walk with her.'

At thirty paces, one of the archers ordered the column to halt. 'State your business,' he called in French.

Lady Anne instructed Ian and Olyver to take her closer. She answered in the same language in a clear, untroubled voice. 'My business is with the steward,' she said. 'Send word that Lady Anne of Develish awaits him at the gate.'

'He'll not come for a woman. He answers only to God and My Lord of Blandeforde.'

'Is Master d'Amiens dead?'

'He is not. Why would you ask such a question?'

'Common soldiers don't normally make decisions for stewards.'

'We have our orders.'

'You do indeed,' she said boldly. 'Send word that Lady Anne of Develish awaits Master d'Amiens at the gate.' She gestured to the crowd behind her. 'Be assured neither I nor these men will leave until I've spoken with him.'

It was a good quarter-hour before a liveried captain climbed up next to the archer and instructed Milady to enter alone. She refused, reiterating her request that the steward be brought to her. After another quarter-hour, the captain returned with new orders. If her entourage dismounted and left their horses and weapons outside, they would be allowed to accompany her. She refused again.

The captain shook his head. 'I urge you not to try Master d'Amiens' patience further, milady. It's only out of courtesy to your dead husband's status that he agrees to see you at all.'

She smiled slightly. 'My request is a reasonable one, captain. Before I enter, I ask that the steward presents himself in person so that I can be assured he lives and has true charge of his master's estates.'

'You have my word that he does, milady.'

'Does your word count for more than the men of Blandeforde's, sir? They tell me they haven't seen Master d'Amiens in months. Writs, purporting to be his, are posted by soldiers and all attempts to contact him are met with silence. What should I make of that?'

'Whatever you choose, milady. You've been given the terms on which you may enter. If you accept them, I will open the gates. If you do not, they will remain closed.'

She bent her head in a mocking bow. 'Thank you, sir. I believe that tells me all I need to know.' She twisted around to address the crowd of men behind her, continuing to speak in French so that the captain would understand her. 'You'll find no leadership here. I'll return with you to the town and then ride to Sarum to inform His Grace the bishop that the steward is dead and the house overrun by Norman fighting men. His Grace will know better than I how to reach My Lord of Blandeforde with the news. Meanwhile, I urge you to withhold your taxes for they will surely be stolen by these mercenaries.'

Ian heard a few voices call out for her to speak in English but Master Slater quickly hushed them. ''Er woords be for the Franky gaeky,' he said in Dorset brogue. 'She wan 'en affrighted enow to faetch the stoörd.'

But it seemed the captain was more distressed than afraid. 'Have you not come for your cousin, milady? I felt certain you had. Will you abandon him?'

Both his words and his tone surprised Lady Anne, for they seemed to imply some sympathy with Thaddeus. 'I can't bargain with Norman thieves, sir. However small the ransom you demand for Athelstan's release, it will be above anything Develish can afford. My only recourse is to seek help from the bishop.'

'You malign me and my fighting men unfairly, milady. None of this is our doing.'

'Then bring Master d'Amiens to the gate, sir. I have only to see him for my doubts to be resolved. His appearance is not one that's easily forgotten.'

ᏭᎧ

Thaddeus was thinking the same as he watched d'Amiens rage against the captain. The split nature of the steward's face—more pronounced in anger as blood suffused the livid stain—seemed to mirror his character. His moods swung from light to dark in the blink of an eye. All his earlier triumph in the church to hear that Lady Anne was at the gate had now given way to fury. Yet there was no accounting for the wrath he was unleashing on the unfortunate wretch who stood before him, unless he believed his own authority was strengthened by it.

And perhaps it was. The young guards who'd been ordered to bring Thaddeus to the great hall halted him inside the entranceway, hunching their shoulders and staring at the floor as if fearful of being seen to have sympathy with their captain. For a brief moment, Thaddeus thought about returning outside. With everyone's attention elsewhere, he could walk clear across the forecourt before his absence was noticed. Yet what would it achieve except a few moments of amusement for himself and a torrent of abuse against his guards? There was more to be gained by earning their gratitude than causing them trouble.

D'Amiens seemed most exercised by the captain's inability to implement simple orders. He was a poor, weak-spirited creature. Only a coward would quail before a woman. She was a widow without rights. Blandeforde's terms of entry, as decided by his steward, must always prevail over hers. It mattered nothing that she had townsmen at her side. Were his soldiers incapable of firing arrows?

Thaddeus advanced into the hall with a laugh. 'You attack the wrong person, Master d'Amiens,' he said, lowering himself into the same carved chair the steward had used two nights previously. 'It's hardly your captain's fault that Lady Anne refuses your terms.' He placed his chains on the table. 'Were I less encumbered with iron, I would refuse them also. You have no authority over either of us.'

D'Amiens rounded on him in fury. 'In your case, that is yet to be demonstrated,' he spat. 'As for her, she can only ever be a supplicant in My Lord of Blandeforde's house. Should he choose to grant her a new husband, she will gain status through the marriage, but until then she is subject to my governance as proctor in My Lord's absence.'

Thaddeus felt moved to agree with him, since he had no wish to embroil Lady Anne in his troubles. And yet . . . Just the knowledge of her presence had lightened his heart. 'Perhaps you aren't as knowledgeable as you think you are,' he said mildly. 'Milady draws her status from her father and not her dead husband.' He switched his gaze to the captain. 'What reason does she give for refusing the steward's terms?'

The man turned to him in relief. 'She requests that Master d'Amiens present himself in person to prove he's alive, sire. He so rarely leaves the house that the men of the town are persuaded he's dead.'

'They lie for their own reasons,' said d'Amiens coldly.

Thaddeus doubted that. He thought it more likely the falsehood was Lady Anne's. 'Why do you object to the request?' he asked. 'You demand a great deal of the lady to expect her to enter an armed compound without knowing what awaits her.'

'She's bold enough. The captain tells me she rides on horseback with upwards of fifty men around her . . . and not a chaperone in sight.' A faint smile touched d'Amiens' lips. 'Master de Courtesmain's accusations of harlotry become more credible.'

Thaddeus eased himself back in the chair and placed his feet on the bench that ran lengthways down the table. 'You'll live to regret those words,' he murmured, closing his eyes. 'If the men of Blandeforde don't make you pay for your ill-considered judgements, be sure I will.'

ⱺχⱷ

There was an audible gasp of surprise—and not a little fear—as the gates swung open to reveal the captain and Master d'Amiens standing some twenty paces back. A dozen guards with drawn bows were ranged at their sides.

Ian and Olyver made to raise their own bows, but Lady Anne stretched out her hands to prevent them. 'I cannot believe Norman soldiers are any more desirous of shedding English blood than we theirs,' she said in French, praying most earnestly that she hadn't misread the captain's sympathy. 'God would not have allowed us to survive the pestilence if He intended us to kill each other.'

She dipped her head to d'Amiens. 'I'm pleased to see you looking so well, sir, but saddened that you feel the need to threaten us. We come in peace, not enmity.'

'You bring too many men with you for me to believe that, milady.'

This time she answered in English. 'But most are your people, Master d'Amiens. What reason do you have to fear them? None is armed. They seek only to explain their difficulties to you.'

He responded in the same language. 'We live in perilous times, milady, and from what I've learnt of Develish, you know this better than I. I'm told you defend your demesne with even more fierceness than I defend My Lord's.'

'But never against those I'm pledged to protect, Master d'Amiens,' she said in French. 'The vows of allegiance that bind me to my people are as sacred as those that bind them to me. Would My Lord of Blandeforde say differently? He's a person of great nobility and honour, so I can't believe he would ever ask his captain to order the murder of defenceless men.'

Her words unsettled the guards, and a brief irritation glimmered in d'Amiens' eyes as he instructed them to lower their weapons. He wished he'd paid more heed to Thurkell's assessment of this woman. Dressed in finery, and at the head of a crowd, she bore little resemblance to the timid wife he'd glimpsed on occasion in Develish. 'My Lord would say you attempt to embellish your importance with such statements, milady. You take unwarranted authority to yourself when you claim oaths that were given and received by your husband as your own.'

She smiled and reverted back to English. 'Do you not believe in honouring your lord's pledges, sir?'

'We are talking about you, milady.'

'Yet our positions are similar, are they not? Through the death or absence of our lords, we have both had responsibility thrust upon us. With God's help, I can say I am comfortable with the choices I've made. Is the same true of you?'

D'Amiens felt forced to answer in the same language, since she was so clearly talking to the men behind her. 'It wasn't God who instructed you to bar your husband from his demesne and seize power from his lawful steward, milady,' he snapped. 'Such actions are treasonable. My Lord of Blandeforde would have dealt with you harshly had de Courtesmain brought the news sooner.'

Lady Anne was relieved to have the steward confirm that de Courtesmain was the informer, though it would help her even more to know he'd come for himself and not for Bourne. 'He was free to do so at any time, but he had a greater fear of the pestilence than he did of me,' she said mildly. 'Treasonable or not, he preferred my protection to the danger of riding the roads. What gives him the courage to brave them now?'

D'Amiens shook his head as if to say he didn't know.

'The last I heard he was steward to Bourne.'

'You heard right, milady.'

'Yet these men—' she gestured behind her—'tell me he entered the town on foot. How so? Was Bourne not gracious enough to give him a horse?'

'It would seem not.' D'Amiens shook his head at the flicker of interest in her eyes. 'If you hope to make something out of it, you'll be disappointed, milady. De Courtesmain's disagreements with Bourne are small compared with the faults he finds in you and the man you call "cousin".'

'I don't doubt it. His grudges grow larger the longer he's away from the source. In Develish his complaints were against Foxcote.

In a week or two, his enemy will be Bourne. I have it in my heart to feel sorry for him. He finds it easier to blame his failings on others than on himself.'

'You'll not be so sympathetic when you see his evidence, milady. He has a page from the Develish register to demonstrate that what he says is true.'

She answered with a low laugh. 'Only *one*, Master d'Amiens? How selective he is in the lies he wishes to promote. I trust you'll allow me to question him on them.'

'As long as you accept my terms. Weapons and horses must be left outside the gate, and only you and your men may enter. I will not tolerate a foolish attempt at rescue if de Courtesmain's accusations are proven.'

'And who will decide that? You?'

'I stand for My Lord of Blandeforde in his absence.'

'In your own mind, perhaps, but not in mine. God demands that a lord deals fairly with all men, not just those they favour.' She lifted the parchment from her lap. 'This is the writ you ordered posted on the church door before last quarter day. Do you recall how it begins? Let me remind you. *Notwithstanding loss of life, the town will remit the same amount in tax as heretofore. The penalty for failure will be harsh.* You go on to list the weight of corn you demand in place of silver.' She raised her head. 'How do you record such payments, sir? As grain or coin?'

He frowned. 'I don't understand you, milady.'

'I'm sure you do, Master d'Amiens. Blandeforde is a King's treasurer. If the sovereign's share of the town's tax is recorded as grain, you will have a granary within the compound to store it. Does such a building exist?'

D'Amiens made no response, but Lady Anne saw the captain give a small shake of his head.

'Then you will have recorded the share in coin after using My Lord's private funds to purchase the grain for the household. I know of no law which forbids such a transaction, but the exchange must be documented so that all, including the King, are persuaded a fair price has been paid and the town's tax faithfully accounted. Will you send for the coffer that holds those monies and the ledger that shows how they were transferred? If all is as it should be, I will have confidence that you are capable of judging fairly between an English noble and a Norman steward.'

Ian thought how clever Lady Anne was to avoid vague accusations of dishonesty in favour of a detail that could be demonstrated. He watched conflicting emotions cross d'Amiens' face. Uncertainty. Disbelief. Calculation. The steward seemed to be struggling with the idea that a woman might be his equal in intelligence, and foolishly decided that she couldn't be. He shook his head impatiently. 'You waste my time with this nonsense. Do you think keeping track of My Lord's revenues is as easy as counting kirtles?'

'For your sake, I hope not, Master d'Amiens. Your pride will suffer badly if you lose your place to a chambermaid.'

A ripple of laughter ran through the crowd, and d'Amiens turned angrily to the captain, ordering him to ready his guard.

With a grunt of displeasure, Master Slater pushed himself through the gap between Ian's and Joshua's horses. 'Do you hold the freemen of Blandeforde in the same contempt as you hold Lady Anne of Develish?' he demanded. 'Our skill with accounting is easily the match of yours, for we trade daily and keep clear records of all we take. You inspected our ledgers often enough before the pestilence, now let us inspect yours, sir. Milady's not alone in questioning your honesty.'

Ian always wondered afterwards what would have happened if the captain had given different orders when the crowd, encouraged by Miller, flowed around the horses to align themselves with Slater. It may have been fear of being overrun that persuaded him to instruct his men to stand aside and allow the column through, but the small nod of respect he gave Lady Anne seemed to tell a different story.

∞

The sound of horses' hooves crunching on gravel, and the murmur of many voices, reached the men in the great hall. The priest, newly arrived with de Courtesmain, showed alarm, while the guards merely looked towards the doors with curiosity. It didn't seem to occur to them that a crowd might represent a threat, but it certainly did to Aristide. He rose to his feet from his position at the other end of the table from Thaddeus, and moved hastily up the room, de Courtesmain scurrying behind him. Thaddeus took satisfaction from the fear in their faces.

He studied Aristide with amusement. 'Who frightens you more?' he asked as the man drew close. 'The gentle lady loved by God or the unarmed townsfolk who accompany her?'

'None is cleansed. They carry the seeds of the pestilence within them.'

With a lazy smile, Thaddeus pushed himself from the chair and stepped out to confront him. 'Then why am I here? You know full well that my sins haven't been cleansed. I'd cut out my tongue before I'd confess to a priest such as you.'

'Get out of my way!'

Thaddeus took his chain in his hands and jerked it tight. 'I will not. You owe your lord's steward and his fighting men a better loyalty than to run at the first sign of trouble. They want to believe that God is on their side, not hiding away with a cringing liar for company.'

Aristide turned to the guards. 'This man is in your charge. Remove him from my path.'

But none responded. Perhaps they feared an elbow in their throats or, more simply, saw that obedience was unnecessary. Even as the priest spoke, their captain appeared in the open doorway and called for Father Aristide to join the steward on the forecourt. 'Master d'Amiens asks that you hold a Mass in the open air for the men of the town, Father. There are many who long to hear God's word and feel His presence amongst them again.'

Thaddeus lowered his hands. 'He's cleverer than I thought,' he said with a laugh. 'There's no safer way to soothe unsettled minds than through prayer. Be sure to preach love, Father. The steward won't have reason to thank you otherwise.'

Seventeen

As HE LISTENED TO THE priest recite his well-rehearsed homily, Thaddeus thought of the adage *A person's nature never changes.* A deceiver remains a deceiver; a generous heart remains generous. Even had Aristide wanted to preach God's love, he couldn't have done it, because instilling fear was the only way he knew to maintain his authority. Wrath and hellfire would always slip more easily off his tongue than forgiveness and redemption.

Too frightened to venture far onto the forecourt, he intoned his prayers and exhortations from inside the arched entranceway, and the vaulted ceiling caused his voice to echo back into the great hall. De Courtesmain sat with bent head and praying hands to Thaddeus's left, the guards to his right. All copied de Courtesmain's stance of piety, and Thaddeus watched their faces as they listened to words and phrases they must have heard a hundred times before. Wickedness had brought the pestilence to Blandeforde. Judgement Day was upon them. Absolution was the only salvation.

The young soldier whose sword he'd broken on Saturday night was closest to him, and he fancied the youth seemed more reluctant than his fellows to pretend devotion. Was he too sensible to believe in Little Sparrow's wickedness? And what of de Courtesmain? Where was *his* sense? Had his time in Develish taught him so little that he was happier to believe absolution more effective in keeping the household free of the pestilence than the killing of rats and the barring of gates?

To his left, he saw movement in the shadows around the archway to the kitchen and guessed servants were creeping from their work to listen. He wondered how many more were gathered about windows, and whether fathers, uncles, brothers and cousins were recognised amongst the crowd on the forecourt. If so, were any persuaded by the priest's strident condemnation of thievery and fornication as the twin devils that blighted the town? Did they truly think their men so lost to honesty and decency that they would indulge in such pursuits while the pestilence raged around them?

Perhaps. Oft-repeated doctrines burrowed all too easily into minds when other ideas were suppressed. Thaddeus found himself hoping a challenge would come from the men in the crowd— surely some must resent the slurs—but, if any tried, their voices were lost amongst the chanted responses, and he feared they were as easily swayed as the servants. Each man might know himself to be guiltless but, since he couldn't speak for others, Aristide would succeed in sowing the same doubts and suspicions through the town as he had in the house.

The young soldier leant towards him. 'Why do you shake your head?' he whispered. 'Do you doubt the truth of what the Father says?'

Thaddeus searched his face. 'His certainty surprises me. I wasn't aware he'd ever taken confession in the town.'

'He hasn't.'

'Yet he seems to know their sins. I wonder how.'

'He must have heard them from the Blandeforde priests before they died.'

Thaddeus smiled slightly. 'By committing a sin himself? It's a grave transgression to break the seal of the confessional. He would have expected to die as they did.'

The young man eyed him curiously. 'But there must be a reason why so many in the town have perished.'

'Indeed. And why, by contrast, so many in the household survive. It's a great puzzle.'

'Do you have the answer to it?'

Thaddeus turned to look at de Courtesmain. He was too tense to be at prayer. Every sinew in his body was straining to hear their whispered conversation. Thaddeus spoke louder. 'Ask this man. He knows the truth as well as anyone. Am I not right, Master de Courtesmain?'

A tremor of violent emotion ran through the Frenchman's body. 'Are you so lost to God that you think it right to disturb a man during Mass?'

Thaddeus smiled. 'My apologies. You were so insistent on staying inside that I thought you felt a show of devotion unnecessary. Is it Lady Anne you're trying to avoid? Perhaps you fear her censure? If so, your worries are groundless. She has never judged you unfairly.'

'You lie,' Hugh snapped. 'She judged me even before I arrived in Develish. No one who came from Foxcote would ever be acceptable to her.'

Thaddeus saw that the other guards were listening. 'Not true. She was unhappy to read what Lady Beatrix wrote about your zealotry in flogging serfs, but she made no other judgement. It was your sly manner and many deceits once you were in Develish that caused her to distrust you. You made the error of thinking all women as vicious and scheming as Lady Beatrix and failed to recognise that Milady is different.'

It seemed prayer was less enticing than self-justification, for Hugh dropped his hands to the table. 'She pretended timidity and dressed in homespun. How could a stranger to Develish know it was she and not her husband who ran the demesne?'

'Would you have behaved differently if you'd been told? Did you think it possible that a woman might be your equal in intelligence?'

'She goes against God's natural order by what she does. All should know their place.'

A smile creased Thaddeus's eyes. 'Do you know yours, sir? You switch loyalties so fast it's hard to keep up with you. Last June you were pledged to Sir Richard, in July to Lady Anne and by January to My Lord of Bourne. Should I assume now that you're sworn to Blandeforde? What price has Master d'Amiens demanded in return? Does your allegiance come cheaper each time you bend your neck to a new master?'

Hugh clenched his fists. 'Blame yourself for your imposture before you blame me for exposing it. I speak only the truth.'

'My friend here will be glad to hear it,' Thaddeus murmured, gesturing to the guard. 'He asks why so many have died in the town and so few in the house. Will you give him the answer?'

Such an anger consumed Hugh that he could barely control himself. 'The priest is right to call you the Devil,' he spat. 'I'll not speak your heresies. They corrupt all who hear them.'

He seemed unaware that their audience was growing. Figures were emerging from the shadows behind him as servants crept forward to hear their words above the priest's intoning of the Credo. *Crucifixus etiam pro nobis sub Pontio Pilato, passus et sepultus est, et resurrexit tertia die, secundum Scripturas, et ascendit in caelum, sedet ad dexteram Patris.*

Thaddeus made the sign of the cross. 'Where is the heresy in describing how Lady Anne has protected her people from the pestilence?' he asked mildly. 'Do you doubt God blesses Develish when not a single person there has died of it?'

'You cite God when it pleases you—not otherwise.'

'As do all men, even Father Aristide when he sees wickednesses that don't exist.' Thaddeus turned his head to look at the servants. 'He's taught these people to fear God instead of reminding them of His love. They should know He weeps as surely as they do over every innocent life that is lost.'

The young guard spoke into the silence that followed. 'How can you know the dead were innocent?'

'For the same reason you do, my friend. Our sins are more numerous than Little Sparrow's can ever have been.'

'Would she have lived if she'd been in Develish?'

'I believe so.'

'Why?'

'Milady is skilled in medicine and has taught her people that the best way to cure a disease is never to catch it. The merit of this lesson has been proved many times in Develish. The sick are treated in a hospital away from the village, and by such means illnesses rarely spread.' He paused to see if the guards and the servants understood him. They seemed to. 'When news of the pestilence first reached Develish, Milady reversed the method by secluding the healthy. She withdrew her people inside her moat and barred entry to all others, thereby keeping the sickness out.'

Confiteor unum baptisma in remissionem peccatorum et expecto resurrectionem mortuorum et vitam venturi saeculi.

'And all still live?'

'They do.'

'Was it for the same reason that Master d'Amiens ordered the gates barred here and forbade entry to townsmen?'

'Yes.'

A woman stirred. 'I helped Little Sparrow over the wall one night so that she might visit her mother in the town. It was forbidden to do such a thing but it broke my heart to see her cry. She loved her mother so much and missed her so greatly. Should I blame myself that she died? I thought her too sweet and innocent ever to warrant God's punishment.'

Thaddeus glanced from one to the other. 'Did you all view her in the same way?'

They nodded.

'Then believe in her goodness and know that God loved her as much as He loves you.' He turned back to the woman. 'Don't blame yourself, mistress. If you were persuaded wickedness was the cause of the pestilence, you had no reason to think an act of kindness would cause her death.'

'There were many who wanted to care for her when she fell to the fever,' said another, 'but the priest wouldn't allow it.'

'She was forced out as the three before her were,' said a man. 'Would Lady Anne have done the same had any succumbed in Develish?'

'There would have been no forcing,' Thaddeus answered. 'All were agreed that, for the good of the demesne, sufferers would take themselves willingly across the moat to spend their last days in the hospital. There was no other way to protect the healthy.'

'Are you saying the priest was right to do what he did?' asked the guard.

Thaddeus glanced towards the entranceway. 'He was . . . though his reasons were less than honest. He had no cause to berate the maid and none to berate the townsmen now. They've shown mercy to every sufferer who's come to Blandeforde and their compassion has cost them dear. Any grief you feel for Little Sparrow is far surpassed by theirs for their dead families.'

Whatever he'd hoped to provoke by his statements, it wasn't that Hugh de Courtesmain would pull out a knife and plunge it into the flesh of his shoulder. Thaddeus took the stab for a punch until de Courtesmain rose to his feet with screams of 'heretic' and 'corrupter', and began chopping down at him with a bloodied blade. The assault was so fierce, and Thaddeus so unprepared for it, that he took several more blows in his arm and shoulder before, with a grunt of pain, he thrust himself out of his chair. All was confusion. The Frenchman's cries were overlaid by shouts from the guards and panicked wailing from the maids, and the only thing Thaddeus could think to do was block de Courtesmain's next strike with his left hand.

It may have been a second only that he stared into de Courtesmain's eyes as the steel drove through his palm. It felt longer. He clamped his right hand over the Frenchman's wrist to prevent him withdrawing the weapon, and he had time to wonder if the frenzied creature was acting for himself or the priest. The priest, he thought, when de Courtesmain loosened his grip in order to pull himself free and an embossed cross, much smeared with gore, was revealed on the dagger's haft.

Thaddeus watched dispassionately as the guards wrestled de Courtesmain to the ground and then resumed his seat, placing the edge of his hand on the table. 'Will you be kind enough to bring me a bowl of heated water and some salt, mistress?' he asked the woman who'd spoken first. 'Also clean, boiled rags for binding. The wound will mend faster with a little care.'

She stared at the four-inch blade piercing his palm, and the blood dripping onto the table, then raised her eyes to his, clearly wondering if she would be right to help him. Whatever she saw seemed to persuade her. 'I will, sire,' she said with a nod, beckoning to three young maids to accompany her. 'Whatever the reason for your wounds and shackles, I wouldn't want you thinking My Lord's household less charitable than his town.'

ೲ

Lady Anne had taken Ian's advice to remain mounted during the Mass, which meant they remained at the rear of the crowd, close to where the driveway entered the forecourt. To descend would have put them on the same level as the men of the town, and while none seemed to be showing signs of the pestilence, there was no knowing if they were hiding fevers or carrying fleas. Ian had fewer qualms about entering the house. Like Thaddeus, he took the barricaded gate and the guildsmen's tale of the young maid's expulsion to mean the steward had used the same measures as Lady Anne to keep the pestilence out. Even so, he kept a constant watch for rats.

Lady Anne was more interested in the steward and the priest. She sat with bent head, apparently at prayer, watching them from beneath her lashes. Both gave every indication that they knew the pestilence was caught and not imposed by God. D'Amiens stood well apart from the kneeling crowd on the other side of the forecourt, surrounded by the guards who'd kept the townsmen at a distance as they'd shepherded him up the driveway. The priest remained within the arched porchway, ready to retreat at the first sign of trouble.

She wondered if she'd ever seen a man so nervous. He found every reason to maintain a good space between himself and the crowd, ordering them to their knees at the centre of the forecourt and making it clear at the outset that, without unleavened bread, there could be no Eucharist. All he could offer was the liturgy and a blessing. He chastised the men for their impatience and urged them to leave and return the following day, when the servants had had time to prepare the proper repast; but Master Slater called out that they'd take what Father Aristide could give them now rather than gamble on the morrow. The irony in his tone told everyone they would wait through eternity before the priest found the courage to draw close enough to place bread into their mouths.

Lady Anne's reaction to the homily was similar to Thaddeus's. Though spoken in heavily accented English, she thought it sounded rehearsed, as if Father Aristide had delivered it every day since the pestilence first entered Blandeforde; but, unlike Thaddeus, she saw the impact his accusations of fornication and thievery had on his listeners. They eyed each other in puzzlement, as if to ask where such ideas had come from and, were it not for the ingrained respect they had for the Mass, she felt sure one or more would have asked the question aloud. Certainly, the restless movements of Master Miller and his supporters suggested they were far from pleased to be charged with sins they hadn't committed.

The priest raised his voice at the end of the Credo to remind the crowd of his authority. 'I believe in one Holy, Catholic and

Apostolic Church. I confess one baptism for the remission of sins, and I look for the resurrection of the dead, and the life of the world to come. Amen.' He stood in silence for several long moments as the kneeling men crossed themselves and then began the bidding prayers.

Only Joshua was close enough to hear the shouting in the great hall. Before the Mass began, he'd steered his horse and the pack ponies towards a tethering rail which was attached to the sill of a window to the right of the entranceway. He was too curious not to look inside as he leant forward to loop the ponies' halters around the bar. The sun outside was very bright and the gloom of the interior very dark, but he felt certain he could make out Thaddeus seated at the end of a long table.

Dimness and distance obscured the man's features, but he appeared a head taller than those around him. He seemed at ease and Joshua wondered sourly why they'd wasted so much energy on him since the chances were he'd already convinced the steward he was Athelstan. He willed Thaddeus to look in his direction, but his friend's interest was fixed on the priest in the entranceway.

Joshua's position left him exposed to the eyes of the townsmen, and he felt obliged to pretend a greater devotion than his companions, who were behind them. He lowered his head and closed his eyes but, being deeply weary after two anxiety-filled nights, the dreary drone of the priest's sermonising sent him to sleep. He couldn't say what woke him unless it was his dogs' restlessness. They were ranged as a pack slightly in front of his mount, hindquarters quivering and muzzles pointing towards the entranceway.

His immediate assumption was that the priest's decision to advance onto the forecourt was unsettling them. His black cope fluttered around him as he walked and his chants grew louder and more strident. For those in front of him, the sound of his voice drowned out all others, but Joshua distinctly heard the wailing cries of women from inside the house. He turned in alarm towards the window, but the sun was reflecting off the panes and there was no seeing through them. He guessed there were other cries he couldn't hear when one of the mastiffs began to inch forward with growls rumbling in his throat.

Joshua hadn't time to debate the rights and wrongs of what he did. He flung himself from his saddle, drew his sword and ordered the pack on. He might resent this one dog's annoying loyalty to Thaddeus, but he was no more inclined than the animal to stand idly by if his friend was in trouble. As he ran towards the entranceway, he saw the guards around the steward reach for their bows, but he was well inside before any had nocked their arrows.

There was such a confusion of people in the hall that the dogs ran hither and thither, barking ferociously. Joshua saw women and maids scattering in terror towards the walls, while a group of liveried men seemed to be struggling with a prisoner. He thought he recognised him as Hugh de Courtesmain but scarce gave him a glance, for his eyes were fixed firmly on the manacled figure at the end of the table. With a command to his dogs to come to heel, he strode down the room and positioned himself at Thaddeus's side, stationing the pack around him.

'Your mastiff sensed you were in trouble, My Lord, and he would seem to have been right.' He looked at the knife through Thaddeus's hand and the seeping gashes in his coat. 'Did the guards do this?'

'No, Buckler. They've shown me only courtesy. You may lower your sword. No harm will come to us from them, though you have my permission to set the pack on de Courtesmain if he slips their clutches.'

Joshua stared at the Frenchman for a moment. 'They'd make short work of him, sire. There's not enough flesh on him to satisfy one dog, let alone seven. Should I pull the knife from your hand?'

'Not yet, my young friend. It's all that's staunching the flow. I've been promised water and bandages by a kindly servant.'

'You're bleeding from other places, My Lord, and those wounds might be as bad. We should remove your coat so that Lady Anne can tend to you. She is outside and will know better than servants what to do.'

A faint smile lifted Thaddeus's mouth. 'Indeed, but even she will have to remove my shackles first.' He watched the doors darken as the captain and several fighting men entered the hall with swords raised. 'Place your weapons on the table and step away from me,' he murmured. 'Let them see you're not a threat. There's no reason for any more blood to be spilt.'

∞

Lady Anne placed a warning hand on Ian's wrist as half the men surrounding the steward set off in pursuit of Joshua. 'Do nothing,' she whispered. 'To fight would be madness. Thaddeus will be saying the same to Joshua.'

'What if he can't, milady? Joshua wouldn't have entered unless he thought him in danger. They could both be in trouble.'

'Then they must help each other. I will not allow you to imperil the lives of the townsmen by acting foolishly. I gave a pledge of peace and will not break it.'

She said no more and Ian sensed rebellion coming from his twin as the dreary Latin ritual continued. *Why had she refused*

*the steward's orders for them to disarm if she wasn't prepared to
let them fight?* Perhaps the question was his own, for he felt the
same frustration. But he also knew the answer. No lord would
have accepted orders from a man of lower status. For Lady Anne
to obey d'Amiens would have been to acknowledge that his rank
was above hers, and she would have lost the townsmen's respect.

But was their respect worth having, Ian wondered, as he
watched the dutiful crowd respond to every prompt the priest
gave? Not one seemed to wonder why he had advanced onto the
forecourt and raised his voice. To Ian it was obvious that some
noise had erupted inside the house which the priest was trying
to hide. But what? Had Thaddeus called for help? Was Joshua
expecting his friends to follow him? Ian knew he hadn't imagined
the barking of the dogs afterwards.

He observed the captain emerge from the entranceway, relieved
to see that his sword was sheathed and his livery unruffled.
Nevertheless, the man appeared a reluctant bearer of news as he
whispered a hesitant explanation into the steward's ear. Whatever
he said was met with anger. D'Amiens' eyes narrowed to slits
before he whispered a command and then dismissed the captain
with an abrupt nod.

'Keep faith,' Lady Anne breathed as the captain set off at a
run towards the western end of the building. 'If anyone is dead
or dying, the steward would have ordered him brought outside
to the priest. They both hold too fast to Church ritual to deny a
man the last rites.'

'What if you're wrong?' whispered Olyver.

'Better two die than fifty.'

In her own way she was as ruthless as Thaddeus, Ian thought,
and he wondered if she would react as coldly if he challenged her

decision. 'As Athelstan's men, we should be at his side, milady. A lord's soldiers are pledged to protect him. The steward must be wondering why only Joshua has gone to his master's aid.'

'Did you honour your pledge two nights ago?'

Ian shifted uncomfortably. 'You know we did not, milady. Thaddeus wouldn't allow it.'

'And wouldn't now. It's not force that can release him, only persuasion.' She nodded to the far corner of the house. 'I see the captain returning. Can you make out what he has in his hand?'

'A ring of keys, milady.'

'How strange,' she murmured. 'I wonder what purpose they have if they're kept outside.'

❧

The captain refused to approach until Joshua and his dogs had retreated ten paces. 'I need your parole, sire,' he told Thaddeus. 'The steward won't allow me to release you from your chains unless you make your pledge before witnesses. Speak loud enough for the servants to hear.'

Thaddeus glanced towards the assembled household. 'You are the captain's witnesses that I give my parole gladly and will make no attempt to escape.' He turned back. 'Will that suffice? In truth, I'm too tired even to stand at the moment.'

The captain tut-tutted as he used one of the keys to unscrew the metal bar that held the manacle in place on Thaddeus's left hand. 'I hope you don't blame my men, sire. They thought he was slapping you until they saw the knife.'

'I also. Take care not to touch it. I doubt the pain will be so easily borne if the blade moves.'

The captain eased off the hoop of the shackle and dropped it onto Thaddeus's lap. 'It can't stay there forever, sire,' he said, moving around the chair to unlock the other manacle. 'Would you have me draw it for you?'

'No thank you, my friend. I'll do it myself when the servants bring me the means to cleanse and bind it. What keeps them so long?'

A woman stepped forward. 'You asked for clean, boiled rags, My Lord.'

'Is that an unusual request?'

'It is, sire. We have no store of clean rags. Mistress Wilde is scrubbing a threadbare kirtle with tallow soap in order to cut it into strips for boiling. She begs your pardon for the time it is taking.'

'And I hers for putting her to the trouble.' Thaddeus thought for a moment. 'Is my charger outside, Buckler?' he asked.

'He is, My Lord. He carries Lady Anne.'

'Then perhaps the captain will allow you to retrieve the packs from behind the saddle. There are some linen braies inside which I know to be clean since I've yet to find a use for them.' He smiled at the ripple of laughter that ran through the women at this mention of undergarments. 'You would pity me if you knew of the folds linen braies form inside my britches when I'm riding. They rub most severely.'

'My Lord says the same, sire,' called a man. 'He too refuses to wear them, never mind how much Milady begs him to follow the customs of the King and his court.'

'Milady would beg even harder if she had to launder his britches,' said a woman's voice.

The jest brought laughter from all the servants, but there was a tinge of wildness to their merriment which seemed to speak less to humour than the release of long pent-up emotions. Thaddeus beckoned Joshua forward as the sound rippled on. 'Will you permit my man to go?' he asked the captain. 'This blade will be harder to pull the longer it stays in place and I need clean wadding to stem the flow of blood.'

The captain gathered the chain and shackles into a pile on the table. 'I'll have to accompany him, My Lord. The steward won't allow him to approach your cousin alone. There's no knowing how she'll react if he speaks to her of what's happened here.'

'She'll learn soon enough.'

'Maybe so, sire, but Master d'Amiens won't want her inciting the townsmen. He fears the admiration they seem to have for her. We live in strange times. Such people wouldn't normally accept the leadership of a woman.'

Eighteen

JOSHUA KEPT TO HIMSELF THAT he'd moved all the bags from Killer to one of the pack ponies before the descent into Blandeforde. This might be his only chance to pass information to Lady Anne and he had no intention of foregoing it. Yet the plan looked like coming to nought when the captain noticed there was nothing before or behind Milady's saddle. He stood with Joshua inside the vaulted porch, waiting for the priest to end a prayer, and even with her skirts draping her mount's loins, she was too slight and small to hide the absence of bulky leather packs. When he asked for an explanation, Joshua explained in a whisper that My Lord's bags had been shared amongst his fighting men in order to give Milady a more comfortable ride. He gestured towards Edmund and Peter, positioned some fifteen paces behind Lady Anne, as the carriers.

This information pleased the captain. He instructed Joshua to follow him down the great hall and through the archway to the kitchen. It was uninhabited except for Mistress Wilde and the maid servants who bobbed worried curtsies when they came in, only to resume their scrubbing in relief when nothing was said about their tardiness. The captain opened a door and ushered Joshua outside.

'We're at the eastern end of the house, and your two companions are well to the rear of the crowd. We'll not be seen by the townsmen if we approach from this direction. You understand there's to be no conversation. Your single task is to retrieve your master's packs.'

Joshua stared at the ground for a moment, wondering whether it was better to defy the man now or later. He raised his eyes to look directly into the captain's. 'I understand those are *your* wishes, sir, but My Lord gave no such instructions, and his is the only authority I recognise.'

The man sighed. 'Then I can't let you fetch the packs. My orders are to keep Milady from Athelstan until the steward's had time to question her.'

'How does my speaking with my companions break that command?'

'He looks to catch Milady in a lie and will believe you're delivering a message from Athelstan if he sees you talking with any in her entourage.'

Joshua hid his curiosity well, but his thoughts were racing. 'I have no message to give except that My Lord has been wounded,' he said slowly. 'Is that the news Master d'Amiens hopes to keep secret?'

'The wounds don't interest him—only what was said in the church. He gave the order to keep them apart when he first learnt of Lady Anne's arrival. It has to do with a pledge your master made to Milady. Only she can release him from it.'

Joshua made a good pretence at puzzlement. 'Then you have nothing to fear. Such secrets are never shared with fighting men.

I seek only to repeat My Lord's request that no more blood is to be shed. What fault would the steward find in that?'

'None if he knew what you were saying.'

'Then where's the harm? You can tell him afterwards that that is all I said.'

'He'll not believe me unless Milady's story conflicts with your lord's.'

Joshua measured the distance between him and Edmund. Twenty paces? Thirty paces? 'He needn't see me at all if you shield me from his view as we cross the forecourt,' he said reasonably. 'I'll be well hidden once I'm between the horses.'

The captain gave a grunt of derision. 'And how do I achieve that? We're of a similar height, and my girth is not so large that it will cover yours.'

Joshua glanced into the kitchen. 'A group of four women in skirts would hide me as long as I walk in a crouch at their side. Has Mistress Wilde the authority to offer cordial to Lady Anne? It would be what hospitality demands for anyone who's ridden as far as she has this day.'

'Mass is being said.'

'All the more reason to show a small act of charity.' Joshua searched the other's face. 'If you have no sympathy for Milady's weariness, at least find some for My Lord. He was more than fair to excuse your guards from blame in his wounding. You owe him a debt of gratitude for that at least.'

With a shrug, the captain stepped back into the kitchen. 'But not you,' he warned. 'Remember that when the steward orders your arrest.' He paused. 'You'd be wise to take off your tabard. You might pass for a servant in tunic and britches.'

Well to the rear of the crowd, Edmund had felt no obligation to feign interest in the Mass. Instead, he'd spent his time studying the house and the land around it. From where he was positioned, he could see both the guards' quarters and the church tower and, though he didn't know what function the smaller building performed, he made a good guess when the captain hurried towards it and two liveried men opened the door to him. After a brief conversation, another appeared in the opening with a ring of keys in his hand.

It was a small step to connect the keys with imprisonment. Edmund recalled an occasion from his childhood when Peter's father, the Develish blacksmith, had forged and hammered iron manacles into hinges for the latrine door after Sir Richard issued an edict that they were never to be used again for the purpose of punishing serfs. Few believed Sir Richard had known what he was signing, but everyone took pleasure in watching the hoops being converted to better use.

Had the captain returned with chains as well as keys, Edmund would have believed they were intended for Joshua, but keys alone suggested unlocking rather than locking. And the thought occurred to him that Joshua and his dogs had somehow effected Thaddeus's release. If the irritating churl had said once that his dogs were worth an army, he'd said it a hundred times, and Edmund pictured him strutting like a cockerel as d'Amiens' guards trembled before ferocious teeth. He watched the entranceway to see who emerged, though in truth he couldn't decide whether he wanted to see Joshua come out in triumph or with his tail between his legs.

A quarter-hour passed before he caught the flutter of women's skirts out of the corner of his eye. He looked to his right and saw a strange procession make its way from the side of the house towards him and Peter. A matronly servant, carrying a silver goblet, was at the head and three young maids, clutching flagons and bonbons, followed close behind. They approached so close to Peter's mount that the animal became restless and Edmund had only the briefest impression of a figure slipping from their midst as Peter laid a soothing hand on his horse's neck.

'Face forward and say nothing,' whispered Joshua, dropping to a crouch between him and Peter. 'All will come to nought if the steward knows I'm here.'

Edmund did as he was bid, watching the servants move in front of Lady Anne's and the twins' horses. Across the heads of the crowd, he saw that d'Amiens' gaze was upon them and, while the steward frowned at their offering of cordial to Milady, he made no move to prevent it. Perhaps he feared the townsmen's reaction if he denied her refreshment. She was most gracious in her acceptance, winning smiles and curtsies from the women.

'I have messages,' Joshua breathed next. 'Thaddeus is wounded but not dying. His attacker was Master de Courtesmain. The guards seem to have a liking for Thaddeus because his shackles have been removed. The servants, too, since they wish to tend his cuts. Thaddeus has told them all that he wants no more blood to be shed and this has increased their sympathy for him. Lady Anne should play on that while remaining wary of the steward. He looks to catch her in a lie by questioning her before she has a chance to speak with Thaddeus. I am told by the captain that the issue concerns a pledge Thaddeus made to Milady and from which only she can release him. But I'm guessing Thaddeus fabricated the story and Milady will be as ignorant as I of what this pledge concerns.'

Edmund leant forward to adjust his horse's noseband. 'Why did the Frenchman attack Thaddeus?'

'I don't know; perhaps anger that the guards are treating him as a lord. De Courtesmain's own status seems much reduced since we last saw him.'

Edmund watched the matron gather the maids together again. 'Make ready,' he muttered. 'The servants are returning. Stay sharp, my friend.'

'You, too,' came the whispered response before Joshua's stooping figure was hidden once again amidst the swirl and rustle of skirts.

The next Edmund saw of him was when he and the captain came out through the entranceway. Joshua, fully dressed again in livery, hurried to the pack ponies to remove Thaddeus's crested leather bags and then hastened back inside the house. The captain turned to follow, but not before dropping to one knee and crossing himself as the priest began the absolution.

Deus, Pater misericordiarum, qui per mortem et resurrectionem Filii . . .

Edmund nudged his mount towards Peter's. 'How do we close the gap between us and Lady Anne without making the steward suspicious?' he murmured. 'We must give her the messages before the service ends. There may not be a chance afterwards.'

Peter nodded. 'A spooked horse won't raise suspicions,' he said, studying the fifteen-yard distance. Without warning, he slid his left boot from his stirrup and drove a sharp kick into the soft flesh between the chest and foreleg of Edward's mount.

Idiot, thought Edmund, as the animal skittered sideways instead of forwards. It took all his skill to turn the creature's head and dance it broadside on towards the rear of Ian's horse while making a pretence of trying to calm it.

The nervous scraping of hooves infected Killer, and Ian turned with an angry order for Edmund to bring his horse under control before Milady was thrown. Edmund made to obey but his handling of the reins was so inept that the animal was alongside Ian's before he had enough command to drop from the saddle. He ducked beneath its neck to make a clumsy bow of apology to Lady Anne and then, with his back to the steward, took hold of its nose collar and ran a soothing hand down its shoulder.

'Can you hear me, milady?' he whispered.

෨ඏ

Thaddeus locked his gaze with Hugh de Courtesmain's as he gripped the haft of the knife and pulled the four-inch blade through his palm. He needed the other's hatred to act as a spur because he knew before he began that the pain would be severe. Yet no amount of imagining had told him how severe. The rawness of the wound, dulled by the length of time he'd kept his hand rigid and unmoving on the table, blazed to life again as the steel ripped through already clotting blood. He was unaware of how pale he became as his mind reacted in shock to this second slicing of tender flesh but he made no sound as he placed the knife on the table and clenched his fist around a balled linen braie to stop the flow of blood. He took satisfaction from the disbelief in de Courtesmain's eyes. If he'd achieved nothing else, he'd demonstrated to the Frenchman that, in a battle of wills between them, his was the stronger.

He allowed Joshua to ease the left sleeve of his coat down his arm and then do the same with his embroidered jerkin. Beneath, the white fabric of the shirt showed seven saturated tears on the upper arm and shoulder where the blade had penetrated. Thaddeus shook his head when Joshua urged him to draw his arm from that sleeve as well. 'Let's wait for Mistress Wilde and her bandages. The wounds are no more than pinpricks thanks to the thickness of my coat and jerkin.' He stirred the knife with his right hand. 'Did you steal this or was it given to you?' he asked de Courtesmain. 'I see that the haft is embossed with a cross.'

When De Courtesmain remained silent, the captain, who was standing to Thaddeus's right, ordered him to speak.

'I'll not answer questions from a slave.'

'You'll wear these if you don't,' said the captain coolly, jerking his chin at the shackles on the table. 'My Lord's not alone in wanting answers. You involved my men in your madness when you attacked their prisoner.'

'They should have remembered what he was when they chose to sit at the table with him. A prisoner should know his place and so should the men who guard him.'

The captain eyed him thoughtfully for a moment. 'You're strangely arrogant for a would-be murderer,' he murmured, leaning forward to push the shackles and keys across the table. 'But you're right to remind me that a prisoner should know his place.' He beckoned to the young guard to pick them up. 'Wrap the chain around a pillar before you secure the manacles.'

From outside came the blessing. *Benedicat vos omnipotens Deus, Pater et Filius et Spiritus Sanctus.*

◌

Lady Anne watched the townsmen rise to their feet and clasp each other's hands in friendship. How clever d'Amiens had been to call a Mass, she thought. Knees might be sore and creaking after an hour at prayer on hard ground, but animosities and grievances were forgotten in the spirit of forgiveness that came with absolution and blessing. Several of the men glanced towards the sun, recalling tasks that needed performing, then turned towards the driveway in preparation for departure. Even if she knew the words that might persuade them to stay, she doubted the wisdom of introducing a woman's voice into the solemn quiet that possessed them. The respect they'd shown her in the town would not be replicated if she assumed the right to speak in a place which, however briefly, had served them as a church.

The priest understood this well, for he remained where he was, head bent in prayer and hands folded about the bejewelled cross that he wore on a chain around his neck. Lady Anne wondered if he'd sought permission from his bishop to adorn himself with such a showy ornament or if the idea had been his. Either way, his continued communion with God prolonged the townsmen's sense that the forecourt was a holy place and deterred any from approaching him. Seeing this, d'Amiens did the same, closing his eyes and pressing his palms together beneath his lowered chin, and within minutes the men at the margins of the crowd began to disperse, their appetite for confrontation dispelled as they walked past Lady Anne and Thaddeus's companions towards the driveway.

'If the rest leave, we must go with them,' murmured Lady Anne. 'To stay will be to accept the power of the priest, and through him the governance of Church law. Do you understand?'

'Yes, milady,' said Ian, Olyver and Edmund in unison.

'Then make ready. My hope is the steward is eager enough to speak with me to request that we stay; I can make better terms with him than with the priest.'

'But what if he doesn't, milady?' Ian asked anxiously. 'Who will tend Thaddeus's wounds?'

'He must manage them himself.'

'What of Joshua?'

'He must stay with Thaddeus. There'll be no bargaining either's release from a position of weakness.'

She took Miller and his supporters as her guide. When they began to stray from the forecourt, she instructed Ian to follow. He paused only to beckon Peter forward and order him and Edmund to retrieve Joshua's horse and the pack ponies before nodding to Olyver to draw Killer into a turn. The dirt road was behind them, and they had barely circled their mounts to face it when a guard hurried across the gravel to address Lady Anne.

'The steward forbids your departure, milady.'

'Has he ordered you to make me your prisoner?'

'I'm ordered to prevent you leaving, milady.'

'Then you have my sympathies,' she said. 'I trust he will be understanding of your failure.'

The man reached nervously for his sword but thought better of it when Ian shook his head. 'Only a fool starts a war for no reason,' he murmured, listening to the stamp of hooves as Edmund and Peter came up behind them. 'Be good enough to step aside. You'll not survive a trampling from eight horses.'

The guard retreated in front of them, creating enough of a delay for d'Amiens and the remaining guards to make their way around the forecourt and form a line across the driveway. By doing so, they split the townsmen into two groups, with Miller and his supporters on one side and the rest on the other. Ian wondered whether this was by accident or design. Did the steward hope to intimidate those confined with Lady Anne? If so, he prayed that

Miller, yet to round the bend in the road, would look back to see what was happening.

D'Amiens sketched a small bow. 'Why this sudden urge to depart, milady?' he asked in French. 'Was the Mass not to your liking?'

She answered in English, her voice carrying well in the still air. 'It was hardly a Mass, Master d'Amiens. In Develish, our priest would not deny supplicants the Eucharist for want of unleavened bread.'

'Father Aristide is obedient to the teachings of Christ, milady.'

She smiled. 'Yet I don't recall Jesus telling us what form the bread should take. All the gospels use the same words. *He took bread and when He had given thanks, He brake it and gave it to them, saying, "This is my body which is given for you."* Is Father Aristide's Bible different from mine that he thinks yeasted bread forbidden?'

D'Amiens refused to be drawn. 'I asked about your sudden urge to depart, milady. It's but two hours since you were demanding entrance. What has changed?'

'My hope that you can ever be an honest judge, sir. You led me to believe you would bring out your ledgers for inspection, but instead you summoned the priest to denounce the townsmen as wicked. For what reason unless to divert attention from your own guilt?'

D'Amiens watched the crowd turn their heads to listen more closely. 'Most seemed comforted by the Mass, milady,' he said in French. 'Only you appear troubled by it. Could it be you heard your own sins mentioned by the priest?'

She searched his face for a moment and then pressed her right palm to her breast. 'I don't know what might lead you to make such an accusation, Master d'Amiens,' she answered in English, 'but I can swear, hand on heart and with Almighty God as my witness, that I have never committed the sins of fornication and thievery. I would go further, and say I am grievously offended that you would cast such slurs against me.'

A murmur came from the crowd, and Ian glanced round to see Slater step forward. 'I, too, am offended,' he said, pressing his own palm to his chest. 'And will likewise swear before Almighty God that I am innocent of what the priest accuses me. My wife, now dead, is the only woman I have loved, and stealing has never tempted me.'

The voices of his fellows rose in agreement as hand after hand thumped against chests, and their cries of innocence brought Miller and his supporters hurrying back. They skirted around the guards and lined themselves beside the greybeard, assuming the same stance of right palm to left breast.

'If fornication and thievery brought the pestilence to Blandeforde,' Miller called, 'then the culprits must be here and not in the town. Father Aristide blames us unfairly.'

Andrew Tench moved forward to join their rank. 'Our priests knew our weaknesses better than he, and they rarely sermonised about mortal sin even before the pestilence came.'

'They were good men all,' said Slater. 'Before they died, they begged us to hold to the path of righteousness, and we have tried to do so. No man here would claim to know another's secrets, but we can all speak of the kindness and care our town has shown the many sufferers who have sought sanctuary over the last half-year. Have you and My Lord's household been as generous, Master d'Amiens? Has the priest?'

D'Amiens stared hard at him as if committing his face to memory. 'You stray into heresy with such questions. Only God knows why the house is blessed and the town condemned.' He raised his voice. 'Am I not right, Father Aristide?'

When no answer came, all turned to look for the black-robed figure. But he was gone, and his absence gave Slater courage.

'Where's the heresy in asking how many sufferers you've tended?' he asked d'Amiens. 'We don't question God's plan for us, only why you sent your sick to us instead of caring for them yourselves. We know of four you expelled but none that you've kept and cared for.'

'None was expelled. They left of their own free will.'

The lie was so blatant—as evidenced by the discomfort of the guards—that a silence followed. It fell to Lady Anne, who had heard the story of the little maid from Edmund, to break it, but rather than challenge d'Amiens on his falsehood, she questioned his judgement.

'Did you not have a duty to stop them?' she asked. 'I cannot believe My Lord of Blandeforde would have wanted more sufferers inflicted on his town when they had taken in so many already.'

D'Amiens eyed her with dislike. 'Do not to try my patience too far,' he said in French. 'You delude yourself if you think can incite these men to support you against my guards.'

'I wouldn't ask it of them,' she answered in the same language. 'I have more care for their lives than you do. Your guards also. I wish harm to no man. Yourself included.'

He gave a contemptuous laugh. 'We can all speak brave words from the back of a horse, milady. If lives matter so much to you, descend and stand amongst the townsmen. Your presence on the ground is their best protection, for I'll not order my soldiers to make war on Lady Anne of Develish.'

'You may come to regret that promise, Master d'Amiens.'

He shook his head. 'You haven't kept your people free of the pestilence all these months to act the fool now. Cease your stirring and encourage this rabble to return to their homes. I give my word that you and Thurkell will receive a fair hearing.'

Lady Anne held his gaze for a moment and then turned to Ian. 'Oblige me by assisting me from my saddle,' she said in English. 'I have more faith that Master d'Amiens' guards will honour his first pledge than I do that he will uphold his second.'

Ian's resistance was obvious. 'Are you sure, milady? I doubt the men of Blandeforde would expect you to act as their shield.'

She nodded. 'In Develish, we set fourteen days as the period of exclusion for a man to prove he was well. Here, eight weeks have passed without a death. Do you ask me to show less friendship to these worthy people than to My Lord of Bourne or the serfs of Pedle Hinton?'

Ian nudged his mount backwards and passed his reins to Peter before swinging himself to the ground. 'No, milady,' he said, reaching up to support her dismount. 'My Lord of Athelstan would say the same. Will you allow me the privilege of accompanying you?'

Nineteen

GYLES STARTOUT BROUGHT HIS SMALL convoy to a halt as they breasted the hill above Blandeforde. To his right rode his brother Alleyn, to his left James Buckler. All wore threadbare tabards with the crest of Sir Richard of Develish, these being the only garments left in Develish that might lift them above the level of serfs. The livery looked well enough from a distance but Gyles didn't doubt the moth-eaten fabric would invite derision at close quarters. He had no greater hopes that their mounts, stolen from Holcombe by Lord Bourne, would strike a more commanding appearance. Two seasons on the pastureland by the moat had left them unbrushed and unkempt, giving them more the air of carthorses than chargers.

They certainly hadn't made for a comfortable journey. So long unridden, they had responded poorly to their bits and, with no time to soften the saddle leather with oil and tallow, all three men had suffered. It led Gyles to wonder if Lady Anne could possibly have reached Blandeforde. Was she capable of riding so far when even he, the most experienced horseman, winced with every unexpected lurch in his brute's uneven gait? The only sounds that had come from James and Alleyn's mouths had been full-throated oaths, and both gave sighs of relief as the town came into sight below them.

By the sun, Gyles estimated it was an hour past noon, and he questioned again whether Lady Anne could be ahead of them. She may have had an eight-hour start on him and his companions, having left Develish at midnight, but they had ridden at a fast gallop and her lack of horsemanship would have kept her to a slow walk until dawn. He cursed himself for not insisting that John ask sensible questions of his son instead of spending his time berating the youth about misplaced loyalty. If Gyles knew where Edmund had left his companions, he would have a better idea of Lady Anne's progress.

James Buckler stood in his stirrups to relieve the pressure on his aching groin. 'What's worrying you?' he asked.

'That we've arrived before Lady Anne. I've known her fifteen years but I've never seen her on horseback. She told me she'd manage with Edmund's help but . . .' He shook his head.

'You think she's given up?'

'There's a good chance.'

Alleyn was studying the verge to the left of the highway. 'Horses have stopped here recently,' he said. 'Do you see how the grass has been trampled? I'm guessing they were allowed to graze while their riders looked down on Blandeforde. Who else could it be but Lady Anne and your sons?'

'The steward's fighting men?' suggested Gyles. 'For all we know they've been scouring the countryside since Thaddeus was arrested.'

There was a thoughtful silence, broken by James Buckler. 'Then what are we doing here?' he asked. 'You could have foreseen all this before we left Develish.'

'I felt I had to try.'

'For Lady Eleanor's sake?'

'Isabella's, too. Her pleas were as heartfelt.' Gyles glanced at Alleyn. 'I even had your Robert joining in.'

'The lad's in search of adventure. He'd have taken my place if you'd permitted it.'

Gyles shook his head. 'It's more than that. He fears Eleanor will harm herself if anything happens to Lady Anne. Both he and Isabella say she'll blame herself if Milady is taken in charge for heresy.'

'With good cause,' said James. 'She should have had more sense than to denounce Lady Anne in front of de Courtesmain.'

'Would you have her kill herself over it now? Robert assures me that's what she'll do if harm comes to Lady Anne through her fault.'

James nodded to the leather knapsack behind Gyles's saddle. 'Will the documents you're carrying prevent that?'

'Isabella believes so—as long as it's Master de Courtesmain who betrays us and I can place them in Lady Anne's hands before she's obliged to answer to him.'

'Hence your fussing over whether she's behind or ahead of us.'

Gyles nodded. 'She must read them first. They'll serve no purpose at all if her dreams were misguided and it's Bourne who informs against Thaddeus.'

James grinned. 'You never think anything she does misguided.'

'There's always a first time.'

'But not today,' Alleyn murmured, jerking his chin towards the right-hand edge of the highway. 'That pile of turd looks like dog excrement to me.' He turned his gaze on Blandeforde. 'You must have more faith, brother—if not in Lady Anne, then in God and your sons. The boys will have found a way to make the journey easier for her, and God loves her too much to lead her wrong now.'

❧

The town appeared empty of life. There were no guards on the bridge and no people in the streets. Gyles was reminded of riding through Dorchester in the early days of the pestilence, when a pall of death had hung over the streets, but he didn't have that same sense here. There were too many signs of recent industry— broached barrels of ale outside tavern doors, the scent of newly baked bread, sheep carcasses hanging from a beam outside a shop.

He knew Blandeforde well from visits he'd made in the past as part of Sir Richard's retinue, and needed no directions on how to find the manor house. Nevertheless, as they neared the turning which led to it he had a growing fear that they were riding towards a flogging. Or worse.

The whip had been banned in Develish for a decade and a half, but he could still remember when Sir Richard had insisted on every serf being summoned to watch a fellow's skin being flayed. Lady Anne's arrival had brought an end to such punishment but the sport had remained common in neighbouring demesnes. Countless times Gyles had been forced to witness a public scourging while lords laid wagers on how many lashes a serf could endure. His darkest memory was of watching a youth hanged for absconding. Thin and undersized, he had dangled at the end of a rope, his legs twitching through more than three hundred beats of a drum before he breathed his last. The spoils had gone to Sir Richard for guessing that the boy's puny weight would keep him from strangling sooner.

'You should prepare yourselves,' he told James and Alleyn. 'I can think of only one reason why bread has been baked but the streets are empty. The people have been ordered to the house. I pray the steward wants their attendance at a trial, though I fear it's more likely they've been summoned to witness a punishment.'

He led them on to the approach road and urged his mount to a trot. Even from two hundred yards, he could see guards along the walls, but his attention was drawn to the throng of women and children blocking the entrance. He guessed the gates must have been closed against them and wondered why. Had the steward ordered a penance so terrible that only men were able to stomach it? The thought alarmed him, and he nudged his horse to a canter, calling on James and Alleyn to do the same. The clatter of hooves on the road caused the crowd to turn and then scurry to the verges, and Gyles saw with relief that he'd guessed wrongly. The gates stood wide with nothing to impede their progress except a straggle of townsmen on the driveway beyond.

If he'd learnt anything from riding with Sir Richard, it was that Norman soldiers had more proficiency with dice than weapons. Few took the trouble to train once they realised how easily Dorseteshire folk were intimidated. There was no call to draw bows or swords when a charging horse or a flailing whip served the purpose better. At fifty yards, he saw that the guards on the walls to either side of the entrance were of an age with his twins, and he gambled they'd had little practice at firing on a moving target. With a shout to the crowd to stand clear, he took his mount to a gallop, and stretched himself along the animal's neck.

The townsmen on the driveway scattered as he thundered through the pillars with James and Alleyn close on his heels, and only when the bend in the driveway was too close for comfort did he straighten and pull hard on his reins. He took a few deep breaths. 'Compose yourselves as best you can,' he told his companions, straightening his tabard and settling his bow across his shoulder. 'Once around that corner, you will be judged by the way you display yourselves. Recall how well Thaddeus has taught our sons and you'll not go wrong.'

James held his finger to his lips. 'Someone comes,' he murmured, giving a small jerk of his head to the rear.

Gyles glanced behind him and then wheeled his horse to face the approaching townsmen. There were ten or twelve, the same who had been making their way towards the gates before the horses set them running.

'I know your crest,' said one. 'I wove it into a tapestry for Sir Richard of Develish three years back. If it's Milady you seek, you'll find her on the forecourt.'

'Thank you, sir. Has she been there long?'

'As long as the Mass lasted. An hour and a half perhaps.'

Gyles took what he could from these answers. 'Does your priest always hold Mass in the open?'

Another man answered. 'He's the steward's priest and had but one reason to sermonise outside: he fears being close to us. Mind, he absolved us of our sins, and that's a gift we haven't had in nigh on half a year.' He eyed Gyles curiously. 'The soldiers who accompany Milady wear a different crest. How so?'

'Their lord is Athelstan, cousin to Lady Anne. His men rode to Develish to inform her of his arrest.'

'She spoke of him in the town. It seems the steward has made an error by taking him in charge.'

'He has,' said Gyles, tapping the pack behind his saddle. 'And I bring the documents to prove it.' He studied the upturned faces. 'Were you summoned here for a trial or just a Mass?'

'Neither,' said the first man. 'We joined our fellow townsmen when Matthew Miller called on us to escort Lady Anne.'

'There are more of you?'

'Many more . . . and all still on the forecourt with your mistress. We have tasks to perform or would have remained with them.'

'Why do the women and children wait at the gate?'

The man shrugged. 'Entry has been forbidden for many months now. We're only here ourselves because of Milady's determination to gain access.'

Gyles's weathered face creased in a smile. 'She has a powerful way with her. I don't doubt the steward is already regretting the permission.' He pulled on his left rein and nudged his horse into motion again. 'I bid you farewell, sirs. May God go with you.'

He expected to hear the response 'And with you', but it seemed the men were regretting their early departure. As he led James and Alleyn at a walk towards the bend, the group chose to follow, their curiosity stronger than their need to work.

☙❧

Thaddeus was grateful the servants had the same curiosity. Those who were closest to the windows called out descriptions of what they were seeing, and together they painted a clear picture of the battle for authority between Lady Anne and d'Amiens. Thaddeus had little difficulty interpreting Milady's actions, or indeed the steward's, but he found it harder to understand Aristide's. A maid, peering to her right, spoke of him hastening across the bridge to the church, and Thaddeus wondered what was taking him there. He had no need to retrieve de Courtesmain's scrolls, which lay on the table where the steward had tossed them before venturing out to confront Lady Anne.

The news that three mounted men in livery with a dozen townsmen behind them had rounded the bend in the driveway prompted the captain to move to the window. He clearly knew the Develish crest, because he asked Thaddeus if they could expect more of Lady Anne's men to join her. And why had these not accompanied her this morning rather than place her in the care of Athelstan's troop?

'I'm as ignorant as you of what's been happening in Develish this day,' said Thaddeus lightly, turning his hand in the bowl of warm briny water that Mistress Wilde had brought him. 'You'll get better answers by going outside and addressing these incomers directly.'

'To do that, I must trust you to hold to your parole, sire. Your master of hounds knows his way to the kitchen and the woodland beyond, and for all I know there are more of Lady Anne's people at the bottom of the driveway.'

'Then take him and the dogs with you. I cannot escape the guards and servants alone.' Thaddeus glanced at the matronly woman who hovered at his side with a salver of boiled rags. 'And nor would I wish to while Mistress Wilde shows me such kindness.'

Joshua ducked his head in a small bow. 'I would prefer to remain at your side, My Lord.'

Thaddeus looked deep into his eyes. 'You will serve a better purpose if you help the captain make sense of Develish speech,

Buckler. I wager these incomers will try to befuddle him with brogue. They did the same often enough with Master de Courtesmain, which is why he's so confused about my status.'

He couldn't tell if Joshua grasped his full meaning, but de Courtesmain certainly did, and Thaddeus counted the Frenchman's angry reaction a victory. For a quarter-hour, the hall had been subjected to his mummery of martyrdom: a sinking to his knees as he was chained to a pillar, the mouthing of prayers and his calling on God to chastise heretics. But it seemed he had too much conceit to allow Thaddeus's slur against his intellect to go unchallenged.

'Are there any lies you won't tell?' he hissed in French. 'Your precious whore has taught her people too well to have them grunt like pigs. Even the harlot you call mother knows how to fashion speech that can be understood.'

Thaddeus studied him with amusement. 'Take care whom you offend, Master de Courtesmain. You'll not be shown kindness by Dorseteshire folk if you call them pigs.'

'Tha' be the truth,' said Mistress Wilde with disgust. 'I zee but woone grunting hog here an' 'e be a Franky. The stoöard shoulda roped him in a sty avore he let him into My Lord's home to snabble his food an' spread his pwoison.' She stared de Courtesmain down as the servants in the hall greeted her brogue with laughter. 'Your soul is full of malice,' she finished in French. 'Good people will always hide their thoughts from you.'

☙☞

Gyles halted his convoy thirty paces short of where d'Amiens and his guards had formed a line across the driveway. He was content to wait until he was noticed, but realised quickly that the wait might be a long one. The attention of all was directed at Lady Anne, who walked amongst a large crowd of men on the forecourt, taking each by the hand and listening gravely as they told her their names and numbered their dead. At her sides were his twin sons, Ian and Olyver.

Away to Gyles's left, on the grassland close to the river's edge, Edmund Trueblood and Peter Catchpole were bent to the task of hobbling eight horses. Ahead, a dozen guards stumbled from the guard house, shrugging on tabards and pulling fingers through sleep-tousled hair. There was no sign of Thaddeus or Joshua.

Gyles thought it a strangely peaceful scene. For more than a decade, he had watched Milady use kindness and reason to quell the anger in men's hearts, but he marvelled that she had the courage to walk alone amongst so many strangers. Few lords would dare. He was reminded of some lines from Isaiah which Milady was fond of quoting. *And the wolf will dwell with the lamb, and the leopard will lie down with the kid. And the calf and the young lion and the fatling together; and a little boy will lead them.* She said it was a foretelling of the coming of Christ, but was it blasphemous to think it spoke of her as well? She displayed more honest love for people than was ever shown by men of the Church.

As if Gyles's thoughts had summoned him, the black-robed figure of the priest emerged from the woodland near the guard house. He seemed weighed down with care, or perhaps by the bag he cradled in his arms, but his rage at the sluggishness of the half-awake soldiers was clear. He struck the nearest across his face when the man was slow to buckle on his sword belt.

'The priest prepares an army,' whispered Alleyn behind him.

Gyles nodded. 'I see him. He looks to make himself their captain and they're not comfortable with it.'

'They're obeying him nonetheless.'

But not willingly, Gyles thought, casting about for the man who should be in charge.

'To your right,' murmured James. 'My son brings company.'

Joshua gave no indication that he recognised any in the convoy as he walked with the captain from the kitchen quarters. He called his pack to heel and addressed Gyles in French. 'I am Buckler, master of hounds to My Lord of Athelstan. This officer is captain of arms to My Lord of Blandeforde's steward. From the crest you wear, he believes you to be from Develish and has asked me to help him understand your speech.' He made a small bow to the captain. 'Will you allow me to explain that in words which are easier for them to understand?'

'As long as you don't play me false.'

Joshua nodded to the small group of townsmen. 'These men will tell you if I do. It's only Normans like Master de Courtesmain who find the brogue hard to understand.' He turned his attention back to Gyles. 'Our big woone a-got the likin' o' this man an' all the maëdes, an' our laëdy a-got the trust o' the v'ok vrom the town. Our Franky stoöard a-got the likin' o' none. The big woone a-told all that the Franky be zo baffled by our zpeech that 'e knows nowt o' truth in Develish. This be why 'e is so mistaëken abou' the big woone's naëme 'n status. Do 'e unnerstan'?'

'Ees,' answered Gyles with a nod. 'But I mun speak wi' the cap'n mysel'. Tell 'im I know Frankish.'

Joshua turned to his escort. 'This man speaks French and is ready to answer any question you have for him, sir.'

Gyles spoke before the captain could. 'I'm the same rank as you, sir, and am willing to give you any information you require, but I believe your own men's need of you is more urgent.' He gestured over the heads of the crowd. 'A dozen approach with swords at the ready and all look nervous. They appear to be under instruction from a priest who walks in their midst. Unless you share his blood lust, I suggest you free them from his command.' He stretched down a hand as a stream of curses issued from the other's mouth. 'Assist him up behind me, Buckler. Together, we'll reach them quicker than if he goes by foot.'

ೞ

Peter straightened from hobbling Killer and looked up to see a horse emerge from between the trees that lined the driveway and race at speed across the grass between the forecourt and the river. He barely had time to register that two men were astride it before it came to a quivering halt some twenty paces from a troop of armed soldiers. With no idea who the riders were, or where they had come from, he took them to be as much of a threat as the soldiers and cupped his hands about his mouth to give the warning cry of a fox—a sharp screech that burst upon the air. When he saw he had Ian's attention, he extended his arms, palms together, pointing in the direction Ian should look.

Ian turned in time to watch the captain leap to the ground and confront soldiers with drawn swords, but he was more interested in the crest of Sir Richard, which was emblazoned on the back of the rider's tabard. He knew from the way the man sat his horse that this was his father and, startled, he glanced towards d'Amiens, wondering what he made of Gyles's sudden appearance. But there was nothing to read in the steward's face.

'He's undecided what to do,' murmured Olyver in Ian's ear. 'He's asking himself how many more Develish men have come and whether he still has his captain's loyalty.'

Ian watched the captain pull his men forcibly from around the priest, ordering them angrily to sheathe their swords and form a line at his side. It was strange, made stranger by Lady Anne's soft, untroubled voice continuing to greet the townsmen as if nothing out of the ordinary was happening. Yet there was such a froth of anticipation in the air that Ian was sure every person on the forecourt knew something was amiss.

He chose to be unresponsive himself, watching impassively as the captain sent his men back to the guard house and took on the duty of escorting the priest himself. He pretended indifference when his father fell in behind them, and gave only a small nod of greeting to Edmund and Peter who returned, unbidden across the grass, to range themselves alongside him and Olyver. All the while, he studied d'Amiens out of the corner of his eye, certain he would not abide by his promise to keep from waging war on Lady Anne of Develish.

'Step clear of the crowd and make ready to face towards the driveway,' he whispered to his companions. 'We must be first to our bows when the steward instructs his guards to prepare theirs. Loose one arrow into the ground at his feet and aim the second at his heart.'

☙

The captain watched in disbelief as Athelstan's men ringed the steward's feet with shafts and nocked and aimed a second arrow even as his own men were struggling to find the string with their first. Two of the guards made a half-hearted attempt to block him as he strode around the forecourt, but he cursed them angrily and ordered them back into line. Their expressions of relief gave him momentary pause, but he was more intent on preventing further shafts from being released.

'What madness is this?' he demanded, planting himself squarely in front of Ian. 'Do you forget that Milady has pledged herself to peace?'

'I do not,' said Ian, taking a step to the side in order to keep d'Amiens in his sights, 'but your argument is with the steward. He questions your reasons for depriving the priest of his guard and seeks to prevent you doing the same with his. He ordered your men to take you in charge.'

'He speaks false,' said d'Amiens coldly. 'Recall your oath to protect your lord and be sure you understand where the real threat lies. These men are Develish serfs who wear livery to mask their banditry and thieving. They are here with the single purpose of forcing the release of the one who calls himself Athelstan. If you aid their attempts at rescue, you will give succour to felons.'

The captain stared at the ground for a moment and then appealed to Lady Anne, who stood a few paces behind Ian. 'Master d'Amiens is correct to remind me that I am bound by oath to protect my lord—or, in his absence, the steward who stands for him. If you value peace, milady, instruct these archers to lower their weapons.'

She shook her head regretfully. 'I cannot, sir, for they answer to Athelstan. You should know their leader speaks the truth, however. Master d'Amiens was the first to offer threat.' She held his gaze. 'It needs only for you to give your surety that it won't happen again. There can be no conflict if both sides are pledged to peace.'

The captain's lips twisted in a wry smile. 'And how do I give such surety, milady? I am a captain who is obliged to obey whatever instructions his lord's representative gives him.'

'Except when they're foolish,' she said with an answering smile. 'If the purpose of these soldiers was to release my cousin by force, they would have made Master d'Amiens their prisoner and bargained his freedom against their master's. The guards on either side of him would be dead and he would have a knife at his throat.' She paused. 'You have authority over your men, sir. I beg you to use it wisely. Athelstan's people ask only that he be allowed to prove his title free of duress and in the hearing of honest men.'

৩৫

Thaddeus had dressed his hand himself, placing small wads of boiled rag, steeped in brine, on either side of the wound and binding a long strip of the kirtle tightly about his palm to hold them in place. As the maids at the window reported the captain mounting behind a Develish man and riding at speed across the grass, he allowed Mistress Wilde to tie off the ends and help him ease his left arm from the sleeve of his shirt. He forbade her on the grounds of decency from removing the garment completely and refused her suggestion that they leave the great hall so that she might tend his wounds in private. Now was not the time to absent himself if what the maids at the window were describing was true.

Mistress Wilde sucked her teeth to see the blood begin to flow again as the scabs came away with his shirt sleeve, but in truth the blade hadn't penetrated far. Thaddeus urged her to clean the cuts with salted water before she bound them, thanking her kindly when she'd finished. She seemed unused to gratitude and her cheeks flushed rosy red as she assisted him back into his clothing. She asked if it was the custom where he came from to cleanse and treat open wounds in such a way and he answered that it was.

'And where would that be, sire?'

Thaddeus stared at de Courtesmain as he answered. 'My mother's family came from a town called Alexandria in Africa. It was she who taught me the value of salt in the cleansing of wounds.'

Angry spittle formed on the Frenchman's lips at this barefaced lie, but any retort he made was lost beneath a cry from the window that the steward had seized the captain and was threatening him with his own sword. The guards who remained in the great hall looked at each other in alarm and then turned their anxious faces to Thaddeus, looking to him for instruction.

With a sigh, he rose to his feet, taking the dagger from the table and dropping it into the pocket of his coat. 'She also taught me that men make poor decisions when they're afraid,' he murmured, ducking his head to Mistress Wilde before beckoning the guards to accompany him. 'I believe we'll serve peace better by going outside,' he said. 'The steward's quarrel is with me, not with your captain.'

The younger guard gestured towards the archway. 'Would the better route not be through the kitchen, sire? We'll likely meet the priest if we go by the front door and he'll not let you pass if he can prevent it.'

Thaddeus gave an approving nod. 'Lead on and I'll follow.'

Twenty

IAN DOUBTED HE AND HIS companions could maintain tension on their strings for much longer. With the captain's body shielding the steward's, they had aimed their arrows at the guards on either side to warn them against entering the fray, but the effort was taking its toll. As each second passed, Ian felt his fingers loosen and his arms tremble under the strain of holding them at shoulder height.

A stillness had fallen on the forecourt as this new threat unfolded, broken only by Joshua and his dogs emerging from the trees that lined the driveway and crossing the grass to join his friends. He commanded the pack to form up in front of them and nocked an arrow in his own bow. His presence gave Ian heart, but in truth he could see no way out of the impasse except surrender. Neither Lady Anne nor the townsmen would tolerate the killing of defenceless guards or the death of the captain who had permitted them to enter the compound. Perhaps Olyver read his thoughts, for he urged him to hold fast.

'I see movement on the driveway,' he whispered.

And so it seemed did Joshua, for he gave a low whistle to set his dogs moving forward, hackles raised and growls rumbling in their throats. It mattered not that this was a trick like any other, performed in return for titbits; so loud were their snarls and so alarming their lowered heads and stalking tread that the attention of every guard in the line was fixed on them. D'Amiens ordered Ian to call them off or bear responsibility for the captain's life.

'You're mighty keen on killing innocent men, sir,' Alleyn Startout said in French, seizing the steward's sword arm from behind and forcing it away from the captain. He cracked d'Amiens wrist across his knee to dislodge the weapon and watched in satisfaction as it clattered to the ground.

James Buckler prised the steward's other arm from the captain's throat and twisted it behind his back. 'Your servant, sir,' he said to the captain in the same language. 'My Lord of Athelstan follows with his guards and a dozen townsmen. He asked me to tell you that he continues to honour his parole.'

The captain took a moment to regain his balance. The dogs had dropped to their bellies on a second whistle from Joshua, but Ian and his companions still kept the tension on their bows. 'Did he give orders for his men to stand down?'

'As long as you give the surety Milady asked for,' said Alleyn. 'He believes you think conflict as senseless as she does.'

'I do,' said the captain grimly, stooping to retrieve his sword. 'As would My Lord of Blandeforde were he here.' He replaced the weapon in its sheath. 'You have my surety,' he told Ian. 'Now oblige me by honouring Milady's pledge of peace.'

'Gladly, sir,' said Ian, lowering his bow and ordering his companions to do the same. He nodded towards the driveway beyond. 'My Lord approaches now.'

The captain turned to watch Thaddeus and his guards cover the last few paces. 'Will you order these men to release the steward, My Lord?' he asked. 'I have no authority to hold him, and nor do you or Milady.'

'Indeed.' Thaddeus motioned James and Alleyn to step away. 'I trust it's only your pride that's hurt, Master d'Amiens.'

'Your men were wrong to threaten me.'

'I could say the same about de Courtesmain.'

'Your wounding was none of my doing.'

'I don't doubt you, sir. It's the priest who holds the power here.' Thaddeus took the dagger from his pocket and balanced it on his bandaged left palm. 'I believe this is Aristide's. De Courtesmain was easily persuaded to wield it on his behalf.'

D'Amiens stared uneasily at the stained blade and the bloodied gashes in Thaddeus's left sleeve. 'You blame the Father unfairly. The intent to harm was clearly de Courtesmain's. He believes you to be a bastard serf from Develish so attacked your sinister side—the side that denotes illegitimacy.'

Thaddeus shook his head in amusement before flicking the knife into the air and catching it neatly in his right hand. 'De Courtesmain's thoughts are never so fanciful. He was simply obeying the priest's command to prevent me speaking to the household of how the pestilence can be avoided. Your confessor fears having his duplicity exposed. Withal, he's a poor judge of character. Whatever de Courtesmain's faults, he hasn't the stomach for murder . . . with or without a promise of absolution.'

D'Amiens chose to answer with bluster. He rounded on the captain. 'This man is a prisoner,' he snapped. 'Why is it he who's in possession of this weapon and not you or one of his guards?'

'It transfixed his palm from side to side, sir. He waited a half-hour before he could withdraw it.'

'Why did you not take it from him then?'

'It wasn't necessary, sir. My Lord had already given me his parole.'

'His status is yet to be determined.'

The captain shrugged. 'Then determine it, Master d'Amiens, and allow us all to resume our lives in peace. There'll be no need for violence once every grievance is resolved.'

'This man has been the cause of the violence and will provoke more once he's shown to be an imposter.'

'Not while my surety stands, sir. Worry more for yourself if his accuser is found to be a liar. You and the priest took much on faith when you chose to believe a stranger's stories of heresy and insurrection in Develish. My Lord of Blandeforde would have demanded stronger proof before he arrested a fellow noble who posed no threat to him.'

ↀ

The closest and most interested observer of that day's happenings was Matthew Miller. Despite his name, his trade was woodworking and there had been precious little call for his services these past two seasons. Lack of work had pushed him into idleness, and lack of revenue had made him resentful of those who had put money aside when times were good. To be witness to something out of the ordinary—more, to be given a sense of purpose and a belief in the future by a woman he'd never met—had raised his spirits higher than they'd been in months.

He prided himself on knowing a deceiver just by looking at him—perhaps because he wasn't above a little duplicity himself when a customer was too green to know the value of what he was purchasing—and he had the feeling that none of the men who rode with or for Lady Anne was what he pretended to be. Yet he couldn't place their class. They gave themselves too much licence to be peasants or mercenaries. The timid hesitancy of the Norman guards was in stark contrast to the Doreseteshire men's confident threatening and disarming of the steward.

Out of the corner of his eye, Miller saw the mounted soldier, who had taken the captain at speed across the grass, pen the priest inside the angle made by the entranceway and the house. Ahead, he watched the approach of Athelstan. Andrew Tench had said he'd never seen so fine a noble, and Miller agreed. Athelstan's height set him above the men around him and the calmness of his manner gave him authority. He appeared as unaffected by d'Amiens calling him a bastard serf as he was to have had a knife pierce his palm.

Yet Miller questioned whether lords were ever so forbearing of discomfort and insolence. Over the years, he'd watched many pass through the town and he remembered them more for their angry complaining and petulance than their patience. But there was no doubting the captain's belief in the man's nobility. Had his words to the steward not made that clear, the respect he showed Athelstan certainly did.

Jeremiah Slater, too, seemed persuaded, though Miller guessed his sudden intervention was inspired by some hastily whispered words from Lady Anne when the steward ordered the captain to send Athelstan under guard to the church and to escort Milady to his office.

The greybeard stepped forward and raised his voice. 'Begging your pardon, sir,' he called to d'Amiens, 'but there are many on this forecourt who would wish to hear the reasons for this man being taken in charge. The guildsmen who accompanied the priest on Saturday night found no fault in him. Why do you?'

'You will know the explanation once his status has been determined.'

'By whom, sir? And on whose word? We can all see the gore on his sleeve and can guess he's been badly injured. Is his attacker the same who accuses him of imposture? If so, he has the right in law to demand justice for himself first. The claims against him will stand for nothing if a jury decides his accuser had murderous intent.'

A murmur of agreement rippled through the crowd of townsmen and Miller watched angry blood suffuse the paler skin in d'Amiens' face. But what offended him more? Miller wondered. To have his decisions challenged, or to see people he'd forsaken for so long speak with a single voice? Lady Anne had said it took courage and generosity to keep a community alive, and Miller saw that Jeremiah Slater had both. The greybeard showed more courage than younger men by once again drawing the steward's attention to himself.

'My friend speaks with knowledge, for he has served as a juryman in the manor court,' Miller said, thrusting forward to stand with Slater. 'All the townsmen here can claim a similar knowledge because of their obligation to attend—and some have seen it from the other side. You know this, Master d'Amiens, for it's your duty to preside over the court and mete out fines for late payment of taxes.' He gestured towards Thaddeus. 'This man is entitled to be heard before twelve good men who will bring fairness and reason to their verdicts.'

'But not in the manor court, which deals only with infractions against Blandeforde by-laws,' d'Amiens snapped. 'I remember you well, Miller. Your infringements have been many, and more often concern false description of goods than late payment of taxes.'

Miller laughed. 'Hardly infringements, sir, since I never lost those cases. A bowl is a bowl whether it costs a groat or a farthing. It's not the vendor's fault if the purchaser's a fool.' He gestured again to Thaddeus. 'Have you not laid the same charge against this man? There can be no falser description of goods than a bastard serf claiming the title of Athelstan and cousinship with Lady Anne of Develish. Why deny him the manor court when you were so generous in allowing me the use of it?'

'There are other issues involved.'

'But none so difficult that a jury of free townsmen can't decide them. You've insulted our intelligence once, sir. Will you do so again? We are as able to understand argument as we are to read ledgers.'

'Which you've still to show us,' called Andrew Tench. 'The convening of the manor court will give you that opportunity.'

Voices cried out in approval, and the captain stirred uneasily, perhaps worried that the fragile peace was about to be broken. Thaddeus laid a calming hand on his arm and addressed d'Amiens.

'We both know my arrest was unlawful,' he said without animosity, 'and were I able to lay my grievances before a jury of my peers—as is my right—I would do so gladly. Nevertheless, I have no quarrel with the good men of Blandeforde deciding my truthfulness. Do you hesitate to summon the court out of fear of having to answer questions yourself, Master d'Amiens? Or is it the priest who decides such matters?'

D'Amiens frowned at him, but whether in perplexity or dislike it was hard to say. 'The court building is in the town and we heard a half-year ago that all the officers were dead. There's been no manor court since, because verdicts reached by jurymen, not approved by officers, are deemed null and void. Is that your wish, Thurkell? To waste time arguing your case before men who lack the authority to free you?'

Thaddeus gave a grunt of amusement. 'You give away your powers too easily, Master d'Amiens.' He turned to Slater and Miller. 'I'm in your hands, good sirs. Are you elders of this town? If so, I believe you have the necessary standing to select jurymen.'

'We are, sire,' said Miller without hesitation. 'Master Slater is leader of our council and I am one of its members.'

'Andrew Tench also,' said Slater, beckoning the man forward. 'In addition, Roger Wright—' he pointed to one of the men beyond Thaddeus—'and Mark Summerlee.' He nodded towards his right. 'We all have knowledge of the manor court, sire, and, with respect to Master d'Amiens, he is mistaken on how jurymen are selected. It used to be that the officers picked the names until rumours began that favourable verdicts could be bought with money. Thereafter, My Lord of Blandeforde decreed that the choice should be made by lot.'

Roger Wright, the man behind Thaddeus, spoke up. 'You should know, too, that there's no requirement for the court to sit in the town building, Master d'Amiens. I've attended three trials in the great hall here, and my father spoke of several being held on this forecourt. Your predecessor thought it right that as many as possible should be allowed to witness the workings of the law, and the courtroom holds a bare forty.'

Andrew Tench raised his hand. 'As steward and presiding officer, you have but to call us to order and the court is convened,' he said. 'Your captain of arms can serve as bailiff and I as clerk of the rolls. I have a better script than most and will need but the use of a table, quill and parchment to make a true record of what is said. In addition, a Bible to take the oaths of truth. My Lord of Blandeforde summoned us in such a way five years ago and no questions were raised about the legality of the verdicts.'

Briefly, d'Amiens closed his eyes as if to shut out the townsmen's words. 'Do you have no care for Milady's people?' he asked Thaddeus. 'You may save yourself by these means but not them. De Courtesmain accuses the whole demesne of crimes.'

'Indeed. He glories in vaunting his self-proclaimed virtue . . . much like your priest.' Thaddeus turned the dagger in his fingers and then dropped it back into his pocket. 'The serfs of Develish will have nothing to answer for once de Courtesmain's lies are exposed. The truth will release them from suspicion, as it will me.'

'Then you can have no objection to my hearing what Milady has to say first. I will assemble the court here in one hour, and she may sit with me in the steward's office until that time comes. The delay will allow the servants to carry tables and benches outside, and the townsmen to draw lots.' D'Amiens dropped his head in a small bow to Lady Anne. 'Is that acceptable to you, milady?'

There was no hesitation in her reply. 'Quite acceptable, Master d'Amiens, but my journey was long and tiring, and I would beg the courtesy of a moment or two in private with a maid first. May I ask for the kindly matron who brought me cordial? I will need a chaperone when I'm in your office and would have more confidence in an older woman.'

D'Amiens' mouth twisted. 'You seem to have managed without a protectress so far, milady.'

'I haven't needed one,' she answered lightly. 'Apart from my husband, you're the only man who's ever invited me to enter his chamber unaccompanied.'

He scowled ferociously as the forecourt erupted in laughter. 'I was referring to your travelling alone with soldiers, milady.'

'I didn't doubt it, sir, but in truth I couldn't have asked for more chivalrous companions. They have learnt their respect and courtesy from their lord.' She turned to Thaddeus. 'I wish we were meeting again under happier circumstances, cousin, but be assured I shall not reveal the details of our pledge unless you have done so already.'

Thaddeus bent forward, touching his fingers to his forehead in order to hide the relief in his eyes. He had no idea how Milady had come by this knowledge, but he blessed her cleverness in raising it. 'I have not, dear friend. The pledge between us was a sacred one and only you have the right to speak of it.' He raised his head. 'Nevertheless, I would urge you to keep your counsel. Blandeforde's proxy has no better right than de Courtesmain to know my reasons for entering Develish last spring in the guise of a peasant called Thurkell.'

She was as adept at hiding understanding as he was. 'Is it but a year that has passed? So much has happened since that it seems longer.' She switched her attention back to d'Amiens. 'Shall we proceed, sir? I would hate to keep these good townsmen from their work longer than is necessary.'

⚬⚬

Once inside the privacy of a chamber, Lady Anne took Mistress Wilde's hands in hers and searched her eyes. The woman must have some sympathy for Thaddeus, she thought, or she wouldn't have lent herself to Joshua's passing of a message to Edmund.

'Did my cousin speak of me to you, mistress?'

'He did, milady, and most highly. Everyone in the household has learnt of your care for your serfs and how you have saved them from the pestilence.'

Everything about her reminded Lady Anne of Clara Trueblood—her stocky stature, her smiling, plump-cheeked face, the straightforward way she spoke—and she followed her instinct that the woman would not betray her to the steward.

'I need your help, Mistress Wilde, but we have a short time only before I must present myself for questioning,' she said.

'What would have you me do, milady?'

'Tell me all you can about Master de Courtesmain. What does the household gossip say about him? How and where does he pass his days? Have promises been made to him in return for accusing my cousin? What happened here this morning? Why did I see him chained to a pillar in the great hall?' She gave a small laugh. 'But all this must be told in the few minutes it takes for me to use a chamber pot and rearrange my gown.'

Mistress Wilde laughed in return. 'There's no need to trouble yourself in that regard, milady. The steward's arse is so tight it takes him a quarter-hour to pass a turd. I'll remind him of that if he chafes at your tardiness.'

She shepherded Lady Anne towards a low chair with a hole in the seat and a chamber pot beneath it, and then brought forward a bowl of water, some cloths and a hairbrush, which she placed on a stool beside the seat. All the while she talked of what she knew. The priest had allowed the Frenchman through the gates some dozen days earlier when a guard reported a messenger speaking of heretical practices in My Lord of Blandeforde's vassal demesnes. A maid had overheard a later conversation between the priest and the steward which suggested the heresy concerned the illegal freeing of serfs. The Frenchman had remained seven days in the church before being given a room inside the house. He had shown great distrust of the servants and had been overly arrogant in the demanding of washing water and victuals.

On the evening of Easter Saturday, a messenger had come from the bridge to report the arrival of one who called himself Athelstan. Shortly afterwards, the priest, the steward and some twenty guards had proceeded down the driveway with flaming torches. The priest was clothed in the steward's attire and the steward was hiding his disfigured face inside the hood of his cloak.

As to what happened during the rest of that night or on Easter Sunday, Mistress Wilde couldn't say. Being head of the kitchen, her task had been to prepare the Easter feast. A rumour said that a prisoner was lodged in the guard house, awaiting trial once the Holy Day had passed; another that he was brought to the house after dark to prevent him corrupting the guards. Both rumours may have been true, because the servants were banned from showing themselves in the great hall or on the forecourt from nightfall on Sunday for fear they, too, would become corrupted by the prisoner's lies and blandishments.

The first Mistress Wilde knew of that morning's happenings was the steward's ranting at his captain of arms for showing cowardice before a woman. So loud was his voice that it could be heard in the kitchen and she had been curious enough to peep through the archway. Imagine her surprise when a tall, handsome man, laden with shackles, had come through the entranceway and chastised the steward for his intemperate speech, saying it wasn't the captain's fault if Lady Anne of Develish had refused his terms.

She spoke of Thaddeus with respect, describing him as calm and unafraid even when the Frenchman attacked him for saying that wickedness wasn't the cause of the pestilence. In truth, few of the servants had thought it was, since there were many more spiteful and cruel folk in their midst than the four who had succumbed. She added that few believed either that the town was as steeped in sin as Father Arisitide claimed.

'Most of us have family there . . . or *had*,' she said, laying aside the brush with which she'd neatened Lady Anne's hair. 'We've never been allowed to know their fate, or the fate of those the priest expelled, but it's hard to think of any of them so wicked that God would want them dead.' She assisted Lady Anne to her feet and knelt to arrange the folds of her gown.

'What reason does Father Aristide give for so few in the household dying?'

'His daily reciting of the liturgy of the hours and the giving of general absolution, milady. By such means he sanctifies the land inside the wall and cleanses us all of our wickedness.'

'Does he sleep in the church?'

Mistress Wilde shook her head. 'The tower's cold and he likes his comforts too much.'

'Was My Lord of Athelstan told of the cleansing rituals?'

'I believe so, milady, for he said Father Aristide has been less than honest in his explanations about why the house remains free of the pestilence.' She stood with a grunt of satisfaction. 'You are truly beautiful. No one would think you'd made a journey this day.'

Lady Anne pulled a wry smile. 'I could wish my tired wits as easily refreshed, Mistress Wilde. I'll need a sharp mind if I'm to avoid the traps the steward and priest set for me.'

The matron chuckled. 'You'll be more at ease than they, milady. The priest's knowledge of women is limited to the confessional, and the steward's to chastising us for wastage. They'll not know how to handle one such as you.'

Lady Anne reached for the woman's hands again. 'I have asked that you stay with me as my chaperone. Do you feel able to do that? I have no wish to cause difficulties between you and Master d'Amiens, but your presence would give me confidence that what he says is truthful. He will surely hesitate to speak falsehoods before a member of the household.'

Mistress Wilde gave her fingers a tight squeeze. 'It'll not cause difficulties, milady. He has too much need of me in the kitchen.' Her eyes gleamed with sudden mischief. 'And if he or the Father wander from the truth, I'll let you know by crossing my wrists in front of my kirtle. It's past time some light was shed on the secrets of this house.'

☙❧

The priest stood in a corner of the office and the steward behind the desk with his back to the window. Both faces were in shade, and Lady Anne wondered if this was deliberate when d'Amiens invited her to sit on a stool which was placed in such a way that she must look towards the light. With a smile, she requested Mistress Wilde to move the stool into the corner on the other side of the window from the priest, begging the steward's pardon for obliging him to turn around.

'I'm sure you're better able to stare into the sun than I am, Master d'Amiens,' she said, settling herself on the stool and giving a nod of acknowledgement to Aristide. 'How may I help you, sirs?'

The priest spoke first. 'Master de Courtesmain has brought us alarming tales of Develish, milady. He speaks of an abandonment of God, thievery and murder by a serf called Thurkell, and bonded men and women claiming to be the equal of lords. He reserves his worst accusation for you, saying you practise heresy.'

'How very strange of him.'

'These are serious charges, milady,' said d'Amiens.

'Indeed,' she answered gravely. 'As serious as the charges Sir Richard made against you some five years since, when you miswrote Develish's taxes. It was fortunate our steward of the time noticed the error before you departed. Sir Richard would have been obliged to raise the matter with My Lord of Blandeforde otherwise.'

'It was a small mistake in calculation, milady.'

'Hardly small, sir. By recollection you left twenty gold nobles out of your addition. Sir Richard would have ordered you flogged for thievery had I not persuaded him that error was more likely than deceit. He was quite convinced you planned to pocket the nobles yourself.'

D'Amiens eyed her with dislike. The knowledge he had of her now told him it was she who had seen the inaccuracy and sent her husband to rage against him. 'There was no deceit, milady.'

'Of course there wasn't,' she agreed. 'No one else thought as badly of you as Sir Richard did. I felt for you that his intemperate language meant we only saw your deputies thereafter.'

There was a short silence.

'I see no comparison between de Courtesmain's accusations and the false one that was levelled against Jacques d'Amiens,' the priest said then.

'You would if you'd ever been accused of a crime you hadn't committed, Father. Master d'Amiens was deeply distressed to have Sir Richard call him a thief.'

'What reason would de Courtesmain have to make up such tales?'

Lady Anne gave a whisper of a laugh. 'How else could he gain entry here? He was a stranger without place or position. What better way to ensure a welcome than to tell a compelling story about one of Blandeforde's vassal demesnes.' She glanced at d'Amiens. 'The bigger mystery is how he persuaded you he wasn't carrying the pestilence. In Develish, we insist on fourteen days' exclusion before we allow people across the moat.'

'He was confined to the church for a week. The Father took him his food and spoke to him through the door.'

'That must have frightened the household.'

'Why? They had no contact with him.'

Lady Anne showed surprise. 'Do they know that contact is dangerous? I thought they were persuaded that absolution and the liturgy of the hours keeps them safe. To have Father Aristide shut from his church for seven days, and the cleansing rituals abandoned, must have worried them.'

The priest stirred angrily. 'These are insignificant matters beside the godlessness of Develish,' he snapped, gesturing to some scrolls on the desk. 'The details are written here, inscribed by de Courtesmain. Your priest has been silenced, your serfs promised freedom and your daughter declared illegitimate so that you and the son of a Develish harlot can govern the demesne together.'

'You make me quite faint with these words, Father. Master de Courtesmain lived amongst us for eight months and I never once guessed his mind was so disturbed. If you'll allow Mistress Wilde to fetch my bag from outside, I can show you the steward's ledger from Develish which tells the true story of my demesne.'

'As written by you and Thurkell.'

She shook her head. 'There are many hands, for the record dates back twenty years. The most recent are mine, Athelstan's and de Courtesmain's. You will recognise your informant's in the pages he composed. He was eager to make what contribution he could to Develish's survival while he was amongst us, and it saddens me greatly that he maligns us now in order to win favour here.' She turned to Mistress Wilde. 'Oblige me by asking my captain of arms to give you the bag that contains the ledger, mistress. You will know him by his closely cropped hair and the Develish crest he wears. I don't doubt Master d'Amiens and Father Aristide will agree to wait on the other side of the door during your absence.'

Mistress Wilde gave them no choice, stepping behind the desk and using her broad body to urge them ahead of her. Once outside, she closed the latch securely behind her, bobbed a respectful curtsey and then hurried toward the entranceway. Her mind was spinning with what she'd heard. *Master d'Amiens a thief . . . the liturgy of the hours a lie . . . Develish a godless Hell.* Was any of it true? she wondered, searching the forecourt for Milady's captain of arms. She picked him out immediately, for he stood apart from the crowd with two others, each wearing the same crest on his tabard and holding his horse by its reins.

They were deep in conversation but broke off as she approached. 'Are you Milady's captain, sir?' she asked Gyles.

'I am, mistress.'

'She asks that you give me the bag that contains the ledger. She wishes the priest and steward to see it so they know she speaks the truth.'

Gyles glanced towards the river. 'My Lord of Athelstan's men have charge of it,' he said, nodding to where Ian and his companions stood with their horses. 'I can accompany you on foot or fetch it more speedily by riding. Which would you prefer?'

Mistress Wilde laughed. 'Speed, sir. I'm a slow walker and Milady's too wearied from her journey to endure the company of Master d'Amiens and Father Aristide for long.'

Gyles swung into his saddle. 'If you have Milady's trust, you have ours,' he said, nodding to James and Alleyn. 'Tell my men how she fares. We worry that she has no protection inside the house.'

As he left, Mistress Wilde looked to James. 'There's no cause for worry,' she assured him. 'Milady may be tired but her mind is strong. I believe the steward and priest feel more menaced by her than she by them.'

'It's Master de Courtesmain we fear, mistress. It seems he's already attacked My Lord of Athelstan. We cannot allow the same to happen to Lady Anne. Where is he now? What news do you have of him? Are his accusations believed?'

She needed little prompting to repeat what she knew. For herself, she thought Milady was right to say the Frenchman's mind was disturbed and his claims against Develish merely designed to win him a position in Blandeforde, but it was clear the priest believed them. She asked the men if anything de Courtesmain said was true, and because they spoke with Doreseteshire accents, she gladly accepted their denials. The day would end poorly if it was Lady Anne who was lying and not the malicious Frenchman.

Twenty-one

WHEN D'AMIENS RE-ENTERED THE OFFICE, he looked at the scrolls on the desk before he looked at Lady Anne. If any had been unfurled and read, it wasn't obvious, though he saw humour in her eyes when he raised his gaze to hers. There had been time enough for her to scan them all, and he chided himself for not removing them. He handed her an advantage each time he undervalued her character and intelligence.

Mistress Wilde placed the bag at Lady Anne's feet. 'Your captain sends his compliments, milady, and trusts that all is as it should be. He's concerned that the loose scrolls may have been crushed by the weight of the ledger.'

Lady Anne smiled her gratitude. 'I'm sure he worries un-necessarily,' she said. 'Will you oblige me by turning away, sirs?' she asked d'Amiens and Aristide. 'There are garments personal to a lady in here and it wouldn't be seemly for you to see them. It will take but a moment to retrieve the documents from the bottom.'

They did as she asked but, even so, she was careful to use the flap of the bag to obscure the contents once she'd unbuckled it.

She had no more desire for them to glimpse the britches she'd worn than Gyles's 'loose scrolls' of which she was ignorant. There were two of them lying atop her woollen cloak and she moved them to her lap before pulling out the ledger and placing it above the scrolls. She let the flap drop again and thanked the steward for his patience.

She handed him the ledger. 'You'll find Sir Richard's and my own lineage inscribed at the front, Master d'Amiens. Athelstan is shown as my cousin through direct descent from my grandfather's brother. It gives his date of birth as one year before mine. If you'd rather study the record in private, I'm happy to wait in the chamber Mistress Wilde found for me.'

'That won't be necessary, milady. I'll have queries as I read and you'll be better able to answer them if you remain.' He nodded to the scrolls in her lap. 'What are they?'

Lady Anne unrolled the first and recognised the shaky, ill-formed script as Father Anselm's. 'This is written by my priest and is addressed to His Grace of Sarum. And this—' she unrolled the next and saw that, though the letter was signed with Eleanor's childish hand, the writing was Isabella Startout's—'is from my daughter, Lady Eleanor. It, too, is addressed to His Grace of Sarum.'

'Why is neither sealed?'

'Wax is precious in Develish, sir. We reserve what little we have for the making of altar candles.'

Father Aristide gave a snort of disbelief. 'You lie. I watched Thurkell seal a parchment with wax two nights ago.'

She smiled slightly. 'Would that be when you were claiming to be the steward, Father? The townsmen tell me their fellows found it unnerving to have you speak so many lies about yourself.' She paused. 'If by Thurkell you mean Athelstan, he left Develish with

My Lord of Bourne and Master de Courtesmain on the first day of January—some three and a half months since. I imagine any wax he uses comes from Bourne.'

'You have answers for everything, milady,' said d'Amiens.

'You will find more in the ledger, sir.'

But not the ones you want, she thought, as they bent their heads to the pages. There was no mention of Thaddeus entering the demesne last spring in the guise of a peasant or explanation for why he would do such a thing. She could guess he'd devised the idea of a 'pledge' to avoid having to give a reason himself and had then cursed mightily to hear that the person who could release him from his promise was at the gate. But where did that leave her? What possible reason could Milady of Develish have had to ask her cousin to pose as a peasant before her husband and his new steward?

Every story she and Thaddeus had composed had been designed to convince d'Amiens of Athelstan's nobility. Not once had they thought to invent explanations for why he might have feigned being a serf in front of de Courtesmain. She understood why he'd had no choice but to admit knowledge of the Frenchman— de Courtesmain's descriptions in his scrolls were so precise that anyone would recognise Thurkell in Athelstan—but she had no idea what to do about it without knowing what else Thaddeus had claimed. Had he said all in Develish believed him a serf? And why would he not have declared himself after Sir Richard's death?

With an inward sigh, she lowered her gaze to Eleanor's letter. It was a fickle irony that in order to defend Thaddeus against one accusation of imposture she must prove him capable of maintaining another.

৩৩

Easter Monday, 1349

Your Most Reverend Grace,

I am Eleanor of Develish, daughter to Sir Richard (now deceased) and his widow Lady Anne. I pray that you are well and that this letter reaches you, for I am greatly troubled in mind over the whereabouts and fate of my beloved mother and her cousin My Lord of Athelstan.

News reached us yesterday in the midst of our joyous celebrations of Christ's resurrection that My Lord of Athelstan had been taken prisoner in Blandeforde. This alarming message was brought by one of his fighting men who spoke of accusations of imposture being made against My Lord. The soldier could not say who the accuser was, but Lady Anne knows of only one person who would level such charges against her cousin. He goes by the name of Hugh de Courtesmain and holds deep grudges against My Lord of Athelstan.

Honoured Sir, I beg you to believe that Master de Courtesmain is not to be trusted. He came to Develish at the behest of my father, who believed he would make a loyal and able steward. This proved to be untrue. Master de Courtesmain was so afeared for himself when Sir Richard died of the pestilence that he handed government to my mother and reduced himself to the class of peasant in order to escape responsibility.

It was by God's mercy that our cousin, Athelstan, was on a visit from Spain when this happened, for he was able to assist Lady Anne in the management of Sir Richard's estate. Being much travelled, he has more knowledge of the world than she, and his different customs and ease of manner endeared him greatly to my father's people in our time of trouble. Together, he and Lady Anne used their wisdom to keep Develish safe, and this caused jealousy and resentment in Master de Courtesmain who saw that he'd been foolish to relinquish his authority so hastily.

Lady Anne has journeyed to Blandeforde to demand My Lord of Athelstan's release but I have grave concerns for her safety. We had word that My Lord of Blandeforde travelled west last year and I do not know who governs in his place. Whoever that person is, I fear Master de Courtesmain has filled his head with falsehoods, and the blame for that is mine. I am more childish than a girl of fourteen years should be and, out of scorn for his cowardice, teased Master de Courtesmain daily with stories that were not true. To my shame, I laughed to see his expressions, for his jealous nature led him to believe the most foolish absurdities.

If you be willing, I beg you to send an envoy to Blandeforde to discover what is happening there. I have such dread that my ill-considered teasing of a man too craven to honour his pledge to my father has led to terrible error. In true contrition, I have performed every penance Father Anselm has asked of me for my falsehoods, but only you have the power to redeem my intemperate words. My Lord of Athelstan is ill-versed in English law, and, being but a woman, my mother may not be given a hearing.

I entreat you to believe that Almighty God blessed Develish twice when He gave charge of the demesne to

Lady Anne and ordained that My Lord of Athelstan was at hand to help her. In great humility and obedience to God, and assisted by the prayers of our priest Father Anselm, they have protected my father's people and welcomed those from other demesnes who have come seeking sanctuary. My Lord of Bourne from Wiltshire was one such and will testify to the truth of what I write.

Your most contrite and humble servant,
In nomine Patris et Filii et Spiritus Sancti
Eleanor of Develish

の

Lady Anne saw more than Isabella's hand in the letter. The cleverness of the ideas and phrasing were surely hers, for Eleanor would never have thought to write of de Courtesmain looking 'to escape responsibility' or Thaddeus having 'different customs' and being 'ill-versed in English law'. Perhaps Isabella had helped, too, in the construction of Father Anselm's letter for, though the hand was his, the expressions of praise were quite foreign to his nature, and she wondered if Gyles and Clara had had the foresight to soften his mood with drink before he began—or, more simply, Gyles had threatened to oust him from his comfortable quarters in the church.

She watched d'Amiens flick through the pages of the ledger, reading some but ignoring most, and it was clear to her that he was searching for the crimes and heresies that de Courtesmain had listed by date in his scrolls. He wouldn't find them, for they were in her private journal, buried at the bottom of a coffer in her chamber. Nevertheless, she knew there was mention of Thaddeus Thurkell in this ledger, often in her own hand.

After a quarter-hour, d'Amiens raised his head. 'This tells me nothing except that Develish's days are filled with tedium. The only pages of interest are those that refer to Thaddeus Thurkell.'

'Would those be the ones written by Master de Courtesmain?' she asked calmly. 'He cuts his quill very fine so his hand is distinctive. You will know it from his scrolls.'

'Why does he not refer to Thurkell as Athelstan?'

'Because Thurkell is the name by which he knew him.' Lady Anne lifted Father Anselm's letter from her lap and offered it to him. 'This may help you understand. It's addressed to His Grace of Sarum but, since it's unsealed, I see no reason why you shouldn't read it.'

'The date is today's. How did you come by it?'

'Father Anselm entrusted it to my captain of arms. Should I and Athelstan be denied justice here, he will ride with it to Sarum.'

◌◌◌

Easter Monday, 1349

Most Reverend Sir,

> *I am Anselm of Develish. If this letter reaches you, I beg you to pray for me as I pray for you each morning and night. With God's blessing we will both survive the pestilence.*
>
> *This letter will accompany one from Lady Eleanor of Develish, who beseeches you on her knees to intercede on behalf of Lady Anne, her beloved mother, and Lord Athelstan, her admired cousin. Since time is pressing, I will not repeat the reasons for her request, which she has*

*set out well enough, but will say only that I lend my pleas
to hers out of a sincere belief that the light of God shines
strongly in the two persons she entreats you to help.*

*Lady Anne is a noblewoman of great love and
kindness who has striven to honour her deceased
husband's pledge to protect his people. She has done so
in humility, following St Francis's example of wearing
simple homespun and sharing all she has with her serfs
so that they might better understand how beloved they
are by God. In this endeavour, she has had the support of
My Lord of Athelstan, whose presence has been a source
of hope and belief in God and the future. He, too, adopts
the ways of St Francis, taking a simple name, choosing
humbleness over extravagance and paying heed to all
men, regardless of their class.*

*It is a cause for joy that none in Develish has died of
the pestilence since Sir Richard passed. Yesterday, as we
celebrated His glorious resurrection, every voice was raised
in praise and gratitude to Christ Our Lord. He has shown
us nothing but love and we repay Him a thousandfold in
the care we have for each other.*

*Honoured sir, I commit Lady Anne and My Lord of
Athelstan to your mercy and beg that you respond to Lady
Eleanor's entreaties.*

*Your humble servant,
In nomine Patris et Filii et Spiritus Sancti
Anselm*

☙

D'Amiens laid the letter aside and examined the page from the Develish register of births. 'The hand is the same,' he said, placing both before Aristide. 'But the thinking and spelling in one is better controlled than the other.'

Aristide took the page of births and deaths from d'Amiens and handed it to Lady Anne. 'How do you explain this, milady? It was written by your priest, was it not?'

She looked at it and nodded. 'Did Master de Courtesmain steal it from us? How very unkind of him. He should have given more thought to families who might want reminding of when their parents and grandparents died.'

'I'm more interested in the birth of Thaddeus Thurkell, milady.'

Lady Anne read the words aloud. '*A sun, Thades, was bor this second week of June, thirteen twenty-eight, to Wil and Ev Thkell.*' She laid the vellum in her lap. 'Poor Eva. It was all too common for children to die early before I arrived in Develish. Did de Courtesmain not think to search for the notification of death? He must surely have questioned why Athelstan looks so much older than a serf born twenty years ago.'

There was a brief hesitation before the priest spoke again. 'Why should he? Thurkell was alive.'

'My *cousin* was alive, Father. Several serfs offered to lend him a name but he chose Thaddeus Thurkell when Eva begged him to take her firstborn's. It pleased her, I think. She loves to picture her lost son as tall and fine as Athelstan.'

'It makes no sense,' the priest snapped. 'Why would a noble pose as a serf? There's no quicker way to incite rebellion than to give such people a sense of importance.'

'Your husband wouldn't have allowed it,' said d'Amiens. 'He had a great hatred of the peasant class.'

Lady Anne smiled. 'He had a hatred of many things, sir. Myself most of all.'

D'Amiens had no doubt then that she had read the scrolls. She wouldn't have admitted Sir Richard's dislike of her had de Courtesmain not revealed it. 'That doesn't answer Father Aristide's question, milady.'

'Perhaps not,' she agreed, 'but it may answer yours. Sir Richard would not have given my cousin entry had he known who he was. He cut me off from my family when we married so that he could do as he pleased with both me and my dowry.'

'You had no rights in the marriage, milady. Few women do.'

'Indeed. He often called me the lowest of his serfs. It's fortunate I can read and write and that kinder stewards than de Courtesmain enabled me to send and receive letters in secret. My situation would have been unbearable otherwise.'

The priest was shocked. 'You abused your husband's trust? The vows of matrimony bound you by sacred oath to honour and obey him.'

Lady Anne nodded. 'And I learnt sympathy for his serfs because of it, Father. Our plights were similar.'

She found an unexpected ally in Mistress Wilde who gave an involuntary laugh. 'Milady of Blandeforde says the same. We're no different, you and I, except in the way we dress, she tells me. We both have to run when the master calls.'

D'Amiens ignored her. 'Do you wish us to understand that you invited your cousin to enter Develish as a peasant in order to deceive your husband, milady?'

'Not so much to deceive as to be invisible,' she answered mildly. 'Had he been noticed by Sir Richard and forced to give a name, you could rightly accuse him of deception . . . but it never happened. Sir Richard had better recognition of his horses than his people.'

'Develish is not so big that a stranger wouldn't stand out, particularly one as distinctive as Athelstan. The steward and bailiff must have seen him. And why would the priest turn a blind eye to the imposture? He owed a duty to be honest with his lord just as you did.'

Lady Anne nodded. 'And so he would have been had Sir Richard asked him directly who the newcomer was. The bailiff also. I made no request of anyone in Develish to tell lies to Sir Richard, only to give a welcome to Athelstan while he was amongst us. None saw harm in it, for they all knew they wouldn't be questioned. Sir Richard was absent from the demesne more often than he was in it, and Athelstan slept in our hospital which my husband never visited. The chances of them meeting were very small.'

'What of the steward?'

'He'd been dead three months. We were awaiting the arrival of de Courtesmain from Foxcote.'

'Explain.'

Lady Anne sighed. 'I doubt you'll understand the reasons if I do, sir, any more than you understand why Milady of Blandeforde likens herself to a servant.'

'There's no avoiding an explanation, milady. If Athelstan is who you say he is, then I'm willing to accept Sir Richard was never told falsehoods about him. But de Courtesmain certainly was. In both his written and spoken word, he affirms that my prisoner is a bastard serf called Thaddeus Thurkell who was born and raised in Develish. How so unless the whole demesne was in league to mislead him?'

Lady Anne lifted Eleanor's letter from her lap and placed it on the desk. 'It was only my daughter who led him false, sir. He sought to ingratiate himself with her after Sir Richard died and she despised him for it. You may blame me and Athelstan for not correcting the misconception but, as God is my witness, de Courtesmain never once asked if the man he believed to be Thurkell was a serf. Had he done so, all Develish would have told him no.'

Grudgingly, d'Amiens read the second letter. 'Why should I believe this? Your daughter will always take your side.'

Lady Anne wondered if he realised how much he was accepting with these words when de Courtesmain had dedicated an entire scroll to Eleanor's hatred and denunciation of her mother. 'I could as easily ask why you believe de Courtesmain, Master d'Amiens.'

'I haven't said I do, milady, but he accuses you and Thurkell of conspiring with others to win freedom for the serfs of Develish. Do you expect me, as Blandeforde's proctor, to ignore such an allegation when every man, woman and child in Develish is as bound to My Lord through sacred oath as they were to his vassal Sir Richard?'

She shook her head. 'I would not, but nor would I expect you to act on such an allegation without first questioning the honesty of the man who makes it. Does his attack on Athelstan not tell you he has great dislike of my cousin and give you cause to wonder whether truth or bitterness drives him?'

When d'Amiens made no response, Father Aristide stepped forward to place a hand on his arm. 'It's easily established, my son,' he said. 'Fetch de Courtesmain here and allow him to make his accusations to Milady. God will tell us which of the two is the perjurer.'

꧁꧂

Mistress Wilde wondered at Lady Anne's calmness when the steward returned with de Courtesmain, freed of his shackles. For herself, she was alarmed to be in a small room with him, unchained and unguarded. She took comfort from the knowledge that his weapon had been removed by My Lord of Athelstan, but her comfort was short-lived when the priest untied a hessian roll on the desk to reveal a large bejewelled cross and silver-bound Bible. In the hands of a lunatic, either was heavy enough to crush a skull.

In her mind, she was urging Milady to protest against the steward bringing so dangerous a man into her presence, but Lady Anne did the opposite. She greeted Master de Courtesmain with a gentle nod of welcome and asked how he fared. 'It saddens me to see you here, sir. I had hoped you would find contentment in Bourne.'

How strangely he looked at her, Mistress Wilde thought. Had she thought it possible, she would have said there was a yearning for Milady in his eyes. 'Thurkell destroyed that chance, milady. He turned Bourne against me.'

She shook her head. 'It was he who gave you the chance. Bourne was unpersuaded of your abilities until Athelstan spoke in praise of you. We both had every expectation you would make a success of the post.'

'You wanted rid of me, milady.'

'Not I, sir. I would have preferred you to remain in Develish. We had need of your cleverness these last three months. Our numbers have swelled with starving serfs from Pedle Hinton, and there's too little room for so many. It's been hard to find places for them to sleep.'

'Did you make use of the church, milady? I said many times that upwards of forty could sleep there in comfort.'

She smiled. 'I remembered, and Father Anselm has been most generous in allowing us the benefit of it. He takes particular care of an elder called Harold Talbot whose wits have become scattered through age. Harold addresses us all with titles from his last demesne. I am Milady of Pedle Hinton and Father Anselm is Father Jean. Were you still with us, you would have to answer to Master Marron, whom Harold assures me is quite the best steward in Dorseteshire.'

D'Amiens saw all too well what she was doing: using smiles and honeyed tones to weaken de Courtesmain's resolve. 'Marron has been dead a decade,' he said coldly. 'He was gone even before I became steward here.'

Lady Anne's eyes lit with amusement. 'Indeed. Poor Harold's confusion is very great. He believes his daughter to be his wife, and the head of our kitchen, who chastises him regularly for taking more food than he should, to be his mother—never mind she's fifteen years his junior. We answer to whatever he wants to call us for fear of upsetting him. A name is not so important that I cannot be Milady of Pedle Hinton when the need arises.'

D'Amiens made an ironic bow. 'Cleverly done, milady. Now tell us why it was necessary to keep Athelstan's name and status from de Courtesmain.'

Before she could answer, the priest advanced with the cross and the Bible. 'Kneel and place your hands on these as you swear before Almighty God that you will speak only the truth. Know that both have been blessed by the Holy Father and are as infallible as he at discovering error. Do not imperil your soul by seeking to deceive us.'

Lady Anne did as she was bid, bowing her head and saying the words aloud while begging God in her mind to forgive her. Had the cross and Bible been made from simpler, humbler materials, her conscience might have pricked her more, but she found it as hard to see Christ's love in richly ornate jewels and silver as she did in Father Aristide's thin, judgemental face. In any case, if it was indeed a mortal sin to give a fatherless child a name and family he could be proud of, her soul had been lost to her the day she inscribed Athelstan's lineage.

She placed herself on the stool again. 'Master de Courtesmain came to Develish while Sir Richard was still alive,' she said. 'Had he been made aware of Athelstan's status then, he would have informed my husband. His gratitude at being raised from bailiff in Foxcote to steward in Develish made him intensely loyal to his new master.'

'As was his duty,' said d'Amiens.

'Indeed, and I had no wish to make his position more difficult by revealing a secret he didn't need to know.'

'How was it difficult?'

'Sir Richard employed him for the single purpose of increasing the levy on Develish serfs in order to raise his personal share by another tenth. I believe Master de Courtesmain found that order troubling.'

'He should. My Lord of Blandeforde has a great dislike of extortion.' D'Amiens glanced at de Courtesmain. 'Was that made known to you by Sir Richard?'

Hugh ran his tongue across his lips. 'It was not, sir.'

D'Amiens eyed him for a moment and then instructed the priest to have him swear to the truth as Lady Anne had done. To Mistress Wilde, de Courtesmain's oath sounded false and insincere, being delivered in the same self-righteous tone with which he'd condemned Athelstan's heresy. Perhaps d'Amiens agreed, because he turned again to Lady Anne for answers.

'What other reason might he have had for finding the order troubling?'

Lady Anne's soft gaze held Hugh's for a moment. 'Sir Richard's sister wrote from Foxcote of Master de Courtesmain's zealotry in whipping serfs who could not or would not pay upwards of three-quarters of what they grew. Since my husband was illiterate, I was obliged to read the letter to him and saw how eager he was to acquire such a person. It made me distrustful of Master de Courtesmain before he arrived, though I came to understand later that he had felt debased by the vile regime in Foxcote and had no wish to repeat it in Develish.'

'Is this true, Master de Courtesmain?'

Hugh closed his eyes as if in agony. 'It grieved me greatly that Sir Richard thought I was willing to bring Foxcote's cruelty to Develish. I tried to make him understand that one half of a bounteous demesne's yield would always exceed three-quarters of one that struggled through death and hunger, but his knowledge of letters and numbers was so poor that such thinking was beyond him.'

'Are you a heretic, sir?'

'By no means,' Hugh cried, his eyes rolling in terror.

'Yet throughout your scrolls you accuse Milady and Thurkell of dissent for speaking ill of Sir Richard. How is it different when you do it?'

'I sought only to explain why his orders troubled me. My loyalty to him was never in question. The same cannot be said of Milady and Thurkell, who refused him entry when he returned from Bradmayne.'

'You were his steward. Why did you not override Milady's order and grant him admittance?'

'The serfs conspired against me. Had I tried, they would have prevented me.'

'There was nothing to stop you crossing the moat and informing Sir Richard of his people's insurrection. You wrote of Thurkell offering the raft to anyone who feared his master's anger. Why did you not take advantage of that offer yourself if you were as loyal as you claim?'

'Thurkell would have stopped me.'

'Is that true, milady?'

Lady Anne shook her head. 'Master de Courtesmain was free to leave whenever he chose. I offered him the chance to return to Foxcote after Sir Richard's death but he refused. He preferred to remain in Develish until My Lord of Bourne offered him the position of steward on his estates, which, being larger and wealthier, suited his ambitions better. I imagine he hopes to find a post here now that Bourne has let him go.'

Time passed as d'Amiens stared at one then the other, assessing their credibility. Perhaps the little Frenchman's obvious discomfort to be in Lady Anne's presence tilted the balance, for he seemed suddenly to make up his mind.

'You and Athelstan both spoke of a pledge, milady. If you give me the reasons for it, and I find them acceptable, I'll be more inclined to believe you than de Courtesmain. He has only a page from a register and self-inscribed scrolls to support his story. You have a ledger—in some places written by him—testimony from your priest and daughter, and the clear loyalty of eight fighting men to support yours. Explain why you asked your cousin to live in Develish as a peasant so that I might better reach a judgement.'

'The fighting men are her serfs,' protested Hugh. 'Their word cannot be trusted.'

'But yours *can*, sir?' Lady Anne asked. 'That was never my experience while you were living in Develish.' She turned to d'Amiens. 'I'm within my rights to refuse your request and ask the men of the town to make the judgement. Athelstan has already agreed to accept their verdict.'

'If that's your choice, all Blandeforde will learn your business, milady.'

She smiled. 'They will anyway. Once shared, a secret becomes yet another piece of gossip.' She pressed her fingers to her eyes for a moment and then dropped her hands to her lap. 'My husband was incapable of managing Develish, Master d'Amiens. You may have guessed this from your visits, though I doubt you knew it was I and not the stewards who managed in his stead. Sir Richard was quite ignorant of my involvement. He believed it was his stewards who made the decisions.'

'But they were yours?'

She nodded. 'For the most part, and always with the stewards' agreement. Before de Courtesmain, they were English freemen who saw sense in helping serfs increase their yields through improved health and the teaching of better work practices, because it made their job of collecting the King's taxes and the Church's tithes easier.' She paused. 'Sir Richard was never content with his portion, even though it always surpassed his neighbours who'd been granted larger demesnes. He pestered every steward to increase his personal levy on his people. Each resisted for the reasons Master de Courtesmain gave you, but when I read Lady

Beatrix's letter, I feared he'd finally found a man who would not. It was for this reason I asked Athelstan to come to Develish.'

'To do what?'

'Protect me from my husband when he learnt I was trying to help his serfs buy themselves out of bondage. To lose at dice was enough provocation for Sir Richard to strike me. To lose control of his people would have caused my death, I think.'

D'Amiens eyed her thoughtfully. Perhaps he was recalling Sir Richard's intemperate rage at the missing twenty nobles. 'De Courtesmain accuses you of worse. He says your plan is to take your serfs out of Develish, leaving false evidence that all have died of the pestilence, so that they can live elsewhere and gain their liberty for nothing.'

Lady Anne gave a small shrug. 'If such a plan existed, I wouldn't be here,' she answered. 'Where's the sense in telling you that all in Develish live if, in truth, I want you to believe us dead?'

'Master de Courtesmain tells a chilling tale of you inciting your people to break their oaths of fealty and your daughter denouncing you as a heretic because of it. Is he lying?'

She glanced at Hugh. 'Would you have me make such cruel allegations against you, sir?' she asked him. 'You cannot deny you tried to gain entry to Lady Eleanor's chamber when you knew her to be unchaperoned. By recollection, you told her I had lost my authority, that the serfs were in control of the demesne and only you could protect her from them. Your falsehoods caused her great distress, Master de Courtesmain.'

'Well?' d'Amiens demanded when de Courtesmain stayed silent.

'She twists everything—just as Thurkell did in the church this morning.' De Courtesmain's hands writhed in front of his chest. 'She was planning her serfs' freedom long before the pestilence came. I read in the records that more than just Sir Richard's grain was being sold to visiting merchants in the two years prior.'

'How is that unlawful?' Lady Anne asked. 'Every serf has the right to buy his way out of bondage if he can save enough gold to satisfy his lord. They all knew it would take time, but each man made a judgement on how much he would need to feed his family and sold the surplus. Where's the blame in that? No one was cheated.'

De Courtesmain levelled a trembling finger at her. 'You did it without Sir Richard's knowledge.'

She feigned a soft laugh. 'I did everything without his knowledge, Master de Courtesmain. Had I not, he would have employed a man such as you a decade ago and, together, you would have brought Develish to her knees.'

'You malign me, milady. I argued against the increased levy.'

'Not after he threatened to dismiss you. Sir Richard was so inflamed everyone in the great hall heard the exchange between you. You had to raise your own voice to plead forgiveness and promise to implement faithfully every order he gave you in future.'

Hugh shifted uncomfortably. Too much of what he'd said and done when Sir Richard was alive had been witnessed, and little of it spoke to his credit. 'Sir Richard was not a reasonable man, milady. His rages were alarming.'

'They were,' she agreed. 'Consider yourself blessed that you endured but one and that his death meant you were released from your pledge of obedience. Having surrendered to him once, you could not have resisted his instruction to falsify our yields to My Lord of Blandeforde.' She held his gaze. 'Did you write of that in your scrolls, Master de Courtesmain? Or do you reserve your enmity only for Athelstan? You had evidence of my husband's dishonesty but none at all of my cousin's.'

De Courtesmain stared at her in disbelief. 'He called himself Thaddeus Thurkell and dressed in peasant clothes, milady.'

'Is that what offends you?' she asked gently. 'That he allowed you to think him beneath you? You thought the same of me while Sir Richard lived, believing my fondness for homespun kirtles was evidence of a weak and timid nature. I remember your shock when you discovered how wrong you were.'

He spread his hands in entreaty. 'I believed what I was told, milady. Had you taken me into your confidence when I arrived, all would have been different. Did I not offer you my allegiance on the day you told me Sir Richard had died?'

'You did, sir.'

'Why did you not tell me then who Thurkell was?'

Lady Anne allowed a wry smile to play across her lips. 'You were too afraid of the pestilence to listen to anything I or Athelstan said, sir. When you weren't accusing us of heresy and wickedness, you were wailing that pustules were growing on your neck. There wasn't a moment in the day when you were able to forget your terror long enough to show you had command of yourself.'

'Your lack of fear made mine worse,' he cried. 'I worried that you had no understanding of what you were doing.'

'Yet Athelstan and I did our best to explain it to you. We even asked your advice, and you had no solutions to offer other than constant penance from my people. You found fault in all of us . . . but my serfs most of all. You made your dislike of them so clear I had no desire to give you further cause to distrust them by revealing they'd stayed silent about Athelstan while Sir Richard was alive.'

'But he was the one I distrusted, milady,' Hugh protested. 'I thought such confidence unnatural in a slave and questioned why you were so willing to take his advice. Had you informed me he was of noble birth my concerns would have vanished.'

This time her laugh was genuine. 'Come, sir,' she said with eyes full of amusement. 'You're far too clever to be so ignorant about yourself. I told you at Christmas who Athelstan was and you could barely speak for rage. You were able to tolerate his clever mind and handsome looks while you thought him a slave, but to learn he was superior to you in every way made your jealousy ungovernable.'

Hugh's anguished silence said more than any words could have done.

Twenty-two

ONCE THE JURORS HAD BEEN selected, a table set up for Andrew Tench to act as clerk and benches arranged across the forecourt for seating, Matthew Miller approached Gyles, Alleyn and James. Close up, his sharp eyes noticed the threadbare appearance of their liveries and the shaggy, ungroomed look of their horses, and he saw a passing resemblance between one of the men and Athelstan's master of hounds. Had d'Amiens been right to call them Develish serfs? he wondered. Might he also be right about Athelstan?

'You should intercede with the captain on behalf of Milady's cousin,' he told Gyles. 'He's been standing for well over an hour and his face looks markedly paler than when I first saw him. He's not far off collapse unless I miss my guess.'

Gyles had the same concern but, since soldiers could only serve one master, he nodded towards the river. 'You must raise the matter with his men, sir.'

'He'll drop before I reach them.' Miller gave his ear a thoughtful scratch. 'Mind, he's a rare sort of noble. Any other would have swooned long since from the pain of a knife through his hand.'

'His forebears on his mother's side were Moors,' Gyles said. 'There'll not be another like him outside Spain.'

'How is he related to Lady Anne?'

'Through his grandfather, who was brother to hers.'

Was that the truth? Miller wondered. Perhaps. It was hard to imagine a serf-woman producing such a giant of a man. 'He's struggling nonetheless. If the steward doesn't call the court together shortly, he'll not have the wits to argue his case.'

Gyles had expressed similar worries to Alleyn. They were all troubled by the length of time Milady had been with the steward because none could think of a benign reason why d'Amiens would extend her detention. Yet how to act when they hadn't the authority to enter the house and demand her release? 'What do you suggest, sir? I doubt My Lord will agree to sit on a bench if it means placing himself in a lower position than the people who accuse him.'

'Demand that My Lord of Blandeforde's chair be brought out. It's a hefty carved throne and your man will not lose stature by resting in it.'

Your man . . . ? 'Such a demand would come better from you, sir. You have more acquaintanceship with the captain than I. He'll pay closer heed to your worries for My Lord's welfare than he will to mine.'

Miller shook his head impatiently. 'You make a mistake by distancing yourselves,' he warned. 'Nothing suits d'Amiens better than to rule through division. He has Milady where he wants her, My Lord too weak to stand, and you and these others—' he gestured to where Ian and his companions stood by the river— 'split by a furlong of grass. Do you think your mistress so able she can win this case alone?'

Alleyn was staring towards the entranceway. 'She seems to have persuaded the steward,' he murmured.

Miller turned to watch d'Amiens escort Lady Anne onto the forecourt. Her hand rested lightly on his forearm and they stood for several moments, talking quietly together while servants brought out three armed chairs. Hovering at her other side was a formidable-looking matron who seemed to be daring every man on the forecourt to test her ability to protect her adopted mistress. When the chairs arrived, d'Amiens made an extravagant bow to Milady before helping her to settle in the one to the left. He then called the captain to bring Athelstan forward.

Miller suppressed a laugh as the two men crossed the open ground. 'I wouldn't have believed it if I hadn't seen it with my own eyes,' he muttered as d'Amiens lowered his head in respect to Athelstan and begged him to take the chair on the right. 'You're mighty fortunate in your liege lady, though I pray to God there are no more like her. The world is unsettled enough by the pestilence. We'll lose our way completely if women become our masters.'

'Or find it more easily,' James Buckler countered dryly. 'Your numbers would not be so depleted if you'd had Lady Anne as your guide these last twelve months.'

ලාර

Miller's belief that the eight fighting men were Develish serfs was confirmed by Lady Anne after d'Amiens declared himself satisfied that Athelstan's nobility had been proved. She rose with the assistance of the matron but, despite her clear weariness, her small figure stood strong and firm throughout her speech. She believed the townsmen would better understand the earlier confusion over Athelstan's status if she explained why some of her serfs had been given the liberty of freemen, for she wanted no lingering doubts about her demesne's honour and virtue. Miller expected a tale for the gullible, but she spoke so simply of her people's commitment to her and each other that he found himself greatly moved.

The trappings of nobility had meant nothing when the pestilence arrived at Develish's gate, she said. Fine gowns and embroidered jerkins gave no protection to the wearers, and both she and her cousin had felt it wrong to make a distinction between themselves and the serfs. If the lowest born were willing to share all they had with their masters, then it ill behoved those of higher birth to set themselves apart. For this reason, all in Develish had worn homespun, eaten their meals together and shared the tasks. Only Sir Richard of Develish's steward, Master de Courtesmain, who had come to the demesne as a stranger a bare few weeks before the pestilence struck, had resisted, seemingly out of a belief that to keep company with serfs was demeaning.

She singled out her captain of arms, Gyles Startout, for the greatest praise. Born a serf, he had been elevated to fighting man a decade previously by her husband, and it was he who had brought his master home and given Develish early news of the plague's virulence. The lone survivor of Sir Richard's ill-fated journey to Bradmayne, Gyles had been as determined as she and Athelstan to prevent the sickness entering their compound. To that end, he had tended and buried his master alone and then remained outside the moat for fourteen days, ready to accept whatever fate God had ordained for him.

Her soft eyes searched out Gyles as she spoke and the grizzled serf's face flushed with pleasure as he bent his knee to her. For a brief moment afterwards, her gaze locked with Matthew Miller's and the sweetness of her smile disarmed him. He had no doubt then that she had spoken the truth when she said she and her cousin had made themselves the equals of underlings. In Miller's whole life, he had never felt the warm acceptance that her smile of recognition bestowed on him.

She went on to speak of how the road north had filled with desperate people looking to flee the pestilence, drawing a comparison with the numbers who had passed through Blandeforde. She and Athelstan were happy for the demesne's fields to be raided for food but not to allow strangers carrying the pestilence into the compound. To that end, Athelstan and Gyles Startout had trained every male serf in the use of weapons so that they might defend the moat should the need arise. By God's grace, they'd only had to do it once.

A voice called out, asking if they'd triumphed, and Lady Anne smiled, saying they had. She believed that Develish now had some of the best archers in Dorseteshire, and the most proficient were the five who rode with Athelstan. He had chosen them to travel with him when he left the demesne to learn what was happening in the world outside. It had needed men of courage to make the journey, and it was a source of pride to her that Athelstan had found them amongst her serfs.

'Why did he have no fighting men of his own?' the same voice called.

'For the reason you heard before,' she answered. 'He came to Develish in the guise of a serf. A retinue would have proclaimed him as a noble.'

'Why didn't he want that?' called another.

'He knew my husband would have prevented my speaking with him if he'd known of his presence.'

A clamour of further questions rose on the air—Miller's louder than most—and Gyles felt his heart sink. What possible explanation could Milady give that would appease sceptical freemen? For himself, he thought she was only making this speech to help Thaddeus understand what she'd told the steward, but the big man's quickly veiled look of disquiet suggested he, too, thought she had backed herself into a corner. Certainly, neither he nor Gyles expected the doughty matron to rescue her.

Mistress Wilde glared at the crowd and then harangued them in Dorseteshire brogue. It was better *she* satisfy their vulgar curiosity than that Milady be obliged to do it, she declared. The poor soul had been forced to endure much from her brutal husband, not least his disdain for her Saxon lineage. Were English men so much less able than English women to understand the pain of being taken from their families and made to suffer under a Norman yoke? It was no wonder she had sympathy for her serfs, whose treatment at the hands of their master had been as vile as hers. Did the men of Blandeforde not ask themselves why Sir Richard had brought a vicious criminal to govern his estates? If de Courtesmain thought nothing of a driving a blade into the arm and hand of My Lord of Athelstan, consider the punishments he would have inflicted on Milady's people if they had been unable to meet her husband's demands for a higher levy on their crops. Praise God for her kindness in trying to protect them, and praise God for sending Athelstan to protect Milady.

She directed her last remark at Jeremiah Slater. 'Your life 'a not bin zo eazy you canna unnerstan 'ow badly hurt a wife is from a beäten or 'ow close they serfs are to starvin when en crop is ta'en.'

'I unnerstan it well,' he answered. 'What be the reason for the Franky's haëtred o' milor'?'

Mistress Wilde tapped her heart. 'Jalousie.'

She went on to tell the townsmen what de Courtesmain had said when he withdrew his accusations against Athelstan. He took no fault to himself, blaming Milady and her serfs for allowing him to believe that Athelstan was inferior to him. It made no matter that he should have guessed so unusual a man could never be a serf. To be tricked had caused him heartache and grief, for he felt he had done nothing to merit their mockery. He admitted trying to turn Milady's daughter and her people against her after Athelstan's departure, but only to restore himself to his rightful position as steward. Bereft of Athelstan's support, and with her serfs in revolt, she would have leant on de Courtesmain as she should have done from the start.

Jeremiah Slater looked amused. 'Be he smitten wi' 'er?'

'He be.'

'He mus be blin' to 'issel'.'

Just witless, said Mistress Wilde dismissively. Despite all he had said and done, he had still fallen to his knees before Milady, begging her forgiveness and pleading with her to allow him to return to Develish.

∞

From where they were standing, Ian and his companions felt a deep discomfort to see de Courtesmain dragged in chains from the house to face trial for his attack on Thaddeus. They could tell from the respect d'Amiens showed Milady when he brought her outside that she must have prevailed, but they questioned whether that victory should be at the expense of the Frenchman.

'He was a fool to stab Thaddeus,' said Peter. 'It wouldn't be happening otherwise.'

'Except Thaddeus probably drove him to it,' muttered Edmund. 'He can be mighty provoking when he has a mind to it.'

The same thoughts were in Gyles's mind. He had no liking for de Courtesmain, whose duplicitous ways had been the cause of Isabella's wounding by Lady Eleanor, but he had no wish to see the snivelling creature flogged. Far more lies had been told and written against him than any he had conceived. Alleyn and James showed their unease in the guilty shifting of their feet, and Gyles was grateful Miller had joined the townsmen on the benches and wasn't close enough to feel their discomfort.

Gyles wouldn't have recognised de Courtesmain in the sad appearance the little Frenchman presented now. Gone was the well-oiled hair, clean-shaven face and prettiness of dress, and in their place were straggled locks, a scruffy beard and peasant clothes. Runnels of tears glistened on his cheeks and he clasped a small wooden cross between his shackled hands as if to show penitence. Behind him walked the priest, his face harsh and unsmiling.

There was a blood lust in the air if the caterwauls that came from the back of the crowd were any guide. Perhaps floggings appealed to these men, or they'd grown bored with the interminable wait for something to happen. For once, Gyles felt himself disappointed in Milady, who watched without emotion as de Courtesmain was forced to his knees in the centre of the forecourt. And what of Thaddeus? Was he untroubled by his conscience?

It seemed not. With a brief nod to Lady Anne, as if to acknowledge an agreement between them, he rose lazily to his feet and asked d'Amiens' permission to address the court. His pallor was less marked from sitting for a quarter-hour, and he made an impressive figure, towering as he did over every seated person on the forecourt. He stood for a moment or two in silence, and then bent his head in respect to the assembled men, touching his fingers to his forehead as he had to Lady Anne.

'I am your humble servant, sirs. Should a time arise when one or more of you has need of my help, you have but to ask.' He smiled to see their surprise. 'Not all traditions are the same. That part of me which is Moorish requires me to repay kindness with kindness, and I offer you my services gladly in return for the courtesy you've shown me.' He paused to collect his thoughts. 'I count myself fortunate that I was raised in the customs of two traditions, because both have taught me wisdom. The giving of charity is common to each, but I have yet to meet a person, English or Moor, who is as steeped in human kindness as Lady Anne of Develish.'

He turned to bend his knee to her. 'God was gracious when he permitted your letter to reach me, cousin. We have written to each other many times down the years, but you had never before asked for my help. I bless God that you did and that He allowed me to make the journey in advance of the pestilence. It was my honour to help you defend your people against this terrible disease, and a greater honour to take your message of hope to the men and women of Dorseteshire. From what I have witnessed in my travels these past months, I believe the worst has passed, and through God's grace we can all begin to dream of a future.'

He faced the crowd again, walking forward to stand in front of de Courtesmain's kneeling figure. 'English justice demands that this man be punished for the crime he has committed against me. Do any of the jurymen doubt that he wounded me most gravely?'

'We do not, sire,' called their foreman. 'But we will hear his explanation if he has one.'

The priest placed his hand on de Courtesmain's head. 'It's an offence against God to attack a noble,' he declared loudly. 'There is no excuse. The prisoner has expressed penitence and will accept his punishment.'

Thaddeus smiled slightly. 'He thought me a serf, Father. Should we condemn him for being wrong?'

'He believed what he wanted to believe.'

'As did you.' Thaddeus produced the dagger from his pocket. 'Is this yours? It has the cross of Christ on its haft, though I question how de Courtesmain came by it.'

Aristide's eyes narrowed. 'Would you have me divulge the secrets of the confessional? I say again, the prisoner has expressed penitence and will accept his punishment.'

'Yet I'm curious to know why he didn't attack me inside the church. He had good reason after I knocked him to the ground. If the knife had been in his possession then, would he not have used it to defend himself?'

Aristide stepped past de Courtesmain to speak in an undertone. 'Desist now,' he hissed. 'Your position is not so secure that you can question a priest.'

Thaddeus's answer wasn't loud enough to carry to the townsmen. 'I saw your fear when the captain brought news of Milady's arrival. You knew I'd reveal your deceits if she gained me a public hearing.' He dropped the knife to the ground between them. 'You may have need of it when the people of Blandeforde learn how shamelessly you saved your own skin at the expense of theirs. They won't thank you for accusing them of wickedness when the closing of the bridge was all that was needed to keep their families from dying.'

The priest's hatred was powerful. 'You're everything de Courtesmain claims you to be.'

'And he somewhat wiser than I painted him. He'd have used the blade sooner and with more passion if he'd thought your promises of a position here would be kept.' Thaddeus reached down to place his hand under de Courtesmain's elbow and raise him to his feet, looking beyond Aristide to the crowd. 'I beg a further kindness of you, my friends,' he called. 'The priest tells me this man's mind is so disturbed he has no understanding of what he's done. Allow me to sentence him according to Moorish justice. It's against our custom to take vengeance on the helpless without offering mercy first.'

'What form would the sentence take?' asked the foreman of the jury.

'The court must order him to recompense me through service. He will be without rights or home to call his own until I judge his penance to be over.'

'You would make him your slave?'

'Or offer him to another. Moorish tradition demands that debts be paid, be they debts of honour or dishonour, and it's the entitlement of the victim to decide who should benefit from the reparation. By such means even monetary obligations are met.'

'Do you choose to offer him to another?'

'Only to one who has shown me kindness.' He touched his forehead to Jeremiah Slater. 'Do you request him, sir?'

The greybeard gave a surprised laugh. 'He'll be of no use to me if his wits have gone.'

'Nor to anyone else,' said Miller. 'He'll likely kill the man who takes him in. You should worry about that yourself, My Lord. If he's attacked you once, he'll do it again.'

'Then his life will be forfeit, for I will not be so merciful a second time.' Thaddeus looked towards the jury. 'What is your decision, sirs? Will you allow Moorish justice to prevail?'

They whispered amongst themselves for several minutes before the foreman signalled agreement, and Thaddeus made the now-familiar gesture of touching his forehead in respect. Lady Anne wondered where he had learnt it and why it was so effective at disarming hostility. He performed the obeisance with such easy grace that he might have been born to it, and she marvelled at how quickly the simple courtesy won the townsmen's trust. None seemed to doubt he'd been raised a Moor or that the customs he cited were genuine.

Clearly, d'Amiens saw danger in allowing Athelstan's influence to grow, for his quickness in accepting the jurymen's decision verged on the unseemly. He instructed Andrew Tench to draw up an order, binding de Courtesmain to Athelstan's service, and then commanded the captain to escort My Lord and his prisoner to the riverbank, where his men awaited him.

'You'll be keen to depart, sire,' he said, bending his neck. 'I regret my error in arresting you but entreat you to believe that the decision was made in good faith. As proctor to My Lord of Blandeforde, I am bound by duty to investigate all and every allegation that is laid before me.'

Lady Anne hid her dismay as Thaddeus turned towards him with disdain in his eyes, afeared that her friend was about to overplay his hand and jeopardise their escape. They had both told too many falsehoods to continue this mummery further. Nevertheless, it was arguable whether she or d'Amiens was the more surprised by his response.

'You have stolen two days of my life, Master d'Amiens. Will you hear my terms of reparation before the worthy men of Blandeforde or would you rather accompany me to the river and discuss them as we walk?'

ᏇᎧ

There was a lengthy silence while every person on the forecourt turned to watch the procession make its way across the stretch of grass. Athelstan walked with the steward; the captain led de Courtesmain by his chains. Finding herself forsaken, Lady Anne folded her hands in her lap and retained what composure she could by pretending interest in the ground at her feet. She was quite bereft of ideas on what to say or do, and only the stalwart bulk of Mistress Wilde behind her chair gave her any sense of protection.

The priest's animosity was so strong she could feel it from where he was standing, but whether his anger was directed at her or Thaddeus she couldn't tell. Whichever, he would not stay silent with her at his mercy, exposed and abandoned in front of the crowd, and she doubted she had the strength to keep fighting him, for her sleepless night and painful journey had taken their toll. The sound of footsteps on the forecourt caused her to turn her head, and a surge of relief rose in her heart to see Gyles and Alleyn approach. They paused to bow in unison and then took up position on either side of her chair, staring solemnly at Aristide.

'Is this another fanciful Moorish custom?' he demanded in French of Lady Anne. 'The menacing of priests?'

She studied him curiously. Was it Thaddeus's acts of obeisance that had angered him? she wondered. Could it be that his pride was offended because he hadn't received one himself? 'I doubt their intention is to discomfort you, Father,' she answered. 'They follow the English custom of standing guard to their liege lord.'

He shook his fist at her. 'You are not their liege lord, milady, and serfs have no right to enter a manor court. Will you instruct them to withdraw or must I?'

Gyles took a step forward to place himself between the two. 'If you give such an order it will not be obeyed, Father,' he said in French. 'I have no wish to challenge your authority, but I will if I deem it necessary. Milady's safety is all that concerns me.'

Aristide pointed towards the guards who stood around the forecourt. 'These soldiers will take you in charge if you resist.'

Gyles placed his hand on the bow which lay diagonally across his chest. 'Then be it on your head if the captain's peace is broken, sir.'

Jeremiah Slater pushed himself to his feet. He, too, spoke in French. 'You make trouble where there is none, Father,' he said irritably. 'I know of no by-law that precludes serfs from the manor court. If such an injunction existed, the steward would have barred Mistress Wilde's attendance.' He turned to address his fellows, reverting to English. 'I'm minded to follow My Lord of Athelstan's example and demand reparation for the losses we've endured. It impresses me as a better custom than anything the Church or French law offers us. How think the rest of you?'

Had she been a distant observer to the heated discussion that followed, Lady Anne would have found it amusing to watch this group of men argue the merits of invented Moorish customs with the priest. As it was, she was at the heart of it, with the townsmen begging her to support them as fervently as she had supported her people. To avoid antagonising the priest, she reminded them that the court was still in session and that, as an invited guest, her words carried no authority. The men of Blandeforde must decide and argue the case for themselves.

After her fourth such careful response, Aristide accused her of inciting heresy. 'Why do you encourage these thoughts instead of condemning them? Where is your responsibility?'

She bent her head in apology. 'Forgive me, Father. I thought you believed the views of a woman to be of no account. Would you have me answer as a liege lord who is bound by duty to support her King and the Church?'

His lips thinned. 'Not if your ambition is to add to this mockery. The Moors are a heathen race and should be exposed as such.'

'My only knowledge of them comes from Athelstan, and he is far from heathen. Nevertheless, I will do my best to assist you.' She rose to her feet. 'Good sirs, Father Aristide sees heresy in your ideas and urges you to abandon them. I would ask only that you bring reason to your thinking. For each of you, your greatest loss has been the death of your wife and children. I hear the sorrow in your voices when you say you wish God had taken you and not them.'

'We all feel that, milady,' said Slater.

'As does every man and woman in Doreseteshire who has suffered similarly,' she answered gently. 'You are not alone in looking for someone to blame for your grief. But who should that person be? And how much will you demand from him? One noble? Ten? A thousand? What price do you put on the lives of your families?'

'More than any man can pay.'

'Then talk of monetary reparation is foolish, is it not? Your hearts will mend sooner with kindly companions than bags of uncaring gold. You can insist Master d'Amiens choose widows for you as payment for your wives, but are you not better able to manage these affairs yourselves?'

Slater and most of the crowd expressed agreement, but Miller was less easily placated. 'The steward should have given us the same protection he gave the household, milady. How is it right that freemen were left to die while servants were helped to live? I, for one, demand reparation for that.'

'In what form, Master Miller? My cousin has told you that the custom of the Moors is to repay in kind. Would you have Mistress Wilde lose her life because she obeyed the steward's orders?'

His mouth twisted in a sour smile. 'I would have the men responsible pay. And if reparation must be made in kind, there are countless dead in a pit—the little servant girl from here amongst them—who were tossed in without ceremony after the last of our priests died.' He looked at Aristide. 'It's past due they were disinterred and reburied with their names recorded and the proper rites performed—and the priest and the steward are the men to do it.'

Aristide ignored him to address Lady Anne. 'I barely understand his speech,' he said in French. 'You must make the answers for me.'

She thought he'd understood perfectly well. Nevertheless . . . 'It's a poor vengeance that comes back to bite you, Master Miller,' she said. 'I doubt it's wise to unearth the dead when the town has been free of the pestilence for eight weeks.'

'You think we'll catch it from corpses?'

'It's not something I would risk in Develish.'

'Nor I in Blandeforde,' said Slater firmly. 'The dead will rest peacefully enough if Father Aristide consecrates the pit and the land around it. As to their names, Master d'Amiens can supply them from his own register once a census has been taken of the living.'

Miller gave a grunt of disgust when the townsmen voiced agreement yet again. 'You're overly quick to give up on your losses. If reparation is what we want, we must demand it.'

'Then offer sensible ideas,' called a voice from the back.

'Perhaps Milady has a suggestion,' said Andrew Tench. 'She knows the custom better than we, for her cousin will have explained it to her.'

But Lady Anne was drained of both strength and answers. She placed a trembling hand on the arm of her chair to steady herself, and it fell to Gyles to answer for her. 'You would do better to put your questions to My Lord,' he said, nodding towards the grass beyond the forecourt. 'Unless I miss my guess, he and Master d'Amiens are returning.'

Twenty-three

JAMES BUCKLER, STANDING WITH THE horses, didn't need Gyles's hard stare and fractional movement of his head towards Thaddeus to know he must act. He'd heard the exchanges on the forecourt and could see as well as his friend that Milady was too fatigued to continue. Yet he doubted Thaddeus was in any better condition to offer solutions. What had seemed like a good idea to save tender Develish consciences was set to become a millstone around their necks.

With quick, practised movements, he hobbled his mount and then attached the halters of the others to its breast collar before stepping away to stand in Thaddeus and d'Amiens' path. Five paces back walked the captain, carrying the manacles he'd removed from de Courtesmain, and behind him came Ian and Edmund, leading a pony with leather bags slung across its withers. James recognised them as those that carried Lady Eleanor's dowry and, praying they presaged good fortune, he forced himself to bend his knee to Thaddeus.

The bandage on Thaddeus's hand was soaked with blood and his face had paled again, but the brief flicker of humour in his eyes said he understood James's reluctance. James had barely been able to show deference to Sir Richard, and to bow before a man he'd known from birth as a bastard changeling was an even greater humiliation. Thaddeus gestured for him to rise. 'You have a message for me?'

'Milady of Develish requests your assistance when your business with the steward is concluded, sire. The townsmen have questions about the Moorish custom of reparation and, being most wearied from her journey and the events of this day, she believes you will answer them better than she can.'

He watched Thaddeus take his left hand in his right and dig his thumb and forefinger into the bandage around his wound. Was it any surprise the bandage was wet with blood if this was the way he was staying alert? The pain must have been severe, but his voice gave no indication of it when he addressed the steward. 'How long will it take to prepare the writs of transfer, Master d'Amiens?'

'Not above an hour, My Lord. The wording is standard and needs but the name of the holder to be changed. I foresee no difficulties as long as the gold reaches the required weight.'

'It will. My men will carry the bags inside and watch as you weigh the amounts. When the documents are ready, bring them to the forecourt so that I may sign them.' He smiled to see d'Amiens' immediate resistance. 'It's never wise to let grievances fester, sir. The townsmen's anger will be harder to appease if you oblige them to wait for Blandeforde's return. You've suffered nothing by honouring your debt to me—indeed, most would say you've gained by it through the added revenue to Blandeforde's coffers—so why fear accord with your own people?'

D'Amiens searched out Matthew Miller. 'Some will break their side of the bargain as soon as it's made.'

'I'm sure they believe the same about you, sir. It's a sad world where trust is in such short supply. Aren't you grieved that a woman finds it easier to win the townsmen's respect than you or the priest? Even with my limited understanding of English customs, that would seem unusual. How do you account for it?'

'You said it yourself, sire. Milady is a rare woman.'

'So rare that she was willing to take the hand of every man on the forecourt. Will you do likewise if I find a way to soothe their sense of injustice? You will win their confidence if you do.'

'Milady was foolhardy.'

'Or wise enough to recognise that two months without a death means the pestilence has passed. If she believes the time has come to abandon fear and embrace the future, should you not also?'

D'Amiens watched irritably as Thaddeus strode towards the forecourt and then, with a muttered command to the captain, he beckoned Ian and Edmund to follow him to the house. As they left, he said crossly that the sooner they finished their business the better he'd be pleased.

The remark won sympathy from James. He may not have known it, but he was as beset by dread as his son had been the first time Thaddeus had claimed to be a noble. So much could still go wrong, yet Thaddeus seemed determined to test God's patience. The wiser course would surely have been to distance himself and Milady from the crowd, but, instead, he lowered himself to his chair and engaged with them.

The captain moved to stand beside James. 'My Lord is power-fully persuasive,' he said, watching Thaddeus touch his forehead to Aristide. 'He'll have the priest reconciled to Moorish customs before he's done.' He motioned towards the guard house. 'Will you accompany me, sir? Master d'Amiens has granted My Lord the use of a carriage and horses so that Milady may return home tonight. The stabling is beyond the house and there are three wagons to choose from. I will order my men to assist you in preparing one.'

James looked at the sun. 'There's scarce three hours of light left.'

'My Lord intends to travel with torches.' A teasing smile lit the captain's eyes. 'Having sampled it himself, he believes Milady will find the highway less arduous than Master d'Amiens' hospitality.'

⁊

Olyver shrugged when Peter asked what they were supposed to do with de Courtesmain. The Frenchman lay curled on the grass, sobbing like a child, and nothing he said was intelligible.

'What's he afraid of?' asked Joshua.

'Develish's anger?' suggested Olyver.

'More likely being abandoned along the way,' said Peter. 'He'll have nothing if Thaddeus decides to set him loose two miles outside Blandeforde.' He knelt to shake de Courtesmain's shoulder. 'You must cease your crying, sir. You shame yourself by it.'

A whisper reached his ear. 'I am already shamed.'

'Maybe so, but none of us has slept enough to have patience with your whining. You're wrong if you think it'll win Milady's or Athelstan's sympathy. They'll respect you more if you take your punishment bravely.'

'I'm lower than a serf.'

'Only because you behaved like a weasel.' Peter grasped the neck of the Frenchman's tunic and hauled him to his feet. 'What do you say to me taking him out ahead of time and talking some sense into him?' he asked Olyver. 'Milady shouldn't have to deal with him in this state.'

'Where will you go?'

'Along the highway.' Peter set to unbuckling the second pack pony's harness. 'He can use this for a mount. The other will be able to carry the load once its rid of the gold. If you haven't caught up with me before the light fades, which you won't with a wagon in tow, I'll make camp near the road's edge. You'll likely see my fire before I see your torches.'

Olyver helped him lift the load to the ground. 'Then make yourself useful while you wait for us,' he said, loosening the knot that held the cauldron and a bag of butchered mutton before attaching them to Peter's saddle. 'I'll not be the only one slitting my throat if I don't see food this night.'

'These, too,' added Joshua, removing a sack of beans and another of dried fruit. 'You can wear them around your neck the way we've had to,' he told de Courtesmain, stringing the rope across his shoulders. 'Peter won't welcome your company, but I don't doubt he'd rather listen to your grudges than have you cause Milady further irritation here.'

Olyver stooped to lace his hands beneath de Courtesmain's foot. 'You should count yourself lucky that God saw fit to inflict you upon us,' he said severely. 'You'd have died long since if He hadn't sent you to Develish.'

ꙮ

The crowd of women and children at the gate had dispersed, leaving only a handful of youths to witness Peter and de Courtesmain's departure. Two or three walked with them, agog with curiosity to know what was happening. Peter answered their questions honestly but shook his head in disgust when they expressed disappointment to hear there'd be no flogging.

'Is that what you've been waiting for?' he asked.

'There's nothing else to do.'

Peter instructed Hugh to take a firm hold of the pony's mane and led him at a fast trot to the end of the approach road. From there, he slowed to a walk. They received curious glances from the women they passed in the streets but none was emboldened enough to speak. He expected to find guards on the bridge, and advised Hugh to speak and act like a freeman if he didn't want to be returned to the steward as an absconder, but the road was empty and they crossed without trouble.

As they made their way up the gentle incline of the hill, Hugh found his voice. 'Do you plan to kill me?'

Peter glanced at him. 'Why would I want to?'

'To spare Milady further worry. I can't speak of what I know if I'm dead.'

'You've already spoken,' said Peter. 'What use would your death be now? The time to kill you was before you entered Blandeforde. I don't say I wouldn't have been tempted. We'd all have been saved a lot of trouble if you'd met with an accident on the road from Bourne.'

'Others may believe me.'

'Not while you're bonded to Athelstan, they won't. No one will hear you unless he gives you permission to speak. Be grateful he kept you alive. You know from the lashes you inflicted on the serfs of Foxcote that you'd not have survived. We had word before you ever reached Develish that five of the men you scourged died from having their skin torn from their ribs.'

Hugh closed his eyes. 'I did what I was commanded to do.'

Peter thought of the numerous times Thaddeus had chastised his companions for blaming their faults on others instead of taking responsibility themselves. 'Is that your defence for every bad act you commit? "Someone else made me do it." I'll wager you blame God for your misfortunes as often as you blame men.'

'I fear His wrath too much to chastise Him.'

'Then I'd not wish to live a second in your shoes, Master de Courtesmain. You must struggle with terror every day. An angry God's as hard to please as an angry lord.'

A flicker of irritation flared in Hugh's heart. 'What knowledge do you have of either? Develish serfs are ignorant of the meaning of wrath or fear.'

Peter gave a grunt of amusement. 'As were you while you lived amongst us. Was that not more pleasurable than where you find yourself now?'

It was a moment before Hugh could produce the words. 'I fear returning to Develish.'

'Because you're a traitor or because you're a slave?'

'Both,' came the whispered reply. 'I'll be a figure of hatred and mockery through what I've done. It would be a kindness to end my life now.'

Peter led him over the breast of the hill. 'You give up too easily, Master de Courtesmain. If the steward honours his promise to grant Athelstan title to Pedle Hinton, you'll be making your home there rather than Develish.' He saw relief enter de Courtesmain's face. 'You won't be so keen when you see it,' he warned. 'The village is destroyed and the roof of the house half-burnt. Your hands will grow calluses cutting timber and mixing daub before they ever lift a pen again.'

The rest of their conversation took place beside a fire while Peter cooked mutton and watched the highway for approaching torches. For his part, Hugh felt compelled to keep revisiting his sins of omission and commission, and the confessions he made to Peter were more honest than any he'd made to a priest. His greatest wretchedness was to lose his status, but Peter advised him to cease fretting about an order made in Blandeforde. Milady and Athelstan would never reduce a man to slavery. They had striven too long to win freedom for their people to take a backward step now.

'You must learn new skills and work with the rest of us to promote the good of all,' he told Hugh. 'When Milady and Athelstan succeed in their plans to turn Develish and Pedle Hinton into communities of freemen and merchants, you'll profit along with the rest of us. If you cling to your one talent, you'll be left behind.'

Lady Anne had said the same on the morning of the great storm, and Hugh had dismissed the idea as fanciful. But he saw that she and Peter were right when the glimmer of torchlight appeared on the highway. As the convoy approached, there was no mistaking Thurkell astride his black charger. He rode between the Startout twins, both holding flares above their heads. On their flanks, Joshua and Edmund steered their mounts with their knees to leave their hands free to operate the bows they were carrying; ahead of them loped the dogs, questing to and fro across the road to sniff out miscreants amongst the trees.

Had they been strangers, Hugh would have taken them for what they appeared to be, a lord and his fighting men, and to cling to the comforting idea that they were serfs—and therefore beneath him—would be as foolish as Peter had warned. Even the older Develish men who followed with Milady's wagon rode with assurance, and Hugh's cheeks heated to recall how he had disparaged them to her, saying none had the wisdom or ability to sit on her council.

Panic engulfed him as they drew closer, and such strong pains struck at his chest that he thought he was dying. He prayed he was. Dead, he would not have to take their derision or search in vain for ways to atone. It was a mystery to him now that he had been so unable to accept that the education which had benefited him might also benefit those whom the Church had ruled beneath him.

He felt Peter's hand grip his arm and heard the youth's call of welcome to Thurkell.

'You're a sight for sore eyes,' came the laughing retort. 'I'm told you have a veritable feast for us.' As the charger brought him level, he gave a nod to Hugh. 'I trust I find you well, Master de Courtesmain.'

Hugh felt tears prick behind his eyes. 'You do, sire.'

Thaddeus swung from his saddle. 'I'm glad to hear it. You were in safe hands with Peter.' He passed his reins to Ian. 'Let me speak with Milady. If she's happy to spend the night in the open, I say we make camp here. For myself, I haven't the energy to travel to Develish this night.'

⚬⚬

As the flames of the fire flickered across the smiling faces of the people around it, Hugh was reminded of when Lady Anne had danced with her serfs to celebrate their victory over Bourne's archers. He had condemned her for it, believing she was endangering her daughter and him by lowering herself to their level. To offer friendship to base-born people was to encourage rebellion, and he'd feared that he and Lady Eleanor, being Normans, would become the butts of their hatred.

He wished now that he had followed her advice and sought closeness with these men. Lady Anne had lost no respect through her care for them. Indeed, their admiration for her showed in everything they said and did. When she stepped from the carriage, taking Thurkell's hand to steady herself, she was dressed once again in homespun, and Hugh had felt an absurd relief to see the simple kirtle. It made his own peasant tunic and britches less noticeable amidst the Athelstan and Develish liveries.

Behind her had come Mistress Wilde, her face wreathed in shy smiles as Thurkell assisted her to the ground. Her belief that he was Athelstan was reinforced by the Develish men's constant use of his title, and Hugh saw that they found it easy to do. Whatever the truth of his birth, there was little doubt they accepted him as a worthy leader beside Milady.

Mistress Wilde was presented as Lady Anne's chaperone for the journey, but when the woman spoke of her excitement to spend a few days in Develish before returning home, Hugh guessed that Milady's reason for bringing her was to remove any lingering uncertainties d'Amiens might have about Thurkell's status. The people of Develish were as committed to upholding the imposture as every man here, and Mistress Wilde would take her belief in his nobility back to Blandeforde. It seemed she was also the bearer of clean rags to re-dress Thurkell's wounds, and Hugh was grateful to Peter for drawing him away while that task was performed.

'We'll serve a better purpose collecting wood,' he said, beckoning to Edmund to bring a torch. After a hundred paces, he asked Edmund if Athelstan had succeeded.

The other youth grinned. 'He did. In return for a pledge of fealty to Blandeforde, Athelstan bears writs granting him vassal status over Pedle Hinton.'

'Will they hold?'

'No reason why not. D'Amiens wanted the gold more than he wanted a demesne devoid of people. Ian said he warned Athelstan he'd give him no quarter if the estate failed in its tax obligations.'

'How did My Lord answer?'

'He advised d'Amiens to concern himself with his own affairs. He was fortunate to have Athelstan's gold to plug the holes in Blandeforde's revenue today, but the shortfalls will increase if the townsmen can't find the confidence to reopen the markets and resume trading. He's persuaded d'Amiens to meet with their council and hear their ideas. It seems they're proposing to hold markets outside their boundaries until they're sure the pestilence has passed.'

'Will that help?'

'Athelstan believes so. Their greatest fear is to allow sufferers into the town again. He's advised all to keep their distance and toss their money onto the ground rather than touch hands. If customers and visiting merchants do the same, confidence will grow on both sides.'

'What else did he say?'

'That he and Milady will set an example by sending their surplus stock to Blandeforde as soon as the markets open. Where Develish and Pedle Hinton lead, others will follow. The townsmen cheered him, but he told us afterwards that it will benefit us as well as them. D'Amiens will be reassured that both demesnes can submit taxes if he sees us trading regularly in Blandeforde.'

Peter saw Hugh shake his head. 'You don't agree, Master de Courtesmain?'

'If the dead are as numerous as Athelstan says, there won't be enough hungry mouths to fetch a good price on meat. To satisfy d'Amiens, he'll need to show another source of wealth.'

'What do you suggest?'

'That he brings in reserves of gold from his Spanish demesnes as soon as foreign ships make entry to England's harbours again. A receipt, properly set out and signed by a ship's captain, will be all that is needed to convince d'Amiens the transaction took place.'

Edmund exchanged a glance with Peter, neither sure what de Courtesmain meant by this. That he believed Athelstan had reserves of gold or that a receipt could be easily forged? Both could see the merit of forgery to explain the wealth they'd plundered from abandoned demesnes this last month. Their biggest haul had come from Bradmayne. For all his professed need of Lady Eleanor's dowry, My Lord of Bradmayne had still left a sizeable fortune behind in his treasury. It should have been stolen by bandits, since the demesne was deserted, but as Thaddeus had said, he and his companions seemed to be the only bandits left in south Dorseteshire.

The fruits of their labour were buried deep in a sand dune overlooking the sea near Poole. Used carefully and wisely, Thaddeus believed there was enough dead men's gold to rebuild Pedle Hinton and set all in Develish on the path to freedom. Nevertheless, he had yet to find a way to excuse his thieving. Certainly, the idea of forging receipts hadn't occurred to him.

'Do you think ships will return soon, Master de Courtesmain?' Edmund asked.

Hugh wondered afterwards if that was the moment he chose to embrace change, or if the desire to do so hadn't been with him from the moment a chattel wife took control of Develish. 'My Lord of Bourne thought so,' he answered. 'I prepared several receipts for him in expectation of trade resuming before too long. He thought it wise to divide his stolen gold across several ships, and I still remember the names I gave the vessels. Will Athelstan be interested to learn them? His own transactions might carry more credence if another lord has used the same ships.'

Peter gave a friendly nod. 'Be sure he will,' he said.

୧୦

As the meal was eaten, Hugh kept his head lowered for fear of meeting Lady Anne's or Thurkell's gaze. He had little confidence that Peter spoke for either of them, and believed it was a matter of time only before one or both forced him to account for his actions. He feared that time had come when Thurkell laid aside his plate and asked Ian to bring his writing desk. He opened the lid and revealed the scrolls Hugh had taken to Blandeforde. He handed Lady Anne the page from the Develish register. 'This is part of your people's history and belongs to you, milady.'

Lady Anne took a moment to read it again and then leant forward to feed the cracked vellum into the fire. 'A small part only,' she said, 'and since there's no way of threading it back into the ledger, it will be lost to us anyway. Better it adds to our warmth than crumbles to dust through neglect.'

Thaddeus watched a lick of flame destroy the evidence of his birth and then raised his eyes to Hugh's. 'The rest are yours, sir, even the letter I left for you in Bourne. Master d'Amiens had no interest in keeping them so I asked for their return. Do you wish to retain them or shall we allow cleansing fire to do its work? I suggest we'll build a better future on new foundations than ones that have become twisted over time.'

Hugh was too nervous to answer. Was he included in this future, he wondered, or did Thurkell speak only for the people of Develish? If the man's intention was to cast him aside, would he not do better to keep the scrolls and threaten to use them as Lady Anne had threatened to use Bourne's letters?

'Perhaps Master de Courtesmain will find the decision easier if you burn the writ of slavery first,' Lady Anne advised quietly.

'Indeed.' Thaddeus lifted the writ and passed it to Peter. 'Allow Master de Courtesmain to reassure himself it's the correct document and then place it in the flames. Blandeforde's seal at the bottom should help it burn.'

Hugh took the page from Peter in trembling hands and ran his tongue around his mouth to produce some words. 'I wounded you badly and had malice in my heart when I did it. What punishment will you demand of me in place of this?'

With a sigh of impatience, as if despairing of Hugh's ability to understand anything, Peter seized back the parchment and thrust it into the fire. 'If it's pain you seek, you'll find it soon enough by working without complaint at whatever you're asked to do,' he said sternly. 'I wasn't jesting when I said your hands will grow calluses cutting timber before they ever lift a pen again.' He stood to retrieve the scrolls from Thaddeus's writing desk. 'All Athelstan asks is whether you wish to make your future with us or forge it alone. There's few would offer you the choice after the trouble you've caused, but Athelstan does. What's your decision?'

'I would join you,' Hugh whispered.

Peter tossed the scrolls into the flames and resumed his seat, tapping the Frenchman's shoulder by way of welcome. 'You'll likely change your mind after you've eaten Joshua's stew five nights in a row, but that's a penance we all have to pay.'

When the laughter subsided, the conversation turned to the ending of Develish's isolation. Thurkell said that there was no knowing how the rest of England fared but he believed it would be safe for Lady Anne to cross the moat on the morrow. She agreed so readily that Hugh knew she must have come to the same decision herself. Perhaps her journey to Blandeforde had been all that was needed to confirm what she and Thurkell had believed all along: that the pestilence would end as surely as the pox or the flux. Hugh wondered that he had been so unwilling to see the soundness of their arguments when even a priest like Aristide had preferred reason over the teachings of the Church.

Lady Anne promised Mistress Wilde a fine celebration, and the woman's plump face was wreathed in smiles to be invited as an equal. It seemed, however, that Thurkell would not be part of the festivities because he gave instructions on where the convoy would divide the following day. Lady Anne, Mistress Wilde and Milady's men would take the highway to Develish, while he and his, together with Master de Courtesmain, would ride to Pedle Hinton. With God's grace, he hoped to invite Milady and her daughter for a visit in the summer, when the forget-me-nots were in full bloom and the beginnings of a fine new demesne were underway.

Hugh felt Lady Anne's gaze upon him. 'Do you look forward to helping My Lord rebuild Pedle Hinton, Master de Courtesmain?' she asked.

Tongue-tied by nerves again, he could only nod.

'I shall ask the women of Develish to stay with me to till and plant our fields, and the men to cross the hills to assist in Pedle Hinton. Master Miller and several more have already promised to make the journey from Blandeforde, and My Lord hopes to attract others in return for wages. He looks to create a community of freemen who can use their wits and skills to improve their lives and the lives of their children. When the time comes, he will need a person knowledgeable in figures to keep a tally of their earnings. Would you be comfortable in such a post, Master de Courtesmain?'

Hugh stared at his hands so that he wouldn't have to look at her. His greatest regret was that he had accepted her illiterate husband's view of her instead of deciding her character for himself. 'I doubt you and My Lord would be right to trust my judgement, milady. I have been wrong about everything.'

'Not everything,' she answered gently. 'Your only real error was to believe that God judges a man by his birth and not by his deeds.'

☙❧

When the moon was three hours from midnight, Gyles Startout lit a torch from the fire and instructed the men to follow him into the woodland in search of bracken for beds. He invited Mistress Wilde to accompany them, raising her forcefully to her feet with his free hand cupped beneath her elbow when she expressed reluctance to leave the warmth of the flames. Alleyn moved to assist him, marching her unceremoniously into the trees while telling her amiably that she must make herself responsible for Milady's mattress in the wagon.

She wrestled herself free after a hundred paces and glared indignantly at the amused faces around her. 'If your purpose is malign, be sure I shall scream,' she warned. 'Lady Anne will be shocked if her chaperone is ill-treated by men she trusts and will send My Lord to rescue me.'

Gyles raised his hand in apology. 'Forgive us, mistress. Our hearts are pure and our purpose good. It's many weeks since My Lord and Milady were able to speak in private. They will welcome some time alone, I think.'

She made a pretence of patting down her cloak to restore some dignity. 'You had but to say. Are they close as cousins? I sense a strong bond between them.'

'Their cousinship is distant but their friendship close. There is admiration and respect on both sides.'

'Grown stronger since her husband's death, I don't doubt. Neither was free to express regard while Sir Richard lived.'

'Indeed . . . and have had little opportunity since.'

Mistress Wilde heard the wry note in Gyles's voice, and looked from one man to the other. Sudden understanding appeared in her eyes. 'Do you hope for more than expressions of regard? A betrothal perhaps?' A laugh rumbled in her throat when none of them answered. 'Go look for bracken and let God do His work,' she said, shooing them away. 'If ever a union was ordained, it was surely this one.'

Develish, the evening of the fifteenth day of April, 1349

We received such a welcome when we returned this noon that I wept for the gladness our people displayed. So loud were the cheers from across the moat that it was several minutes before Gyles could announce that our time of exclusion is over and Athelstan has been granted title to Pedle Hinton. At the forefront of the crowd was Eleanor, clasping the hands of Isabella and Robert as naturally as if they were her brother and sister, and I cannot recall ever seeing her so happy. It was a sweet moment when I stepped from the raft and she allowed me to embrace her as a mother; sweeter still when she begged me to accept the embraces of our serfs.

I have promised to give an account of our time in Blandeforde when we assemble to eat, though I doubt it will be necessary. Clara Trueblood has invited Mistress Wilde to the kitchen, claiming quite shamelessly that she needs a woman of experience to help in the preparation of the meal. From the noisy gasps of astonishment which echo through the great hall, Mistress Wilde's rendering of the tale is more enthralling than mine can ever be. Who, except Thaddeus, will understand that the most exciting of yesterday's events was to ride at speed along a deserted highway?

I have no fear that our people will reveal the truth about Athelstan. They and I have talked it through many times and none resents Thaddeus's assumption of nobility. All have confidence that his single purpose is to secure their freedom and future prosperity, not least Will and Eva. It's 3 months since he pledged to support them in idleness if they maintained the fiction, and Will has been counting his good fortune ever since. He tells me now that he always had confidence the son he raised would succeed in acquiring a demesne of his own!

It matters not if the name Thaddeus is used by accident. Mistress Wilde is so enchanted by Athelstan's Moorish ways and thoughtful courtesy that she is quite persuaded he encouraged all to call him Thaddeus while he lived as a serf. Gyles, Alleyn and James have tasked themselves with spreading the story that Athelstan entered Develish last spring as a peasant, and as long as enough repeat it, Mistress Wilde will confirm that truth to d'Amiens upon her return to Blandeforde. I don't doubt he will question her thoroughly, for a man such as he does not abandon his suspicions lightly.

I cannot say what caused de Courtesmain to fall to his knees and beg me to forgive his errors and lies but we would not have escaped so easily if he hadn't. In truth, I had expected him to hold even more strongly to his accusations after d'Amiens threatened him with a flogging, and I am sure the

priest expected the same, because he was most put out when
de Courtesmain chose retraction instead. Mistress Wilde assures
me God stepped in to prick de Courtesmain's conscience, but I
think it more likely de Courtesmain looked to prick mine. If so,
he's fortunate Thaddeus is able to read my thoughts and found a
convincing reason to spare his attacker.

I pray de Courtesmain has the sense to bury his animosities
and work with Thaddeus in Pedle Hinton. Gyles says he'll have
little choice, since the only audience for his whispered poison
in the next few weeks will be Ian, Olyver, Edmund, Joshua and
Peter, and not one of them will waver in loyalty to the man
who is taking them from bondage to freedom. I don't doubt for
a moment that Gyles is correct. His sons and their friends are
as worthy as their fathers and wholly committed to the path
Thaddeus has chosen for them.

Dear Gyles. He has been my kindest and most generous
supporter since I came to Develish. Mistress Wilde tells me I
have him to thank for allowing me some moments alone with
Thaddeus last night. How precious they were, for it is many
weeks since my beautiful Moor last held me in his arms. Then,
we could only dream that a day might come when a vassal
widow might marry a bastard slave, but now we dare to hope
that the dream will be realised. Thaddeus tells me he finds his
Moorish part easier to play than his noble English part, but in

truth he plays both with such ease that God must surely have intended him to be Athelstan.

It will be a few months yet before Pedle Hinton is restored and My Lord of Athelstan in a position to ask permission from Blandeforde to unite his demesne with Develish. That time will allow me to help Eleanor make peace with herself so that she gains in confidence and her mind becomes calm. I worry less than Clara and Isabella about her seizure because her character is not as frail as they believe. She needs only to understand that love is not diminished through being shared, and I see evidence of that lesson already being learnt through her nurturing of the cats and the happiness her friendship with Robert brings her. I even dare to hope that it won't be long before Isabella, too, becomes a loved and trusted confidante.

Robert tells me it was he who helped Father Anselm compose his letter, by keeping the old man's tankard replenished with wine. He says the more the Father drank the better his ideas and handwriting became! I can believe the second claim but not the first. The sweet praise could only have come from Robert. He assures me that his ambition now is to be a merchant and not a fighting man, but I've made a small wager with his father that he will reach even greater heights. He has the same cleverness and thirst for knowledge as Thaddeus and

Isabella at the same age, and it will not be long before he has learnt all that I can teach him.

I bless God daily for the bonds of affection that have held us together and brought us through the pestilence. To be loved and honoured for who we are, and not what our status represents, is surely the lesson He wanted us to learn when he sent His son to live as a carpenter and not as a king.

The future will be bright indeed when even the humblest are given the chance to prove their worth.

In nomine Patris et Filii et Spiritus Sanctus